from that flame

MaryAnn T. Beverly

KALLISTI PUBLISHING

WILKES-BARRE, PA

Kallisti Publishing, Inc.
332 Center Street
Wilkes-Barre, PA 18702
Phone (877) 444-6188 • Fax (419) 781-1907
www.kallistipublishing.com

Kallisti Publishing, Inc. titles may be purchased for business or promotional use or for special sales. Please contact Kallisti Publishing for more information.

Kallisti Publishing, Inc. and its logo are trademarks of Kallisti Publishing, Inc.

10 9 8 7 6 5 4 3 2 1

Library of Congress Control Number: 2007932817
ISBN 0-9761111-8-7
ISBN-13 978-0-9761111-8-4

DESIGNED & PRINTED IN THE UNITED STATES OF AMF

Dedicated with thanks to Mark, Mom and Dad, Isaac, David, Rita and John, Marsha, Kate, Suzzie, Patricia, Alice, Eddie, and all the family and friends who never lost faith in my dream

and

Dedicated to the memory of Ahmed Shah Massoud (1953 - 2001)

With special thanks to Abdullah Qazi and Danielle Bogard for their help with the foreign words in Dari and French and to Zahir Sajanie for use of his photo of Massoud.

Ahmed Shah Massoud
September 2, 1953 – September 9, 2001
Photograph by Zahir Sajanie ©2000

Contents

Author's Note

In November 2001 while at my doctor's office, I picked up a copy of National Geographic's *Adventure* magazine. Flipping through it, I came across a picture of a man. My reaction to seeing this picture surprised me because I seemed to recognize his face although I was fairly certain I had never met him. The sensation of somehow "knowing" this Afghan *mujahidin* was so powerful, I borrowed the magazine and went home to do research about him on the Internet. His name was Ahmed Shah Massoud.

There is a great deal of information available about Massoud. His world-wide recognition began in the 1980s when he lead many successful defensive and offensive battles against the Soviet Union after it invaded Afghanistan. *The Wall Street Journal* credited him as being the Afghan who ended the Cold War. After the departure of the Soviet troops, Massoud became the Defense Minister in the newly formed Rabbani government, a position he held until his death in 2001.

Commander Massoud's battles continued as Afghanistan suffered a civil war soon after the new government took office. He remained locked in battle as the Taliban and al-Qaeda began to take over his country. He implored the world's assistance to defeat the terrorists who had infiltrated Afghanistan, but precious little help came his way until it was too late. On September 9, 2001, Ahmed Shah Massoud was assassinated by suicide bombers reportedly under the orders of Osama bin Laden. Two days later, the terrorism "beyond comprehension" of which Massoud had warned, came to pass on America's shores. The events of September 11, 2001, proved how horrifyingly true Massoud's predictions had been.

Two weeks after his funeral, US bombs began to fall on Afghanistan. Massoud's Northern Alliance became American forces' closest ally in the region. They fought along side the American troops to drive the Taliban and al-Qaeda from the country. The freedom which came at last to Afghanistan would be bittersweet because after twenty years of fighting for that freedom, the leader known as *Amer Saheb* was not there to share in the victory.

When I decided to write a book about Massoud, I wanted to do something other than merely report dates and facts. There are many nonfiction books already written about him. I wanted to grasp the many complexities of the man's personality as well as his historically recorded accomplishments. That is when the idea of writing historic fiction occurred to me. Fiction would grant me the freedom to portray Ahmed Shah Massoud and his companions as I envisioned them. All of the characters in the book would be products of my imagination, and, with an historic skeleton as the framework for the tale, I would be able to write a story which portrayed Ahmed Shah Massoud in settings of my choosing.

While many of the events, such as Massoud's visit to Paris, actually occurred, my interpretation of those events and the people involved in them is fictional. Many events are chimerical. The Massoud who exists in *From That Flame* does not exist outside its pages. None of the words spoken by any of the characters should be taken as historically accurate in their entirety. Quotations of Massoud's have been translated from the original Dari by others than the author. While considerable research was conducted so that incidents are represented as accurately as possible, the story is one of historic fiction rather than historic fact.

It is my hope that as you read *From That Flame*, you not only get to know Massoud as the "Lion of Panjshir," the leader, the military genius; but that you get to know Ahmed Shah Massoud—the *man*.

MaryAnn T. Beverly
Columbia, SC
June 2007

Preface

In the winter of 2001, Osama bin Laden ordered two things: an assassination and an attack. In September of that year, both happened.

Map

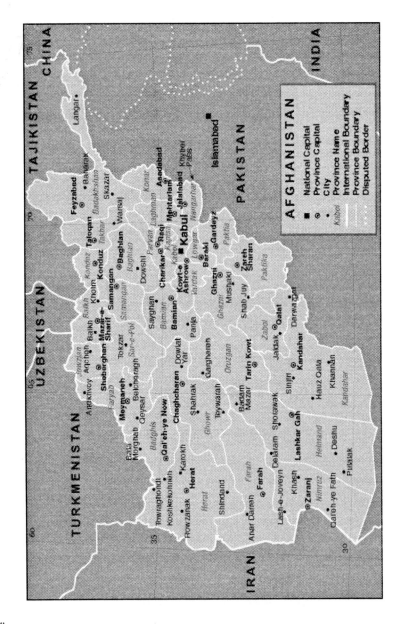

from

that

flame

From that flame, that existence,
that wonderful man
who can burn beneath the water.
No other kind of light
will cook the food you need.

—Hafiz

1. Journalist

D r. Abdullah stuck his head inside the open flap of the tent in which Commander Ahmed Shah Massoud sat studying a Soviet-era map of the Afghan terrain by the weak afternoon sunlight and an old lantern.

"There is a journalist here."

Commander Massoud looked up with a frown. "Another one? Another Westerner?"

"Yes," Dr. Abdullah replied. He ran his hand over his smoothly trimmed beard.

"They come and they come and ask questions, but nothing ever happens. Nothing ever changes." Massoud sighed deeply. "I ask for help, and they send me journalists. Send him away. I need soldiers and weapons, not writers and cameras."

Abdullah shrugged. "All right. But it's not a man; it's a woman."

"A woman? Alone?" The Commander's eyebrows shot up in surprise.

"Yes. She said she was in Pakistan researching a story on the plight of the women in Afghanistan. She talked to some women from RAWA."

"Then what's she doing here? We don't have women here, not even women from RAWA. Doesn't she know how foolish she is to travel alone in this part of the country? How did she get here?"

Abdullah raised his hand against the onslaught of questions. "Apparently she heard about you while she was in Peshawar. Some of the women in RAWA told her that your vision for women in Afghanistan is different from that of the Taliban, and she came to verify the facts. She had escorts from Peshawar to Shoghot, and they brought her through the Derah Pass to Ghowrayd Gharami. She found new escorts from there to here, but they just left her."

A wry smile crossed Massoud's rakishly handsome face. "I see. We are not the top story, only a sidebar." He scratched his head just beneath the lip of the *pakol* he always wore. "That might make the interview questions different from those we usually get. Besides, after the trip she took to get here, it would be wrong to send her away without an interview. Send this female journalist to me, will you, my friend?"

"Are you sure?" Abdullah asked. "It's late in the day. If we don't send her back to Ghowrayd Gharami now, we will have to provide accommodations for her to spend the night."

"We can't send her back now under any circumstances. If she's been left here, she is under our protection whether we like it or not. I don't want her traveling at night even with our men as escorts. Better to wait until morning. Ask Hani to bunk in with Abdul. We'll let her have his tent for the night. Bring her to me, will you?"

Abdullah nodded and ducked back out of the tent. Ahmed Shah was his best friend as well as the Commander of the resistance, and although Abdullah loved and trusted him completely, he sometimes didn't understand the way his friend's mind worked. Right now a journalist—especially a female journalist—was the last thing they needed. The Taliban's fighters had been moving closer, encroaching on more Northern Alliance-held territory. Massoud should be focusing on his battle plans to drive the enemy back, not granting yet another interview to a Western journalist.

"He'll see you," Dr. Abdullah said to Michelle Garrett. "You will spend the night in our camp, and tomorrow we will have someone take you back to Pakistan."

"Thank you, Doctor," the journalist answered, not prepared to announce that she had other plans in mind. This man's face was too stern at the moment to brook a discussion. "I do realize that my unannounced arrival caught you at a bad time. I appreciate your hospitality."

from that flame

"Every day in Afghanistan is a bad time since the Taliban took over," Dr. Abdullah said, but his attitude towards her softened a little. "Still, you are welcome. This way," he said and gestured. He turned and led her back to the tent where Commander Massoud waited for her. Dressed in Western-style clothing, the doctor seemed out of place among the rugged *mujahidin* fighters who wore either camouflage or traditional Afghan clothes. It also struck her as odd that, despite the cold, the doctor wore no hat on his slightly balding head.

"Miss Michelle Garrett," Dr. Abdullah began the introduction in Dari, "this is Ahmed Shah Massoud. Commander Massoud, Michelle Garrett."

"*Salaam.*" Massoud offered his hand to her without rising and shook hers warmly. "Do we need a translator?" He also spoke in Dari as he looked at Abdullah.

"She speaks French," Dr. Abdullah said.

Guessing what the Commander had asked of the doctor, Michelle simultaneously asked, "You speak French, don't you? I speak a little."

"*Oui,*" Massoud replied. "*Comment allez vous?* Please sit down." He indicated a space of carpet to his left as he switched from Dari to French.

"*Très bien.* Thank you for agreeing to see me, Commander," Michelle said as she settled into the offered space. "It is an honor to meet you." She squirmed a little under the intensity of his gaze. She saw the old maps spread out before him on the ground. "Are you preparing for battle?" she asked to get the conversation started. She glanced covertly around the battered, old tent. Except for a few neatly rolled rugs and blankets and an ancient-looking teapot, there was little else. She looked again at the man whose face was brightened by the single lantern as he hunched over his well-creased maps.

"*Oui,*" Massoud nodded. "The Taliban soldiers are advancing against us. I am preparing to deploy my troops to a different location." He saw the interest in her expression and pointed to the map. "We are here," he pointed to a spot on the map, "and I am going to move the troops here, to Jorm." His finger pointed to another spot on the map.

"Why?" Michelle leaned forward to look at the map where

he pointed. Her eyes were beginning to adjust to the lesser light within the large, musty tent, but it was still nearly impossible to see the tiny markings that had been handwritten all over it.

"Because it will be easier for us to defend ourselves from that location. We have arms and munitions stored there as well as food and water," Commander Massoud explained patiently. "There are more caves and hiding places. We are engaged in guerrilla fighting, Miss Garrett. We must gain an advantage where we can find one." He began to fold the map. "Now may I ask you a question? Did you really come through the northwest frontier of Pakistan?"

"Is that what it's called? In Islamabad I hired a translator and bodyguard. When I heard about you, they made arrangements for me to travel to Shoghot with some other men. In Shoghot, those men found men to bring me here. I was relayed along the route."

"It was an exceedingly dangerous trip." Commander Massoud shook his head in disbelief. "It is amazing you are alive. You risked your life and property."

"My mother always said I never had enough sense to know when I should be afraid," Michelle answered with a laugh. "Once I decided I needed to meet you, I did whatever was necessary to get here." She spoke matter-of-factly with a smile and a shrug.

"So I understand," the Commander returned her smile. "Now that you are here, how may I help you?"

Michelle studied the face of the man before her. He wore his *pakol* a little off to one side of his head as if it were a beret. His black hair was thick beneath the hat. He had an especially wide streak of gray running over his left temple. A traditional *paktou* was casually flung over the shoulders of the dark canvas military-style jacket he wore against the cold that penetrated the old tent. He was somewhere in his late forties, she guessed. Around his eyes there were deep lines and creases caused by both harsh weather and grave concerns. Topped by dense lashes, the almond shaped, dark eyes themselves were penetrating and bright with intelligence. His face was long, his nose Aquiline, his complexion swarthy. He wore his facial hair in a roughly trimmed beard and moustache, and when he smiled, Michelle felt the charismatic power that made him a legend of near mythic proportions. Since Massoud was seated, the journalist was unable to determine his height, but she did observe that he was very slender with a wiry sort of strength. He is a very handsome man, Michelle thought, and she was again flustered by his steady gaze and her own inappropriate thought. She groped for her pen and paper.

"While I was in Pakistan researching this article, your name came up. I was told that you disapprove of the Taliban's policies towards women. Is this true?"

"Yes, I disapprove of the oppression and brutality with which the Taliban treats women." His answer was well rehearsed but sincere. "There is nothing in Islam to support the extreme view they hold. There is nothing in the *Qur'an* that says women should not get an education, receive medical attention, or hold a job outside the home if they wish." Massoud's slender, quick hands punctuated his sentences. "Women are equal to men. They deserve a voice in their government and in all things affecting their lives. The members of the Revolutionary Afghan Women's Association have my respect for the courage and bravery they have shown in their fight."

"I'm sure they will appreciate knowing that," Michelle answered automatically before pressing on with her next question. "Commander, if the *Qur'an* does not support the belief that women are inferior to men, where does the Taliban get its view that women have no value beyond their ability to give birth?" Michelle tore her eyes away from the mesmerizing action of the man's hands.

Massoud shrugged. "I don't know. It is some twisted, perverted form of extremist Islam that I have never seen or read—and I have studied with some of the great *mullahs*."

"I was told that when your government was in Kabul, things were not much better for women," the journalist stated bluntly. "Wasn't it the Taliban's promise to bring law and order to the country after you were unable to provide it that won them acceptance among the Afghan population in the first place?"

Massoud nodded slightly, surprised by her candor but also appreciative of it. "The government for which I was the Defense Minister was unable to provide the security the people craved. There were many complicated factors working against us. One of them was Pakistan, who first sent the Taliban to my country, by the way. In the beginning, the people hoped the Taliban would provide peace and safety. It did not take long for the Taliban to reveal its true intentions. The Taliban is an intolerant gang of thugs that is trying to impose an extreme form of Islam on my country and my people. Equally as bad is the fact that they are allowing terrorist groups like al-Qaeda to make their homes in Afghanistan. They must be driven from the land."

"What if the majority of people still prefer the Taliban?" the journalist queried.

"My people do not prefer the Taliban. Years ago, perhaps, when my government had failed, but not now." Massoud's hand again cut through the air to emphasize his words.

"Then why don't the people help you drive them out?" Michelle asked.

"They can't. The Taliban is brutal. They think nothing of killing all the women and children in a village in order to make the point that they must not be defied. The people are terrified of them."

Michelle was scribbling her notes furiously. "You said that Pakistan was instrumental in bringing the Taliban to power?"

"*Oui.* Pakistan has long interfered in Afghanistan's internal politics."

"How was your government ousted?" Michelle asked next. "After fighting the Soviets for ten, long years and ultimately seizing control from the Communists, I can't imagine that you went without a fight."

"I did without much of a fight," Commander Massoud answered softly, measuring his words. Even now the troubled history of his beloved country hurt him. "After we finally drove the Soviets out, Burhanuddin Rabbani became president. We tried to establish a working, central government. We had little support from the international community." Commander Massoud looked at Michelle Garrett directly. "We were good enough to supply tanks and missiles as long as we were fighting the Soviets, but we were not good enough to support and assist once the Soviets were defeated." His tone was matter-of-fact. If he was angry or bitter, he hid it well.

Michelle didn't want to get sidetracked by a different subject. "That doesn't explain what happened to your government. I heard horror stories from the women in RAWA about the raping and killing in Kabul while Rabbani was the president. Are they

from that flame

untrue?"

"Sadly, no. Afghanistan is filled with tribal warlords who are still vying for power. Tribal wars broke out and caused great devastation in Kabul. I am grieved to say that many of the stories you've heard are true. There was fighting between various factions. Many people were harmed or killed. Many fled to Pakistan and Iran." The regret in the Commander's eyes was unmistakable. Michelle suspected that he blamed himself although she had heard from several sources that neither Massoud nor those closest to him had anything to do with the atrocities committed against the people of Afghanistan at that time.

"The government in Pakistan decided to get involved," the Commander continued. "Pakistani leaders have their own plans for Afghanistan which are connected to their conflict with India. We are to be their rear guard in case of an invasion. A fallback position, so to speak. In any event, Pakistan had its own interests at heart when it interfered with us.

"Pakistan also supports *madrassas,* religious schools that teach radical Islam to men. The *madrassas* are where the Taliban was born. The people of Afghanistan were weary of war, and when the Taliban came in and promised peace, the people were willing to give them a chance. Those of us who were *mujahidin* could not live under the teaching and rule of the Taliban. We resisted their influence and control. In the end, however, we were unable to maintain control of Kabul. Rather than risk more civilian casualties and complete destruction of the city, we retreated to Panjshir.

"It did not take long for the people to realize what a mistake had been made by allowing the Taliban to gain control, but by then it was too late. We in the resistance had been pushed into this northern corner of our own country. From here we will fight until the Taliban and their foreign dogs, the al-Qaeda, are driven from Afghanistan."

"How will you do this?" Michelle asked. "You are so few, and they are so many."

"We will because we must." Massoud spoke with grim determination. His hands cut the air in sharp, hard gestures and his eyes glittered with resolve. "We drove back the Soviet Union when we were outnumbered ten to one. We will do the same with the Taliban."

from that flame

"What will happen if you fail?" Michelle asked quietly and watched his face closely.

"If we lose control of this part of the country and the Taliban rules all of Afghanistan, I fear the United Nations will relent and recognize them rather than us as the official government of the country. That would be a terrible thing. My people cannot live the way the Taliban is forcing them to live." Massoud heaved a weary sigh, and Michelle could almost see a physical burden of enormous proportions resting on his shoulders. "We need the West to join us in getting rid of the Taliban and their al-Qaeda henchmen," he concluded softly.

"Why would the West want to get involved in Afghanistan's civil war?" Michelle asked gently, inquisitively. "It doesn't sound like US policy to me."

"Because it is not merely a civil war." Massoud spoke with conviction. "It is a war that is going to bleed out into the rest of the world. Does the West think the Taliban and al-Qaeda are happy to stay in this country alone? What a fool's paradise! They want their fanatical views and hatred to be Afghanistan's primary export."

Abdullah appeared in the entrance of the tent. Massoud suddenly stood up. "I apologize, but there is work I must do. You will remain in the camp for the night. Abdullah is arranging sleeping quarters for you." He realized that the woman, weighted down with her camera bag and the backpack she had not bothered to remove, was having a hard time getting up. He extended his hand again, this time to help her to her feet. She grasped his hand and allowed him to help pull her up. Now that they were both standing, Michelle decided he was taller than she guessed when he was seated. In reality, he was only a few inches taller than she but carried himself in such a way as to appear well over six feet.

"Will you return and join me for dinner a little later?" Massoud asked. "We can talk more."

"I would be honored. Thank you for your kind hospitality." Michelle smiled at him.

He returned her smile before turning his attention to Abdullah. "Did you arrange a tent for her?" Massoud asked his friend in Dari.

"Yes, but Hani is not happy that a *kafir*, especially a female

8

from that flame

kafir, will be using his tent. Those are his words, not mine."

"He shouldn't call her that," Massoud frowned slightly.

"Well, don't forget that we still have work to do, and a journalist is a distraction right now." His disapproval indicated that he agreed more with Hani than with his friend.

"I never forget," Massoud answered more sharply than he intended.

"Is something wrong?" Michelle asked in French from where she stood in Massoud's tent. "I don't need a tent if it is causing a problem. I have a sleeping bag."

"Of course you need a tent," Massoud answered her in French. "There is no problem. Abdullah will show you where to put your things." He glanced at his friend again and spoke in Dari under his breath. "Ask Abdul to guard her. I want her kept safe if there is trouble tonight."

He turned back to Michelle and flashed his charismatic smile at her. "Please go with Doctor Abdullah. *Khuda hafiz.* Good-bye. I will see you for dinner in about two hours." Without waiting for her response, he disappeared back into his tent.

Michelle looked at Dr. Abdullah. "Is he upset with me about something?" she asked him in English. She was relieved he spoke English. She feared that her French was not what it should be, and she worried that she might have misspoken in her conversation with Massoud.

"How would I know? I wasn't in the tent. Did you say something to upset him?"

"No, I don't think so. He answered my questions very candidly. But just now he seemed rather abrupt."

"He's fighting a war," Dr. Abdullah said dryly. "He gave you time he could ill afford, and he will give you more later. Excuse him if he must return to his work."

"I'm sorry," Michelle stammered. She had an uneasy feeling that this man did not like her, but she had no idea why.

"No apology is necessary," the doctor replied, shaking his head. "Just please understand that what Commander Massoud does or doesn't do may mean the life or death of thousands." He pointed down a narrow path. "Let's go this way."

"Would it be all right if I walked around camp and took some pictures? The mountains are magnificent."

Dr. Abdullah looked as if he might object but instead nodded and told her to wait where she was. He returned a moment later, followed by an armed *mujahidin* soldier. "This is Abdul. He doesn't speak French or English, but he will stay with you and protect you with his own life. If he indicates that you must come back immediately, please don't resist or argue with him. Remember that you are in a war zone. Let him do his job and keep you alive while you take your pictures."

Michelle smiled and nodded at the handsome youth with an AK-47 flung over his shoulder. He did not acknowledge her smile. She turned her attention back to Abdullah and looked squarely in the doctor's eyes. She cocked her head and studied him openly. She decided that under different circumstances, she would find him quite sophisticated and debonair. "You really don't want me here, do you?"

"That hardly matters since you are here," Abdullah pointed out.

"But why?" Michelle pressed. "Because of the danger?"

"Partly, yes." Dr. Abdullah looked down at the ground for a few seconds before meeting her gaze. He thought a moment longer and decided to be honest with her.

"Every time a journalist comes here—and there have been many over the years—Commander Massoud allows himself to hope yet again that someone in the outside world might actually hear what he's saying and come to help. No one ever does, and my friend is repeatedly disappointed. I don't like to see him disappointed again and again. I wouldn't want him to have a false hope that something you write might be heard when nothing else written ever has." The doctor couldn't completely hide his anger and frustration.

"I've barely asked him half a dozen questions," Michelle asserted. "Why would he have any hope about what I might write?"

"I know him. He likes your approach. He thinks there is something unique about you. If he persists in that thinking, he will have his false hope, and he will be disappointed." Abdullah frowned. He should not be having this conversation with this foreign woman. Still more angry words spilled from his mouth as the color rose in his regal face. His wide-set, dark eyes flashed with emotion although his voice was barely above a whisper. "Take your pictures of the colorful *mujahidin* soldiers and write your deep, introspective words about the struggles of Afghanistan. While you do that, Commander Massoud and I will know that thousands more of our people are being displaced, tortured, and killed. We'll go into many more battles and have a dozen or two of our friends blown up or gunned down. We will fight and die to gain a few more meters of bombed-out land. We will kill a few more Taliban and al-Qaeda soldiers. And in the end, nothing will change. Your pictures and words will do no good except to line your own pockets."

"That's not fair!" Michelle protested. "I came—"

"You came for RAWA and got Commander Massoud because he was an interesting sidebar to your story," Abdullah charged. "That amuses Commander Massoud. I, however, am not amused." He waved his arm in a dismissive gesture and strode away back in the direction of Massoud's tent.

Michelle shook her head, smiled at a grim-faced Abdul, and started walking farther down the rocky path with her camera in hand. Abdul quickly followed after her.

"Noshe jaan. Bon appetite," Commander Massoud said as he passed a bowl of rice and mutton and a slice of Afghan flat bread, *nan,* to Michelle Garrett. Dr. Abdullah had already handed her a glass cup of hot, green tea. "Tell me what you thought about the women from RAWA you met in Pakistan."

As was the Afghan custom for dining, they sat in a circle on the floor with a tablecloth spread among them. Michelle was vaguely aware of how unlike Afghan custom it was for her to be seated and eating with the men. In a country where the different sexes rarely mixed except with close family members, Michelle was being given unprecedented freedom.

As she accepted the bowl, Michelle gave Dr. Abdullah, who was sitting across from her, a defiant glance before turning her attention to Commander Massoud. "They are some of the bravest women I've ever met. Did you know that some of them dared to wear hidden cameras around Kabul? They documented the things the Taliban was doing to them."

"I have heard about their videos," Massoud nodded, and he looked at her with new interest. "You actually saw them?"

"*Oui*, and they were extraordinary, sad, and terrifying. They showed executions that took place in the soccer stadium in Kabul. A woman was shot in the head."

"The Taliban likes public executions. They use terror to govern." Massoud dipped his bread into his bowl as he spoke.

"They beat women if the wind blows and their ankles are exposed for a moment. The women have no right to legal recourse."

"Women have no rights under the Taliban," Massoud said and nodded in agreement. "This is one of the areas in which my government always differs sharply from theirs."

"There is a woman in Kabul I want to talk to," Michelle said. "The women—"

"Impossible," Massoud interrupted. "You cannot go to Kabul. You would be killed or, at the very least, arrested immediately."

"Couldn't I wear a *burqa* and disguise myself?"

Commander Massoud shook his head. "If you are discovered dressed as an Afghan woman, the Taliban will think you are an American spy. Nothing could save you then."

"I have to go," Michelle insisted. "I can't finish my story if I don't."

"Then you had better change your story," Massoud said firmly. "You cannot go to Kabul."

"You can't stop me from going," Michelle said defiantly.

Massoud looked at her squarely, and when he spoke, there was no mistaking the authority in his soft voice. "Yes, I can, and I will stop you. You will not go to Kabul."

"Are you going to…?" She couldn't think of the word she wanted in French and turned to Dr. Abdullah.

"How do you say 'detain' in French?" she asked him in English.

"*Retenir*," Dr. Abdullah answered.

"*Non*," Massoud replied immediately. "Not detained."

"What do you call it if you won't let me go where I want?"

Michelle demanded. She was not afraid that this man would hurt her, but she was increasingly worried that her freedom of movement was about to be restricted.

Massoud looked at her directly and spoke sharply. "Alive. I call it keeping you alive. I will have some of my men take you back to Peshawar in the morning."

"I don't want to go back to Pakistan. I just left there. My story is in Kabul."

"Your story may be in Kabul, but *you* will not be. There is no more discussion." Massoud waved his hand to dismiss her further arguments.

Michelle suddenly understood why so many people obeyed this man. He had a commanding presence that was quite powerful, and although he had not raised his voice when he spoke, it was almost impossible to consider arguing with him. Almost, but not quite.

"Fine. Then I will go to Pakistan and reenter Afghanistan from a different direction. I'll go through the Khyber Pass. I won't be your responsibility."

"Western women," Massoud muttered under his breath in Dari. While on many levels he admired Michelle's fierce independence, he was also annoyed by it. No Afghan woman would argue with him this way. He looked over at the journalist who was suddenly complicating his life.

The head scarf she was wearing when she first arrived had slipped from its position, and the soft flicker of firelight highlighted her blonde-brown hair as is cascaded down over her shoulders. He guessed she was in her mid-thirties. Her features were small and irregular but pleasing. Her hazel eyes were flecked with green and gold as they glared at him obstinately. Her long, upper lip was firmly planted against the lower lip, and he suspected that the small movement at the back of her jaw was caused by her teeth grinding in determination. She was a small woman, this Western journalist who, unlike any other woman in the country, was clad in jeans and boots and a heavy, bright red sweater. She suddenly reminded Massoud of a mother bird he once saw fly fearlessly into the face of a hungry dog who was getting too close to her nest of eggs. Yes, he recognized the expression on her face and sighed deeply. He would have to make better use of his diplomatic skills. Soldier. Statesman. Diplomat. They were hats he switched and wore with ease.

"You are correct," he said softly. "You could come right back and go to Kabul, and I could not stop you. Please understand that I am asking you not to go to Kabul, at least not right now, because I do not wish to see you arrested or killed. That is my only concern. I understand about the importance of your story, and I will try to make arrangements for you to see this woman from RAWA as soon as it is safe. Perhaps it would be possible to bring her to you. Give me her name, and I can send a message to her in Kabul. Will you allow me to look into this matter a little more before you go to Kabul on your own? Please?"

In spite of herself, Michelle was charmed and intrigued by Massoud. Just when she was girding up for a fight, he became reasonable. As her voice grew louder, his became softer. While her body language became more confrontational, his grew increasingly more serene. She felt her anger start to slip away.

"What am I supposed to do while you 'look into this matter'?" She tried to hang onto her exasperation, but she knew she was fighting a losing battle.

"Write about me, of course!" He flashed a wide, irresistible grin at her and began to laugh. The gleam in his eye indicated that he was teasing her. His laughter was so contagious, Michelle began to laugh too.

"What in the world could I find to write about you?"

"I will think of something spectacular to do," he said with a smile. Laughing again, he handed her some of his sugared almonds called *noql*. "I am rumored to have done one or two spectacular things before." He shrugged noncommittally, but his eyes twinkled with humor.

"Yes, I've heard," Michelle said dryly as she smiled and shook her head. She knew there was a story here, a story every bit as interesting and important as one about RAWA alone. Could she combine them and do both justice? She glanced at Dr. Abdullah. Her face sobered at his frown.

Commander Massoud's eyes followed her gaze over to his friend. "Where did you lose your sense of humor, my friend?" he asked.

"My wife took it with her when she fled Afghanistan with

my children," Abdullah snapped. "Besides, there is no humor in war."

"We must laugh when we can," Massoud said softly, "or we will weep all day and night. But I know your sorrow, and I am vulnerable to it myself."

"Is your wife not in Afghanistan either?" Michelle asked Massoud.

"She is now although I have sent her to Tajikistan from time to time when there have been too many death threats against her and my children. I recently moved them into a house in Saricha overlooking the Panjshir Valley."

"The Taliban threatened your children?" Michelle asked in horror.

"Mine. Abdullah's. Many of our top leaders'. They think it will intimidate us. It doesn't. It only serves to make us more determined."

"How many children do you have, Commander?"

"Six beautiful, glorious children, praise God. I am a blessed man."

"It's late, and we must break camp early," Abdullah said as he stood up, his bad humor still wrapped around him like a warm blanket on this cold night. "I will escort you to your tent," he said pointedly to Michelle.

"All right," she agreed and rose immediately. "Thank you, Doctor. And thank you very kindly for your time, company, and the meal, Commander. I appreciate them all very much."

"I will see you in the morning. *Bonne nuit.* Good night. May God watch over you as you sleep."

Abdul appeared as if by magic at the exact moment Massoud tossed open the tent flap. Abdullah said something softly to him in Dari. Abdul nodded and left.

"Shall we go?" Dr. Abdullah said pointing toward the path.

"How many languages do you speak, Doctor Abdullah?" Michelle asked as they walked. She slipped a little on the icy earth. Abdullah's hand shot out, grabbed her elbow, and steadied her. He kept his hand on her arm as he answered.

"Dari. English. French. German. Pashtu. A little Russian. And you?" he asked because politeness required it.

from that flame

"English, of course. Enough French to get by. Survival Spanish. I admire your ability with languages. Would you consider teaching me some Dari? At least enough so that I'm not completely helpless if you or Massoud isn't around? I don't want to rely on a translator every minute of the day."

Abdullah forced a smile. "Of course, it would be my honor to be your instructor. Here is your tent. Abdul brought extra blankets. As you may have noticed, Afghanistan's mountains are bitterly cold at night in early March."

"I have a sleeping bag good to minus thirty…" Upon seeing his expression, she abruptly added, "You are very kind. Thank you for the blankets. I'm sure I can use them."

"Abdul will be outside watching—no, guarding—you throughout the night."

"But won't he get cold?"

"He has his orders. You need not worry about him."

"He could stay inside the tent. It's large enough…" Michelle's voice trailed off when she saw the horrified expression on Abdullah's face. "I meant no disrespect," she stammered as she felt her cheeks flush a hot red in the darkness. Even the cold night air could not remove the heat of embarrassment she felt rising in her face.

"Good night, Miss Garrett," Abdullah said and walked away.

Michelle shivered in the frigid, thin air, but she still stopped to look up at the stars before going into her tent. The clear night made the stars seem impossibly close, as if she could reach out and pluck one from its spot in the sky. They looked as if the hand of God had cast diamonds across a dark blue velvet backdrop that were now hers for the taking.

From the corner of her eye she saw a shadow move and assumed it was Abdul. She knew she would be as safe as Massoud could keep her while she spent her first night in this hostile land and rugged terrain. Perhaps she could give the extra blankets to Abdul later. She opened the flap of the tent and saw her backpack and sleeping bag neatly laid beside a small pile of blankets and rugs. A lantern cast a dim light barely bright enough for her to arrange the rugs and blankets and add her sleeping bag to the top.

Suddenly Michelle felt the day's exertion catching up with her. She was exhausted.

from that flame

She untied her boots and set them aside. She tossed her coat beside them and climbed into the sleeping bag before extinguishing the lantern. As she curled up inside the bag, she could hear muffled sounds from outside, low male voices and sometimes someone walking on the frozen path not far from her tent. She had planned on running the two conversations she had with Commander Massoud through her mind, but sleep began to overtake her almost immediately. Outside her tent, Abdul silently stared off into the black night.

2. Attack

Michelle heard an impossibly loud noise outside her tent, a noise loud enough to wake her from a very deep sleep. A moment later she felt the earth tremble beneath her. An explosion sounded nearby, shaking the ground and jolting her forward as she struggled to free herself from the tangle of her sleeping bag. She heard the shouts of men and the pounding of running feet on hard ground not far from her tent. She had been sleeping in most of her clothes and hastily pulled on the rest. Her boots and coat were on in a moment as well. Grabbing a single camera, she stuck her head out the flap of her tent and into a night that had been turned from tranquility to hell without a moment's notice.

Abdul, who had been standing just outside the tent trying to figure out how best to extricate the sleeping journalist, clutched Michelle by the front of her coat, jerked her from the tent, and pulled her to her feet. He released her coat, grabbed her wrist, and began pulling her up the path. He was speaking to her quickly and loudly. Michelle couldn't understand a word he said, but his intent was obvious. They had to move, and move fast.

Abdul half-dragged her up the steep, rocky path. Michelle, who had been looking up at the bright mortar tracers that filled the sky and made it almost as light as day, stumbled over a loose rock and nearly fell, twisting her ankle and crying out in pain. Abdul didn't stop pulling her along with him, and she was forced to hobble along as quickly as she could. They reached a small group of rocks, and Abdul shoved her behind them. He pointed to a small hollowed-out spot and indicated that she should sit there. Michelle remembered what Abdullah had told her about obeying Abdul's instructions, and she did as he requested. Crouching down inside the hollow, she looked up at Abdul and smiled weakly. He unceremoniously shoved her head down lower and positioned himself so that she was trapped between the rock and his legs. A loud, shrieking noise nearby ended with the sound of metal exploding and men screaming. Michelle screamed too and brought her hands to her ears.

There were several more explosions in rapid succession, none more than two hundred yards away. Rocks and debris dusted them as earthen rain came down from the mountain directly behind them as it suffered repeated blows. Abdul leaned over farther so that he could cover Michelle's head with his body. Someone joined Abdul near the rocks, but from her poor vantage point, all Michelle could see was pant legs and shoes which she recognized as Dr. Abdullah's because of their Western design.

"Are you all right?" Abdullah asked her in English as he touched her shoulder.

"Define 'all right,'" Michelle snapped through teeth that chattered as much from fear as from the cold. "Who's shooting at us?"

"Taliban or al-Qaeda, of course," Dr. Abdullah replied tersely. He was out of breath.

Michelle didn't say anything as she watched Abdul lift a rocket launcher to his shoulder, take aim at an enemy she could not see, and fire. She had never been so terrified. She pressed her body as tightly against the rock as she could, closed her eyes, clamped her hands over her ears again, and prayed it would be over soon. An RPG landed close enough to brighten the night sky with a surreal light.

"Come," she felt large fingers curling around her wrist as Abdullah pulled her to her feet and forced her to move with him. "Keep your head down," he shouted as he ran, dragging her behind him. Her small wrist was completely encircled by his large hand. He forced her to move rapidly despite the pain that jolted through her every time the sprained ankle hit the ground. They ran over the broken ground until they reached another gathering of rocks about fifty yards up the mountain. More *mujahidin* fighters were behind the boulders.

"Do you want a weapon?" Abdullah asked Michelle. He held out his hand, and someone handed him a hand gun.

from that flame

"I have never fired a gun in my life," Michelle protested.

"It isn't hard," Abdullah said as he pushed an ancient Makarov into her hands. "Point and pull the trigger. Try to hit the other guys rather than ours."

"I can't," she said and shoved the gun back at him. "I'd end up shooting myself." The ugly, steel color suddenly wore a rainbow of yellows and oranges as tracer light reflected on the barrel.

Abdullah accepted the gun back. Responsibility for this woman on the front line of the battle was the last thing he wanted or needed, but nevertheless, it was his. He slipped the weapon into his pocket.

"Come," he said as he again grabbed her wrist and began to pull her away from the relative safety of the rocks.

"Where are we going?" Michelle yelled as the force of a nearby explosion nearly knocked her off her feet. Do all these men grab and drag? she wondered to herself. Then aloud she asked hopefully, "To Commander Massoud?"

"Massoud is organizing the defense," Abdullah answered. "I am going to put you in the safest place I can think, and I want you to stay there. I have to get back to the Commander, and I can't keep worrying about you."

"You're leaving me alone?" Michelle asked in terror. Abdullah didn't answer.

They reached a rusted, burned-out, Soviet-era tank, a long abandoned relic from another war. "Get under there," Abdullah said, pointing to the space beneath what was left of the vehicle. "Whatever you do, don't move until someone comes to get you. I mean it. Don't move."

Dr. Abdullah was gone before she could answer. More explosions in the vicinity caused Michelle to dive under the tank's charred shell. The ground beneath the tank was littered with shrapnel, stones, and various bits of metal fragments. She cleared a space as best she could, cursing herself for not bringing her gloves every time a sharp sliver of metal nipped at her cold fingers. Finally, Michelle curled up into a fetal position on the hard, cold ground, her camera pressed to her chest. Freezing and terrified, she berated herself for ever coming to this wild, hostile land.

from that flame

In the command tent, Dr. Abdullah huddled over the old Soviet map with Commander Massoud. He peered more closely in the dim light before lightly touching his finger to the map. "The RPGs are coming from here and here," Abdullah said and pointed to two spots not far from their present location. "There is also gunfire coming from here," he confirmed, pointing to a third spot on the map. "They are fairly close together in this large valley."

Massoud peered more closely at the map, straining to see in the dim light provided by the lantern. "They have us well triangulated. Are there men positioned elsewhere?"

"Here," Abdullah pointed at yet another spot, "but I think they are moving closer to the others here." His hand swept back to a previously indicated spot.

"I need to know for sure. Send Mohammed to scout the area. And our men have positioned themselves where?"

Abdullah jabbed at the map again "Here, here, and here."

"How well are they armed?"

"Moderately well. Half a dozen rocket launchers and missiles, two light cannons, about fourteen DshKs. Everyone has an AK- 47. At least a hundred rounds each, I would guess."

"No mortars?

"We only had a few, and they were used first."

Massoud was grim as he studied the map searching for a small strategic advantage.

He glanced at Abdullah. "Send Mohammed to reconnoiter this area, and then find Commanders Mehmet, Amin, and Ollah, and bring them here."

Massoud suddenly remembered the journalist. "Abdullah, were is Michelle Garrett? Surely she is not in her tent?"

"No, I took her to that rusted out Soviet tank behind the southern ridge that we saw yesterday. She'll be safe there."

"You should have brought her here," Commander Massoud said. "She must be frightened half to death."

"I thought she would be safer farther away from the front line," Abdullah explained.

Commander Massoud nodded and dismissed her from his mind. "Go get the Commanders, will you please?"

As Abdullah left, Commander Massoud bent even closer to

the map and coaxed its secrets from the well creased folds.

"I want you to take your men and go this way." Massoud's finger traced a path on the map. He looked at Commander Ollah to be certain he understood and then turned to the next man. "Mehmet, you will take your men and go this way," he instructed as his finger traced another route.

"We will move to their rear flank and come from behind," Mehmet said and nodded in agreement.

"Yes," Commander Massoud said. "You will come this way with your men, and you, Commander Ollah, will approach this way with your men. Commander Amin, you will spread your men out across this ridge here." His finger swept a long trail on the map. "They will keep the Taliban fighters pinned down while the others move into position.

"Commander Ollah, avoid this strip of land." Massoud's finger jabbed the map. "It is heavily mined. Be certain to go this way." His finger slid down a geographic mountain. He looked from one man to the other. "Does everyone understand?" They all nodded. "Good." Massoud shifted his position from sitting to kneeling. "We will pray for God's blessing before you go."

All night Michelle lie listening to explosions and gunfire, constantly wondering if the next grenade or rocket would land on the tank. Sometimes the concussions were so close, rust fragments from the tank rained down on her head. Other times, the booms were so far away, they sounded like a faint rumbling of thunder. Finally, at dawn's first light, the world became silent. After the quiet was unbroken for half an hour, Michelle fell asleep from nervous exhaustion.

She didn't know how long she had been asleep when she awoke with a start, but the day's light seemed brighter. A scorched tree that she could see from her vantage point was casting a long shadow, and she guessed that it was still very early. Her muscles were cramped, and her back ached from a night spent on the cold ground. More than anything, she wanted to crawl out from beneath the tank, stretch, and warm herself in the sun's meager heat. But Dr. Abdullah had told her to stay there until someone came for her, and no one had come. Her teeth began to chatter uncontrollably.

What if they are all dead? she thought with alarm. What if they retreated and forgot about me? What if Doctor Abdullah was killed, and no one knows where he hid me? What if no one comes looking for me?

Michelle tortured herself with thoughts like these until she was half mad with fear. Still, she was afraid to leave the relative safety of the tank's belly. She looked at the tree again. The shadow was shorter. The day was growing older, and still no one came. She was beginning to think about climbing out from under the tank despite Abdullah's warning when she suddenly lifted her head from the ground and listened intently. Was that the sound of footfalls? She curled back into a fetal position, her senses on alert, and listened.

"Miss Garrett?" a voice called out softly. "Are you here?" the voice continued in French. "It's Ahmed Shah Massoud."

"I'm here," Michelle called out and started to drag herself out from under the tank.

Every muscle screamed in protest. When she was able to stand, her head began to pound with blinding pain. She felt dizzy and sick to her stomach. When she put weight on her sprained ankle, shock waves shot through her body.

Commander Massoud had planned on teasing her about her dirty face and her wild, rust-covered hair, but when he saw how pale she had became and how ill she looked, the laughing words fell away unspoken.

"Are you hurt?" he asked with genuine concern.

"I'm fine," she answered a half second before she pitched forward in a dead faint.

Michelle felt someone pressing a cold, damp cloth against her forehead. Slowly she opened her eyes. An unknown man sat beside her where she lay on a pallet on the ground inside a tattered tent. The man smiled in relief. Over his shoulder she saw Ahmed Shah Massoud come into view.

"What happened?" she asked him.

"You fainted," Massoud answered. "I brought you to my medic's tent."

"I never fainted before in my life," Michelle protested and tried to sit up. The medic pressed a restraining hand against her shoulder with a kindly shake of his head.

"Please rest a moment longer," Massoud urged her. "I want to make certain that you're all right."

"I'm fine. Really," Michelle insisted. "My dignity is bruised, but the rest of me is fine." If she had been completely honest, she would have to admit that the musty tent started to spin before her eyes the moment she tried to sit up.

"There is no need to be embarrassed," Massoud said gently. "It was a fierce battle even for us. I can't imagine what the experience must have been like for someone unaccustomed to war. Your camera did not fare as well as you did." He held up a broken lens.

"I have another. I admit, I was sacred half to death," Michelle answered. "After Doctor Abdullah left me under the tank, I kept expecting a mortar to land on me at any minute."

"He should not have left you there alone." A small frown crossed Massoud's face.

"He was worried about getting back to the fight, and he thought it was the safest, most out-of-the-way place for me," Michelle observed. "I know he meant to do the best thing for all of us."

"Yes, he did," Massoud agreed pleasantly. Michelle couldn't tell if his change of tone was genuine or not. He said something to the medic that Michelle didn't understand.

"*Amer Saheb*," the man nodded to Massoud and left the tent.

"He has other patients," Massoud explained. "We suffered several injuries last night."

"And he had to leave them to attend to my fainting spell? Now I feel terrible as well as ridiculous." Michelle took the cold cloth from her forehead and frowned.

"Nonsense. You are our guest. He was glad to help you. Abdul mentioned that you had sprained your ankle, and the medic bandaged it. Now, if you promise me that you will continue to stay here and rest, I will check on my men and then come back with some tea." He was gone before Michelle had time to protest or agree.

Wondering if she was now alone in the tent, Michelle craned her neck to look around its dim recesses. From what she could see, the medic had little equipment available. A low, portable table stood against the back wall. Resting on it was an old lantern and ancient-looking instruments, presumably all the medic had at his disposal with which to perform minor surgery. Since there was no autoclave visible, Michelle guessed that the old man had to boil water to sterilize his equipment, such as it was. On the table also were several rolls of bandages, clean cloths, and a leather belt. Michelle didn't even want to think what the belt might be used to do. She also saw several small bottles of pills that she assumed were antibiotics.

There were several rugs spread on the floor to keep damaged bodies off the cold ground. Also in this tent was something she never expected to see, a *sandali*: the traditional heating apparatus comprised of a square, wooden table covered by a big cotton quilt with a charcoal fire underneath in the *mankal* or brazier. No wonder she was warm for the first time in the past twenty-four hours. True, this one was about half the size of others she had seen, but even so, she couldn't imagine how the medic managed to haul that contraption around the mountains. However he did it, she was absolutely certain that his patients appreciated it. They would also enjoy whatever it was that had been tossed onto the charcoal embers to fill the tent with the fragrance of sandalwood. The problem, as Michelle saw it, was that there was no one else around to share the warmth and scent. She felt completely isolated and alone and wondered if it had been handled that way by design. Probably. The *mujahidin* soldiers might object to sharing a tent with a Western female. There is no way to change it, she decided. Warm and relaxed, Michelle dozed off into a far more peaceful sleep than she had had the night before.

"Miss Garrett?"

Michelle opened her eyes at the sound of her name. Commander Massoud had returned with two cups of hot, green tea. He sat near her pallet, waited for her to sit up, and handed her a cup of the steaming drink.

from that flame

"*Merci. S'il vous plaît,* Commander, won't you call me Michelle? Not only did I faint into your arms, you had to drag me all the way back here. I think you have earned the right to call me by my first name"

He returned her smile with a warm one of his own. "Only if you call me Ahmed Shah. After all, I am not your commander."

"I think you could command all of Afghanistan," she said with genuine respect.

He smiled again but shook his head slightly. "I have no wish to command this country. I fight so that my people may one day command themselves."

"Surely you must want something more than that? Something for yourself?"

"As much leisure time as I want to read poetry," he answered honestly, a softness creeping into his eyes and voice.

"Poetry?" Michelle repeated in surprise. "What type of poetry?"

"Persian. The most beautiful poetry in the world," he answered as his wistful expression traveled from his eyes to his mouth. He shook his head as if to cast away those things he could not have and looked at her directly. "Tell me about yourself, will you?"

Michelle sipped the hot tea as she thought about what to tell this man. She had considered her life rather interesting and exciting, but compared to his, her own life actually seemed quite ordinary.

"I wanted to be a journalist since I was a little girl. My parents discouraged me. They wanted me to be a teacher. They thought journalism was too unsure, too dangerous a field for a woman. But I can be pretty stubborn."

"*Non! C'est vrai?* Really?" Massoud said in mock surprise.

"Yeah, yeah," Michelle waved her hand dismissively. "You can call it stubborn if you wish. I prefer to think I am determined."

"That you are," he agreed, but a chuckle took any sting from his words. His hand swept the room. "And look where it landed you. Did you attend college for journalism?"

"Yes, but it didn't do me much good. I ran into the old trick bag about experience."

Massoud was puzzled. "Excuse me, but what is a 'trick bag'?"

"No one wants to hire you to be a journalist until you have experience as a journalist, but how can you get experience if no one will hire you? There is no answer. It's a trick bag with no way out."

"Ah, I see," Massoud nodded. "But you found a way out?"

"Eventually. I was hired by a small town newspaper and was bored out of my mind after less than a year. A person can only write so many obituaries before it becomes routine." Michelle saw the pained expression on Massoud's face and realized what she had said.

"I am sorry. That was terribly insensitive of me. Please forgive me."

"There is nothing to forgive. Our life's experiences are different, that's all. For the difference, I thank God for your sake."

"You're the one who might—or rather should—be jaded about death. You've seen so much of it. How do you not become immune?" Michelle finished the last of her tea.

"I suppose I have in a way," Massoud said slowly. "If I allowed myself to become bogged down in grief, I would not be able to carry on the battle. Yet when my men die, as some did last night, I stop to realize that a life, a gift from Allah, has been taken, and the realization causes me sorrow. Today when we bury them, I will allow myself time to mourn for just a little while. I mourn for every life these twenty years of war have taken from us."

They sat in silence for several moments. Finally Michelle spoke again. "I think I should go back to Peshawar. You have too many other concerns to be worried about protecting me too."

"I am very sorry, Michele *Jaan*, but I'm afraid that's not possible right now. You will have to remain with us a while longer, at least until we reach Jorm."

"Why? What happened last night?"

"We had heavy casualties. I can't afford to send four or five of my men with you to Peshawar right now. The Taliban will regroup and attack again soon. We need to move to more defensible ground immediately."

"What will I do?"

"You will stay with us as my special guest. We will gradually make our way to Khwaja Bahauddin. You will go with us as far as Jorm. I will be able to get more men and re-supply them. From there I will be able to send men with you to Peshawar. I doubt I will be able to arrange to locate and bring to you the RAWA woman in Kabul."

Michelle forced a smile to her face and tried to hide her fear and worry. "Don't worry about that. As you said yesterday, I think I can find something to write about you."

"Then it is settled." Massoud got to his feet. "I had someone bring your things," he said and pointed to her belongings in another part of the tent. "Please stay here and continue to rest while we conduct our burials. Someone will come for you when we break camp and prepare to go."

"Will I see you then?"

"Yes, of course." He stopped at the opening and turned back to her. "I have a proposition for you."

"What sort of proposition?" Michelle asked with mock suspicion in her voice. "Don't tell me you're going to make me learn how to shoot a rocket launcher."

Massoud laughed at the suggestion. "No, nothing quite that drastic although learning to shoot a small, personal weapon would be a good idea. I was going to propose that in exchange for Abdullah giving you lessons in Dari, you give me lessons in English."

"What does Dr. Abdullah get out of that arrangement?" Michelle smiled.

Massoud thought for a moment. "Time when neither of us is asking him to do something for either of us?"

"I am certain he would appreciate that," Michelle laughed aloud. She realized that she felt much better than she had earlier. His kindness and warmth had distracted her and made her feel safe again.

"*Ahmed Shah?*" she called to his retreating back. He turned to look at her. "*Merci,*" she said softly.

"You are welcome," he said in English, smiled, and left to bury his dead.

from that flame

"Miss Garrett?" Dr. Abdullah's voice came from outside the medic's tent. "May I come in?"

"Yes, of course," Michelle answered. She watched the broad shouldered, bearded man come through the flap. "Are we ready to go?"

"Soon," Abdullah nodded. "Commander Massoud has a favor to ask."

"Anything. What can I do for him?"

"Wear these." Dr. Abdullah handed her a neatly folded stack of clothes, a *pakol* on top. "Please," he added as an afterthought.

Michelle held up the camouflage pants. "He wants to me dress like a *mujahidin*?" she asked in bewilderment.

"We will be traveling through some dangerous areas," Abdullah explained. "The Commander thought it would be better if you didn't stand out as much. Consider it a disguise to keep you safe."

Michelle shrugged. "That makes sense, I guess." She looked at Abdullah who stood still as if waiting. "Is there something else, Doctor?"

"No," Abdullah answered.

"Are you going to stand there and watch me change?" Michelle asked pointedly.

"Oh, no!" Abdullah flushed a deep red. "Forgive me. I will wait outside."

"I was kidding!" Michelle called after him, but he was gone. The man was a conundrum to her. She had tried half a dozen different approaches in order to get him to relax and drop his guard around her, but nothing worked. She didn't know why he disliked or resented her, or even if he had any opinion of her at all. Whenever he was around, though, she felt tense and cautious. She couldn't imagine laughing and teasing with him the way she did with Commander Massoud. Still, the man must have something of value, or Massoud wouldn't keep him as close as he did. She sighed and held the *pakol* in her hands. She never liked hats. Resolutely, she began to unbutton her sweater.

Ahmed Shah Massoud swallowed a smile and arranged his

face in pleasant, approving lines. "You look...um..." He searched for a word to use in this extraordinary situation.

"*Une idiote?*" Michelle finished the sentence for him as she tucked the rest of her hair up under the *pakol*. The clothes provided her were several sizes too large.

"*Intéressante,*" Commander Massoud smiled in spite of himself.

"Interesting like a strange zoo specimen no one has ever seen before." She caught his eye and saw the merriment dancing there. "This is your fault," she said, bursting into laughter.

"Guilty as charged, but I hope it will keep you safer. Are you ready to go?"

Michelle nodded, ducked back into the tent to get her pack, and emerged again. "Ready," she pronounced. She fell into step next to the Commander.

"I know what a burden I have become to you," she said. "I am sorry. That was never my intention."

"I know that," Massoud said kindly. "Things often happen that are beyond our control. It is life. And death."

"How many men did you lose last night?"

"Fourteen killed and eight wounded."

"So many! You blame yourself, don't you?" Michelle said with a sudden flash of insight. She saw the deep lines around his eyes and wondered what horrors those eyes had seen.

"Yes and no. I know we fight for a worthy cause. I know it was the Taliban who started the battle. But I also know those men fought and died because I asked them."

"But in the end it was their choice, wasn't it?" Michelle tread carefully. "They fought and died for what they believed, for what they held dear. Would they have gone away if you had told them to go? Or would they have stayed anyway and said to you, 'This is where we belong. This is our fight too'?"

"They would have stayed," Massoud said in a voice barely above a whisper.

"Then if you blame yourself for their deaths, do you not diminish their right to make these important decisions for themselves?"

"You are being philosophical," Massoud said with a shake his head. "I am talking about flesh-and-blood men I knew and loved. Men who will never return home to their families. It is not easy to be philosophical about them."

"I know," Michelle agreed and said no more. They walked in silence for several kilometers. Eventually Commander Massoud went ahead, and Dr. Abdullah stepped into the space beside the journalist. She would rather Massoud had stayed. Dr. Abdullah did not speak as they walked.

By Michelle's estimate they had traveled at least eighteen kilometers by the time night began to fall. She was more tired than she ever remembered being. Her feet hurt. Her legs hurt. Her back, under the weight of the heavy pack, hurt.

Several times Commander Massoud stopped his convoy so that he could climb to a higher point and survey the landscape with his binoculars. Satisfied that the Taliban was not in direct pursuit, they continued on their way.

"How much farther to Jorm?" Michelle asked Dr. Abdullah.

The doctor thought for a moment before answering. "Three times as far as we traveled today," he said at last. "But men have been sent ahead who will barely stop to sleep and will get there in two days. They will return and meet us along the road with a car or another vehicle."

"How does the Northern Alliance get its financing?" Michelle asked unexpectedly. "I mean, these men don't fight for free, do they? You all need to eat. You need to be re-supplied. I can't imagine how much it costs to finance a war for so many years, but it must be expensive."

"We do not deal in heroin if that is what you are implying," Abdullah replied sharply.

"I didn't say anything about heroin," Michelle protested. "I asked a legitimate question. If you don't want to answer, I'll ask the Commander later." Will this man ever stop being suspicious of me? Michelle wondered with exasperation.

"Many of the men are volunteers. We get some weapons from, shall we say, 'interested' governments. We also have a gem mining operation," Abdullah answered.

"Gems?" Michelle repeated in surprise.

from that flame

"Emeralds and lapis lazuli. Commander Massoud has means to market them internationally."

Michelle shook her head. "He is an amazing man. Run a war. Run an international business. Run a country. Is there anything he can't do?"

"No, not the country," Dr. Abdullah answered. "Commander Massoud is Tajik. Too many tribes would never accept a Tajik leader. It is a minority, you know."

"I thought he got along with everyone. Except the Taliban, I mean."

"There are…friendships of convenience and partnerships of necessity," Abdullah spoke carefully. "This is a war we fight. Trying to build a peace with these same friends and partners would be nearly impossible." Abdullah rubbed his beard. "Although," he continued quietly, "there are times I think that if anyone could unite all the factions of this land, it is Ahmed Shah Massoud."

Michelle didn't answer. She certainly had no argument with Abdullah's conclusion. She saw Massoud himself approaching them.

"How are you doing?" he asked her.

"Fine, thanks," she lied. "Are we stopping for the night?"

"There are caves up there." The Commander pointed to a spot with a slightly higher elevation. "They will provide both shelter and protection."

"I'm right behind you." Michelle smiled steadily although her teeth were clenched. They began the rocky ascent.

Michelle looked around the encampment. She knew there were at least sixty men in their party, but she could only see four or five. She guessed the others had scattered into various foxholes and depressions where they would keep watch throughout the long, cold night. While walking, she asked Dr. Abdullah about the phrase she had heard the medic use to address the Commander at the other camp.

"What does 'Amer Saheb' mean?" she asked.

"Loosely translated it would mean 'dear boss.' You must have heard someone address the Commander that way. It is a nick-

from that flame

name used by many people in the region and especially by his men."

"Yes, the medic addressed him by that name. I saw great respect in the man's eyes when he looked at the Commander."

"I think Commander Massoud reminds the old man of his dead son. But do not mistake me. The Commander is respected and loved by all his men. Any of them would gladly give his life in order to save him or march to their own deaths on his order."

Michelle reflected on that conversation as she watched Abdullah approach the medic and speak to him. The medic nodded and hurried off quickly in the direction of the cave in which Massoud was setting up his command center.

"Is the Commander ill?" Michelle asked as she walked over to Dr. Abdullah.

"He has chronic back pain. It has been serious enough in the past that he has had to be in hospital. He tries to hide the pain, but I can tell from the way he walks when it hurts him. This was a long hike for him today."

"I noticed that he wears heavy military boots. Is that best?"

"No, unless they were especially designed to support his back and relieve some of the pain. I suggested he have some made, but he thinks they would be an extravagance."

"What will the medic do for him now?"

"Apply hot compresses—if the Commander agrees to lie down long enough to be treated." Dr. Abdullah shook his head in resignation.

"You're a doctor. Why don't you take care of him?"

"I do when his health concerns are serious. I was first signed on to be the medical practitioner for the resistance, but then other responsibilities came my way. Now the medic handles almost all of the health concerns, and my position is advisory. Will you help me find a safe place to build a small fire so that Commander Massoud can have his compresses and the men can have their dinner?"

"Yes, of course," Michelle agreed immediately. The doctor was suddenly more open and approachable than he had been all day.

After she had eaten, Michelle went to the mouth of the cave

but stopped in hesitation. "Commander Massoud? May I come in?" she called out. "I have food for you."

"Yes, of course, come in," the Commander answered. "I thought we had reached an agreement about using first names, Miss Garrett?"

By the pale light of the very small fire on the floor near him, Michelle could see him grimace as he struggled to sit up.

"Please stay resting," she said hastily. "I won't think your manners are bad if you don't get up, Ahmed Shah *Jaan*."

"Thank you, Michelle *Jaan*." He sighed with relief and eased himself onto the pallet he used as a bed. "Do you have tea?" Michelle had asked Abdullah about the word *jaan* and learned it was an Afghan term that signified respect and friendship.

"Yes," Michelle moved closer and carefully handed him a full cup of hot tea. He raised his head high enough to sip it before setting the cup on the ground next to him.

"It doesn't look like the compresses helped your back very much," Michelle observed.

"You know about that, do you? My secret is out." Massoud smiled at her. Nothing could diminish the warmth of his smile. "Promise me that you won't tell my enemies about this weakness."

"I promise," Michelle agreed solemnly. "May I sit down?" She pointed to the ground next to him.

"My coat is over there," the Commander said and pointed to his other side. "Please use it as a cushion."

"Here." Michelle set the small bowl of rice and mutton and a piece of bread on his chest before going around him to get the coat.

"I'm not hungry." Massoud set the dish next to the teacup.

"Nevertheless, you must eat." Michelle sat down, retrieved the bowl, and handed it back to him.

His slender fingers grasped the bread, dipped it into the bowl, and withdrew a small amount of the contents. He obediently put the food in his mouth and chewed. "Happy?" he said when he finished.

"Hardly. Ahmed Shah *Jaan*, you have done so much for me. Will you allow me to try to help you with your pain?"

from that flame

Massoud smiled again. "Do you have an American aspirin?" The lines around his eyes deepened, but the light in his eyes brightened with his smile.

"Yes, actually, I do," Michelle said in surprise because she had forgotten all about the small bottle buried in her pack. "I'll go get them."

"No, stay. You weren't thinking about aspirin. How else were you going to help me?"

"My father had a bad back. He suffered terrible pain. Whenever he was in physical therapy, he seemed to improve. When his health insurance started to run out, the physical therapist taught me the massage techniques she used to ease his pain. I could try those techniques on you, if you wish."

"You would do that for me? Your hands are small. Will they not tire? I don't want you to exert yourself on my behalf."

"Who was it that dragged me back to base camp after I fainted? Having to cart me back probably aggravated your condition worse than walking did. I owe you."

"No, of course not," Commander Massoud protested immediately. "But if you would do the massage for me, I would be very grateful."

"I will have to touch you."

"Yes, I imagine it would be difficult to give someone a massage without touching him," he said and laughed softly. "But wait," a new thought crossed his mind. "Would it be improper for you? What are your customs in a situation such as this?"

"I've never been in a situation like this. I'm making things up as I go along."

Commander Massoud laughed again but more loudly. The laughter alone was a healing gift for him. "As am I. 'Making it up' as we go along, I mean. All right. Let us do it this way. Please go find my medic. I will tell him that I want him to observe this massage technique. Then, when you are no longer with us, he will be able to perform the therapy. Meanwhile, his presence here will discourage anyone from thinking impure thoughts."

"You think of everything. While I'm gone, will you eat something?"

Commander Massoud nodded and obediently picked up the bowl containing his dinner. Michelle nodded in satisfaction and then hurried out in search of the older man. A few minutes later she returned carrying her backpack, the medic close on her heels.

"I do have aspirin," Michelle said as she dug in her pack. "They might help a little."

Massoud raised his hand to stop her before she dumped the entire contents of her pack onto the ground. "Let's save them in case tomorrow is worse, all right? The massage will be enough in itself. I am very grateful for your kind offer."

Massoud turned to his medic and spoke to him softly in Dari. The older man carefully helped the Commander remove his shirt and roll over onto his stomach. The medic looked at Michelle and made a gesture indicating that it was time for her to begin.

The medic sat a short distance away and watched with great interest while the foreign woman rubbed her hands together to warm them before touching the Commander's back.

"Where does the pain seem to have its origin?" Michelle asked.

"I think it is the sciatic nerve," Massoud's muffled voice answered, "but then the pain emanates out in every direction."

"Okay, I'll see if I can find the bad spots," Michelle said and finally laid her hands on him. Carefully, gently, her fingers began to probe the muscles of his back.

"Good grief," she proclaimed shortly. "Your muscles are bunched and tied in knots." She began to knead two of the worst. "Can you try to relax?"

"I'm sorry. I was trying to remember where I left my maps."

"No battle plans right now, Commander," Michelle scolded him. "You have to think relaxing thoughts. Tell me something pleasant. What do you like to do when you're at home?"

"If I were at home right now, I would find my baby daughter and give her the bedtime bath. She likes to splash water at my face. I tickle her feet, and she kicks them in the water and makes big splashes until I am soaked too."

"What happens next?" Michelle prompted softly.

"She likes for me to read stories to her. One night I let her pick a story, and the next night it is my turn to choose. She always picks fairy tales, and I always pick poetry. I read until she falls asleep. I tuck her blankets in around her. I love to sit and watch her sleep. There is such beauty and innocence in children. We must leave the world a better place for them."

"Don't you have a son too?" Michelle kept her voice low and soft as her hands continued to seek the source of his pain. The medic closely observed her movements.

"Ahmad. He's twelve. I have been away too much of his life. Once I couldn't get home for an entire year."

"I'm sure he is very proud of his father."

"He said he wanted to be a soldier like me. I told him not to become one because then he will be away from home all the time just as I am. I told him to be a medical doctor instead. One of my daughters said she wanted to be a pilot. I told her that she might be shot down, and I would lose a daughter. Better she become a teacher."

"A doctor, a teacher; you want your children to have safe jobs and good lives."

"Yes, of course. What parent does not want that for his children? It's one of the reasons we must drive the Taliban from this land. My daughters must be free to have an education and career, not only in Panjshir, but in Kabul as well."

"You mentioned the Taliban, and a dozen more muscles bunched up," Michelle scolded. She stopped massaging his back and started to dig through her pack again.

"Are you finished?" Commander Massoud asked with disappointment in his voice.

"No, not yet," Michelle muttered as she continued to search for something. "Ha! Here it is. Better than aspirin."

"What?" Massoud twisted his head around and tried to see what she had in her hands. He couldn't clearly see what she was holding.

"Lay back down," Michelle commanded. She slipped a lightweight set of headphones over his ears and pressed a button on her CD player. "Beethoven. If this string quartet doesn't relax you, nothing will. No more talking. Just listen to the music." She began to knead his back again. This time she felt the tense muscles begin to relax beneath her skilled hands. Within fifteen minutes she felt his breathing pattern change. Her touch grew lighter and slower and finally stopped. She smiled and nodded at the medic who gave her an approving nod.

"Sleep well," Michelle whispered as she began to stand. She almost touched his hair but withdrew her hand before she did. Despite his kindness and friendliness towards her, and she did believe he was genuine and sincere in his attitude, she knew there was a line of over-familiarity that she must not cross no matter how natural it might seem under these unusual circumstances. Despite his friendliness towards her, he was still a great warrior and military genius. He was still Afghanistan's only hope in holding back the sweeping flood of a Taliban takeover. He was still the *mujahidin* fighter who was largely responsible for driving the Soviet Union from the land. No matter how badly his back may hurt him, his spine was made of steel. She knew instinctively that it would be a serious error to mistake his kindness for weakness. Massoud was forged iron and capable of doing whatever was necessary under any situation that presented itself. Only a fool would underestimate the power and strength of this man, and Michelle was not a fool.

She stood up, shook out his coat, and carefully covered him with it. Smiling and nodding at the old medic, she left the sleeping Commander to his dreams of a day when he would no longer be called upon to wage war.

Outside the cave entrance, Michelle bumped into Dr. Abdullah. "He's asleep," she warned the doctor, hoping he had not come to talk to the commander.

"Good," Abdullah said with satisfaction. "Thank you for helping him."

"I'm grateful for the opportunity to do something in return for his many kind acts," Michelle answered. "Is there anything I can do for you, Doctor?"

"Thank you, no." Abdullah smiled at her genuinely for the first time. "Let me walk with you to where you will be sleeping. You should rest now too. Tomorrow will be another long day."

Michelle began to hope that the doctor's coldness towards her was gone for good.

"I haven't slept so well in a long time," Massoud said to Michelle the next morning as he handed her the CD player. "I missed writing in my journal and reading my poetry as I do every night, but it was worth it. Thank you for your kindness to me."

"And we all stayed safe and sound despite the fact that you didn't get to find your map and spend hours studying it," Michelle teased. "I am glad I was able to give you some relief." She pulled the *pakol* onto her head and began tucking her hair beneath it. "We can do it again tonight if you want."

"Thank you. Let us wait to see what kind of conditions we have tonight, all right?" Massoud nodded at her. "Now if you will excuse me, I must go study the maps I failed to study last night."

"How long until we pull out?" Michelle asked.

Massoud calculated in his mind. "About two hours. Why? Are you eager to resume the hike through our beautiful mountains?" he concluded with a smile.

"I was wondering if I had time to wander around and take some pictures, that's all," Michelle said. "It is beautiful here, and I may never pass this way again."

"Take Abdul with you, and don't go too far. Remember, the land is heavily mined. Stick to the paths, and don't wander off them whatever you do. Be back in an hour."

"Yes, sir." Michelle made a mock salute. Massoud laughed. He couldn't remember the last time he had laughed so often. He was unaccustomed to this Western woman's easy, casual, manner and her sense of irreverent fun, and the novelty of it amused him. During many of their grimmest days there was no reason to smile, much less laugh. Massoud was sure he would know those days again. Meanwhile, he intended to enjoy every moment of light-hearted fun brought his way by her. He motioned for Dr. Abdullah to join him in the temporary command center but paused a moment before going in so that he could watch Michelle walk over to Abdul. Satisfied that she would be okay, he dismissed her from his mind and prepared to focus on the serious matters at hand.

Commander Massoud poured over the old Soviet-era maps spread on the ground in front of him and Abdullah. His commanders sat on the floor in a circle around him. Massoud went around the circle asking each commander precise questions about what had happened during the last battle. He listened carefully to each man's answer. Often there were follow-up questions, references to the map, or animated discussions about various strategic options for the next battle. Once Massoud was satisfied with the end result of one commander's explanations and comments, he would move on to the next man.

Occasionally, Massoud would go outside, climb a little higher up the mountain side, raise his binoculars to his eyes, and carefully scan the terrain for Taliban movement. He had rear guards deployed, but they might not see what he could from his higher vantage point. Everything seemed quiet, but he knew better than to trust appearances.

Back in the cave-turned-command center, Commander Massoud continued discussing his plans. They were going to wage an offensive attack against the Taliban troops they knew were close behind them. Even if they could not kill them all, killing some would make the others retreat long enough to regroup. That would give the Northern Alliance a few extra hours to reach the next staging ground. Where were the tanks positioned? Where were the few remaining helicopters? Were the stockpiled munitions dumps full? Did the men fully understand the ground plan?

Finally satisfied that all was ready, Massoud called two of his most trusted soldiers to the command center. He gave the men a lengthy, detailed message to be delivered in person, and made each one repeat it back to him. These men brought messages to the other *mujahidin* commanders and troops positioned on the opposite side of the Panjshir Valley. At this juncture, Massoud didn't want to risk the interception of a satellite phone call or radio message. It would be absolutely essential that at least one of them made it through to the other side. The ultimate offensive plan depended on everyone positioning himself in an exact location.

Massoud invited the soldier-messengers to join him and his commanders in prayer before they left. He personally helped load them with supplies of bread, water, and dried mulberries. He made sure that their Kalashnikovs had full clips. Finally, he embraced each one as he would his own son and prayed that God would protect them and bless their efforts with success. He climbed to his vantage point on the mountain once more, searched the countryside through his binoculars, and signaled that it was safe for them to proceed towards the southeast. He watched them leave the camp and prayed again that they would remain safe throughout their dangerous journey.

"Ahmed Shah?" Dr. Abdullah said.

"Hmmm?" Commander Massoud answered absently as he watched the soldiers disappear from sight.

"You have us traveling through some very difficult terrain on the route you've selected. The path is narrow and steep with out-croppings of jagged rock. Are you certain we shouldn't look for a different route? One that is less treacherous and demanding?"

"I'm sure," the Commander answered firmly. "We have sup-plies stockpiled on that route. As dangerous as it may be for us, it will be even more precarious for the Taliban fighters who are coming after us. They are not familiar with it at all. Why are you concerned?"

"Partly because of your back, and partly because of your jour-nalist."

"She is not *my* journalist."

"Well, she is certainly not mine. Nevertheless, she is with us. Will she be able to make the climb? Will you?"

"Of course I will, and so shall she. She has a lot of spirit and determination."

"All right," Abdullah agreed, "but what about you? I saw how much pain you were in after yesterday's hike, and this path you've laid out for us will be worse."

"I'll be all right, Doctor," the Commander said and patted his friend's arm. "Now let's get this camp broken down and head out. As you said, it is not going to be a pleasant or easy climb." Massoud chuckled to himself.

"What are you laughing about?" Abdullah demanded to know.

"I was just wondering what it would be like to live in a place where there were no mountains. Can you imagine? I barely can. I think when this war is over, I would like to lie on warm sand on a beach somewhere without a mountain in sight."

"You would feel like a fish out of water," Dr. Abdullah laughed himself.

from that flame

"Quite probably, but I would still like to try it."

"So would I," Dr. Abdullah admitted. The two friends went into the command center and began packing up their supplies as they had done at least a thousand times before.

Michelle raised the camera to her eye, framed the picture she wanted to take in the lens, and depressed the button. The electronic whir of the film advancing was the only sound in the still countryside. She lowered the camera and looked at the vast expanse of snow- covered, unimaginably high mountains of the Hindu Kush range. They were beautiful and forbidding at the same time, and she feared she was heading straight into them.

She turned around and looked back over the area through which they had traveled the day before. To the south and west spread the Panjshir Valley which was sliced in half by the Panjshir River. Even in late winter, this land held the promise of verdant fields and abundant crops. She could barely make out terraced acreage that would be plowed and seeded in a few months. Houses standing alone and in clusters dotted the landscape. She knew this area—Massoud's native region of Afghanistan—had absorbed hundreds of thousands of refugees as families fled the advancing Taliban. Michelle wondered where they had been housed and how they were fed. She knew from the women in RAWA that women in Panjshir could work and even ran schools and hospitals, and she wondered again how a man as forward-thinking as Ahmed Shah Massoud could come from the same land as men who viewed women as little more than chattel. It was a question she hoped to answer before she parted ways with him.

Abdul tugged at her coat sleeve and indicated that it was time for them to go back to camp. Michelle smiled and nodded, took one final look around, and followed her guide back down the slippery path they had taken up.

"May I ask a question?" Commander Massoud fell into step with Michelle when they reached a relatively smooth stretch of land.

"Of course, anything." Michelle nodded in agreement.

from that flame

"What makes you choose the job you have? I mean, why did you risk your life coming into a war zone when you could just as easily have stayed somewhere safe?"

Michelle thought for a moment before answering. It was a question she had been asked before but never under these difficult circumstances. It was the same question she had been asking herself.

"You must realize that I am not a war correspondent in the way many of the other journalists who have come to see you are," she spoke slowly as she carefully chose her words. "They can reel off a million facts about the Afghan struggle over the past twenty years, and I know very few of those facts. I don't know very much about your brilliant, military career. You are going to have to explain to me how you managed to defeat the Soviet Union because all I know is that you are credited with having done it."

"I remember that the reason you came to see me had to do with my efforts on behalf of the women of Afghanistan and not the war itself," Commander Massoud said.

"Yes," Michelle agreed. "I seek the truth, Commander. I try to learn and understand something different or new and then explain it to other people in the articles I write. I try to give a voice to those who may not have one. This assignment to meet with the women from RAWA and learn about the plight of women under the Taliban's rule is an important one."

"I agree," the Commander nodded. "I hope that I have been able to contribute to that story. The women of my country are suffering terribly. They need a voice to share their sorrows and tribulations with the world. I am grateful that yours will be that voice."

"Meeting you has added a new depth to the original story," Michelle observed.

"Oh? How is that?"

"The two stories are inexorably linked," Michelle said thoughtfully. "I think the women of your country will continue to suffer until you are successful. I was very distressed by everything I learned while in Pakistan. The entire situation appeared hopeless. The women are isolated, disenfranchised, and seemingly alone in their struggle. I admired their courage, bravery, and determination, but I also feared that those noble qualities would be beaten out of them over time. That was when I heard about you. That was when I knew I needed to come talk to you for myself."

"Weren't you at all afraid to come here alone? You couldn't have known what to expect. It is a dangerous route even before you get to the front lines."

"I was afraid," Michelle admitted. "As you say, I didn't know what to expect. You could have been a horrible man who threw me out of his camp or have simply refused to even speak to a female journalist." Michelle flashed a quick smile at the Commander before becoming serious again. "What I did know was that if there was going to be an element of hope in the story, and that hope had some basis in truth, I had to come, meet you face to face, and hear from your own mouth in your own words that at least part of what you are fighting for is the women."

"And now you know that is true?"

"Yes. And I also know that the struggle of RAWA and your struggle for all of Afghanistan are one and the same. A happy ending for one depends completely on a happy ending for the other."

"I wish I could promise a happy ending to both stories, but this is not one of my daughter's fairy tales." Commander Massoud's face was grim as he spoke, but his soft voice did not change its tone.

"Don't you think you can win?" Michelle asked quietly.

"I don't know," the Commander answered honestly. "It gets harder and harder to keep up the fight. If we don't get resupplied soon, and if we don't get help from the West, the day may come when all we have left is Panjshir. That we will never surrender. As for the rest of the country, I cannot promise to deliver it from the Taliban and al-Qaeda. All I can promise is that I will never stop trying."

"No one can do more than that, Commander."

"But what if it's not enough?" he muttered under his breath. For a fleeting moment an expression crossed his face that Michelle had not seen before. It was as if the light had suddenly been turned off in his eyes. Then the look was gone, and he smiled again. "Excuse me, please. I need to use my binoculars to survey the land behind and in front of us. There is a good vantage point ahead."

from that flame

Michelle watched the Commander stride off as Dr. Abdullah, who had been following a few feet behind them, fell into step with Michelle.

"He won't let himself give in to despair, will he?" Michelle asked the doctor.

"No, he won't. Giving in to despair would mean giving up his faith that God will help him. Ahmed Shah Massoud has amazing faith."

Michelle nodded but said nothing. Dr. Abdullah looked at her more closely. "Are you all right?"

"Yes, thank you," Michelle said and smiled mechanically. "My mind was wandering, that's all."

"How about if we put that mind to work? Are you ready for your first lesson in Dari? You can learn a few phrases and surprise the Commander at dinner."

Michelle flashed a genuine smile this time. "That would be great." She was not only grateful for the diversion, she was also grateful that the doctor seemed to be warming up to her. She wanted him as a friend. She would prove to him that she was a worthy student. She listened with careful attention as he began a basic grammar lesson.

3. Treason

"I'm afraid we don't have much variety in our food," Commander Massoud explained as bowls of rice and mutton, known as *gorma pilau*, were passed around. He, Michelle, and Dr. Abdullah were settled on rugs around a small fire inside a fairly large cave.

"I'm so hungry, I could eat a camel's foot," Michelle pronounced and eagerly accepted the bowl offered her.

"Hopefully it will never come to that," the Commander said with a laugh. "You must be exhausted as well as starving. You did well on our long hike today."

"Did I have another option?" Michelle asked with a straight face. "I mean, what else could I have done but continue hiking? Wait on the side of the path for the Taliban to come along? You've convinced me that would not be a good idea."

"You could have let one of the men carry your pack, at least. It is nearly as big as you are when you add the sleeping bag to the bottom of the frame."

"No way." Michelle shook her head vehemently. "I'll carry my own weight—and the weight of my pack. Thanks just the same."

"As you wish. Remember, however, that the higher we get, the thinner the air gets, and it will be more difficult for you to breathe. Should you need someone to help you, promise me that you will ask."

"I promise," Michelle agreed. "How about you? How is your back? Climbing and climbing can't be easy for you."

"Did I have another option?" Massoud smiled at his guest. "I suppose I could have waited for the Taliban too. Perhaps tomorrow you and I will sit on the side of the trail and see what happens when they show up."

Dr. Abdullah smiled as he spoke, but his voice was serious. "You didn't answer her question, my friend. It is something I would like to know as well. How is your back? Are you in pain?"

"Great, now I have two of you worrying about me as if I were a sick child," Massoud shook his head in disbelief. "Are you going to take turns or gang up on me at the same time?"

"And still you do not answer the question," Dr. Abdullah persisted.

Massoud threw up his hands in resignation. "All right, yes, I am in some pain. It was a very long hike. But I will rest now, and by morning I'll be fine and ready to go. Satisfied?"

"I will massage your back again," Michelle said. "It seemed to help."

"It did help," the Commander agreed, "but you are weary, and I do not want you to exert yourself any further on my behalf."

"Is he always so hardheaded?" Michelle asked Dr. Abdullah.

"Yes," Abdullah said and nodded in agreement. "He's right, you know. We are ganging up on him. I think I rather enjoy it."

"You would," Massoud said dryly, but with a soft chuckle.

Michelle stood up. "I need to go outside for a few minutes to…um…when I come back, I'll give you that massage. I have another CD you'll enjoy hearing."

"I really should study the maps and review tomorrow's route," Massoud countered.

"You can check them in the morning before we leave," Dr. Abdullah said in his pragmatic doctor's voice. "Tonight, I prescribe the massage, the music, and a good night's sleep."

"I can see that from now on I don't dare leave you two alone to plan your plots against me." Massoud frowned, but his eyes twinkled. "All right. This night we will do it your way. Just this once. Michelle *Jaan*, be careful out there."

"I will," she said. "I'll be right back." The men watched her leave.

"You like her very much, don't you?" Abdullah asked his friend.

from that flame

"Yes, I do," Commander Massoud said candidly. "She is unlike anyone I have ever met. Almost all the other Westerners, and certainly all the other journalists, have been men. Such a woman is completely new to my experience. Her mind works differently. I never quite know what she will say, and I enjoy the unpredictability of that."

"That's it? You enjoy her unpredictability?" Abdullah teased.

"Perhaps there is a little more than that," Commander Massoud said as he smiled in agreement. "I admire her spirit too. She is undaunted, isn't she? Perhaps it is not unusual for American women to be fearless and bold, but, as I said, it is new to my experience."

"She's not afraid of you," Dr. Abdullah observed. "She teases you and makes you laugh more than I have ever heard you laugh. She respects and admires you very much, yet at the same time she is irreverent. She considers herself an equal—and a friend."

"She is both," the Commander agreed. "She is also open-minded, warm, generous, and kind. I admire her easy, relaxed ability to take so many new experiences in stride." His face grew somber. "I want to see our women have that same joy in life again. We must do that for them, my friend. It is incumbent upon us."

"We will," Dr. Abdullah said, patting his friend's arm. "But not tonight. Tonight you rest so that you will be strong to lead us into battle another day. And now I am going to retire. Does it matter which of the inner chambers I use?"

"I think Michelle put her things in the one on the left. You may choose either of the others. May Allah watch over you as you sleep, my friend."

"And may His blessings be on you. *Shab bakhair.* Good night."

"Where did Doctor Abdullah go? Should I go find the medic?" Michelle asked a moment later when she returned.

"The poor fellow is probably sound asleep by now. Let's not disturb him."

"Okay. I'll go get the CD player and come right back. Can you take your shirt off by yourself?"

from that flame

"If you don't mind, I would rather talk with you than listen to music or have the massage. Would that be all right?"

"Only if I can get you to relax while listening to my chatter. And you must lie down." Once the commander obeyed, she asked, "What would you like to talk about?"

"Tell me a story about the most amazing place you've ever been."

Michelle made a thoughtful noise as she considered her answer. She knew that she had been blessed in her life to have visited many countries and to have had many wonderful experiences. "That would have to be a volcanic pool high in the Andes Mountains, a place called Cocanuco in Colombia, South America, " she answered at last. "It's a place that would do you a world of good right about now."

"Tell me about it, please. How did you come to be there? Were you in Colombia on an assignment?"

"I was there on assignment one year and made friends. I went back a year later on vacation."

"What was the assignment that took you there? Colombia's guerrilla army?"

"No. I told you, I'm not a war correspondent. I like writing about people. There is a special school in the southwest of the country, a school that teaches mentally handicapped children. I went there to write about the school and became good friends with the people who work there.

"One evening after an especially long, difficult day, the director of the school decided that everyone needed to do something fun to relax. We all piled into his old van and went high into the Andes. The air was very cold, much like it is here right now. We parked the van on the side of the road and walked through what appeared to be some sort of small park. It was very dark and silent out there in the middle of nowhere.

"Suddenly I heard the faint sound of running water and smelled something strange in the air. The closer we got to the sound of the water, the stronger the smell of sulfur became. We finally reached a small clearing. There was a natural bridge of rocks in front of us, and to the right of the bridge was a pool of water with steam rising from it. My friend told me that it was volcanic-fed. Even the rocks that formed the bridge were hot from the water flowing beneath them."

Michelle's voice had taken on a soothing monotone as she softly spoke, and she saw the Commander begin to relax as he listened to her and tried to envision what she described.

"We were high in the mountains, probably as high as we are here, and the stars appeared to be so close, I thought if I stretched far enough, I might be able to grasp one in my hand and pluck it from the sky. I had the same feeling the first night I was in your camp. Anyway, that night was cold and quiet except for the gurgle of the water and the hiss of the steam rising from the pool.

"We took off most of our clothes and eased into the very hot water. The water was deep enough to cover my shoulders, and the pool was long enough to swim several strokes. I think there were seven of us in the pool, and once we all had time to adjust to the temperature, we played. We had splashing fights and races from one side to the other. The water no longer felt painfully hot, but rather soothingly warm and revitalizing. When we would tire from our games, everyone would cling to the side and rest.

"There was a magical quality to the place. Perhaps that quality was caused by the seeming contradictions. The water was hot, yet the air was cold. We were on land though we felt closer to the sky. The silence was profound, but beneath the silence were the whispering sounds of the water and the creatures of the night in the dense, wooded area that surrounded us."

"It sounds splendid," the Commander murmured, nearly asleep.

"It was," Michelle made her voice even more quiet. "When I got out of the water, I laid on the rocks that made the bridge. It was impossible to stay still. Whichever side of my body came in contact with the rocks burned while the other side, which was exposed to the cold air, froze. I flopped from one side to the other like a fish on land before finally giving up and getting dressed. All in all, it was an amazing experience."

Michelle could tell from the rise and fall of his body that his breathing had changed. He was asleep. She stopped speaking, leaned over, and covered him with his coat. This time she allowed her hand a single, light stroke over his dark, gray-streaked hair. She asked God to bless this man upon whom so many burdens rested. After checking the low-burning fire, she found her way to

from that flame

the cave's chamber that was to serve as her sleeping quarters for the night.

Feeling slightly claustrophobic in the close quarters of her inner chamber, Michelle rolled over in her sleeping bag so that she could see the firelight dimly lighting the mouth of the main chamber. Her eyes were heavy with sleep. She closed them and tried to relax even as the sound of her own, shallow breathing seemed to fill the small space of the inner chamber. There was a damp, earthy smell from the ground beneath her, and it caused Michelle's imagination to wander as she thought about the others who had, over the past thousands of years, slept in this same spot. Thinking about Alexander the Great, Michelle drifted off to sleep.

The shaking of the ground was so powerful, bits of rock broke loose from the walls of the cave and cascaded to the ground. Michelle felt the earth move beneath her as she struggled to free herself from her sleeping bag. She had no idea how long she had been asleep, but it felt like only minutes. A shadow appeared in the mouth of the opening to her chamber, blocking the dim light that filtered through from the adjoining room.

"Michelle *Jaan*," she heard Commander Massoud's voice, "stay here. I will return for you when it is safe. Please, stay here."

"Are we under attack again?"

"Yes, but my men are mobilizing. You'll be safe if you stay here." He was gone before Michelle could say anything else. She brought her knees up to her chin and wrapped her arms around her legs. Her eyes strained in the darkness to see something that was not there even as her ears tried to shut out the sounds of the bombs falling close to the cave that sheltered her.

Commander Massoud grabbed his Kalishnikov and hurried to the cave's main entrance. He looked up into the night sky filled with red-orange tracers from the incoming and outgoing ordinance. From the light they cast, he could see his men scrambling into defensible positions.

"How close are they?" Dr. Abdullah asked from behind.

"Two, maybe three kilometers," the Commander answered.

"They shouldn't have been able to get this close without one of our sentries noticing." He cast his friend a worried look. "They shouldn't be so close," he repeated.

Commander Mehmet hurried toward Commander Massoud. "Should I deploy my men in the flanking formation we used last time?"

"No." Massoud shook his head slowly, his eyes scanning and searching the countryside. "Something is not right. Tell your men to hold their positions. Tell Ollah and Amin to have their men do the same. Do not launch an offensive maneuver. Just hold your ground."

Mehmet looked skeptical but agreed. "All right. We need someone on the 82mm."

"Send Zahir there, and then go and relay the message for everyone to hold his ground," Commander Massoud answered.

Mehmet ran off to do as he was ordered. "I'll take the 82mm," Dr. Abdullah said to Commander Massoud.

"No, Let Zahir handle it."

"What do you want me to do?"

"Stay here. Defend this position in case any of the fighters break through our lines."

"Is Michelle Garrett inside?"

"Yes." Commander Massoud glanced at his friend. "Don't let anything happen to her." He handed the Kalishnikov rifle to the doctor.

"I can fight," the doctor argued.

"I know you can, but I need you here. Besides, we will have wounded. You can triage here at the cave." Commander Massoud was gone into the night to make certain that his orders were being followed. Dr. Abdullah lifted the rifle across his chest.

"Abdullah?" Michelle came up behind him and laid her hand on his back.

Abdullah glanced over his shoulder. "Go back inside. It isn't safe here."

"I don't like being alone in the dark. The explosions sound so close, I'm afraid the cave is going to blow up and crash down on top of my head. Please don't make me go back in there all by myself."

from that flame

"All right, stay, but remain well behind me."

"I will," Michelle said fervently. She grasped the back of his heavy coat in each hand. Holding onto the cloth, knowing there was a living, breathing person just on the other side of it, comforted her. Still, every time a bomb or grenade exploded, she jumped a little and tightened her grip.

Abdullah did not complain. He thought back fifteen years ago to a time before war had become a daily occurrence for him, and he remembered how scared he had been during his first days of battle. There was something about an RPG exploding in one's vicinity that was inevitably a reminder of life's fragile brevity. He looked over his shoulder at her again.

"You'll be okay," he said reassuringly as another explosion shook the ground upon which they stood. Michelle buried her face in his coat and said nothing.

As suddenly as the fighting began, it stopped. An unsettling silence fell over the camp. Michelle lifted her head. "Is it over?" she whispered through teeth that chattered.

"*Shhh*," Abdullah hushed her as his ears strained to hear any sound that might give away the enemy's intention. Nothing but silence. Finally, he heard a sound from above and behind him and turned to see Commander Massoud sliding down the end of the path on the heels of his boots. The Commander reached the lip of the short drop off, skidded to a stop, and stepped down the rest of the way.

"What happened?" Dr. Abdullah asked in a low voice.

Massoud gestured towards the interior of the cave. "Let's go inside. I want to check something on the map." He saw Michelle peeking around from Abdullah's back. The Commander switched to French.

"Are you all right? I thought I told you to stay inside the cave."

"I told her it was all right to stay with me," Abdullah said. "She was afraid."

Commander Massoud nodded. "That might have been a better idea all along." He went deeper into the cave, selected the map he wanted, and began to unroll it. Abdullah grabbed one end and

53

helped to smooth it out and hold it flat. Massoud drew a lantern closer to the map and peered at it intently.

"What do you think happened?" Abdullah asked while he watched Commander Massoud nod his head as if what he saw on the map confirmed the thoughts in his mind.

"We are here. We had lookouts stationed here, here, and here." His finger jabbed sharply at three areas on the map. The attack came from this area," he said, pointing to a fourth mark.

"Within our perimeter?" Dr. Abdullah asked in surprise. He pointed to one of the positions Massoud had indicated. "How did they get past the lookout stationed here?"

Commander Massoud's face was grim when he looked at his friend. "That is exactly the question I need answered."

"You think we have a traitor in our midst, don't you?" Abdullah asked in Dari, worry filling his voice. "Someone who knew about the flanking maneuver you used two days ago and was trying to lure our men into a trap?"

Massoud shrugged. "It is the most logical explanation, but let us wait until we hear from the parties involved before jumping to conclusions. Will you please go find Mehmet, Amin, and Ollah and bring them here? We will get to the bottom of this."

As Dr. Abdullah left, Commander Massoud looked at Michelle. "Are you all right?" he asked again. "I know how frightening it must have been for you."

"It was," Michelle said and knelt down next to where he sat. "What's going on? Where did Abdullah go?"

"Michelle *Jaan*, I am going to ask you to please return to your sleeping area, and this time you absolutely must remain there. Abdullah is bringing my commanders here for a serious meeting. It would be better if you were not here."

Michelle shrugged. "If you speak in Dari, I won't be able to understand what is being said anyway."

"They will not speak freely, even in Dari. Your presence at a war council will make them very uncomfortable, and there is a vitally important matter we must discuss. All of our lives could depend on it. Will you go?"

"Yes, of course I will." Michelle stood up immediately. "You look very troubled, and that worries me. Tomorrow will you tell me what you can so that my imagination doesn't run wild?"

from that flame

"If I can, I will. Good night, Michelle *Jaan*. Thank you for understanding." Massoud returned to his map, and Michelle felt dismissed. Reluctantly, she headed back into the darker interior of the cave.

Commanders Mehmet, Amin, and Ollah sat in a circle around the map facing Commander Massoud and Dr. Abdullah. "Show me where you stationed your men," Massoud looked at Mehmet. His eyes followed Mehmet's finger as it traced over a small segment of the map.

"As you instructed, I stationed the perimeter guards on this ridge."

"About five kilometers from base camp," Commander Massoud noted. "How many?"

"Five men who would have been rotated out after a four-hour shift. I used our standard protocol, Commander."

"No one had been rotated out before the attack began?"

"No."

Massoud nodded and looked at Commander Amin. "Where are your men?"

Amin leaned forward and studied the map for a moment until he located the correct locations. "Here, along the base of this mountain, and here, near the river bed." He glanced at Commander Massoud and continued before the question was asked. "Seven men on a standard rotation."

Commander Massoud looked at Commander Ollah next. The Commander studied the map, but he also squirmed a little and shifted his weight around on the rug.

"Here and here," he poked at the map without clearly identifying the locations. He glanced at Massoud. "Four men."

"Had any been rotated out?"

"Yes. Kahn and Hamid came to me after dinner. They asked if they could switch patrols two hours early."

"Did they give a reason for their request?"

"Kahn said they had been asked by Azid and Mohammed to relieve them a little early. They were doing it as a favor because Azid and Mohammed had the late rotation last night and barely had any sleep."

"Was that true?"

"I didn't think it was," Commander Ollah said and shrugged, "but then I thought maybe I was mistaken. I told them to make the rotation early, to relieve Azid and Mohammed so that they could sleep."

"Where are Azid and Mohammed now?" Massoud asked.

"Probably trying to get some sleep now that the fighting is over," Ollah answered.

"And Kahn and Hamid? Where are they?"

"Still on patrol as far as I know."

"I need to see Azid and Mohammed." Massoud watched Commander Ollah get up and then glanced at Abdullah. He saw his own suspicions reflected back at him.

In a few minutes Commander Ollah returned with the soldiers following close behind him. Both men looked worried.

"Sit," Commander Massoud motioned to the soldiers. "Tell me what happened tonight."

"What do you mean, Commander?" Mohammed asked.

"You were on perimeter patrol, correct?"

"Yes."

"What happened after that?"

Mohammed glanced at Azid and then looked back at Commander Massoud. "We were on perimeter patrol for about two hours. Everything seemed quiet." Mohammed stopped speaking for a moment and glanced at Azid again. "Kahn and Hamid showed up and said they had come to relieve us."

Ollah opened his mouth as if to speak. Commander Massoud held up a restraining hand to silence him and asked his own question. "Did they tell you why they were relieving you early?"

"Did we do something wrong, Commander?" Azid asked.

"Did Kahn and Hamid tell you why they were relieving you early?" Massoud repeated.

"They said that Commander Ollah assigned them a six-hour shift as punishment for falling behind during today's travel."

"Had they fallen behind? Did you notice?"

"No, *Amer Saheb*. They were near the end of the caravan all

from that flame

day, but I didn't notice if they actually fell behind or not."

"What did you do when you returned to base camp?"

"We got something to eat and went to sleep until the fighting started."

"Thank you. Speak of this to no one. You may go." Commander Massoud dismissed them.

Mohammed stopped at the mouth of the cave and looked back. "Did we do something wrong, Commander? Were we wrong to let them relieve us early?"

Commander Massoud shook his head. "No, you did nothing wrong. Go get some sleep. Tomorrow will be another long day."

"What's this all about, Commander Massoud?" Mehmet asked once the senior leaders were alone. "What do you think happened out there?"

Massoud rubbed his hands over his face. "The Taliban fighters were within what should have been our secure perimeter. That would suggest that someone let them in." He looked at Ollah. "Don't you agree?"

"I didn't know," Ollah said hoarsely.

"I never thought you did," Massoud replied quickly.

"If the Taliban fighters breached our perimeter, why didn't they attack?" Mehmet asked. "Why did they stay in the valley?"

"I think only a few dozen breached the perimeter. Enough to get our attention," Commander Massoud answered. "My guess is that they were hoping we would send men out into a flanking maneuver the way we did two nights ago. That would mean that the rest of the Taliban fighters would have been somewhere around here," Massoud said and pointed to the map. "They were setting a trap. Had our men gone in to outflank this smaller group, they would have been trapped between the two divisions."

"Why didn't you send the men into that maneuver?" Mehmet asked. "I kept expecting that you would issue the command to do that. How did you know?"

Commander Massoud shrugged. "I was acting on a hunch. Once I realized that our perimeter had been breached, I wondered how that might have happened without any warning shots being fired. There could only have been two explanations. Either all the men in that patrol had been silently killed before any of them could fire a single shot, or the Taliban fighters had help getting through." Commander Massoud looked again at Ollah. "What do you think should be done?" he asked.

"Let me bring Kahn and Hamid here. Maybe there is an explanation we have not yet considered," General Ollah offered.

"All right," Commander Massoud agreed. "Send someone to relieve them and have Kahn and Hamid brought back."

"I'll get them myself," Commander Ollah said.

"No," Massoud said firmly. "If they have betrayed us, they would be alarmed if you showed up in person. That would threaten your own safety. Send two men to relieve them as you would in a normal rotation. Do not tell the others anything about what has transpired here. We do not want to tip our hand." Ollah nodded and left.

"*Ahmed Shah*," Dr. Abdullah said in a low voice as his eyes anxiously searched his friend's face, "it will take at least an hour for the fighters to complete the rotation and Kahn and Hamid return. It is nearly dawn. Go into the back chamber and sleep for a while. I will get you as soon as the others return."

Commander Massoud rubbed his eyes before looking at Abdullah. "I don't think I could sleep." He rubbed his hands over his face again. He was weary to the core of his being.

"Then rest at least," Abdullah urged. "Who knows what the day will bring? You should rest while you can."

Commander Massoud nodded woodenly. Lack of sleep was an enemy to be avoided whenever possible. Slowly he stood up. "Why?" he asked in a voice heavy with both sorrow and bewilderment. "Why would they betray our cause?"

"We don't know for certain that they did. You won't have answers to your question for at least an hour. Go rest until then."

Commander Massoud patted his friend on the shoulder as he passed. No matter what else in the world happened, he would never doubt the loyalty of Abdullah. As certain as the sun lighted the Eastern sky each morning, Abdullah's devotion and friendship would persist. For fifteen years Abdullah had been at his side, advising, counseling, cautioning, and sharing his visions and dreams for their homeland. He counted Abdullah among the greatest blessings God had given him in life.

"Get me as soon as they return." He turned left at the back

of the cave and peered into the small chamber Michelle was using. In the dim light he could see her huddled up in her sleeping bag, apparently asleep. He turned around and went into the other chamber where Abdullah had been sleeping until the fighting broke out. He knelt and prayed and then laid down to uneasy minutes of broken sleep.

Dawn was breaking when Commander Massoud was back in the front section of the cave. Again Abdullah, Mehmet, and Amin sat around him. Commander Ollah and Kahn stood before them.

"*Eenja Beyaa*. Come here. Where is Hamid?" Massoud asked Kahn.

"He is dead, killed in last night's fighting." Kahn shifted his weight from foot to foot. His hands fidgeted at his sides. Commander Ollah reached over and took the younger man's sidearm out of the belt at his waist.

Commander Massoud looked at Abdullah and nodded slightly. Dr. Abdullah immediately got up and left the cave. He was back a moment later, his orders issued.

"You and Hamid told Commander Ollah that Azid and Mohammed asked you to relieve them early. Is that correct?"

"Yes," Kahn mumbled. He kept his eyes down and seemed to be studying with great interest the pattern of the small rug beneath him on the cave floor.

"Was that the true reason?"

Kahn cast a covert look at Commander Ollah. "Not exactly. It's what we told the Commander."

"You lied to your commander? Why?"

"We didn't think he would let us go if he knew the real reason."

"And what was the real reason?" Commander Massoud asked patiently.

"Azid and Mohammed said they would share tomorrow—today's—dinner rations with us if we relieved them early so that they could get some extra sleep." Kahn looked at Commander Massoud defiantly. "You always lecture us about eating and sleeping in proportionate amounts. We didn't think you or Commander Ollah would like it if the four of us traded."

Commander Massoud nodded as if he accepted this explanation. "I see. Tell me what happened next."

"You know what happened next. We were on patrol when the fighting broke out. We fought back. Hamid was killed."

"Come and look at this map, and then answer a question for me, if you will." Commander Massoud pointed to a dot on the map. "You were here. Is that correct?"

"Yes," Kahn agreed warily. "Just about there."

"Good." Massoud made eye contact with Kahn, who began to shift his weight uneasily. "Now here is my question. How did the Taliban fighters get past you and Hamid? How had they reached this point when they opened fire?"

"I don't know…" Kahn's voice trailed off. "They must have slipped past us."

"More than a dozen men?" Commander Massoud said in disbelief. "Were you asleep?"

"No…" Kahn began to squirm more urgently. The Commander's eyes were burning holes into him and could see straight into his brain, he was certain.

Another soldier appeared at the cave's opening. Abdullah went over to him, listened to what the man said, and turned back to the assembled men. "Hamid's body was found. His throat was cut."

Commander Massoud shifted his gaze from Abdullah back to Kahn. There was a mixture of expressions from rage to grief etched on it, but his voice remained calm. "I will ask again. How did the Taliban fighters get past you?"

Kahn threw back his head defiantly, knowing he was caught. "I let them. I killed Hamid, and I let the Taliban pass through the checkpoint."

"Why?" Commander Massoud asked with genuine shock and horror even though it was the answer he expected. "Why would you kill your brother-in-arms, another *mujahidin* fighter, and betray us all to the Taliban?"

"Commander Massoud?" Michelle's voice came from the back of the cave. The Commander turned his head and looked over his shoulder.

"Go back inside," he said quietly in French. When he saw her hesitate, he turned so that he could see her better and so that she could see his face. *"Partez vite!"* his voice thundered and echoed through the cave. Michelle jumped and darted back like a scared rabbit into its hole. Massoud turned back and again froze Kahn with the coldness of his stare.

"Why? *Chee shod?* What happened?"

Kahn's momentary bravado began to leave him. His survival now depended on the mercy of Ahmed Shah Massoud. He put his hands in his pockets and pulled out rolls of money. Tears began to roll down his dusty cheeks.

"They gave me money. They told me I could slip away and go home. I wanted to go home, *Amer Saheb*. I haven't been home in eight months. I just wanted to see my wife and son. I wanted to go home." The man began to sob. He dropped the money to the ground and fell to his knees. "Forgive me, *Amer Saheb*. I'm sorry. I was wrong."

Commander Massoud shook his head slowly. "You confessed to murder and treason. You killed your friend and betrayed us all. Ask God for forgiveness, not me—I have none to give. It is not within my power." He looked from one commander to the next. "Does anyone offer forgiveness to this man?"

No one spoke.

Massoud stood up and turned to Commander Ollah. "He is your man. You are responsible for him and must decide what to do with him."

Commander Ollah grabbed the weeping man by the shoulders and pushed him out the cave's opening. Grim-faced, Commanders Amin and Mehmet followed after them. Commander Massoud turned to Dr. Abdullah with deep sorrow in his eyes.

"Tell me how I failed Kahn. He would not have done what he did unless I failed to see something I should have seen, do something I should have done, or known something I should have known. Why didn't he tell me how badly he wanted to return home?"

Dr. Abdullah spoke vehemently. "You are not responsible for this. You have four thousand men under your command. You know them all by name. You agonize over each man lost in battle.

from that flame

You care for them as if they were your sons. You have never failed any of them—any of us. This was Kahn's choice, *Ahmed Shah*. He choose to do what he did. His reasons for not telling you of his desire to return home are invalid, whatever they may be. Besides, he didn't betray just you. He betrayed us all."

Massoud buried his face in his hands and didn't look up for several minutes. When he did drop his hands, his face was calm and resolved. Prayer always had that influence on him. "We need to break camp and get out of here fast," Massoud said with his usual, quiet authority. "The Taliban may have made a short, tactical retreat when we didn't walk into their trap, but they are still out there, and they will attack again."

"What if there are other traitors within our ranks?" Abdullah asked.

"I will mount an offensive this evening. We will not again be as trusting or vulnerable as we were last night. Come on, let's get out of here."

4. Exhaustion

r. Abdullah stood in the small opening of the cave's alcove where the journalist sat huddled and miserable. "Michelle *Jaan*, we're leaving." Without saying anything, the woman grabbed her backpack, dragged it through the opening after her, and followed Dr. Abdullah into the front section of the cave. It was completely empty.

"Where is Commander Massoud?"

"He's gone on ahead. Here, let me help you with that." Dr. Abdullah lifted the backpack so that Michelle could slip her arms through the straps.

"Doctor Abdullah, what happened to that man?"

"Which man?" Abdullah asked evasively.

"The one who looked like he was on trial."

"Kahn was on trial. He confessed to murder and treason."

"Where is he?"

"I don't know," Abdullah answered honestly. He studied Michelle's face and tried to determine how much truth she could handle. "I would assume he has been executed for his crimes." Michelle paled but said nothing. "He cut the throat of his friend, and he accepted money in exchange for letting the Taliban past a checkpoint into our camp."

"I understand," Michelle said weakly.

"I know this brand of instant justice isn't what you're used to seeing. We don't have the luxury of a complicated legal system with lawyers and courts and appeals."

"I said I understood."

"I hope you do. There was nothing else that could have been

done. He committed a crime, and a just punishment was meted out."

"Can we please just drop the subject?" Michelle pleaded. "Please?"

"All right. We must leave now. Commander Massoud is looking for a point from which he can mount an offensive attack tonight. We want to get you well behind the front line before it begins."

"Another battle?" Michelle paled even more. "How do you live like this every day?"

"It's all we've known for twenty years. This is Afghanistan."

Dr. Abdullah walked side-by-side with Michelle in silence for several kilometers. He scrutinized her face from time to time and could see that she was troubled.

"Are you all right?" he asked at last.

"Do you realize that either you or Commander Massoud asks me that every single day? *Ça va!* I'm fine," she snapped in exasperation.

"The Commander described you as 'undaunted.' Our questions about your well-being should not be construed as a signal that we think you are weak. It's just that we know you have never experienced anything quite like what you've gone through this past week. Please consider our concern as a sign of friendship. That is the intention," the doctor concluded.

Michelle nodded absently. She had only been half listening to him. "Abdullah *Jaan*," she said suddenly as if the question forced itself from her lips against her will, "did Commander Massoud kill that man himself?"

"No. He was one of Commander Ollah's men. It was Ollah's responsibility to hand down the punishment. But do not mistake me; Commander Massoud gave his consent to the execution. We all did. Kahn was judged by a 'jury of his peers.' Isn't that what you call it in America?"

"Yes," Michelle confirmed, "that's what we call it. What did Commander Massoud think about what that man—Kahn, did you say his name was? What did Massoud think about what Kahn did?"

"You tell me," Abdullah replied. "You should know him well enough by now. What did he think? The Commander has been very open with you. You tell me."

"He probably found some way to blame himself," Michelle answered. "And I would imagine that the betrayal hurt him very much."

"You are correct on both counts. Commander Massoud feels grief over the death of every one of our men—no matter the circumstances of his death. And he tortures himself thinking that there might have been a way to avoid the casualty."

"Yet with every new day, he finds a way to leave the most recent deaths behind him and go on to a new battle and face even more death," Michelle said. She continued her struggle to understand this enigma named Commander Ahmed Shah Massoud.

"What choice does he have, Michelle *Jaan*? We all depend on him. It is Massoud who always has a plan. It is Massoud who always has a vision. It is Massoud who always has a strategy. He didn't ask for any of this, but when it was laid on his shoulders, he accepted the responsibility and has never shrugged it off. If he ever decided to walk away from it all—and who could blame him if he did that after twenty years of fighting?—what would happen to Afghanistan? Would there be less death? Don't fool yourself. The Taliban has done ethnic cleansing in the past. They would do it again. They want all the territory held by all the minority groups in the country, and they would kill everyone who tried to stop them. Commander Massoud and the *mujahidin* are all that stand between the Taliban and the slaughter of tens of thousands of innocent people. You can't judge him. You haven't earned that right."

"I don't want to judge him," Michelle protested, shocked that the doctor thought that was what she had been doing. "I don't judge him. You misunderstood me! I was wondering how and where he finds the strength to do what he does day after day, year after year. Why hasn't he been broken yet? Why hasn't he given up, thrown his hands in the air, and walked away? You're right: no one could blame him. How does he do what he does?"

"I'm sorry. It was I who judged you. Misjudged. Explaining and defending has become second nature to me after all these years." Abdullah smiled as he apologized. "To answer your question, his faith is a source of deep strength and comfort for him. He believes that he is doing the work Allah has placed before him. The *Qur'an* teaches that 'God loves those who are firm and steadfast,' and it also says that we should 'bear patiently whatever may befall' us. War—first against the Soviets and then against the Taliban—is what has befallen Ahmed Shah Massoud, and he is determined to remain firm and steadfast."

"And then there is Afghanistan itself," Michelle added softly.

"Yes, there is his country and his people, and he could never abandon them. He will never cease fighting for them until they are free to live as God intended them to live."

"Thank you, Abdullah *Jaan*," Michelle said and smiled at her walking companion.

"I apologize if I was harsh. I didn't mean it quite the way it sounded."

"Your duty is to defend your friend and Commander. No apology is necessary. Commander Massoud is fortunate to have such loyal friends, especially when considering recent events."

"Are you ready for a lesson in Dari?" Abdullah asked as he dug in his pocket and withdrew something. He held it up for Michelle to see.

"It's a pistachio," she observed with a smile, happy to change the topic.

"Close," Dr. Abdullah said, returning her smile. "Shorten the word just a little. *Pista*."

It was a long day of hard hiking, and as Commander Massoud had predicted, it became increasingly difficult for Michelle to breathe. The air became thinner as they climbed higher and higher in the Hindu Kush mountains. Her backpack felt as if it weighed more than she did. Her twisted ankle ached with every step. She was so short of breath, she could barely speak. The air was colder, and her fingers, despite the gloves she wore, were growing numb. Too exhausted to take another step, she finally dropped onto a flat rock near the side of the trail, rested her arms on her knees, and let her head drop down between her shoulders. Dr. Abdullah, who had been walking and talking with another man, was at her side in an instant.

"Too tired," was all Michelle managed to gasp in the thin, cold air.

"You can't stay here," Abdullah said firmly. "If you don't freeze first, the Taliban will get you. And assuming that doesn't happen, you'll be right at the front line when the fighting breaks out tonight."

"I'm so cold." Michelle started to shiver.

Dr. Abdullah sighed. "Rudaki," he called to a fighter who was passing nearby and motioned for him to come over. "Michelle, unbuckle the straps on your pack." As he spoke Dr. Abdullah began to unfasten the ties that held her sleeping bag to the bottom of the pack's frame.

Michelle's fingers fumbled at the buckles. She took off her gloves and tried again. Her fingers were too cold to obey her command.

"I can't." She looked over her shoulder at the doctor. "My fingers won't work."

"Okay, stand up and let me see." Abdullah helped her to her feet, turned her around, and unfastened the buckles himself. He pulled the backpack from her shoulders and handed it to Rudaki as he explained something in Dari. The soldier nodded, swung the pack onto his own back, and took off walking again.

"It's not fair to make him carry my things," Michelle gasped.

"I don't have many options here," Dr. Abdullah began to unzip the zipper on Michelle's sleeping bag so that it would open like a blanket. "We can let Rudaki carry your pack and see if you can continue the hike, or we can unload one of the mules, make the men carry all that artillery, and put you on the mule. Or, he can carry you." He flung the sleeping bag over her shoulders and draped it in front of her. "Give me your hands."

Michelle held her hands out. Dr. Abdullah stripped off his own gloves and then hers. He stuffed them all into his pockets, took her hands in his, and began to rub them briskly.

"I'm sorry I'm so much trouble," Michelle wheezed.

"Don't talk," the doctor instructed as he continued to warm her hands. "Keep all your strength for breathing and hiking." Satisfied that blood was again circulating in her hands, he handed Michelle her gloves. He slipped on his own gloves and pulled the sleeping bag tighter around Michelle's shoulders. A light snow was beginning to fall.

"Will you let me help you?" Dr. Abdullah asked. Michelle nodded mutely. "All right, good." Dr. Abdullah wrapped his free arm around her so that he could support part of her weight and assist her in walking. "We don't have to walk fast, but we do have to keep moving."

By the time dusk was falling, they had reached what would serve as a base camp for the night. Abdullah was half dragging Michelle when they reached the cave designated by Commander Massoud as his headquarters. When they came in, Massoud looked up from his maps.

"*Chee shod?* What happened?" he asked with concern.

"Exposure and exhaustion," Abdullah answered. He began grabbing rugs to make a pallet near the fire. He lead Michelle to it and had her lie down. Although she was still rolled up in her sleeping bag, the doctor piled blankets on top of her.

Massoud studied her with concern. "Will she be all right?"

Dr. Abdullah dug through the blankets until he could find her wrist. "I think so." He tilted his watch towards the firelight and took her pulse. He looked over at Commander Massoud's anxious face. "I'll get her warm; she'll be fine once she has slept. You don't need to worry."

"All right. Do whatever you need for her, and then join me. I want to discuss something with you." The Commander glanced once more at Michelle and then turned back to his maps. Everything was going to depend on precise movements. He needed to know where every gully and hill was located.

"I'll be there in a few minutes," Abdullah answered as he struggled to untie the wet, frozen laces of Michelle's boots. When he got her boots off, he put them near the fire to dry and rubbed her feet. Finally, he forced her to drink a small amount of hot green tea. He was a little concerned to see how violently she was shivering, but he knew there was little else he could do for her at that moment. He felt her forehead and cheeks.

"Sleep while you can," he told her. "It's the best thing for you right now."

from that flame

Michelle caught his hand in hers before he moved it away. "Thank you, Abdullah," she said through teeth that chattered.

He gave her hand a gentle squeeze before releasing it. "You are welcome. Sleep now."

He noted with satisfaction that her eyes were already closing. He went to join Commander Massoud at the maps.

Two hours later, Commander Massoud finished his meeting. He looked around the circle of well-known, well-trusted faces. "Does everyone understand the plan?" His eyes swept from Amin to Mehmet to Ollah. All the men nodded.

"And the weapons cache was all there?" Massoud turned to Mehmet.

"Yes," Mehmet laughed. "For the third time, yes, everything was exactly where we hid it last fall. My men should just about be finished getting it distributed."

"And all the men have eaten?" Massoud looked at Amin.

"They go into battle with full stomachs, *Amer Saheb*," Amin nodded.

"All right. Let's pray, and then you will go to your men." Massoud shifted from sitting to kneeling. "We will ask God to hold you all safe in the palm of His hand."

For Michelle, the night seemed to go on forever. She would open her eyes and see the vague outlines of Commander Massoud and Dr. Abdullah huddled near the fire listening to words in Dari coming to them over a two-way radio. Sometimes they spoke softly to each other, and sometimes she could hear the sounds of ordinance exploding. In her feverish state, she couldn't tell if the sounds were coming from close outside the cave or over the radio. She couldn't stay awake for more than a few minutes at a time, and as she slept, all the sensory input blended together into dreams that inevitably turned into nightmares. Every so often she would awaken to find Dr. Abdullah beside her, his hand on her wrist or cheek as he monitored his patient. Once he tried to get her to eat something, but she fell asleep before she finished chewing the bread. Another time he forced some water down her throat, and once he wiped her face with a cool, damp cloth.

With dawn came silence at last. Whatever happened on the battlefield, it was over.

Commander Massoud pulled a blanket over his coat and went out into the snowy morning to meet his troops as they returned to camp. Dr. Abdullah also wrapped himself in a blanket, but instead of going outside, he sat near Michelle, leaned against the cave wall, and closed his eyes. Michelle fell into a peaceful sleep for the first time in two days.

"What happened last night?" Michelle asked Commander Massoud as soon as she opened her eyes and saw him sitting near the fire.

"It went well, praise Allah," he answered and smiled with relief when she spoke to him. She looked much better. The feverish glow was gone from her eyes. "How are you feeling today? Better?"

"*Oui*, very much better, thank you." Michelle struggled to get out from under all the blankets piled on her.

"I don't think you should get up until Doctor Abdullah says you can," Commander Massoud admonished her. "You had us very worried yesterday."

"I'm sorry." Michelle gave up fighting the blankets and laid flat again.

"Would you like some tea?" Massoud poured a cup and brought it over to her. "You must be starving. I'll have someone prepare food for you."

"No, don't go. Please tell me what happened last night. Were there heavy casualties?"

The Commander shook his head. "*Non*. We lost three men. The Taliban lost two hundred. Those that were left, fled. Our position here is secure enough that we can stay over until tomorrow."

"I thought you never stayed in the same place two nights in a row."

Massoud smiled at her genially. "I am making an exception.

Everyone is exhausted. No one has slept more than two hours in the last two days. My men need to rest. So do I."

"You look very tired," Michelle observed.

"I am. I must speak to you about a few things, and then I will go to sleep." He settled himself more comfortably before continuing. "First, I wish to apologize for raising my voice to you yesterday morning."

"You had every right to be angry with me. You told me to stay in my sleeping chamber. I didn't mean to disobey you. I didn't know the meeting was still going on. I'm sorry."

Commander Massoud shook his head. "The prophet teaches us to speak justly whether we are angry or pleased. I did not speak justly to you. My anger was not towards you but rather towards Kahn. It was wrong of me to raise my voice to you under any circumstances. I hope you will forgive me."

"There is nothing to forgive. What else did you need to talk to me about?"

"Now that we have some breathing space from the Taliban, I can spare enough men to take you to Peshawar. You could be there in a week."

Michelle struggled to hide her disappointment. "I understand why you want me to go," she said slowly. "And of course I will. I've caused you enough trouble already, and you have been marvelously kind to me."

Commander Massoud shook his head and laughed softly to himself. "I don't think I will ever understand how your mind works. I thought you would jump at the chance to get out of the war zone. Should I infer that you would rather stay in these mountains than go back to Pakistan?"

"If it is all right with you, *balay*. Yes, of course I would rather stay."

"But why 'of course'? I do not understand. You have been half frozen and starved not to mention physically exhausted from hiking day after day. Night after night you have been awakened by the sound of artillery exploding around you. If you stay, your life will be in perpetual danger. You will have to continue hiking in the cold, eating the bare minimum of food to keep body and soul together. If I were you, I would be on my way to Pakistan before the noon sun reached its summit. Yet you say 'of course' you would rather stay. Why?"

"Because you are here and not in Pakistan," Michelle answered honestly. "If I am going to find the right words to give voice to who you are and what you are trying to accomplish , there is much more I need to know. There is much more I need to understand. I suppose I could go back to Pakistan and interview other people about you, but I would rather learn about you from you."

"You are welcome to stay if that is your desire. We should be around Feyzabad in a day or two. You can leave from there or stay, whichever you wish." Massoud shook his head in disbelief.

"Are you sure? I am aware that having me along adds to the responsibilities for both you and Doctor Abdullah."

Commander Massoud dismissed her words with a wave of his hand. "You are our guest, and we are happy to do whatever we can for you."

"I feel as if I am taking advantage of your cultural hospitality. I know that by custom, Afghans never turn away a guest. Is that why you will allow me to stay?"

"That was the reason when you first arrived," the Commander admitted. "Now I have a vested interest in your story too. I think we need more time to discuss what you should know." He stood up. "And now I shall sleep for a little while."

"Please take these blankets." Michelle started to peel off several of the blankets Dr. Abdullah had piled on top of her.

"You need them," the Commander shook his head.

"Are you kidding? They are so heavy I can barely move, and I'm so hot, I'm sweating. Abdullah not only thawed me out, he has me half-baked."

Massoud chuckled at the thought. "All right." He started to take the blankets from her and make a pallet a few feet away. "But if you get cold, you must tell me so that I can give them back."

"Would you like me to massage your back?"

"Absolutely not. You must restore and conserve all your strength and energy, not expend it on me." He laid down and pulled a blanket over him. He saw the she was looking at him with an expression he didn't understand. "Did I offend you by refusing your offer? I didn't mean…"

from that flame

"No," Michelle interrupted him, "I wasn't offended. I am amazed, that's all. In the midst of all this insanity that makes up your life, you somehow manage to remain one of the kindest people I have ever met. I don't know how you do it, and that's one of those things I need to understand before I can write an accurate story. Thank you for letting me stay."

"*Qaabilay tashakur nayst.* You are welcome. May I ask a favor of you?"

"Of course. Anything."

"May I listen to more of your music as I go to sleep?"

Michelle grinned broadly. "You bet you can." She pulled her backpack closer to her, removed the portable CD player, and handed it to Massoud. Next she pulled out a handful of CDs. She spread them out like cards in her hand and showed them to the Commander.

"Pick one."

"Will you select one for me? Anything soothing and harmonious."

Michelle studied the CDs for a moment before making her choice. "Here. This is an Italian singer with the voice of an angel. His name is Andrea Bocelli. I think you'll like him."

Massoud put the CD in the player and placed the headphones on his ears. "Thank you for sharing this gift of such rare beauty." He found the on button and closed his eyes as the music filled his ears.

"Sleep well, *Amer Saheb*," Michelle whispered as she laid back down herself. She watched the Commander sleep for a long time before her own exhaustion overtook her, and she slept again herself. There was nothing but blissful silence all afternoon long for the Afghan *mujahidin* commander and the Western, female journalist.

Commander Massoud looked with satisfaction at his quiet encampment. He had ordered extra rations for all of them. Even if they had half empty stomachs the next afternoon, this day they were satiated.

Small ribbons of smoke rose from several fires. Men sat

around each fire talking and laughing softly, enjoying their rare day off as well as the sense of well-being that blanketed the camp. Michelle could hear the faint sounds of a *tambur's* haunting melody, and then someone began to softly blow a *tula*. He coaxed impossibly sweet, mysterious sounds from the instrument. She followed Massoud's gaze around the encampment. These men had little food, shelter, and warmth, and yet she was quite certain that if she asked them, they would, without exception, say that they were prepared to stay with Commander Massoud.

"You inspire great loyalty from your men," Michelle observed.

"Not from all of them." Commander Massoud turned back into the cave and sat beside his own fire.

"You are thinking about Kahn," Michelle said as she settled in next to him.

"*Oui.* I can't help but wonder if I failed him in some way. Why else would he have betrayed our cause?"

"Maybe you didn't have anything to do with it. Maybe he just wasn't as committed as you and the others. He was bought off for money, *Ahmed Shah*. He valued that more than the freedom of his country."

Commander Massoud scratched his beard thoughtfully before meeting Michelle's gaze. "Perhaps. Did Abdullah tell you the whole story?"

"He told me enough. He was concerned that I might not understand the form of justice you have here."

"Do you?" Massoud studied her solemnly.

"Yes. It's true that I am accustomed to huge buildings filled with judges and lawyers, but I know that isn't possible here. In this case, you did what you had to do. You had no other option."

"In this case?"

"The man confessed to two, terrible crimes. What more evidence could you need?"

"Yes," Massoud agreed, but his mind seemed to be elsewhere, thinking back to other men accused of similar crimes and to the punishment handed down to them. "It was easier in this case. There are times when we do not have the luxury of a confession as evidence, and still a verdict must be reached." He looked at

Michelle intently. "I never allow torture, not even to gain a confession, and sometimes that makes it more difficult to learn the truth in a situation. I strive to be fair and just."

"You don't need to tell me that. I already know," Michelle said gently.

Massoud suddenly smiled. "It occurs to me that you know a great deal more about me than I do about you."

Michelle shrugged. "There isn't much to know. We have an expression: 'what you see is what you get.' That applies to me. No mystery here."

"I like what I see. Tell me something more about yourself. Have you a husband or children?"

"No, it's just me. I thought about having a family once, but how could I and still do the work I do? One or the other would suffer. For the time being at least, work is my priority."

"Have you a successful career?" the Commander asked with genuine interest.

"Modest success, I guess," Michelle answered honestly. "I haven't won the Nobel or Pulitzer Prize yet, but I am respected as a journalist in certain circles."

He turned her words back on her with a smile. "You don't need to tell me that. I already know it. Please tell me where else in the world you have been. Which was your best story? I liked the story you told me about the volcanic pool in Colombia. Do you have other stories like that?"

Sensing that his interest was sincere and wanting him to know her better, Michelle began to talk. She told him about her visits to South America, Africa, and Europe. She had a writer's knack for taking even a simple tale and weaving it into a story of grand drama or side-splitting humor. She made him laugh so hard, he felt tears spring to his eyes. At other times her stories moved him to tears of compassion over struggles in other lands. He was interested in every detail, every observation she had. He listened intently to everything she said, sorted through her often mangled French, and asked question after question when he wanted to know more. Finally, she was stopped by Abdullah's appearance at the cave's entrance.

"Is this an inconvenient time?" he asked.

"No, not at all. Come in and rescue our guest. I fear I have

monopolized her time and made her tell me too many stories."
He looked at Michelle with a genial smile. "I enjoyed listening to
you very much. Thank you. It was a most pleasant diversion." He
turned his attention back to his friend and advisor. "What may I
do for you, my friend?"

"I thought this might be a good time for Michelle to learn
how to use a sidearm as we discussed."

"You want me to learn to shoot a gun?" Michelle demanded.
"Isn't it bad enough I have to dress like a *mujahidin*? Now you
want me to shoot like one too?" Both Dr. Abdullah and Commander Massoud chuckled at the look of outrage on her face. It
was Massoud who spoke first.

"We thought we might ask you to lead the next incursion
against the Taliban," he managed to say with a straight face.

"We thought it would be an interesting lead-in to your article," Dr. Abdullah added with an equally sober expression.

"Ha, ha. You two are so funny, you could start your own com-
edy routine" Michelle said sarcastically. "I think it is an awful idea.
Armed journalists are asking for trouble. It simply isn't done."

Dr. Abdullah knelt down and laid a small handgun on the
rug in front of Michelle. She looked at it as if it were some hid-
eous creature.

"What's that?"

"A Soviet PSM," Abdullah answered. "It is an excellent personal weapon for close combat. It is lightweight, reliable, and
easy to use."

"You aren't kidding, are you?" Michelle looked from one man
to the other. She looked down at the gun and back up to the men.
"Didn't I just say that journalists don't carry weapons?"

Commander Massoud leaned forward and looked at her intently. "Michelle *Jaan*, please listen to me. I would not ask you to
do this if it wasn't important. I promise you that I will do everything in my power to keep you safe so that you never have to use
the weapon, but it would be much wiser for you to have the gun
and not need it than to need it and not have it. You know from
the members of RAWA what the Taliban will do to a woman."

"I have someone ready to give you basic shooting lessons,"
Abdullah spoke up. "You trusted us when we asked you to wear
the clothes of the *mujahidin*. Please trust us in this matter too. We

discussed it carefully, and it is not a decision we reached lightly. If we became separated, having a weapon and knowing how to use it would probably mean the difference between life and death."

Michelle reached out and gingerly touched the gun. She looked from Commander Massoud to Dr. Abdullah again before picking the sidearm up.

"It's heavy," she whispered, "and cold." She looked directly at Commander Massoud. "If I were a man, would you insist I carry a gun?"

"I would suggest it, but, no, I would not insist," he answered honestly.

"Then why do I have to?"

"Because you are not a man," the Commander said gently, "and right now Afghanistan is not kind to women."

Michelle nodded and turned the gun over in her hands several times as she studied it. It was abhorrent to her beyond description. She raised her gaze from the gun to Commander Massoud's lean face and intent eyes. There was no laughter in them now. Finally, she looked at Dr. Abdullah. "Well, then I guess we had better get to that lesson." All three of them stood.

"Hey, I don't suppose you have a shoulder holster, do you? I always thought those looked pretty cool," Michelle said with a grin.

Commander Massoud laughed and pointed to the cave's opening. "Go. Now."

Quite a crowd of amused and bemused Northern Alliance soldiers gathered to watch the American woman learn how to shoot the little gun. Some scowled with disapproval. Others laughed quietly. There were those who shook their heads in disbelief over the whole scene. Michelle tried to ignore them all and concentrate on what she was being told.

"Place your feet shoulder width apart," Dr. Abdullah instructed her. "Distribute your weight evenly between both legs and feet. You can bend your knees slightly if that is more comfortable. Keep your center of gravity low. Now drop your arms straight down to your sides." The doctor nodded to another man standing nearby. This man approached them with an old, worn belt and a holster.

from that flame

Abdullah handed the marksman the handgun. He slipped it into the holster, snapped the safety latch over it, and reached around Michelle so that he could settle the holster around her hips. Once the buckle was tightened, he positioned the holster on her thigh and fastened it with a hide strap that would hold it in the proper position on her leg.

"I feel like I'm getting ready for the shootout at the OK Corral," Michelle said to Dr. Abdullah.

"Excuse me?" The doctor looked puzzled.

"You know—the American West? Cowboys? Gun fights?" The doctor studied her as if she had suddenly begun to speak a language he did not understand. Michelle shook her head and gave up. "Never mind."

"You will explain this reference to me later?" Abdullah asked with real interest.

"Sure, we'll save the story for tomorrow's twenty-mile hike with full pack," Michelle said with a sarcasm she did not intend.

"I believe the Commander said he could have you escorted back to Pakistan now if you wished." Dr. Abdullah was confused by the derision in her voice.

"I'm sorry, Abdullah *Jaan*," Michelle said sincerely. "My tone was sharp, and I didn't mean it. I'm a little stressed out about having to learn to shoot this damn gun, that's all. I appreciate everything you are doing for me. Truly I do."

Dr. Abdullah decided he would refrain from asking her to explain exactly what "stressed out" meant. "Shall we continue with the lesson?" he asked.

"Absolutely," Michelle said firmly. "Annie Oakley, move over!"

"Who?" Dr. Abdullah looked around them with concern. This time Michelle burst into laughter and laughed until tears spilled down her cheeks.

"Tomorrow," she said when she was at last able to gasp some air. "Tomorrow on that twenty-mile hike, I will explain everything, I promise."

"All right," Dr. Abdullah agreed and forced a smile to his face. "As I was saying earlier, spread your weight evenly, and keep your center of gravity low. Let your arm drop to your side…"

from that flame

"How did you do?" Commander Massoud asked when Abdullah and Michelle finally made their way back to the cave.

"Let's just say you wouldn't want to recruit me into your army," Michelle answered.

"She did fine," the doctor said.

"Yeah, well, I'd rather arm myself with my pen, if you don't mind," Michelle said as she unbuckled the belt and set the weapon aside. "'The pen is mightier than the sword,' you know."

"Not around here," Massoud said. "Swords may be handy in certain circumstances, but in general I'd rather have a full compliment of tanks, helicopters, RPGs, mortar, and SAMs."

"And this fine instrument," Michelle said holding up her pen, "might help you get more of those. Can we talk a while?" Commander Massoud nodded his agreement. Michelle dug out her notepad and poised her pen to write. She posed her first question.

"Okay, let's start at the beginning. You weren't born a soldier, so how did you get to this point?"

"Actually my earliest ambition was to join the military," Massoud spoke reflectively. "My father was an officer in King Zahir Shah's military. He looked resplendent in his uniform, and I wanted to be just like him."

"Why didn't you join the army?"

"My father would not allow it. He wanted me to become an engineer or a doctor. He sent me to college where I began to study engineering."

"You only began the course of study? You didn't complete it?"

"No," Commander Massoud replied, shaking his head sadly. "The Communists seized control of the Afghan government, and that changed everything."

"Will you tell me a little about this Communist takeover? If that is where you have your roots as a resistance fighter, I need to understand the sequence of events better. I have a general knowledge of Afghan history, but not the details I need to fully understand the whole picture."

from that flame

"In 1973, Daoud Kahn, a cousin of King Zahir, waited until the king left the country on vacation. Daoud and the Afghan Communist Party overthrew the government, exiled King Zahir, abolished the monarchy, and presented a new, communist constitution to Afghanistan. My father was loyal to the king, of course. He resisted this new government. I made many public anti-communist statements, perhaps too many. By 1975, it had become dangerous for me to remain in Kabul. I thought about going to Panjshir, but my father urged me to flee to Pakistan and work from there to dislodge the communist regime in Kabul."

"Did you go?" Michelle asked.

"Yes. Some of my friends and professors and I did go to Pakistan. One of my friends was a man named Gulbuddin Hekmatyar. We belonged to a political party called Jawanan-e-Musulman."

"Wait a minute," Michelle started flipping through her notes. "I wrote something about Hekmatyar earlier. Let me find it."

Commander Massoud and Dr. Abdullah exchanged glances.

"Here it is," Michelle said with satisfaction. "I didn't hear very many good things about him. He has a reputation for being a pretty brutal warlord. He is your friend?"

"Was. He *was* my friend."

"What happened?"

"Can we just say that he and I had a parting of the ways?" Massoud asked. It was obvious that his relationship with the warlord was not something he wanted to discuss.

"Hekmatyar changed his position often," Dr. Abdullah interjected. "Later he actually worked for the Soviet KGB." The doctor was not as reticent to express his views on the former friend-turned-warlord.

Michelle looked from one man to the other. "He started out fighting the Communists and ended up working for the KGB? How did that happen?"

Massoud frowned. "Perhaps we can discuss his story at a later time. I mention him because he is an important figure in the many struggles of this land."

Michelle obediently flipped her tablet back to the page she had been using and looked at her last notes. "So you went to Pakistan. What happened there?"

from that flame

"Pakistani Prime Minister Butto commissioned the Frontier Corp to create unrest in major cities and strategic points within Afghanistan."

"The Frontier Corp?" Michelle asked. "What is that?"

"It was the name for the organization that later became the ISI," Dr. Abdullah explained. "It is Pakistan's intelligence force."

"You were trained to 'create unrest'?" Michelle looked at the Commander quizzically. "What does that mean exactly?"

"By forcing the Communists to spread their troops thin, Butto wanted to pave the way for a *coup d'etat* by the Ikhwani group within his own army. At this time I was still aligned with Gulbuddin Hekmatyar and Jawanan-e-Musulman. Butto set up an anti-West faction headed by Hekmatyar."

"How did you create unrest?"

"We were trained as saboteurs," Commander Massoud said quietly. "We were trained to incite subversion and treason that would undermine the communists."

"Sabotage," Michelle said aloud as she wrote the word. "I've always loved that word. It is surrounded by such mystery."

"There was no mystery surrounding our first mission," Commander Massoud laughed aloud over his memories. "We almost got ourselves killed."

"Really? I can't imagine you failing at anything involving strategy."

Massoud smiled again. "This was twenty-seven years ago, remember. I was only twenty-two years old and thought I had all the answers. I have learned a great deal in the intervening years."

"Tell me about the first mission," Michelle pleaded.

Commander Massoud shook his head as he remembered that experience so many years before. "It was July. My companions and I—there were about ten of us—decided we would seize control of a small community called Rokha. We camped out above the town for two days watching everyone who came in and out of the area. There didn't seem to be much activity, no warlords, no soldiers; in fact, no one who was really in charge as far as we could see. We thought we would have an easy time controlling the population.

"On the morning of the third day we slung our rifles over

our arms and marched into town. We found the local *mullah* and told him that we were going to liberate their community from the Communist regime. He said 'all right' and seemed undisturbed by our presence."

"What was your master plan?" Michelle asked.

The Commander let out a self-deprecating laugh, scratched his beard, and shoved his *pakol* farther back on his head before answering. "Our plan was to sabotage the Communists, of course. We had decided on a two-prong effort. We would try to persuade some of the men close to us in age to join our struggle against the government. We also hoped to find one or two men who would be willing to act as spies. We would then train these men and send them out to integrate within the Afghan army. If they could uncover information about different campaigns, they could report back to us. We would know the enemies' plans and could relay them back to Jawanan-e-Musulman."

"That seems simple enough," Michelle said. "What went wrong?"

Commander Massoud started to laugh aloud again. "Everything! What we didn't know was that the nice, old *mullah* decided we were not 'liberators' but rather a gang of bandits who had really come to plunder the town. None of us paid the least bit of attention to him and never noticed that he was gone."

Michelle started to anticipate what was coming next. "Oh, no!"

"We were strolling around town, talking to people, and congratulating ourselves on how smoothly our campaign was going. We thought we were making real progress in winning over the minds and hearts of a few people who would be useful to our cause. Since we were confident that this first campaign had gone so smoothly, we even discussed asking for a bigger *shahr*, a city with a larger population, the next time. We were so young and foolish and arrogant."

The laughter faded from Commander Massoud's voice as he continued talking. "Allah must have been watching over us is all I can think. A young boy with whom I had been tossing pebbles the day before came running up to me. He pointed down the road where soldiers were beginning to appear. The *mullah* was in front of them, talking and pointing towards the village.

from that flame

"I noticed that several of the village's men were also starting to congregate and glare with angry faces in our direction. Several of them were holding axes and various farming implements, and a few of them waved their weapons at us menacingly."

"Farming instruments?" Michelle repeated with a frown. "I don't know that word in this context."

"*Outils,* farming tools," Dr. Abdullah explained.

"I used the wrong word. I'm sorry," Commander Massoud said.

"No, not the wrong word," Michelle answered. "It's just that your French is much better than mine. Please continue your story. You said you saw men from the village coming towards you waving weapons?"

Massoud nodded and picked up his story from where he had left off. "Bright young man that I was, it didn't take me long to figure out that my companions and I were soon to be in a great deal of trouble. We started racing to gather up our belongings which we had casually left scattered around town. The army was getting closer, and the town's men were looking even angrier.

"We gathered as much as we could hold and took off running like scared rabbits back into the hills. It was the most graceless, hasty retreat you could ever imagine. By the time the army joined the townsmen and they all started coming after us, we were pretty well away. I learned many valuable lessons from that failed effort."

"At least you all got away," Michelle said as she tore her eyes away from the moving hands he used to amplify and punctuate every sentence. She scribbled more notes.

"No, we didn't."

Michelle looked up when she heard his change in tone and studied the Commander's face. The lines and creases around his eyes seemed to deepen with sorrow at the remembrance.

"One of my best friends, Fahad," Massoud continued, "slipped on some loose rocks and broke his leg. I went back and tried to lift and carry him, but he was heavy and the road was steep.

"He pleaded with me to leave him. He said the soldiers would take him back to the town and have his leg set. He said we really hadn't committed any crimes in the town, and the worst that would happen to him would be that he would have to spend a little time in jail. He promised he would meet me back in Pakistan as soon as he could."

Michelle sat quietly, barely breathing for fear of interrupting the narration. When his hands stopped moving, she realized that his mind was far away from the cave in which they were sitting, and that if she jumped up and started to sing, he probably wouldn't notice. Ahmed Shah Massoud, Commander of the feared Northern Alliance, was no longer sitting in a cave high in the Hindu Kush. He was sitting with his best friend on a hot, dusty road outside the small village of Rokha, and his friend was persuading him to go on alone.

Commander Massoud's voice was very low when he began speaking again. "I left him there. I embraced him, told him I would see him in Pakistan, and I left him there. I was about half a kilometer away when I heard a gunshot. I kept climbing.

"When I got to a higher vantage point, I looked back down the mountain and saw two soldiers dragging Fahad behind them as they would a slaughtered animal." Commander Massoud's hands made a small up and down movement. "His head was bouncing on the ground, banging into rocks, bouncing again. I knew he was dead." He fell silent.

Massoud finally focused his intense eyes on Michelle. "I haven't thought about Fahad for many years. It is good to remember my friend. Now if you will excuse me, I must make sure the men have enough food." The Commander rose and quickly left the cave.

Michelle looked over at Dr. Abdullah. "I didn't mean to upset him by asking him to tell the story."

"Of course you didn't. How could you possibly know the effect it would have on him? He'll be all right. Just give him a few minutes with his troops, and he will find his equilibrium again."

"I can't imagine how much loss he has suffered over these years."

"No, you can't," Dr. Abdullah said quietly, "and that is a very good thing. No one should have to endure as much loss as he has. He is a strong man. He will bear even more. But I must tell you, I think he remembers the name of everyone who has gone to Paradise."

from that flame

"I'll ask yet again: why doesn't he give up as so many others who have fled Afghanistan have? Surely he has earned some peace in his life? I struggle to understand, and still I can't. Why doesn't he leave?"

"He will never leave Afghanistan, and there will be no peace for him until there is peace for his people. Surely you know that about him by now?"

Michelle nodded and sighed. "Yes, I do. It just doesn't seem right, that's all."

"It will be 'right' when he gets to set aside the guns and tanks and begin to design the beautiful buildings that will be built here again. It will be 'right' when he sees his people free. It will be 'right' when elections are held and the people have the leaders they choose. It will be 'right' when his name is recorded in our history books as the man who gave Afghanistan back to the Afghan people," the doctor concluded with great passion.

Michelle nodded and smiled a small smile at Abdullah. "And you, you who have been at his side for such a long time and share his every vision, all those same things will make it 'right' for you as well."

"Yes," the doctor said solemnly. "When I can watch my children and his and all the other children of our land live happy, safe, productive lives, then all will be right, and I will know that my life's struggle was worth any price paid."

"You are a good man, Doctor Abdullah," Michelle spoke with genuine admiration. "It has been a wonderful opportunity getting to know you. You have all my respect."

"After the way I behaved the first night, I never dared expect such kind words from you," the doctor smiled a little sheepishly. "I am glad for having had the opportunity to get to know you, too."

"Friends?" Michelle held out her hand. Dr. Abdullah's much larger hand swallowed hers.

"Friends," he answered with a smile.

5. Mountains

What's going on?" Michelle shouted at Dr. Abdullah early the next morning. Her voice had to carry over a harsh, bitter wind that burned her skin and forced her to grab her *pakol* to keep it from flying off. She had come out of the cave to discover that several inches of snow had fallen during the night. She shivered and retreated a step back into the cave. She could still see the doctor but was shielded from the worst of the wind. Traveling today was going to be miserable.

Dr. Abdullah made a gesture to indicate that he would be with her in a moment. He finished giving his orders to the men who were packing the mules. The poor beasts already looked half-frozen.

Abdullah came back into the interior of the cave, snagging Michelle's arm and drawing her in with him. He stamped his feet to knock the snow off and bent over the low burning fire with his hands outstretched.

"We aren't going to be able to travel very far today," Dr. Abdullah said, "but it is important that we leave this location. Commander Massoud and a dozen men have already gone ahead to scout out a place for us to stop again. We are going to need a lot of caves and room enough for all the men and animals."

"Does he have any idea where to look?" Michelle asked anxiously.

Dr. Abdullah smiled reassuringly. "Of course he does. No one knows these mountains better than he does. He said there's a place about seven kilometers from here on the way to the Turghan Pass where we can start crossing west to Khwaja Bahauddin. "

Michelle looked outside. Seven kilometers was less than half

from that flame

the distance they had been covering each day, but in this extreme weather, seven kilometers was going to feel like seven hundred. To make matters worse, she wasn't feeling very well.

"Abdullah, in all fairness, I have to tell you before we leave that I feel weak and sick. I don't want to hold everyone back, but I know you can't leave me here alone either. Maybe a few men could stay with me until the weather clears or until I feel better, and then we could catch up with you?"

Dr. Abdullah put his fingers on her wrist to check her pulse almost before she finished her last sentence. "Tell me what is wrong."

"I have a headache. I'm nauseated. I'm so fatigued, I don't think I can hike seven kilometers."

Dr. Abdullah looked at her eyes, felt her throat and forehead, and checked her pulse again at her carotid artery. Finally he nodded and spoke. "I think it is just altitude sickness. It's not uncommon among people who are unaccustomed to the thin air of the mountains. It is nothing too serious."

"Will it pass?"

The doctor smiled disarmingly. "Of course, as soon as you reach a lower altitude."

"Swell," Michelle said sarcastically, "especially since our day's plan calls for us to keep going up." Her expression changed to one of real concern. "I don't think I can make it."

"After what happened to you the day before yesterday on the way to this camp, I had already made a medical decision that hiking was not on your agenda today."

"Then you will leave me here with a few men?" The thought frightened her, but she was determined to hide her fear at least until Abdullah left.

"Hardly. When you came out, I was having the men redistribute the armament and supplies carried by the mules. Today, one of the mules will carry you and your pack, and before you begin to argue with me, let me say that the mule will think it's lucky to have such a light load. The weight has been distributed evenly enough among the others so that they will not notice the difference."

"I wasn't going to argue. I was going to say *tashakur*. Thank you. You are absolutely correct in thinking that this is the only

87

way I could make today's trip." She looked at him out of the corner of her eye and made a funny face. "I don't argue that much."

Abdullah laughed. "Yes, you do. Constantly. It's one of your charms. I want you to add several layers of your own clothes beneath your fatigues. Nothing too heavy, just a few layers of light cloth that will help to hold in your body heat. Wear multiple pairs of socks. If you have an extra *paktou*, you can wear one over your *pakol* and tie it under your chin. The other can cover the lower half of your face and tie behind your neck. It will protect your nose and throat from breathing the cold air directly."

"You were just looking for an excuse to get me to cover my face," Michelle teased.

"Absolutely," Dr. Abdullah deadpanned. "Get dressed. We pull out in five minutes."

Five minutes later one of the Alliance soldiers was giving Michelle a leg up onto the mule's back. Her pack was snuggly tied to the animal's rear shanks behind her.

"Lean forward over the mule's neck," Abdullah shouted over the wind. After she did as she was asked, the doctor and the *mujahidin* soldier struggled to drape her sleeping bag over her like a tent. The wind kept trying to snatch it out of their hands and blow it off the mountain ridge. Finally the two men managed to get it into position completely covering Michelle from her head to the place behind her where she was braced against her pack. For a moment she was completely gone from sight, and the mule looked as if it was wearing an enormous blanket with a bumpy object beneath it.

Abdullah and the *mujahidin* used straps taken from rifles and looped them together for length to secure the sleeping bag in place around Michelle. The straps were fastened to the mule's harness and girth as well as Michelle's backpack. It was a tangled mess, but Abdullah thought it would keep the woman warm and dry as they traveled. Michelle sat up as much as she dared and peered out from under the sleeping bag.

Dr. Abdullah tapped Michelle's foot. "Pull your legs up so that your feet are sheltered by the bag." Again she did as she was told. With the sleeping bag to block the bitter wind, she was actually quite comfortable.

"All right," Abdullah nodded in satisfaction. "As long as you

from that flame

stay covered, you should be all right. If you get very tired, just lay forward on the mule's neck. It will make adjustments for your weight shift. Do you think you can make it?"

"Yes," Michelle smiled bravely. "I will. Thank you."

"If you start to feel worse, just call Zayed's name. He will be leading the mule. I will be close by, and he will get me if you call his name. Okay? Let's go." Dr. Abdullah nodded to Zayed, and they were on their way.

By the time they reached the end of the first kilometer, Michelle had leaned far over the mule's neck with her arms on either side of its neck. The warmth from the animal's body comforted her as did the gentle, rocking motion it made as it walked. The wind blew the sleeping bag well over her head. She laughed softly to herself when she tried to imagine the odd picture she would present to anyone who saw her. She didn't care how funny she looked. She was reasonably warm, and the large group was moving towards their newest destination, and she had not been left behind. She looked forward to seeing Commander Massoud when they arrived. She wanted to make him laugh to compensate for the sadness her questions had brought to him the night before.

Dr. Abdullah startled her when he pulled her covering away and peered beneath her portable, sleeping bag-tent. "How are you doing?" He had wrapped an additional blanket over his coat. While he was wearing a *paktou* around his neck and lower face as protection from the freezing wind and snow and had a hat jammed low on his head, Michelle could see that small crystals of ice had formed in his eyebrows and more had grasped the wisps of his hair that had blown loose from the hat.

"You are freezing," Michelle said in alarm.

"No." Abdullah shook his head. Michelle couldn't see his mouth beneath the *paktou*, but she suspected that he was smiling. "I just wanted to tell you that we will be stopping much sooner than expected."

"Why?"

"Massoud sent a runner back. He found a set of caves a little to the west that is several kilometers closer. The runner will change our course and lead us there."

"Will we be far enough away from any Taliban who might

still be following us?"

Abdullah shrugged. "They are having the same problems traveling as we are, and they are less well stocked with food and blankets. Besides, there won't be that many of them left until they bring in reinforcements. The battle the night before last greatly reduced their local number. Massoud will handle whomever is left."

Dr. Abdullah pulled the sleeping bag back over Michelle so that she was again completely covered. He was a little worried about her. Her face seemed unnaturally pale, and her eyes were again beginning to have a feverish cast to them. He kept a position directly beside the mule whenever the path was wide enough to accommodate them both.

Michelle was almost dozing when she felt the sure-footed mule begin to slip a little. At first it was barely noticeable, a mere sound of a hoof scrapping on icy rock rather than landing firmly on frozen earth. Then there was the slightest stumble as the mule quickly regained its balance. Her mind began to weigh options. Should she sit up? That would throw her weight towards the animal's hindquarters. Was that good or bad? Should she stay down so that her weight was partially over its shoulders? Did that make it harder or easier for the mule to maintain his balance? Should she dismount altogether? She lifted her head cautiously so that she could peer out from beneath the sleeping bag. She would call to Zayed. He would know far better than she.

They were climbing at a fairly steep rate of ascent, and the narrow path strewn with rocks of all sizes and shapes twisted sharply to accommodate a large outcropping of jagged boulder. As Michelle opened her mouth to call to Zayed, everything started to move as if in slow motion.

Zayed, less sure-footed than the beast he led, slipped on some rocks that were encrusted with snow and ice. As he lost his footing and balance, he fell forward to his knees, still clutching the lead line to the mule. He began to slide backwards down the steep incline and slammed into the mule's front legs setting off a chain reaction.

The animal was knocked off balance and tried valiantly to regain its footing. Michelle, feeling the animal slip and slide beneath her, started to sit up so that she could get off. The straps holding down the sleeping bag both in front and behind her

from that flame

prohibited her from moving freely, but the incline of the mule caused her to start to slip backwards towards the pack behind her. The mule, impacted from the front by Zayed, and suddenly having the weight on its back shifted because of Michelle's movement, had its legs start to go out from under it.

The mule tried to lunge forward, but rather than having its front feet land on solid earth, they landed on Zayed's body. Zayed, his hand nearly frozen on the lead line, tried to get out of the way, but it was too late. Man, woman, and beast all started to fall in a tangle of arms, legs, and leather straps.

Michelle would never be quite certain what happened after that point. She heard dim shouts in Dari. She felt herself being thrown first away from and then back towards the mule's contorting body. She thought she felt a strong hand close on her upper arm and grip as tightly as a band of steel. But then she was free from the grip and rolling, unable to tell where she began and the mule ended as their two bodies crashed to the frozen ground. She was unaware of anything beyond the point of her head hitting the ice-encrusted, rocky earth.

When Michelle regained consciousness, Dr. Abdullah was kneeling beside her packing snow on her forehead and right eye.

"That's cold," she complained weakly.

"I have to stop the bleeding," Abdullah answered.

"How bad is it?"

"I don't know. Head wounds bleed a lot. I couldn't get a good look at the gash because of the blood."

"Is Zayed all right?" Michelle tried to raise herself on her left elbow to look for him.

"Don't move." Dr. Abdullah gently pushed her back down. "Zayed will be fine. He has a broken arm." Abdullah put both of his hands on her arm and started to press and manipulate the bone gently. His hands moved over her clavicle and breast bone to the other clavicle and arm. He checked her ribs, her legs, her feet, her neck, and her back. Finally, he removed the *paktou* and *pakol* from her head and slid his hands over her skull.

"I have a very hard head," Michelle teased, hoping to relieve the tense, worried look from the doctor's face. "Except for half my face being frozen, I'm fine."

"I'm the doctor," Abdullah reminded his patient. "I will decide if you are fine."

"Well, I had better be since lying here in the snow much longer is not going to be an option."

"There you go arguing again."

Michelle smiled. "More proof that I am okay. I have a headache, but except for that and the bump on my head, I do think I'm okay."

"Nothing seems to be broken," the doctor agreed. "Look at me directly. I need a light to check if your pupils are reactive, but I can see that they are the same size."

"See? No concussion. Now may I get up?"

"Only sitting." Dr. Abdullah assisted her. He took a clean handkerchief from his pocket, filled it with fresh snow, tied the corners together, and then laid it on the gash on her face. He brought her hand up to hold the impromptu ice pack for herself.

When Michelle was upright and looking around, she saw one man putting a sling on Zayed's arm. Another man was struggling to free her backpack from the dead mule.

"Oh, the poor thing!" Michelle cried out.

"He broke his leg," Dr. Abdullah said. "He had to be put down."

"I'm sorry." Michelle's eyes filled with tears.

"It wasn't your fault," Abdullah assured her. "It was an accident that could have happened to anyone. This path is treacherous. I thank God that neither you nor Zayed was killed. We can always get another mule. Do you want to try standing now?" Michelle nodded. Abdullah stood first and then helped her to her feet. Leaning heavily on his arm, her head grew dizzy and her vision clouded.

"Well?" the doctor asked.

"I'm fine," Michelle answered in a shaky voice. "I can go on."

"We will take it very slow and easy. I am having another mule prepared for you, but I don't think it would be wise to mount until we reach the ridge up there."

"I think I would rather walk than get on another mule."

"Two more kilometers? Don't argue. You're riding."

from that flame

"I'm not arguing. I'm expressing a preference."

"You're arguing. And keep that pack on your face." He cupped her elbow and forced back up the arm she had been lowering. He replaced her *paktous* and *pakol* and bundled her up with the sleeping bag again. Then, as he had done two days previously, he had her lean on him so that he could support her as she walked.

Michelle brought up one side of her sleeping bag and studied the long gash in it. The doctor saw what she was looking at.

"I had to cut one of the straps that bound you to the mule, and I'm afraid I was not careful of your bag. I'm sorry it was damaged."

"That's okay. The next time you are at The Backpacker in Denver, you can buy me a new one to replace it," Michelle suggested with a small smile.

"I will." Dr. Abdullah answered seriously.

Slowly, carefully, they made their way to the top of the ridge. To their surprise, Commander Massoud was waiting for them.

"You were taking so long…" he began but then saw the handkerchief pressed to Michelle's face. "What happened?" he asked with alarm. "Are you all right?" He looked at Dr. Abdullah. "Is she all right?"

"She will be all right," Dr. Abdullah began.

"I'm fine," Michelle said at the same time.

"What happened?" the Commander asked again.

"I didn't think having a sprained ankle, getting shot at and bombed by the Taliban, and suffering from exposure and altitude sickness was sufficient," Michelle said dryly. "I thought falling off a mountain while strapped to a mule would be an interesting experience to round out my adventure in Afghanistan."

Commander Massoud looked at her blankly for a moment before catching the twinkle in the one eye he could see. When she started to laugh, he joined in with a hearty laugh of his own. He laughed so hard his shoulders shook and his eyes filled with tears.

"Now are you ready to go back to Peshawar?" he said when he could finally speak.

"No way," Michelle said firmly. "I intend to see this through to the end."

from that flame

"She said she has a hard head," Dr. Abdullah laughed along with them.

"I believe it," Commander Massoud said sincerely. "Let's get to the camp, Doctor. You are going to have your hands full with this patient, I fear." They turned and began the dangerous incline, both men keeping a careful eye on their improbable guest.

"Am I your favorite patient yet?" Michelle teased Dr. Abdullah as he finished dressing the nasty cut over her right eyebrow. The fire warmed the interior of the cave, and several lanterns gave him a better light by which to work.

"You are certainly becoming my most frequent patient," the doctor replied absentmindedly as he concentrated on his work. "In the middle of a battle zone, that's saying something. Follow my finger with your eyes." He slowly moved his hand back and forth in front of her face. He nodded in satisfaction. "You're lucky. I don't think you have suffered any permanent injury. After a little rest, you will be as good as new. Provided you don't find a new way to get yourself sick, injured, or otherwise banged up."

"Hey, it's not my fault you like hiking around frozen mountains at ten thousand feet," Michelle protested. "If you and Commander Massoud want to join me on a warm, sandy beach and finish the interviews there, you'd have my vote."

"A warm beach and ocean breezes sound delightful," Abdullah Abdullah sighed. "Not any time soon, I'm afraid."

"Exactly how long have you been with the Commander?" Michelle asked.

Dr. Abdullah thought for a moment. "Since a time almost before I can remember. It feels as if I have always been with him. It was 1985. I joined him to help oust the Soviet Union."

"And stuck around to help oust the Taliban? Sixteen years is a long time."

"Yes, it is. I graduated from medical school in the late seventies and was sent to Panjshir to head up a clinic there. From the first time I met Ahmed Shah Massoud, there was a bond between us. I was a practicing doctor for several years, but ultimately I left the clinic to go with Massoud. I started running field hospitals for him, but after a while my responsibilities became more political and advisory."

"You were part of the Rabbani government in Kabul in 1992?"

"Yes, I was in the Ministry of Defense with Massoud. In 1996 I was named the spokesman for the Northern Alliance. Last year I became the government's Foreign Minister."

"Do you think you'll ever go back to practicing medicine?"

"I didn't think I had stopped." Abdullah smiled at her. "You keep making certain of that."

"You know what I mean."

Abdullah sighed again and got a faraway look in his eyes. "There is nothing I would enjoy more because it would mean that my country is at peace, and I could finally begin to help cure the ailments that affect the people here." He looked at Michelle. "Do you know about the massive number of people who have lost limbs to land mines? There are many cases of malnutrition. Children die from preventable diseases. Diseases run rampant that proper sanitation, sufficient food, clean water, and basic medical care could curb." The doctor smiled sadly as he concluded his thought. "Yes, I would practice medicine again and do whatever I could to help my people."

"I will pray for that day to come soon, my friend," Michelle said quietly. "You have gifted, healing hands. They should be holding a sick child rather than a cold rifle."

"I pray for the same thing." Dr. Abdullah replied. "And, now, the doctor is telling this patient that she needs food and fluid and then some rest. I will find something for you and bring it back before I go to see if they need help getting all of the men, animals, and equipment settled into the caves."

"Michelle *Jaan*?" Commander Massoud looked around the stone curve of the cave into the deep interior where the journalist was stretched out on her battered sleeping bag.

"Hi." Michelle propped herself up on her elbows. "Is everything squared away?"

Massoud looked puzzled as he repeated what Michelle had said. "*Carré loin?* I'm sorry, but I don't understand this phrase."

from that flame

Michelle thought for a moment. *"Prête?"* It was amazing to her that they hadn't encountered many more language problems. More than ever she envied Dr. Abdullah's language skills.

"Ah! Ready. No, not completely." The Commander approached her. "That's why I'm here. I had hoped to give you this space to yourself, but I'm afraid you will have to have someone in here with you. There isn't quite enough room. I'm sorry."

"Please don't be. Who will be my roommate? Human or mule?"

"Both," the Commander smiled. "I need sleeping quarters for Doctor Abdullah, me, and two mules."

"Honestly, I would rather have company than be in here all alone. It would be cold, lonely, and scary if I was here by myself."

"You should have said something," the Commander admonished her.

"Well, I would have except the very first night when I suggested that Abdul could share a tent with me, Abdullah almost had a heart attack. I was afraid to bring it up again."

Commander Massoud chuckled. "That was a little different."

"Yeah? Well you were the one who got the medic to play chaperone the first night I gave you a back massage. I'm just trying to figure out your rules and customs. I don't want to offend anyone."

"You were a stranger then to all of us. You've been with us for what? About a week now? Everyone has become accustomed to your presence. My men have figured out that both Abdullah and I consider you a friend. Besides, everyone realizes the dire circumstances we are all under. Sometimes rules and customs take a backseat to the necessities for survival." Commander Massoud ran his hands over his face, and Michelle suddenly sensed that he was both exhausted and in pain.

"What's wrong?" she asked. "Is it your back?"

"Yes, of course. Always that, but I have a headache too. I am tired, that's all."

"I can't imagine why. Come here," Michelle got on her knees and patted the sleeping bag beneath her.

Massoud shook his head. "I can't sleep now. I have things to do."

"I don't intend for you to sleep. Please, just come here and sit with your back to me."

"It's too cold to take off my coat," the Commander protested.

"Good grief, and Abdullah says I argue all the time." Michelle glared at him. *"Eenja beyaa!* Come here!" She laughed at his startled expression. "Please?" she added with a smile.

Reluctantly Commander Massoud went over to her, turned around, and sat down.

"Will you take off your *pakol*, please?" Michelle asked.

He did as he was asked. Michelle pressed her thumbs against the base of his skull and let her fingers search until they found his temples. She began to apply gentle pressure.

A small moan escaped Commander Massoud's lips. "I think we should get the medic," he said in a hushed voice.

"I thought you said we didn't need a chaperone," Michelle asked.

"I meant so he can learn how to do this. It feels wonderful. What do you call it?"

"Acupressure. Now be quiet and try to relax, will you?" She moved her thumbs a centimeter down his neck.

"When the war is over, will you come back and set up a clinic next to Abdullah's?"

"Only if that clinic is somewhere a heck of a lot warmer than it is here."

"Okay," Commander Massoud said drowsily. "I'll fix the weather right after I finish the war."

"Uh-huh," Michelle said softly. "But not right this minute, Commander."

"No, not right this minute," he murmured in agreement.

Michelle's fingers continued to apply pressure to the bones in the Commanders neck and surrounding muscles. She varied the degree of strength she used and felt his upper body start to respond to the therapy. He started to slump forward a little.

"Lie back," Michelle moved backwards to give him more room. She helped to guide his head to a soft landing on the cushion. "Bring your knees up so that your lower back is pressed flat against the ground," she instructed. When he complied, she switched her technique to a slight tugging on his neck to offer a traction-like stretch.

"I can't sleep now," the Commander muttered.

"Okay," Michelle agreed softly. "Shhh … just relax." It was only a matter of moments before the Commander had drifted off into a light sleep.

Michelle continued the pressure and stretching exercises for fear that he would immediately awaken if she stopped, but she worked with a lighter touch and studied the face of the man whose head she held in her hands.

He was the most extraordinary man she had ever met. There was something as timeless and ageless as Afghanistan itself at the very core of him. He embodied all Afghanistan's tribulations and sufferings, all her fierce pride and independence, all her faith and hope, all her courage and endurance. Like Afghanistan, he had faced hardship and disappointment, failure and frustration. But also like Afghanistan, he had hard-won victories and glorious successes, bountiful blessings, and triumphant conquests. Like his country, he had had his hopes dashed but was not defeated. In the face of bitter foes with overwhelming strength, he found the inventiveness to change, adapt, and ultimately defeat his enemies. He was as strong, steadfast, enduring, and dangerous as the mountains he defended.

For Afghanistan, he became her Sisyphus. He pushed the same rock of freedom up the same mountain time after time only to have it roll down and force him to start again. His life was defined by getting that huge boulder up the hill, and Michelle knew he would continue to struggle with it no matter how weary he became or how hopeless the goal of ever reaching the summit might seem. Even if getting the rock to the top of the mountain and finally seeing his people free to determine their own destiny took him all his life, he would never stop trying.

Massoud pleaded his case over and over again to the outside world. He patiently explained, exhorted, cautioned, and appealed for help. When help did not arrive, he found new words to advance the cause of his beloved country and went back to those who had listened politely but did not help, and again he elucidated, clarified, illustrated, and warned. When few listened and even fewer helped, he rallied his men with their aging, meager weapons, grasped the rock, and began to push it up the mountain one more time.

Will this Sisyphus finally shove his heavy rock to the top of the mountain and receive the rest he has earned? Michelle wondered. She would find a way to help him if she could. She had words, editors, magazines, and publishers, but she also had time and money. She could find a way to make it all work for him.

She leaned over so that her mouth was only an inch from his ear. "I will find a way to help you; I promise," she softly whispered.

"Shhh." Michelle put her finger to her lips when Dr. Abdullah entered the cave five minutes later.

"I'm sorry, but I must wake him. He is needed," Dr. Abdullah said in a normal tone of voice. Commander Massoud's eyes flew open, and he sat straight up. His eyes met those of his friend.

"*Chee shod?*"

"Nothing. Zahir is back. He has a message from General Fahim."

Commander Massoud started to get up, and as he did his eyes caught Michelle's. "I told you I couldn't sleep now." His voice was low, but the words were sharply delivered, and the cold anger in his eyes startled Michelle. She sat back on her heels but said nothing. She felt as if his words had slapped her across the face, and she clamped her teeth together tightly to keep from crying. Massoud snatched up his *pakol*, slammed it on his head, got to his feet, and turned to Dr. Abdullah.

"Take me to Zahir."

Abdullah shot Michelle a sympathetic glance, but she didn't see it. She was studying her hands with great interest, and Abdullah guessed she was trying to hide her tears. She did not lift her head.

"Well?" Commander Massoud barked.

"Let's go." Dr. Abdullah turned to him. The men left the cave and went out into the bitterly cold wind and blowing snow.

"*Ahmed Shah*," Abdullah said as they were walking to another cave in the complex, "you should not have—"

"Not now." Massoud raised his hand to ward off the words he knew his friend was going to say. He quickened his pace.

"You should not have spoken to her—" Abdullah began again.

Commander Massoud stopped walking and turned to face his friend. "I know," he said firmly. "No more discussion about it now. I will talk to her later. Right now I must hear Mohammed Fahim's message."

Abdullah knew when tactical retreat was the best option. "Zahir is waiting. Let's go."

Night was rapidly approaching by the time Commander Massoud made it back to the cave where he would sleep that night. He pushed past the two mules someone had secured near the very front of the cave. The fire was barely burning, and all of the lanterns were giving off only a low light. In the semi-darkness he found the small pile of twigs and dried grasses set aside and fed them to the fire. Once the blaze grew larger, Massoud looked around the cave's interior. He could barely see Michelle where she sat huddled against the cave's deepest recess.

Her knees were drawn up almost under her chin, and her arms were wrapped around her legs. Her head was tilted downwards so that her face was resting on her knees. She remained motionless although he knew she had to be aware he had come in.

"Come warm yourself by the fire," he said gently. When she didn't move, he added, "You'll freeze over there." Still there was no movement from her.

Massoud went over to her and stooped down so that he could look her in the eyes. Michelle did nothing to acknowledge his presence.

"Look at me," he said. Slowly, Michelle raised her head so that he could see her face.

The look of abject misery in her eyes was enhanced by the gash over her right eyebrow and the dark bruise on her right cheek bone.

"Come by the fire," he said quietly. "We can talk and stay warm at the same time." He smiled ruefully at her. "Or I'll talk,

from that flame

and you can listen to my apology. Please?"

Michelle stood up and went closer to the fire. The Commander grabbed several blankets that were neatly piled nearby. When Michelle knelt by the fire with her hands outstretched towards the faint heat, he draped one of the blankets over her shoulders before wrapping one around himself and taking a seat opposite her.

"I'm sorry I spoke to you unkindly," Massoud said sincerely.

"I was only trying to make your headache go away," Michelle said. "I didn't mean to make you fall asleep and miss your meeting."

Commander Massoud swept his hand over his face and rubbed his tired eyes a moment before looking at Michelle again. "I know," he slowly said at last. "It was anger at myself for falling asleep. I was wrong to blame you."

"I bet you haven't slept more than twenty hours altogether in all the time I've been here. You are exhausted, *Ahmed Shah*. You need sleep just like everyone else."

"My circumstances do not allow me to…," he searched for the right words, "to afford myself the luxury of resting, eating, or even sleeping whenever my body asks for those things. If I don't do things that need to be done at the exact times they need to be accomplished, people may suffer or die. I must remain extremely self-disciplined at all times. Falling asleep this afternoon when I knew General Fahim's message was expected was a breech in that self-discipline. I was angry at myself, but I blamed it on you. I was wrong, and I hope you will forgive me."

"There is nothing to forgive," Michelle answered, "but I think you are too hard on yourself. You are human, after all. Even the great Commander Massoud needs a reprieve every now and then."

"Yes," the Commander said, smiling, "and that is what you are. You make me laugh often, a rare gift for me. Laughter heals a bruised and battered mind as prayer heals a bruised and battered soul. You also give me hope, a commodity that can be difficult to find during days like these."

"And I thought I just gave you a headache," Michelle quipped.

Massoud laughed softly. "That's exactly what I mean. You

have a justifiable reason to be angry with me, yet you offer forgiveness and with humor try to take blame that is not yours. If a fraction of the outside world has your kindness and understanding, I find hope for all of us."

Flustered and embarrassed, Michelle hastily sought to divert Massoud. "Who is General Fahim?" she asked abruptly.

Commander Massoud smiled again. "He is my chief intelligence officer," he answered. "I will agree to change the subject if you assure me that no hard feelings about my bad behavior are lingering."

Michelle grinned. "Sure. I figure I have a 'get out of jail free card.'"

"A what?" Commander Massoud knitted his brows.

"Never mind," Michelle laughed. "There are no hard feelings. Tell me about the message from General Fahim, okay?"

"There's not much to tell. Remember a few days ago when I sent two of my men to relay a message to one of the other Alliance commanders? It outlined a strategy for an upcoming battle that needed to be coordinated with Fahim's men. One of my men came back with Fahim's response."

"Only one came back? Did the other stay with the general?"

Commander Massoud shook his head slowly. "No. He was either killed or captured."

"I'm sorry. I know you take each loss to heart." Michelle averted her eyes, warmed her hands, and sat silently for a few moments.

"The news from Fahim was good at least," Commander Massoud said at last.

"I'm glad about that. May I ask how the remaining messenger knew how to find us? We aren't where we were supposed to be."

"We seldom are," Massoud answered. "We should never be where our enemy expects us, only where they don't. I station relay men along our routes so that no matter how our direction may change, the other commanders will always be able to find us."

"You've gotten pretty good at this war commander stuff, haven't you?" Michelle teased in an effort to make him smile again. Instead, Massoud stood up and paced back and forth in the limited space.

from that flame

"I wish I had never been required to learn these things, but this life was thrust upon me, and now I must do the best I can for all involved." Massoud looked over at the journalist and saw the troubled expression on her face. "What's wrong?"

"What you just said reminded me of something one RAWA member said about you." Michelle looked up at the Commander. "I wasn't entirely honest with you when I first got to your camp."

"Oh?" Massoud returned to his seat across from her. "What do you mean? You said RAWA told you that I had a vision for women's life in Afghanistan that differed from that of the Taliban. Was that untrue?"

"No, but it was only half the truth," Michelle admitted.

"Then I think you had better tell me all of it," Massoud encouraged.

Michelle expelled her breath slowly before meeting his eyes. "Okay. Some of the women in RAWA are supportive of your efforts. They believe that you and your Alliance are the best hope they have for a normal life in this country. But there are some—many, in fact—who disagree, and one woman in particular charges that you are worse than the Taliban in allowing violence against women. Another compared you to the Angolan rebel Janos Savambi."

A shadow of hurt fell over Commander Massoud's face. "I see. What else?"

"I was told that you love war, that you crave it, that you will never allow peace. If I remember the exact quote, she said, 'He eats, drinks, and inhales war.' When I came to your camp that first night, it wasn't just to confirm facts. I wanted to figure out for myself which Commander Ahmed Shah Massoud was the real one."

"Did you?"

"I'm working on it. However, I am at a loss to explain why some women made the accusations they did. It doesn't fit with the man I've come to know."

Massoud shook his head. "I'm not at a loss; I understand completely. I made promises I could not keep, and people—women—who were counting on me to deliver peace were hurt when I failed."

"You mean when the Rabbani government took over Kabul?"

"Yes, but before and after as well." Massoud scratched his beard thoughtfully for a moment. It was nearly impossible to explain the complicated machinations of Afghan politics to a foreigner. It was also impossible to explain every decision he had made over a twenty- year period of time. Decisions had been made which, at the time, seemed reasonable. It was only with hindsight that he could understand why so many had turned out badly. Still, he wanted to be as candid with Michelle as he could safely be.

"Once we drove the Soviets out of the country," he began slowly, "my troops joined forces with the troops of many of Afghanistan's warlords. I took Kabul with ten thousand men. We handed power over to Burhanuddin Rabbani and a leadership counsel. Our hope and plan was to one day have a democratic nation in which the people themselves were allowed to select their leaders. In our efforts to form a government, we excluded the political-military establishment of Pakistan's Hekmatyar."

"Him again," Michelle said knowingly. "Is that when the final break came between you and your one time friend and ally?"

Commander Massoud nodded in agreement. "You recall that he and I had already become estranged. This made it worse. Additionally, the exclusion of Hekmatyar angered Pakistan, who supported and backed him. Hekmatyar's troops started lobbing mortars into Kabul. There was great destruction of property and loss of life. We agreed to include Hekmatyar in the new government in a compromise effort.

"Finally, in April of 1992, the *mujahidin* and the Afghan army maintained peaceful control of Kabul. A coalition formed an interim government in Peshawar. A fifty member leadership counsel headed by Professor Mujaddedi was supposed to lead Afghanistan for the first two months. The counsel consisted of thirty Commanders, ten *ulema*, or religious leaders, and one nominated member from each of the ten major *mujahidin* parties. The counsel hoped to transfer power to Rabbani fairly quickly. He would serve for four months until elections could be organized."

"Is that when you were named Defense Minister?" Michelle asked.

from that flame

"Yes." Massoud nodded. "I had been strongly allied with President Rabbani for many years. We trusted each other and were friends."

"It sounds as if everything was in place to work well. What happened? What led to the breakdown of the government?"

"The leader of the National Islamic Front of Afghanistan, Pir Sayed Ahmed Gailani, challenged the government because Hekmatyar, who ultimately represented Pakistan's interests, was still involved. At the same time, Abdul Ali Mazari, who represented the alliance of Iranian-based parties, declared the government unacceptable because his group was not represented."

"You were facing dissention from all over," Michelle observed.

"It was even worse. Next Professor Mujaddedi appointed a warlord from the Mazar area, an ex-Communist Uzbek named Dostum, to the rank of full general. I and all of the other *mujahidin* objected to Dostum being elevated to that status.

"Dostum and his followers became angry and wanted to expand their power base beyond Mazar-i-Sharif. His troops became unruly and violent. They began confiscating property from the residents of Kabul. It was then that the rapes, killings, assaults, and other atrocities really began. We moved from a war against the Soviet Union to a civil war fed by outside interference almost overnight. We destroyed Kabul and shattered the hopes of the Afghan people because we were unable to form a cohesive, cooperative, unity government."

Michelle sat quietly as she considered all that the Commander had told her. She understood better now why some of the women from RAWA were so harsh in their criticism of Ahmed Shah Massoud. They had dared to believe him, had dared to hope when he said he would deliver peace and freedom to their country. What followed would have made anyone bitterly disappointed. Michelle also understood better why the people of Afghanistan might have welcomed the Taliban in the early days. They promised to bring law and order to a country that had been ravaged by war for too many years. When the people of the land had lost faith in the ability of their own leaders to govern fairly and provide them a measure of security, even the Pakistani-supported group must have seemed like a viable replacement. No one could have guessed in the early days how oppressive and cruel the Taliban would become.

"You are thinking that I failed?" Massoud asked.

"No," Michelle answered quickly. "I am only saddened by the story you told. You were very close to establishing a good government in Kabul."

"But I did fail," Massoud repeated with a sigh. "I failed repeatedly. Many of the terrible things that happened were not under my direct control, but that makes them no less my responsibility. I was one of the leaders, and I must accept blame for those under my command."

"Would you have failed if Pakistan and Iran had stayed out of your country's internal affairs? It seems to me that they made it impossible for you and your interim government to succeed," Michelle observed.

Commander Massoud smiled ruefully. "You are being kind and offering me an excuse. There is no doubt that Pakistan and other foreign interventions added to the problem, but the crisis was equally rooted in internal problems. There were too many warlords seeking individual power. I was one of them. I believed my vision for Afghanistan was best. I should have worked harder to make allies through persuasive means rather than enemies through combative means. I hope I have learned from the many mistakes I made. "

"Was what happened in Kabul the worst time for you? It is obvious how painfully it affected you. You were so close to having everything you wanted only to lose it all."

"I've had so many 'worst times' in my life, I can't remember the worst," Massoud answered bleakly. "I have many regrets over Kabul. Regrets for things I have or have not done in the war. Regrets that when I had Kabul, I did not serve the people better. Enough regrets for me to understand why the women of whom you spoke feel as they do. Our country and our noble people were brutalized and became the victims of misplaced greed, hegemonic designs, and ignorance. Our shortcomings were a result of political innocence, inexperience, vulnerability, victimization, bickering, and inflated egos. I wish I could go back and do it differently." His eyes grew dark as his thoughts moved to a time that was the source of some of his deepest regrets in life.

Michelle said, "It is a lesson I have learned too well," and then she began to recite a poem from memory.

> It's good to leave each day behind,
> like flowing water, free of sadness.
> Yesterday is gone and its tale told.
> Today new seeds are growing.

"You know Rumi!" Commander Massoud said with delight.

"I have always loved his writing," Michelle answered. "He was a very wise man as well as a magnificent poet. I think you might heed his words. You can't undo what happened, but you can resolve that the next time you won't make the same mistakes."

"I will remember that wisdom," the Commander agreed.

"I appreciate your candor," Michelle added. " You are an honest man, Ahmed Shah Massoud. Poor Diogenes needed to meet you. Thank you for letting me ask you about this difficult period in your life."

"She knows Greek mythology as well as Persian poets," Commander Massoud said approvingly. His face became serious again. "When you write your story, Michelle *Jaan,* I want you to have all the facts. How could you be persuasive in what you write if you have suspicions that I have only talked about the victories and achievements when you know there have been defeats and failures too? The truth may be harsh and painful, but I am not afraid of it."

Dr. Abdullah pushed past the mules and came into the tent. "Am I interrupting?"

"No, of course not," Massoud welcomed his friend to the fire. "I need you to explain something to me."

"What's that?" Abdullah sat by the fire and looked at his friend.

"Michelle says I owe her a 'get out of jail free card.' What is that?"

Abdullah's gaze went from Massoud to Michelle and back to Massoud. He stared at him blankly. "I have no idea."

Massoud arched an eyebrow and smiled. "I thought you said you spoke the language."

"I do. Fluently," Abdullah looked back at Michelle. "I just

don't know every slang reference she does."

Michelle started to laugh at the expression on Abdullah's face. "I'll have you know that 'get out of jail free card' is not slang. It is a tried and true Americanism. All right, let me explain to you this game called Monopoly."

"You still haven't explained the OK Corral and Annie Oakley references," Abdullah reminded her.

"Who?" Commander Massoud's eyebrows went up again.

"Someone she mentioned when she was having her shooting lesson," Abdullah answered. "By the way," he turned back to Michelle, "where is the gun?" He looked at her leg. The gun was not in sight.

"In my backpack."

"That rather defeats the purpose, don't you think?" Abdullah asked.

"Back to this board game called Monopoly," Michelle said, grinning. "It's a Western Capitalist game all Americans love to play. You get to buy and sell property."

The men leaned back comfortably and let her prattle on even though they barely understood what she was talking about. After months of long, sleepless nights during which fiery tracers lit the sky, mortar concussions shook the ground, and tactical planning or death counts were the only topics of conversation around, the mere sound of her animated voice and laughter was a delightful diversion. They laughed with her, encouraged her to talk longer, and began to dread the day when she would inevitably leave and return to America to write her story.

6. Helicopter

The next morning at dawn's first light, the base camp was a hive of activity as men began to pack up the equipment and prepare for the day's trek. There would not be another series of caves for at least ten kilometers, and they were approaching the path that would bring them to the summit of the mountain. It would be a long, hard day for man and beast.

Michelle was very cold when she awoke. She got up and hastily began to cram her belongings into her backpack. She knew that Commander Massoud would make certain food was left for her breakfast, but what she really wanted was a chance to melt some snow for warm water so that she could wash her face. The moist towelettes she had brought with her were long gone, and she didn't want to use the alcohol swabs in case they would be needed for medicinal purposes. She wanted a bath so badly she could hardly stand it, but since that would be impossible, perhaps it would not be too much to hope for some water to wash her face.

Commander Massoud was overseeing the excavation of munitions and supplies from deep within one of the caves. Michelle had more than enough time to heat her water and repack her personal belongings. She pulled her backpack on, determined that she would hike the miles herself. Except for a faint headache, she felt well and invigorated. Finally, camera in hand, she went to ask permission to take a walk so that she could photograph the area.

"I won't go too far," she explained to the Commander. "I would love to have some good pictures to go along with the story."

from that flame

Commander Massoud consulted his watch. "You must be back in an hour at the latest." He called to Abdul to come over to them and instructed the soldier to accompany the journalist while she took her pictures.

"Where is your gun?" Massoud glanced at Michelle's leg.

"I told you, in my pack."

"You must put it on."

"But Abdul has a rifle," Michelle argued.

Massoud sighed deeply. "If you want to go take pictures, you will strap on the pistol. Otherwise, stay here in the camp where I know you are safe."

"Fine." Annoyed, Michelle slid the pack off her back, opened it, and began to dig through its contents. She pulled out the gun and holster and strapped the belt around her waist. "Happy?" she snapped as she zipped up her pack and flung it back onto her shoulders.

The Commander pointed to her pack. "You could leave that here."

"No thanks. I've got it." Michelle turned on her heel and walked off. Massoud shook his head and waved Abdul after her. He liked this journalist very much, but there were times when she was an aggravation. He shook his head again and turned his attention back to the task at hand.

"Where is Michelle?" Abdullah approached Commander Massoud. "I have a mule ready for her."

"Off taking pictures somewhere." Massoud casually waved his hand in the direction of the western range. "She'll be back soon although she may not want to ride today."

"Is she afraid because of what happened yesterday?"

The Commander shook his head. "No, I don't think so. I made her wear the pistol you gave her. She is not happy."

"What does that have to do with riding the mule?" the doctor was puzzled.

"Nothing. But haven't you noticed that she doesn't like to take commands? One a day is about her limit, and I already used up the one for today. If you insist she ride the mule, she will insist

110

on walking."

"Then I won't insist," Dr. Abdullah smiled. "I will ask very pleasantly."

Commander Massoud started to laugh. "Yes, I need to learn to ask more pleasantly. That would be a good skill to have."

"You're the commander, Commander," the doctor joined in the laughter. "You command, and I'll ask. Between us we'll get her to do what we want."

"What I want right now is for her to return so that we can leave." Commander Massoud's eyes searched the terrain where he had last seen the journalist and his soldier.

"Shall I send someone to find them?" Abdullah asked.

"Let's give her fifteen more minutes. One of the helicopters is hidden only about three kilometers from here. I'll go up and look for her if she doesn't come back soon."

Abdullah heard the concern in his friend's voice. "You're worried. Why?"

"You heard what Zahir said last night. General Fahim sent warning that the Taliban is regrouping near Keshem. That isn't very far from here and is in the direction I saw her heading."

"I think we should send someone after her." Dr. Abdullah was now worried as well. "Who is with her?"

"Abdul. All right, here's what we'll do. Send Nasser and one other man to get the helicopter. I'll take three men and start out after her. Nasser can pick us up on the other side of that mountain." Massoud pointed westward. "Meanwhile, you and the rest of the men head towards Kalan Eylgah. We will wait there for you and make camp for the night. Do you know which caves I mean? The ones near Turghan Pass."

"Yes, I know the ones you mean," Abdullah replied, "but why don't I look for her while you head towards Kalan?"

"She is my responsibility. I'll go for her."

"All right," Abdullah said. "We should be able to reach the caves by nightfall if we press hard." He placed a restraining hand on the Commander who was walking away. "Be careful, my friend. There is no one the Taliban wants more badly than they want you."

Massoud smiled at his friend. "I'll see you tonight." The

from that flame

Commander called to three men and, moving as quickly as he could over the broken terrain, he headed up the mountain with the men close on his heels. He turned back for just a moment and met Abdullah's eyes. The doctor nodded slightly. He knew the plan, and he would not fail his friend.

Commander Massoud hiked up the mountain as fast as he could. His eyes scanned back and forth searching for broken scrub branches or freshly disturbed rocks which would indicate the way Michelle and Abdul had gone. Every five hundred yards he would stop briefly, raise the binoculars hanging around his neck to his eyes, and search the land around him. When they came to a small gorge, he had his men fan out to search behind each outcropping of rock and inside each shallow cave. Nothing.

Finally, the Commander picked up what he believed was a fresh trail. He and his men began moving even more quickly. It was difficult climbing. Their weapons and packs were heavy, and the speed of their ascent was beginning to take a toll on all of them. Massoud was amazed that Michelle had gone so far and that Abdul had let her. He would have a word or two to say to both of them.

Gasping for air, Commander Massoud and his men reached a small, level spot near the top of the mountain. From this vantage point, Massoud was able to see for a great distance. Part of what he saw brought him relief, and part of what he saw chilled him to the bone.

Racing up the other side of the mountain, moving as quickly as they possibly could on the frozen, broken terrain, Abdul was half dragging, half pulling Michelle upwards. Less than a half a kilometer behind them was a group of men; outlaws, Taliban, or al-Qaeda, Commander Massoud didn't know. That they were in pursuit was apparent.

Michelle saw Massoud and his men about a hundred yards above them. The sight of them brought her relief and renewed strength. She found her footing on the ground and started climbing quickly enough so that Abdul didn't have to pull her along with him. Her heart was hammering so hard, she thought it would burst out of her chest. Her lungs were on fire as they tried to intake a sufficient amount of the thin, cold air. Her leg and back muscles screamed in pain and protest as she forced herself to move even faster. Every tortured step brought her closer to the Commander and his weapons.

Commander Massoud shouted something loudly in Dari. The men on either side of him started firing down the mountainside. Abdul practically hurled Michelle to the ground before throwing his own body over hers. The whistle of the bullets made a peculiar sound as they whizzed past over their heads.

Michelle, flattened against the frozen, rocky earth by the weight of the man on top of her, wondered if this was going to be the end of her story. Since her mind was unable to grasp the enormity of what was happening around her, it drifted off to a different place, and she started to laugh to herself. She could not resist the irony of the situation. She had always thought war correspondents were slightly crazy. She could never understand the thrill they received when they were in a battle zone. It seemed so foolish to her. Yet here she was, smack in the middle of a war she barely understood, and now there was a good possibility she was going to be a casualty of that war.

Commander Massoud yelled something else. The weight was off her back, but before she could take a deep breath, Abdul was pulling her to her feet and shoving her the last few feet up to the area where the Northern Alliance soldiers were.

Massoud reached out and grabbed the front of her coat. He literally lifted her off her feet as he brought her up the final foot and pushed her behind him and his men. Hands reached down to assist Abdul and pull him up. The six of them ducked behind an outcropping of rocks as the Commander gave hasty instructions to his men before turning to Michelle.

"We have to move. Are you up to it?"

"I can make it," she said. "I am so sorry I got you into all this."

"We'll talk about blame later. Right now we have to go. The men will hold this position and give us time to get away. We are going there." He pointed towards a curve up ahead.

"Why are we going that way? The camp is in the other direction."

"The camp is already dispersed. A helicopter is going to

pick us up over that ridge. We have to get there quickly." He said something else to his *mujahidin* before grabbing Michelle's coat sleeve.

"Keep low and move as quickly as you can," he instructed. As the two of them headed out, the four remaining fighters stood and started to lay down a hail of bullets as cover so that their commander could escape.

"Will they be able to get away?" Michelle asked.

"Don't talk now. The air is thin. Conserve your energy for climbing," Massoud instructed. "We have to reach the clearing before the helicopter does." He raced along, pulling her with him. Slipping and falling, Michelle had no choice but to keep up with him the best she could. They would climb higher for a while, level out, and then ascend again. Michelle focused all her attention and effort on putting one foot in front of the other as she tried to keep her balance on the precarious terrain. Just when she felt she could not run or climb another step, Commander Massoud stopped in his tracks.

Massoud heard the distinctive *whoup whoup* sound of a chopper's blade slicing through the air. He peered out from the scant trees and rocks behind which he and Michelle had been hiding. It was one of his helicopters with Nasser at the controls.

"Come on." He grabbed Michelle's hand and began to pull her along with him again. They ran out into the clearing. Massoud faced the helicopter and waved his arms in a big gesture that would attract the pilot's attention.

"He isn't going to be able to land here," Michelle shouted over the noise as she looked around the small clearing. "There isn't enough room." She didn't know one kind of helicopter from other, but she saw the Cyrillic writing on this one and assumed that it was Russian. It looked enormous to her.

"No, but he will drop a ladder, and we will climb up," Massoud shouted back.

"I can't climb a rope ladder up into a helicopter!" Michelle's eyes widened in terror.

"You will have to do it. I will help you," Massoud replied as he continued to wave at the helicopter.

Seemingly from out of nowhere came gunfire. Bullets hit the ground near their feet. Chips of frozen dirt and rock spit up-

from that flame

ward. Massoud grabbed Michelle and almost threw her to the ground behind a low outcropping of rocks nearby. He lay prone beside her, his eyes frantically searching for whomever was firing at them. Not seeing anyone, he looked in the other direction for possible cover closer to the location of the hovering helicopter. There was another low grouping of rocks near the northern edge of the clearing.

The helicopter flew overhead and started firing at the ground in the general direction from where the shots had been fired at Massoud. Having cover, Massoud grabbed Michelle's arm and pulled her to her feet.

"Keep your head down," he shouted over the loud noise of the helicopter's engines and gunfire. Taking her with him, he raced to the next small outcropping of rocks. They skidded to a stop and dropped down behind them.

"Stay down," Massoud ordered as he swung the Kalishnikov onto the rocks and, using them as a tripod to steady the gun, started to fire. Return fire skipped off the rocks very near Massoud's head.

Terrified, and with her head flat on the frozen ground, Michelle watched what she could see of Massoud as he continued to fire the gun. It occurred to her that she had never seen him actually use a weapon before, and momentarily she started to think about why that might be. An explosion scattered bits of rock on them and brought her wandering mind back to the matter at hand. She lifted her head just a little only to feel Massoud's hand on her *pakol* pressing it back down. She slid her hand beneath her cheek to cushion her face from the cold earth while her eyes looked up as far as she could make them go and still remain in the same position.

She saw an area on the leg of his pants growing dark and wet. The fabric of his pants was ripped by a small hole. "You've been hit!" Michelle shouted over the racket.

"A flesh wound," Massoud shouted back. "Stay down."

After several more minutes of intense fire, all fell silent over the clearing except for the constant *whoupping* sound made by the helicopter. Massoud risked a moment to look down at Michelle.

"Are you hurt?"

She shook her head slightly. "No."

"We aren't going to be able to climb the rope into the helicopter. There won't be enough time."

"What are we going to do?" Michelle's eyes grew wide with still-growing fear.

"Do you trust me?" Massoud asked.

Michelle studied his face for just an instant. "Yes," she answered, and she did.

Massoud glanced up at the Hind. "My men are lowering the rope. Rather than climbing it before the chopper moves off, we are only going to have time to get on the bottom of the ladder. Nasser will back away and head east. As soon as there is a safe place, they will stop long enough for us to finish climbing the ladder. Do you understand?"

Michelle's eyes scanned the trees and rocky outcroppings of the near mountains. The mighty Hindu Kush lay in the not too distant forward position. And then she looked back into Massoud's eyes. There was a silent pleading in them. He desperately needed her to do as he asked, but if she couldn't or wouldn't, he would remain by her side and face whatever consequences followed.

"Let's do it," she answered and settled her pack on her shoulders.

Massoud smiled encouragingly at her before looking up at the helicopter and signaling for the rope ladder. It came falling down about five feet behind them.

"When I start firing, I want you to run towards the rope. You are going to have to jump high enough to reach at least the bottom rung. Once you get it in your hands, just hang on. Don't worry about trying to pull yourself up. I'll help you once I'm on it myself. I think you should leave your backpack behind."

Michelle thought about the contents of the pack. All of her work from the past month was in it; her notes, her interviews, the many rolls of film she had shot. She glanced at Massoud in panic. She couldn't bring herself to leave it all behind.

"You're going to argue with me again, aren't you?" Massoud asked.

"There are too many valuable things in there. I can't leave it."

"We don't have time to debate the issue. You have to go now,

from that flame

or it will all be moot. Ready?"

"Ready, *Amer Saheb*," Michelle said as would one of his men.

Massoud started emptying what was left in his clip in the direction of the still unseen enemy. "Now!" he thundered at Michelle.

Michelle leaped the several steps to the rope. It tossed from side to side beneath the hulking chopper. The wind and turbulence were making it dance madly in front of her. It was over her head and nearly out of reach. She knew she would only have one chance. She jumped, barely reached the very bottom rung, felt it in her hands, and grabbed it tightly. The weight of the backpack kept her off balance and unable to pull herself higher up the rope.

Michelle was too terrified to look around. Massoud was still on the ground somewhere behind her. The enemy gunmen were hidden from her view. The huge helicopter hung uncomfortably over her head, its rotors shaking the old Soviet–era chopper and flinging her back and forth like a fish on a hook. She was exposed, vulnerable, and felt absolutely terrified. It seemed to her she had been hanging there for several minutes when, in fact, it had only been a matter of seconds.

The gunfire from Massoud stopped, and the helicopter's guns started firing again as Nasser and the Commander exchanged cover fire for one another in a well rehearsed pattern. Massoud ran to the rope ladder and jumped. Even as his body slammed into Michelle's, he reached the third rung and immediately started to pull himself up. Careful not to step on her hands and loosen her grip, he managed to get his feet onto the second rung and reached down for the woman.

"Grab my hand, and I'll pull you up. Put your feet between mine," he shouted loudly to be heard over the din of the helicopter's engines and the *clack-clack* of the guns.

Letting go of her grip on the rope required the largest leap of faith she had ever been asked to make. If she let go and Massoud missed his aim, she wouldn't have the strength to reach her hand back up to the rope. She would fall to the ground, and at that point she would expect Nasser to protect his Commander to the exclusion of everything else. They would be unable to wait for her to make a second or third jump to the rope.

She felt as if her hands were frozen in their grip around the rope's cross tie. She looked up at Commander Massoud with an expression that begged him not to make her let go. Their eyes met, and he saw the terror on her face. Before she could say anything, he spoke.

"I won't let you fall," he shouted. "Please, Michelle *Jaan*, do it now. I won't let you fall."

Michelle released her left hand and reached upwards for his. With great relief and gratitude, she felt his hand close around her wrist and start to pull her up. A moment later, she stood at the same level as Massoud, her feet stepping on his before she found the empty space between them.

Massoud stretched his arm around the rope, slipped his hand between her back and the pack on it, and tightened his grip. "Hold onto me," he shouted.

Clinging tightly to the rope with her left hand, Michelle wrapped her right arm around the rope and reached for Massoud. On this matter, no argument from her would be forthcoming. He looked up at the helicopter and waved. Still firing, the helicopter began to back off.

Return fire came again from the ground and whistled alarmingly close to them. Massoud began to rock his body as a child might rock on a swing to get it moving. The rope ladder began to move and sway. Michelle grasped him even harder, buried her face in his coat, and started to pray. A moving target might be harder to hit, she knew, but dangling precariously beneath a lurching helicopter at this height, Michelle would have been much happier to be a more stationary one.

The helicopter continued to back away while the pilot tried to be careful of the precious cargo hanging so perilously beneath him. Finally, when he guessed that he was out of the range of gunfire, Nasser turned the chopper in the direction he wanted to go and began to move forward. One kilometer slipped away and then another as Nasser started looking for a place where he could hopefully lower the dangling people to the ground and then land, or, at the very least, remain safely stationery long enough for his commander and the journalist to finish climbing up into the chopper. Spotting a small, relatively flat surface about a kilo-

from that flame

meter ahead, he turned in that direction.

Commander Massoud heard an RPG whiz past and looked up in horror just in time to see it clip the back rotor. The chopper began to spin almost immediately. The rope swayed dangerously. Michelle lost her footing on the ladder and felt herself starting to slip. Massoud's arm tightened.

"Hold tightly onto me," he shouted. Michelle practically climbed him the way she used to climb trees as a girl. Her arms in a stranglehold around his shoulders, and pressed her face into his collar.

"Don't let go unless I tell you," Massoud said, his mouth very near her ear.

"Don't worry," she answered and tightened her grip on him even more.

The chopper was tossing wildly. Nasser knew it was going down, and all he hoped to do was find a way to unload his passengers before it did. He fought the chopper for nearly half a kilometer down the steep, northern slope of the mountain. The muscles in his arms bulged like banded steel as he struggled with the controls. Finally, he thought he was close enough to the clearing. By sheer strength of will, he managed to head the chopper in its direction and begin a slight descent even as the helicopter pitched wildly.

Commander Massoud looked up at the chopper and realized that they all were out of time. The helicopter was starting to spin, and once it turned into a full spin, they would all be lost. He looked down at the ground. They were up high and the ground was hard, but there was no choice left for him.

"We are going to have to drop. It's the only way. Can you ease yourself to the lowest rung?" he shouted to Michelle. "Very quickly."

Michelle peeked down towards the ground. Reluctantly she released her grip on Commander Massoud and returned her hands to the rope. Blindly, she began to search for the next rung down. She had just reached her foot down to the second rung when the helicopter lurched and began to turn one hundred and eighty degrees.

Michelle felt the rope rip from her hands. She was flung off the ladder and started falling towards the ground. She screamed and hit the ground on her backpack. The wind was immediately knocked out of her. Momentum sent her heels over her head, and when her head hit the frozen ground with a hard thud, everything went hazy, then black.

For a moment Massoud wondered if she had been killed in the fall. He said a quick prayer, climbed down the remaining two rungs, and dropped to the ground about twenty feet from Michelle. Pain shot though his spine like a lightening bolt, and he sank to his knees for a moment to collect himself before he ran towards Michelle as the helicopter began to climb higher.

Michelle was conscious and breathing although she wasn't moving. Massoud dropped to the frozen ground beside her and felt for a pulse at her carotid artery. It was weak but steady. His eyes traveled upward towards the helicopter which was now moving south in the direction from which they had come. It was pitching and turning violently as Nasser fought for every last moment of control.

Massoud knew what Nasser was doing. "*Inna lillahi wa inna ilayhi raji'un*, Nasser *Jaan*," he said softly. He watched in helpless anguish as the helicopter moved out of his line of sight a moment before it crashed into the side of the mountain and exploded into flames. Commander Massoud lowered his head and prayed again for the soul of the man who had sacrificed himself to save his friend. "Verily we belong to Allah, and truly to Him shall we return."

"You promised you would do something spectacular for me to write about," Michelle said in a voice barely above a whisper. "Was that it?"

"Yes, it was. What do you think?" Massoud said quietly. He tried to force a smile to his face but failed. He was relieved to see color returning to Michelle's face.

"I think it was a bit of overkill," Michelle answered with a small gasp in her voice. "I would have been content with much less."

"Next time I will make sure that the situation is more sedate. Are you all right? Is anything broken? Do you think you can get up? We really need to move from this clearing."

"Okay. Can you help me?" Massoud stood so that he could reach down and help pull her up. When he stood, Michelle saw that the dark blot of blood on his pants had spread from his thigh to his knee. She looked up at him but said nothing. Instead she clasped his hands and allowed him to help her up. When she applied weight to her ankle, she winced in pain.

"What is it?" Massoud asked when he saw her grimace.

"My ankle. It had hardly been bothering me at all. I must have twisted it again sometime during all that running, jumping, and leaping. You really should create much less hazardous storylines, *Amer Saheb.*"

"Shall I carry you?" Massoud asked.

"I don't think so!" Michelle was indignant. "Especially since you are the one bleeding all over the place."

"I told you, it is a flesh wound."

"Well, I'll be glad when your medic can take a look at it. Where did the helicopter land? How far do we have to walk?" Michelle started scanning the sky and the closest mountainsides. Just as she saw the column of dark smoke, the Commander started to explain.

"Michelle," Massoud paused a moment before continuing. "There is no helicopter. It crashed into the mountain and exploded." He looked and pointed at the tall column of smoke arising from the destroyed Hind.

Michelle's face grew pale as she stared in the direction of the smoke. "Did the pilot bail out? Is he okay?"

"Nasser was a very brave man. He made certain that the chopper went down in sight of the enemy. He wanted them to think I perished in the accident as well. He bought us time to get away. Can we talk as we walk? We need to get out of this open space."

"I am very sorry for his death." Michelle hobbled along beside Massoud. "This is all my fault, isn't it?"

"No, it is not," he answered firmly. "You had no idea the Taliban was so close. None of us did. They are responsible for Nasser's death. Right now you and I must focus on what lies ahead rather than look back. It is going to take all of our strength and determination to survive this. Can you do that?"

"Yes," Michelle answered through lips that trembled. Her eyes closed for a moment while she tried to force back the tears that seemed determined to fall. She searched deep within herself to summon whatever courage she had left. She remembered

from that flame

a conversation she once had with an Italian photographer who specialized in war photography. What had Raffaele Ciriello called his pictures? *Postcards from Hell*. That was the most apt description she could imagine at the moment. Had anyone taken a picture of her and Commander Massoud at that instant, it would have been a postcard of two people trapped in a hell on earth. Wearily, with every bone and muscle screaming in pain, she walked.

7. Cave

ichelle looked out at the vast mountain range before them. It was getting darker and colder. Never had she felt so small and vulnerable. If the Taliban didn't kill them, this inhospitable place might. "What's your plan now, Commander?" The question came out more sharply than she intended, but fear was an even closer companion than he.

Massoud pointed above them. "There are caves up there. At least I think there are," he added honestly. Michelle noticed that walking was painful for him as well, but she couldn't tell whether it originated from his back or his gunshot wound.

"Where is your map?"

"I left it behind at camp when I departed to look for you. If there aren't any caves, we'll make some other shelter for the night. I'm sure that Abdullah saw the fireball from the helicopter. He will send out a search and rescue team. If we can survive for twenty-four hours, we'll be okay."

Twenty-four hours? Michelle thought with a sinking heart but said nothing aloud.

Massoud saw her expression. "We will survive this," he assured her. "Just think of the tale we will have to tell tomorrow night when everyone gathers around the fire. Better yet, think of the story you'll write. You will be the talk of the town."

Michelle still said nothing but rather continued to hobble along with new determination. For his part, Massoud's brave words masked two things. He wasn't at all sure that Abdullah had seen the chopper go down, and, he knew that he was still losing blood from the wound in his thigh. To make matters even worse, they had little food or water, a single blanket, Michelle's tattered sleeping bag, and a nearly exhausted supply of ammunition. They were completely without a map or a tent. On top of all that, his back was causing him so much pain, each step was torture almost beyond endurance. He stretched his back the best he could and offered to carry Michelle's backpack as well as the equipment he was already carrying.

"Where is the pistol?" he asked suddenly as she declined his offer.

"In my backpack," Michelle said sheepishly. "I know you made me put it on, but—"

"Never mind that now," the Commander interrupted her. "Turn around so that I can get it. I am so grateful for the extra weapon, I will forego scolding you for not having it strapped on." He located the gun and holster, took them from the backpack, and strapped them to his waist.

"We have to do something to stop your bleeding." Michelle removed the *paktou* from her neck. She folded it into a semblance of a bandage, knelt down, and wrapped it around Massoud's leg. She pulled it tight.

"How's that? Too tight?"

"No, it's fine. Thank you."

"I'm not used to seeing you with weapons," Michelle observed as they started walking again.

"I don't usually wear them under normal circumstances, but today is hardly normal. I assure you, I am quite adept at using them."

"I don't doubt that," Michelle said quickly. "I only meant that since you usually command rather than actually fight, it is unusual to see you armed with a pistol and a rifle."

"These days I command rather than fight. There was a time when I did both. This isn't the first time I've been shot, although the last time was long ago."

"Where? When?"

"You sound just like a journalist with your questions," Massoud said with a slight smile. "In the leg in the late 70s. I almost bled to death."

"That's such a comforting thing to tell me now since you have been shot in the leg and are bleeding." Michelle tried to make

from that flame

light of his predicament, but the Commander heard the real fear in her voice.

"I'm not bleeding that badly, especially since you applied this tourniquet," he said reassuringly. "I'll be fine. We both will."

"From your lips to God's ear," Michelle said under her breath. They were climbing higher, the air was growing very thin again, and to make matters worse, it was starting to snow.

An hour later they had their first piece of luck when they came across a small cave that was narrow but fairly deep. Massoud went in first to check it out. He emerged in time to catch Michelle nervously glancing over her shoulder.

"This will work well," he said with forced cheerfulness. "It's deep enough that we might even dare a small fire without attracting attention."

Michelle dropped the pack from her shoulders. "I'll start gathering small branches. You look worn out. Rest, okay? I'll be back soon." The white lines of pain around his eyes worried her.

"I will help," Massoud argued. "It isn't right for you to gather wood alone when it will keep both of us warm."

"Who are you kidding?" Michelle asked frankly. "Do you think I didn't notice how difficult it was for you to walk? Every step was excruciating. I need you alive and mobile if I am going to survive this. See? Completely selfish motives." She handed him her backpack. "Go in, spread out the sleeping bag, and lie down. If you feel up to it, you could dig out the small first aid kit stashed in the bottom of my bag. As soon as I get back and we build our fire, I'm looking at that 'flesh wound' in your leg."

"I should argue with you, but I am simply too weary and in too much pain," Commander Massoud replied. "I will accept both of your kind offers." He set down her pack and unbuckled the holster around his waist. He held it out to her. "You must take this. Please, use the trees and rocks as cover. Don't let yourself get caught out in the open. And if you see anyone, drop the wood and get back here as fast as you can. Agreed?"

"*Oui, Amer Saheb,*" Michelle answered as she accepted the handgun from him with fingers that felt nearly frozen solid. She doubted she could get the gun out of the holster and shoot it in under five minutes even if her life depended on it. "I'll be careful, and I'll be okay. I promise."

Massoud raised his arm, and for the briefest of moments his hand brushed her bruised cheek. "You are a courageous woman. No one I know could have done better than you did today."

"I'm only alive at all because of everything you've done for me this week," she said quietly. "There will never be enough words of thanks I could say to you." She gave him a gentle push towards the cave. "Now go lie down while I get the wood."

"*Oui, Amer Saheb,*" he said with a smile.

Using one of the few matches he had in his pocket, Massoud carefully nurtured the dried grass Michelle had brought back with her when she brought the wood. She had found the small clump at the base of a pine tree trunk and had packed it into her pocket with care. She knew that some kind of tinder would be vital if they hoped to get the damp wood to burn at all. She had picked up the driest wood she could find, but none of it was what someone who had a choice would want to build a campfire.

The Commander hadn't rested completely while she was gone. He had gathered loose stones from inside the cave and built a small fire ring. He fashioned the side facing the open mouth of the cave higher in the hope that it would prevent the firelight from being as easily seen by someone passing outside the cave. Now that it was growing dark, any light at all would attract attention; however, since the alternative was to freeze, he felt he had to risk a small fire.

Once he was satisfied that the tinder had caught, he slowly added several twigs. The fire caught and dimly illuminated the inside of the cave.

"It's not very big," Michelle observed.

"No, it isn't" Massoud agreed. "However, it is big enough. We not only don't want the light to attract attention, but also we don't want the cave filled with too much smoke. This small fire will give sufficient light and heat without being too hazardous. Now, shall we eat? I have water, bread, and mulberries in my pack."

The cave was so narrow, there wasn't much room to move.

from that flame

Not that she wanted to move away from the fire. Even with its slight heat, she felt as if she was thawing out after many hours of being frozen solid. "I have a few snacks too, but first I want to look at that leg," she said firmly. "Did you have time to find the first aid kit?"

"No, I forgot. I'm sorry."

"Can you split the pants near the wound while I hunt for the kit?" She began pulling items out of her pack. She held up her CD player—crushed. "I think this is done for. I thought I heard something crack when I fell from the helicopter. Better it breaks than my back," she said as she lightly tossed the player aside.

"I'm sorry that is broken. Now you won't be able to listen to your beautiful music."

"You mean you won't be able to listen to my beautiful music," Michelle teased. "Maybe I can run to the local Wal-Mart and buy another one. I'll stop and grab a pizza on the way back."

She never thought she would ever actually miss Wal-Mart and Pizza Hut, but at that moment, she would have given her right arm for either of them.

"I can't imagine the life you live," the Commander said as Michelle turned her attention to his wound. "It must be wonderful to be able to buy anything you want whenever you want it."

"Yeah, well, if I really could buy anything whenever I wanted, I'd be out of here and shopping in a heartbeat," Michelle said absently as she peered more closely at Massoud's leg. "You lied to me," she said with a grimace as she turned the light from her small flashlight on Massoud's leg and stared at the deep, dark hole in his thigh about midway between his knee and hip. "If that's a flesh wound, I'm my Aunt Katherine."

"This is the first time I've seen it too," Massoud protested as he tried to sit up and get a better view, but his back shrieked in pain, and he fell back with a gasp.

"I don't have any means of trying to extract that bullet," Michelle said. "Even if I had the right instruments, I don't have the know-how. The best I can do is clean it, apply an antibiotic ointment, and wrap it."

"If you will do that, I would be very grateful," Massoud answered quietly.

"Okay." Michelle used her teeth to rip open the cleansing pad of alcohol from the first-aid kit and gathered a handful of sterile cotton. "This is going to hurt like the devil."

"An infection would be worse." Massoud clasped his hands together tightly and closed his eyes. "I will pray. You do what you must."

Michelle began gingerly swabbing the bullet wound. Massoud's whole body stiffened and his knuckles turned white as his hands tightened on each other, but he made no sound except a sharp intake of breath. His lips started moving in silent prayer. He didn't stop praying until Michelle stopped swabbing.

"That's as good as I can get it," she said. "The antibiotic ointment shouldn't hurt."

Massoud opened his eyes. "I wish my men all had handy kits like yours," he said to make conversation in a voice that was barely above a hoarse whisper.

"When I get back to the States, I'll send you a box filled with them, okay?" Michelle said as she carefully applied the ointment with a cotton swab.

"That would be very generous. Thank you. I'll give you an address of a friend in Pakistan. If you send them there, he will get them to me in Panjshir."

"I may just bring them back in person. Would that be okay?" Michelle said absentmindedly as she studied the wound to make sure that all of it was well covered with ointment. She moved her small flashlight around and nodded to herself, satisfied with her work.

"That would be best of all," Massoud smiled wanly, "but I can't believe that once out, you would ever want to come back. Selfishly, my friend, I would like to know before you leave that one day I will see you again."

"You can count on it." Michelle pressed some clean gauze against the wound. She dug in her bag, pulled out a white blouse, and began to tear it into long strips. She wrapped the strips around his thigh several times before finally securing it with tape from the medical kit.

"There," she said when she was done. "My first field dressing."

"Thank you for attending to me," Massoud said humbly.

"*Qaabilay tashakur nayst.* No thanks are necessary. It's the least

I could do after you have been so kind to me. Not to mention that you saved my life today. I think I owe you a bandage, don't you?" Michelle was surprised and distressed when her eyes suddenly filled with tears. "What a day, huh?" She forced a brave smile to her mouth, but a tear or two escaped and rolled down her cheeks. She swiped at them angrily. Massoud reached out and caught her hand.

"We will be all right," he said in a low, firm voice.

"I know," Michelle answered as firmly as she could. She shook her head and wiped the tears away with determination. "Don't pay any attention to me. I'm fine, or at least I will be once I get to eat something. Let me get you some aspirin for your pain and then help you get comfortable. After we've had something to eat, I'll work on your back."

"You are very kind to me," Massoud said gently.

"We're in this together," Michelle said firmly. "We'll survive it somehow if we watch out for each other." She smiled at the man who had pain etched all over his face. "And here I am prattling on when you are in dire need of aspirin." She began furiously to upend her backpack in search of the elusive aspirin. Everything came spilling out onto the ground, and only Massoud's quick action prevented things from sliding into the small fire. Michelle scooped everything into a pile and pulled out Bayer aspirin, a wrapped Snickers bar, and a similarly wrapped Nature Valley granola bar. She handed all three to Massoud.

"What are these?" Massoud held the candy in one hand and the granola bar in the other.

"Junk food and health food," Michelle answered.

"Excuse me?" the Commander looked perplexed. "Garbage food?"

Michelle started to laugh. "No. Is that what I said?"

Massoud nodded. "Yes. You said '*détritus*.' That is not what you meant to say?"

"*Ordures?*" Michelle offered.

"Refuse?" Massoud said quizzically. He was beginning to laugh with her as she struggled to find the right word

"Never mind." Michelle snatched the candy bar from his hand. "I'll eat this, and you eat the health food. *Santé*, right?"

"Yes," he agreed pleasantly. "Why is it healthy?" He was enjoying this new game.

"It's granola. It has *miel, avoine,* and *raisins secs. Il n'y a pas de préservatif,*" Michelle concluded happily, fairly certain that this time she had gotten all the words right. She continued to think she had done well right up until she saw the very strange expression on Massoud's face.

"All right," she sighed with resignation, "what did I get wrong this time?"

Massoud opened his mouth to speak, but it snapped shut again without any words coming out. The light was bad, but Michelle would have sworn the man was starting to blush.

"What?" Michelle demanded. "Spit it out. It can't be that bad."

"*Il n'y a pas de préservatif?*" Massoud repeated as he started to chortle. He tried to say something else, but his laughter was building, and wave after wave of guffaws prevented him from catching his breath long enough to speak.

"It has no preservative in it!" Michelle tried again. Massoud's laughter was contagious. Tears were starting to roll down his dusty cheeks, and his chest heaved. Michelle gave up trying not to join in his laughter, although she still didn't know what in the world she had said to bring about this fit of hilarity.

"It has no condoms in it?" Massoud gasped out before dissolving into laughter again. "You said this health food had honey, oats, raisins, and no condoms in it." He carefully pronounced the word in French so that she would understand its meaning.

It was Michelle's turn to blush in the semi-darkness, but Massoud obviously found her mistake genuinely funny rather than offensive. She looked at him, rolled her eyes, and made a face. It set him off in gales of laughter again. He finally held his stomach as if it hurt him and simply gasped for air.

"Are you quite finished?" Michelle said dryly, but humor danced in her eyes.

"I hope so," Massoud managed to say. "I hope you aren't angry with me for laughing. After the day we've had, I was just struck by how fortunate I was to have food with no condoms in it." He set off on another storm of laughter.

Still trying to pretend she was annoyed with him, Michelle

from that flame

grabbed the granola bar from his hand and opened the wrapper. She handed it back to him with flourish. "Your health food, Commander. No condoms included." They laughed their way through the rest of their meager meal. They were still hungry, and they knew they would have to ration what little food they did have, but they were alive; they were warm and sheltered, and they felt reasonably safe. All things considered, they agreed it could have been worse.

"Ahmed Shah *Jaan*?" Michelle had been staring into the small fire since they finished eating.

"Hmmm?" he answered absentmindedly.

"What happens if your men don't come for us tomorrow?" Michelle asked softly.

"They'll come."

"But what if they don't?"

"Then we will find our own way out of here and back to them," Massoud said with conviction.

"Okay," Michelle said with uncertainty. Her brief show of bravado had faded. "By the way, it's still snowing."

Massoud saw a glitter of tears in her eyes again, and it caught him off guard. This fragile, emotional side of her was one he had not seen before. She had been brave and daring during all the challenges the last week had brought; he didn't want to see her lose that tenacity. Fearlessness was one of the traits he had come to admire most in her. He wanted to make her laugh her loud, contagious laugh, but not a single, clever thing came to mind. He knew he had to say something.

"Michelle? Would you look at me?" He saw her swipe at her tears again before she met his gaze. "You remind me of the women of my country," he spoke softly. "They face adversity and hardship and still manage to find a way to remain compassionate and strong. Don't give in to hopelessness or despair. If you can't have faith in me, have faith in yourself. Most of all have faith in God. He will not abandon us."

"It's not that I don't have faith in you and God," Michelle denied vehemently. "Truly. I believe that if any man can get us out of here, it's you. I'm just plain scared. I have never doubted you for a moment, *Amer Saheb*." She forced a smile to her face. "Shall I massage your back now?"

"Can we wait until it is closer to the time we sleep? Right now I would like to talk with you. Is that all right?"

"Sure. About what?"

"I am supposed to attend a conference in Paris early next month. Perhaps you can suggest your favorite places so that I will know what sights to see? I have never been away from the Afghanistan region before and have no idea where to begin—assuming there is some time in which I might visit the city."

"I can suggest several places. You will love Paris, and all of France will go crazy for you, I'm certain."

"I doubt that very much," Massoud said humbly. "My hope is that people in the European Union will hear—truly hear—my words about the plight of the Afghan people and want to help them. If that happens, my trip will be a success even if I never see any of the cities."

"Would you tell me more about yourself?" Michelle asked. "There is so much I still don't know."

"My life is much less interesting than yours. I barely have a year of college study and no degree. I have not traveled to exotic lands. My life has been spent fighting for almost as long as I can remember." A sadness crept into his eyes as he spoke. Michelle could not imagine what he had seen, done, and endured in his endless campaign to free his country from one foreign invader after another. She could imagine that there would have been no boundaries to what this man might have accomplished if his life had been different, if his calling had been to do something other than fight a war.

Michelle didn't want him to be sad, especially after the hearty laugh they had shared earlier, and if introspection would do that now, she would divert him from it. "I have heard that you have one of the largest private libraries in all of Afghanistan," she said. "Is that true?"

"I don't know if it is one of the largest, but it is a respectable size. I love to read."

"What sort of topics interest you?"

"Books on Islam, poetry, philosophy, politics, diplomacy, history, and poetry."

from that flame

"You said poetry twice," Michelle said with a smile.

"Perhaps because I love it twice as much as all the others except the *Qur'an*," he said and returned her smile.

"Do you know any selections by heart?"

"Yes, a few of my favorite ones."

"Will you recite one for me?"

"They are in Persian. You won't understand them. Shall I translate?"

"No, don't translate," Michelle shook her head. "I would like to hear the tone and cadence of the words, feel their original rhythm and movement. Does that make sense?"

"Perfectly well. Let me think for a moment." His hand stroked his beard as he ran through his mental catalog of favorites.

"All right, I have one," he said at last. "It is by my favorite poet, Hafiz. It is called, 'Our Hearts Should Do This More.'" Michelle sat back, watched his face with great expectancy, and anticipated the words in his melodious voice.

> I sit in the streets with the homeless,
> My clothes stained with the wine
> From the vineyards the saints tend.
> Light has painted all acts the same color,
> So I sit around and laugh all day with my friends.

> At night, if I feel a divine loneliness,
> I tear the doors off love's mansion
> And wrestle God onto the floor.
> He becomes so pleased with [me]
> And says,
> "Our hearts should do this more!"

As he spoke the small flames' soft light gently touched his face. His spirit was transported by the words to a place far from the cold cave that imprisoned his pain-stricken body. For him this poem was a prayer, words of love to the God he worshiped with passion and total devotion. The words flowed, and because of Massoud's eloquent recitation, Michelle believed that she knew exactly what the poet was sharing even though she couldn't understand a single word.

"That was exquisite," she said when he finished. "Have you another, or am I being greedy by asking you to recite it?"

"One more, and then we need to sleep."

"After I massage your back," Michelle reminded him.

Massoud shook his head a little. "You offer that kindness in the same breath in which you wonder if you are greedy. There is your answer." He shifted his weight around to find a more comfortable reclining position and began to recite another poem.

Michele closely watched his face as he spoke the beautiful words he knew and loved so well. A myriad of emotions manifested themselves. At times there was sorrow almost too deep to bear. At other times both voice and expression carried unfettered dreams and unfathomable expectations. Still other passages evoked immense joy, unbound reverence, and endless hope. As Massoud's voice rose and fell, and as the words flowed from his tongue, Michelle sat mesmerized.

He was a hero to much of Afghanistan, and he wore that mantle with dignity, modesty, and goodwill. His military genius made him famous outside the boundaries of a country he rarely left. The Lion of Panjshir roared loudly, and the earth shook when he walked. He was respected and feared and loved. His country had needed him, and for her sake, this man with a poet's soul became a warrior. If one day he could bring about a lasting peace, he would gratefully trade his fame and authority for a quiet room, his family, and his beloved books. He would build beautiful buildings instead of reducing them to rubble. He would quietly slip away to live his life in the peace he so desperately craved.

How did such a gentle, kind spirit find within it the ability to become a fearless hero? Michelle wondered. How did one face blood and bullets, death and destruction every single day and still have the sensitivity to quote poetry with such a depth of feeling? Ahmed Shah Massoud was two very different men who found a way to live in harmony within a single mind and heart. This is the dichotomy, the mystery, the allure of him, she thought, and I doubt I will ever fully understand it.

"You are very quiet," Massoud observed. He had finished his recitation a minute earlier, and Michelle had made no comment.

from that flame

"I think I have the approach for my story," Michelle answered. "Shall I tell you what it will be?"

Massoud shook his head. "No. I trust you to write the truth as you see it. I would not want to contaminate your truth by commenting on it prematurely. Perhaps when the piece is published, you will bring it to me so that I may read it then."

"I would be honored, *Amer Saheb*."

Massoud smiled at her. "The honor will be mine."

"All right, roll over." Michelle began to rub her hands together to warm them.

"Hafiz's poems have relaxed me as much as a therapeutic massage would have," the Commander declined her invitation.

"It's too bad the CD player was crushed. Listening to music might have been as beneficial as the poetry and massage."

"Perhaps you could sing something?" the Commander suggested.

"I wouldn't inflict my singing voice on the Taliban," Michelle laughed. "It would be cruel and unusual punishment."

"If you sang to the Taliban, they would have you stoned to death," Massoud sighed sleepily. "They outlawed singing."

"No more talk about the Taliban," Michelle said firmly. "You'll be tense again in a flash. I might dare hum a tune, but if it hurts your ears, you have only yourself to blame." She began to hum a lullaby her mother used to sing to her.

Ten minutes later he was nearly asleep. Michelle stopped humming, added a few more small pieces of wood to the fire, stretched out on the sleeping bag they were using as a mat beneath them, and slid under the thin blanket they had as their only cover. Suddenly she found this part of their predicament funny. She had started out in a tent clear across the camp from him. Then they shared a cave with separate sleeping chambers. Next she ended up sleeping with Massoud, Dr. Abdullah and two mules. And now this. No one would believe it. Her raw nerves found humor in the crazy twists and turns her life had taken since coming to Afghanistan.

"Stay close," Massoud muttered sleepily. "We need to share body heat as well as this thin blanket."

Obediently Michelle curled up and fell into a deep sleep of utter exhaustion.

8. Facts

Their sparse breakfast consisted of water, *nan*, and mulberries from Massoud's pack. He insisted that he could not possibly eat "garbage food" for breakfast. Michelle supplemented her breakfast with the last of her peanut butter crackers.

While Michelle had still been asleep, Commander Massoud had gone outside and gathered another small amount of wood to renew the fire. He said his morning prayers. He also used his binoculars to scan the surrounding countryside. Everything appeared quiet, but his instinct told him that quiet was often an illusion. Now the question he must answer was whether they should stay or go. Both had unimaginable risks.

Michelle saved her last sip of water so that she could brush her teeth. She craved a hot shower or bath but decided she wouldn't complain. She would be content if she could at least brush her teeth. Maybe she could find something to use as a pot and melt some snow for bathing water later. She just wished she knew where "later" would find them. Massoud was looking grim as he hobbled around out in the snow. Michelle was almost afraid to ask him what was happening next.

"What are we going to do now?" she swallowed her fear and found the courage to ask him.

"We will stay here one more day and night. We can gather enough wood for the fire. We have enough food if we are careful to ration it. And, it will give my leg one more day to heal in case we have to hike out."

"And one more day for the bullet to stay in your leg," Michelle reminded him. "I need to redress the wound. It is bleeding again."

"The bullet is the least of my worries right now. If it's too bad, I can go to a hospital in Dushanbe and have it surgically removed. Right now we have to focus on staying alive long enough for the bullet to become a real problem."

"Tell me what you want me to do besides get more firewood," Michelle said. "Whatever it is, I will do it after I have re-wrapped your leg. Come here and sit down."

"I think that if we pile snow in front of the cave's mouth and block off at least three quarters of it, we will be able to retain more warmth inside," the Commander said as he lowered himself onto the sleeping bag. He couldn't prevent a grimace of pain from crossing his face.

"That sounds like a good idea, Mr. Engineer," Michelle agreed as she unwrapped the bloodied cloth from his leg. "When I fell from the mule and got this gash on my forehead, Doctor Abdullah piled snow on it to stop the bleeding. I think we should do that to your leg. You are going to have to stop walking around so much." She removed another clean shirt from her pack and went outside to fill it with snow.

Once the bleeding was stanched, Michelle reapplied the antibiotic ointment and dressed his wound with a fresh bandage. "You are going to stay right here," she instructed Massoud. "I am not going to have you bleed to death on my watch. Doctor Abdullah would have my head."

"But can you construct the wall by yourself?"

"When I was a kid, I was the master snow fort builder in the neighborhood. My forts could withstand several attacks by snowball-wielding, enemy forces. I think I can manage this project alone."

"As a practical matter, then, I will stay here and not move around too much. Thank you, *Amer Saheb*."

"No problem, but if I'm building walls, I expect you to handle lunch," Michelle said with a grin. "Deal?" Michelle offered her hand.

"Deal." Commander Massoud took her outstretched hand and shook it in agreement.

from that flame

It took Michelle the rest of the morning and the early part of the afternoon to construct a makeshift wall that would shelter them from the cold as well as protect them from outside eyes. It ended up being a massive structure. One small side section was left open. It would be their door so that they could get in and out of the cave as needed. Massoud studied the wall with a careful eye and nodded his approval. "That's not half-bad. *Aafareen!* Well done," he pronounced. "Are you hungry? What shall we have for lunch? What are you Americans so fond of eating? Steak and potatoes?"

"I was thinking that melted snow, bread, and dried mulberries would be tasty," Michelle said, returning his smile. "You wouldn't happen to have any on hand, would you?"

"Why, I just might," Massoud nodded and started to arrange the small amounts of food between them.

"Ahmed Shah, may I ask you a favor?"

He smiled at her. "You may ask me any favor you wish. I am in your debt."

"It's only a question I really don't think you'll mind answering. It is just something I need insight on if I am going to write the piece I have in mind for the magazine."

"Before you ask your question, may I ask one? I don't think you ever told me for whom you were working. What magazine will carry this story?"

Michelle blushed slightly. "My story originally was going to be about RAWA, remember? I was writing it for a women's magazine. I don't think they will be interested in what the story has turned into. That means I don't have a guaranteed market for the article I am now writing. I'm going to have to shop around for a publisher. I do think, however, that I have a good chance of selling it. Yours is a fascinating story."

"I wish you luck in your efforts," Commander Massoud said with genuine support.

"If I sell it—when I sell it—I will use the money I earn from the sale to buy those first aid kits you want."

"And you will bring the article and the kits to me personally, right?" Massoud intended to hold her to her promise.

"Yes. And when I come back, will you help me meet the woman from Kabul I need to interview? I don't want the woman's magazine suing me for breech of contract because I didn't finish the story on RAWA."

"I will arrange for you to meet with whomever you wish," he assured her. "And when peace once again is restored to my country, I hope that you will visit yet again and allow me to show you how beautiful it truly is. I'm afraid you've received a very negative introduction to Afghanistan."

"The circumstances might be a lot worse than I bargained for when I first got here, but from now on, when I think of Afghanistan, I will think of you and your brave men, and that is not negative, *Amer Saheb*. This is a once in a lifetime experience."

"Praise Allah, no? Once in a life is enough," Massoud laughed. "Was your question about the woman from Kabul, or do you have another?"

"Another. You told me how your government's rule in Kabul started to fall apart because of both internal and external forces, but you didn't tell me exactly how the Taliban came to power. I thought about them after you mentioned them last night and wondered."

Commander Massoud's face darkened at the mention of the Taliban.

"You don't have to talk to me about them if you'd rather not," Michelle said hastily.

He shook his head. "I told you I would talk about whatever you needed to know to present a full, accurate story. Do you want facts or my feelings about them?"

"Facts first, please." Michelle dug into her pack and pulled out a paper and pen. "I'll use the facts as the skeleton upon which to hang the flesh of your emotions. Okay?"

"Okay," Massoud said. "The facts it is. If you remember, I told you that we had forged an agreement for the formation of the Rabbani government in 1993. You will also remember that there was still a great deal of factional infighting. We were destroying our own cities and people as we fought each other for control of the government and territories throughout the country. It was a disaster. Afghanistan descended into a civil war that killed tens of thousands of people. Millions fled the country and went to refugee camps in Pakistan and Iran. Tens of thousands more became internally displaced people, leaving their land and homes and fleeing each new battle that approached them. It was a disaster of epic proportions. People were starving and dying, and God forgive me, I couldn't prevent it." Massoud rubbed his eyes. His fingers stayed pressed against them for a moment as he tried to push back the frustration, anger, disappointment, and blame he felt each time he thought about those dark days. After several minutes he dropped his hand and looked squarely again at Michelle.

"Two things happened that brought the Taliban to power. First there was a rape in Kandahar. A *mullah* named Omar gathered some men together, took the law into his own hands, captured, and punished the men responsible. The people of Kandahar, sick of war and crime, believed that Omar and his men were the answer to their prayers. He promised them peace and rule of law, and they opened their arms to him. Then, in September of 1994, the newly-formed Taliban was appointed by Pakistan to protect a trade convoy. They had been trained in and had ties to the *madrassas* in Pakistan. They were part of a militant Sunni-Muslim movement I have never understood. I have read and studied the *Qur'an* all my life, and I have found nothing to support their radical teachings or beliefs.

"Be that as it may, they were also heavily armed by Pakistan. They had close ties to that country's intelligence service—the ISI—who re-supplied them as necessary. They soon emerged as a strong fighting faction."

"That was just what you needed," Michelle said sarcastically. "Another foreign fighting force, as if you didn't already have enough with which to contend."

Commander Massoud nodded. "Exactly. In the beginning they acted like a police force. They did things that ingratiated them to the people. They provided a form of law and order the Rabbani government had been unable to provide because of the constant insurrections. The Taliban found its niche and filled it well. I never blamed the people of my country for welcoming the Taliban. Had we been able to work with them, we might have accomplished something."

"So what happened? Why couldn't you work with them?"

Massoud shrugged. "That was never in their plan. They wanted to rule the country according to their own concept of an Islamic caliphate, and that meant those of us who wanted something

from that flame

else had to be eliminated. Omar believed God had spoken to him and wanted him to rule all of Afghanistan, and so all opposition had to be destroyed."

"But didn't you eventually have a cease-fire and agree to talk to Mohammed Omar?"

"Yes. The United Nations brokered a cease-fire in the Spring of 1998, but it did not last for long. We in the resistance were asking for a democratic election. Our thought was that if the people wanted the Taliban, an election would prove it. Omar was afraid. He knew by then that the people hated and feared the Taliban and would never vote them into power. He broke the cease-fire rather than discuss free elections."

"By 1998 the Taliban had been in power for two years, right?" Michelle said looking through her notes. "How did they originally gain control of Kabul in 1996?"

"As I said, they were well armed and powerful. They established themselves in Kandahar and then spread out into other areas of the country. It was easy for them in the Pashtun areas since they were mainly Pashtun themselves. As they went along, they recruited and armed new members. Often they did this by force. If a man refused to join them, they would kill him and his whole family. Many joined them because they had no other choice, not because they agreed with the Taliban's extreme interpretation of Islamic doctrine. Finally, when they had amassed a sufficient number of soldiers, they attacked Kabul. The first time they attacked, we were able to defeat them. The next time..." his voice trailed off.

"As the Minister of Defense, you chose a tactical retreat rather than all-out war?" Michelle asked.

"There had already been too many civilian casualties," Commander Massoud answered. "I feared even more. It seemed better to retreat from the city into the mountains. We knew the Taliban would come after us there, but there would be fewer civilians in the crossfire, and we could better control when and how the battles took place." He looked troubled as if he was second-guessing himself about the wisdom of the retreat. He sighed deeply before continuing. "The Taliban swept into Kabul and immediately executed all of the Rabanni government officials who were still there. They executed Najibullah, the Communist leader. A Saudi named Osama bin Laden was brought in as a negotiator, but he sided with Omar's plan for Afghanistan. Omar offered bin Laden refuge in Afghanistan, and, through him, they brought his terrorist organization into my country."

"I have heard about bin Laden and his al-Qaeda organization. They are being held responsible for bombing the USS Cole in Yemen," Michelle said.

"Among many other acts of terrorism," Commander Massoud said. "Bin Laden hates the West. He wants nothing more than to bring about its destruction in the name of a *jihad*. If he is not stopped, I fear he will be successful."

"Why does Omar and the Taliban want to be associated with him?"

"Partly for ideological reasons. Their fanaticism compliments each other. Their hatred of the West runs parallel. Plus, bin Laden has money. He has a lot of money, and he shares it with the top Taliban leadership for both weapons and their personal use. It is a pragmatic marriage. Bin Laden needed a base of operations. The Taliban needed money and additional military support. It is also an ideological marriage based on mutually shared hatred of the West, and especially the United States."

Michelle sat quietly for a moment. This was obviously an emotional topic for the Commander, and she wanted to tread carefully.

"The Taliban claims to control ninety percent of the country. Do you agree with that number?" she asked when it appeared to her that he was ready for her next question.

"No." Commander Massoud shook his head. "The United Front still maintains between twenty-five and thirty percent of the country. However, you must understand that we would continue to fight even if we only controlled an area as large as my *pakol*."

"One more factual question? We can leave your personal response to them for another time," Michelle said.

"All right." The Commander shifted his weight to get more comfortable.

"What happened in Taloqan? How did you lose it?"

"Who told you about Taloqan?" the Commander asked with a sigh and rested his head on his hand as he studied Michelle's face.

Michelle smiled. "I was in Pakistan for three weeks before I

from that flame

came to see you. I heard a lot of stories. It doesn't matter what I heard or from whom I heard it. What I want is your side of the story."

The Commander's hand traveled up to his head where he rubbed his hair before moving down over his face. His fingers jabbed at his tired eyes and finally ended up at his beard where he scratched his chin. "Can't I tell you a story about a victory rather than a defeat? I have a lot of good stories about victories too," Massoud said ruefully.

Michelle laughed aloud. "I'm sure you do. I witnessed a couple of them firsthand, remember? When we discuss the Soviet invasion, you can tell me a wonderful story of David and Goliath, okay? Right now I'd like to know about Taloqan. It was your last major defeat, wasn't it?"

"Yes, last summer," Commander Massoud sighed. "What do you want to know?"

"Who? What? When? Where? Why? The big five Ws. Come on, you've talked to enough journalists to know those are the questions we always ask." Michelle poised her pen over the pad and gave him her best, objective journalist expression.

Massoud smiled softly. "I suppose I do know the drill by now. All right, then. In August of 2000, the Taliban was reinforced by two Pakistani brigades and an artillery battalion. The makeup of the Taliban fighters by this time included not only Pakistanis but also Arabs, Filipinos, Kashmiris, Chechens, and other foreigners. It was like an invading army all over again.

"I had my headquarters in Taloqan then. The Taliban surged into the Northeast in an effort to take the city and cut my supply lines. The battle lasted for weeks, but we were out-manned, out-supplied, and outgunned. On September fifth, Taloqan fell. We retreated from Taloqan to Khwaja Bahauddin determined to keep the supply line north and south of Taloqan between Takhar and Badakshan provinces open. Winter would give us time to regroup and re-supply."

"And so here you are still guarding that supply line? General Fahim, too? Is that what he is doing from his side?"

"More or less." Commander Massoud smiled a little mysteriously. "Shall I continue answering the five Ws?"

"There's more? I thought you answered them already."

"Oh, well, if you don't want to hear any more—" The Commander moved as if to get up.

"Ha, ha, very funny," Michelle said sarcastically. "Put yourself right back down there. There is no where for you to go anyway. Besides, I am not only a captive audience; I am also a fascinated audience. Talk, *Amer Saheb*. I'm all ears."

He grinned and settled himself again. "What do you want to know?"

"Wait a minute, you were the one who wanted to talk," Michelle laughed. "This is your story. Tell me what you think I should know."

"Last October I met with Ismael Khan and Rashid Dostum, two other commanders who had been fighting the Taliban on their own fronts. We agreed to set aside differences we had had in the past and work together to defeat the Taliban. We decided we would use this winter to rally and train more troops. Now that spring is coming, we will meet again soon and devise a strategy. We will retake Taloqan by this summer."

"You sound very confident."

"I am," Massoud replied. "Certain countries—you'll forgive me if I don't give their names—have promised to help re-supply us with helicopters, RPGs, armored vehicles, surface-to-air missiles, mortar, and ammunition. Even your country is thinking about sending us more Stinger missiles. I will appeal to the European Parliament next month. There may be more help coming."

"I thought you said the US didn't want to get involved in this dispute?"

"The US didn't want to get involved in what they viewed as our civil war. They have their own agenda. I understand this."

"Bin Laden?"

"Yes, Bin Laden and his terrorist dogs. Ever since the bombings at the African embassies, your leaders have become more interested. They won't commit troops, and I wouldn't want them to do that, but they are considering upgrading our weapons, and that I welcome. I wish your government would also increase its humanitarian aid. However, for the moment I will accept whatever help they will offer. I also pray that the international community will apply pressure to Pakistan to stop supporting the Taliban."

from that flame

"You said the United States might send more Stinger missiles. When did they first send them?" Michelle asked.

"When we were fighting the Soviets. They were using an air assault against us, and we had no way to stop them. The United States sent their newly developed Stingers to the *mujahidin* through their sources in Pakistan."

"I see," Michelle scribbled her notes furiously fast. "And now, it has been your *mujahidin* who have prevented the Taliban from gaining acceptance within the international community. Is that how you see it?"

"Yes. I think the brave fighters deserve credit, don't you? It is their blood that is spilled and their lives that are sacrificed."

"Yes," Michelle agreed. "Your holy warriors are devoted to the cause of freedom."

"Holy warriors?" Massoud repeated.

"Yes. Isn't that what *mujahidin* means?" Michelle was perplexed. "That is what I have always heard. Don't tell me I have another word wrong."

"I like that definition," Massoud said with an eyebrow arched, "and I'm sure it is accurate in some ways, but the actual meaning, I believe, is 'one who struggles.'"

"I like that definition better." Michelle smiled and wrote the words in her notebook. "Well, if the US government liked the *mujahidin* well enough to support them when they fought the Soviets, it makes sense that they would also support them in their fight against the Taliban and al Qaeda. Anything more you want to add?"

"I have talked enough," Massoud said. "I want to listen to you. Tell me more about your life." He tossed a few more twigs on their low-burning fire. "*S'il vous plaît?* Or, since Abdullah taught you the word in Dari, *lotfan?*"

Michelle shrugged. "I don't know what to tell you. My life has been so different from yours, we don't even have the same frame of reference. The Annie Oakley and Monopoly stories sort of fell flat."

"No, they didn't," Massoud argued. "I enjoyed hearing about them both. But if you would rather, don't tell me about an event or activity. Tell me something about you. Tell me about what you think and feel on any topic of your choice."

"Why…How could that possibly be of interest to you?" Michelle was flustered.

"Because you interest me." Massoud was amused by her disquiet at the thought of talking about herself. Journalists always wanted to know about the other person rather than reveal anything about themselves. "Come on. It's fair. You know everything about me."

"Hardly," Michelle said dryly. "All right," she scratched at her cheek absentmindedly. "I guess one of the things most important to me is to give an honest voice to those who don't usually have one. The world is filled with people who have interesting, thought-provoking, courageous stories to tell. My work means a lot to me. I know it's just journalism, but it is my small contribution to helping humanity."

"It is a huge responsibility," Massoud observed. "It requires great honesty, an open mind, and a willingness to put yourself in the other person's shoes. You have those qualities." Michelle blushed at the words of praise. Commander Massoud continued. "The women from RAWA need you to finish their story."

"I agree," Michelle said. "I have every intention of finishing the article about those magnificent, courageous women. I am counting on you to help me speak to the last people I need to interview."

"I give you my word that I will help. Now, please tell me a complete story," the Commander suggested. "What is one of your favorite 'voices' heard and stories told?"

"That's easy," Michelle smiled. "Remember I told you about the trip to the volcanic pool in the Andes Mountains?"

"Ah, yes," the Commander said. "The school with the mentally handicapped children. You mentioned that story took you to Colombia."

"The school is the most amazing place," Michelle began. "Traditionally children with mental illness or retardation are shut away and kept out of sight. Money is certainly not allocated by the government to educate them. My friend Ricardo came up with the most innovative means of educating these special students.

"He found an old house, rounded up some seed money, found teachers and equipment, and opened his school. His curriculum exclusively uses the arts to teach the children."

from that flame

"The performing arts?" Commander Massoud asked with great interest.

"Yes, but not only the performing arts, the visual ones, too. The students work with clay to make everything from masks to bowls. The children hand paint greeting cards and sell them to help raise money for the school. They make beautiful *molas,* and—"

"*Mola?* The word is Spanish? What does it mean?" Massoud interjected.

"It is an art object that is usually hung on a wall and is made of fabrics arranged and sewn to make a picture. For example, there may be brown fabric sewn to resemble a tree trunk and green fabric arranged like leaves. In the same *mola,* there might be a house, an animal, and a person. They are quite wonderful."

"So they sound. What else do they do at this school?"

"They learn to dance in order to gain control of their bodies and to express themselves. They have video cameras now. It is extraordinary to watch a movie made by a student who can't express himself in words. Once the students and their dance teacher picked a ballad and created an entire play to tell the song's story. They paint murals and paintings and each other." Michelle ended with a laugh.

"Each other?" Massoud laughed with her. "Tell me."

"One day the teachers spread out enormous pieces of paper and several small pans of bright, beautiful colors. They brought out the younger students, those who were about three or four. They took off all their clothes except their underwear and encouraged the children to use their entire bodies to paint the great paper. How they laughed with delight as they rolled and squished in the paint." Michelle's eyes had a far-away look as if she were no longer in a cold cave in Afghanistan but rather in the warm sun of Colombia.

"When they were finished, the teachers took them one by one to the outdoor showers and washed them off." Michelle started to laugh at the recollection. "You can imagine the challenge of trying to hang onto a paint-covered, wiggling child when cold water is added to the mix."

"You miss them very much, don't you?" Massoud asked softly.

from that flame

"I didn't realize how much until just now. Yes, I miss them. I need to go back."

"What's the first thing you'll do when you get there?"

"Hug and kiss every little face," Michelle said emphatically.

"After you have gone back there, will you come back here and talk to the teachers in Panjshir about the techniques your friend uses so well? I think they would be interested and might find means of adapting some of the ideas."

Michelle agreed with a smile. "I would like that. Let's see…I have to come back with the published story for you. I have to come back to finish the RAWA story. I have to bring back the medical kits, and now I have to come back again to conduct a teaching seminar. Did I forget anything?"

"You might be able to combine one or two of those events into a single trip," Massoud chuckled. "But you did forget one thing: the therapeutic massage center you are going to open next to Doctor Abdullah's clinic."

Michelle slapped her forehead. "How could I forget that! I'm going to be coming and going so often, I should consider buying a house so I'll always have a place to stay."

"You don't like my caves?" Commander Massoud asked solemnly. "I'll let you take your pick. I have the finest caves in all of Afghanistan."

"That's not what I heard," Michelle said wagging her finger at him. "I heard Osama bin Laden has the best caves in the country."

"Yes, but you wouldn't want him as your landlord." Massoud's eyes twinkled as he spoke.

"No, I don't suppose I would," Michelle agreed emphatically. "But I don't want one of your caves either, thank you very much. A nice, little house with an orchard in Panjshir sounds much more to my liking."

"Mine, too. We could be neighbors."

"Okay, neighbor; it's a deal. I will look forward to that day."

"But today is not so pleasant, is it?" the Commander observed with concern. "I will go gather more fuel for the fire if you will assemble something for dinner. Remember, we need to ration."

"Are you sure you won't let me go out? What about your

from that flame

leg?"

"I need to stretch my back," Massoud answered. "I won't walk far." He limped over to the small opening in the snow door Michelle had built.

"Ahmed Shah *Jaan*," Michelle called after him. She went to him when he stopped and looked back. She held out the handgun and her empty backpack.

"You forgot these."

Massoud accepted the weapon. "I know what this is for, but why the pack?"

"You can carry more wood and grass than in your arms, and it might be easier on your back and leg."

"I'll be right back." Massoud smiled and ducked out into the last of the day's light.

Michelle went back into the interior and began to sort through their small rations.

9. Blood

"What is this?" Massoud held up something wrapped in paper so that Michelle could see. There was a teasing twinkle in his eye. "*Ordure?*"

"*Cochonneries,*" Michelle countered with a laugh. "I remembered the phrase for unhealthy food. "That is *C'est une barre chocolatée.* Are you sure you want to eat chocolate?"

"Not nearly as much as you do." He tossed the candy bar to her with a chuckle and stuck the last granola bar in his mouth. The hard, cold grains felt like wood chips in his mouth, but he just smiled and chewed. It was nourishment, and he would not complain.

They talked for a few more hours, sometimes seriously and sometimes with humor.

Despite their dire circumstances, they found many reasons to laugh. Finally, Michelle redressed the Commander's wound and lulled him nearly to sleep with another mindless humming. She stood up.

"Aren't you going to sleep?" Massoud asked drowsily.

"I need to go to the bathroom. I'll be right back."

"I should go with you." The Commander started to get up. "It's dark and dangerous. You might get lost."

"Don't you dare even think about it," Michelle warned. "I can find my own way."

"All right, but please don't wander too far. Stay near the cave. Don't forget about the land mines. Take the pistol."

"I don't need the gun," Michelle protested. "There is nothing but snow out there for fifty miles, and it is pitch dark now. No

from that flame

one could see me even if I was five feet in front of them."

Massoud reached for the gun beside him, slid the safety, and held it out to her. "Here are your choices. Take the gun and shoot anything that moves, or I come with you and stand guard while you...do what you need to do. Which do you prefer?"

Michelle stood over the reclining man and glared down at him.

"All right," Massoud started to get up, "I'll go with you."

"Oh, give me the damn thing." She snatched it out of his hands. "What am I likely to find out there anyway?"

"Wild animals, Taliban, al-Qaeda—all sorts of vermin."

Michelle peered towards the opening of the cave. It was very dark. She looked back at Massoud and almost asked him to accompany her after all. But the wound on his leg had finally stopped bleeding, and she didn't want to risk having it open again. Besides that, he was half asleep. She could do this. After everything she had gone through in the past week, surely she could go to the bathroom by herself. She clicked on her small flashlight. The light was growing weaker as the batteries began to fail. I will have to conserve it, she thought, and turned it off again.

"I'll be right back." She took a deep breath, plunged outside, and was swallowed by the cold darkness.

Michelle relieved herself and headed back to the cave. She decided she'd tell Massoud about the huge bear she scared off. Are there bears in Afghanistan? She wondered. It's so cold, if there are bears, they have to be hibernating. She quickened her pace. She had wandered farther from the cave than she had realized. She really needed trees that were closer.

A movement near the entrance of the cave caught her attention. Had he followed her after all just to make sure she was all right? She wouldn't put it past him to protect her and then hurry back to the cave so that she wouldn't know. She switched off the flashlight and started to creep more silently in the hope that she would catch him up and moving around. She would tease him unmercifully and think of some fun insult she could hurl his way. She only hoped he wasn't bleeding again. I'm going to run out of clean blouses to use as bandages before we get to the medic, she thought. She crept forward silently.

She had just reached the opening of the cave when she heard

a man's voice that was not Massoud's. Her first thought was that they had been found by his men. Then she heard the tone of voice the speaker was using. None of Massoud's men would ever talk to him that way. She couldn't understand what was being said, but it did not sound pleasant. Cautiously she peered into the cave.

Her eyes quickly adapted to the only slightly higher degree of light within than without. What she saw made her heart stop and her breath catch in her throat. A man stood over Massoud, who was still lying on the ground, with a rifle pointed directly at him. Massoud's Kalishnikov was at least three feet away. He would never be able to reach it in time. The man was still yelling angrily, determined to speak his mind before killing the defenseless man beneath him.

Michelle didn't think. Some instinct deep inside her that she didn't even know existed took control. She stepped into the cave, raised the gun, pointed it at the intruder, and fired. The sound of the gunpowder exploding echoed with a ferocious din throughout the small cave. She wasn't sure where the bullet had entered the uninvited man, only that she had hit him. He fell forward as Massoud rolled away from the falling body and reached for the Kalishnikov. He kept rolling, weapon in hand, made it first to his knees, and then struggled to his feet. He raised the gun and pointed it at the motionless man. He dared to take his eyes off the would-be assassin long enough to cast a quick glance in Michelle's direction.

"Are you all right?"

She was shaking and trembling so badly, she could hardly stand. Why her knees hadn't given out on her, she did not know. She lowered the pistol.

"Yes," she managed to whisper at last. "Is he dead?"

Massoud studied the man on the ground before him and looked for a rise and fall in the chest. "I don't know. Yes, I think he is. Can you keep me covered?"

"What?" Michelle said even as she automatically raised the arm whose shaking hand held the pistol.

Massoud took a cautious step forward, bent over, and felt the man's wrist for a pulse. Nothing. He took another step closer and tried to see where the bullet had entered the body. From what he could see, it looked as if the assassin had taken the hit directly be-

from that flame

tween the shoulder blades. He looked at Michelle's stricken face.

"He's dead."

A moan escaped from her mouth, and her knees did buckle. She unceremoniously knelt down hard on the ground. She started shaking uncontrollably.

Massoud hobbled over to her. "Look at me," he ordered her. When she obeyed, he saw tears running down her flushed cheeks. "You saved my life. There is no doubt he would have killed me. You saved my life." His voice was firm and emphatic. He could not afford to have her become hysterical, not when he didn't know who else might be lurking out in the dark night.

"Okay," Michelle stammered in numb agreement.

Massoud set his rifle aside, crouched down the best he could with his injured leg, and took the pistol from her. He set it next to the other gun and took her trembling hands into his. He would will his strength into her if he could.

"Look at me," he said again but gently this time. She did as he asked. "My poor friend." His voice softened when he saw the abject misery and shocked horror on her face. "You have had a lousy initiation into my life. I am sorry for that. I am not sorry that man is dead instead of me."

"I'm not either," Michelle managed to say over the lump in her throat. "Who is he?"

"I don't know his name, only his politics. His name doesn't matter now. He is with Allah trying to explain why he was going to kill an unarmed man." The Commander wondered if she was hearing his words and not just his voice. "He was going to kill me," Massoud repeated firmly and slowly. "He announced that he was, and he took great pleasure in the prospect."

Michelle nodded. "I know. I know I didn't have a choice." Her voice was strangled.

"Your choice was his life or both of ours. He would have killed you as well the moment that he saw you."

"What do we do now?" Michelle asked barely above a whisper.

"We have to move his body. Normally I would never ask you to do something like that, but I need your help. Can you help me, Michelle *Jaan*?"

"Move him where?" Michelle shuddered at the idea of having to touch him.

"Away from the fire and our camp."

"Okay," Michelle said woodenly and stood up abruptly. "I can move him. I don't want you to hurt yourself any worse than you already have."

"Nonsense." Massoud struggled to stand upright. "This is not the same as gathering firewood. This we will do together."

They went to the body, and Massoud set aside the pack the man had dropped when he raised his gun. They rolled him onto his back, and each grabbed an ankle. The man was not heavy, and the cave was small. It only took a few tugs to reposition the body and open up their camp space again. Massoud removed the bedroll from the dead man's pack.

"Now we will have another cover," he said as he hastily covered the large blood spill on the ground with the blanket he had been using. He rearranged the blankets and sleeping bag so that she wouldn't have to see what would be beneath them when they slept.

Michelle opened her mouth to say that she could not use the assassin's blanket, but her mouth snapped shut before she said anything. She would use it. She was shaking from trauma and cold. All she wanted to do was lie down, close her eyes, and escape into the peace sleep would bring.

"Could there be more men out there?" Michelle asked suddenly. The thought that occurred to Commander Massoud a moment after the shot was fired only now dawned on her.

"Perhaps," Massoud said honestly. "I think it would be best if we slept in shifts tonight so that one of us can keep watch."

"All right," Michelle agreed. "You can sleep first, and I'll keep guard."

"I think it would be better if you slept," Massoud countered. "Your nerves had quite a shock and need time to recover. "

"You aren't going to leave the cave, are you?" Michelle asked anxiously.

"Of course not. I am going to be right here." He added a little more fuel to their small fire and then struggled to get down onto the ground again. He didn't think his leg had resumed bleeding, but after dragging the corpse, his back was screaming insults at him. Finally he was as comfortable as the hard ground would allow. Michelle laid beside him and curled up into a fetal position with her back towards him.

Massoud arranged the other thin blanket first over her and then over himself. Everything was quiet except for the soft crackle of the small fire. He looked down at Michelle, saw her shoulders wracked with a jerking movement, and knew that she was weeping. He wished there was something he could do that would make her pain go away.

"I'm sorry," he spoke quietly. "If I could undo what happened tonight, I would. I wish it could have been I who killed him rather than have you suffer this way."

Michelle looked backward over her shoulder so that she could see his face. "I'm not sorry that you're alive. I am only sorry that I had to kill him in order to keep you alive. I've never killed anyone before," she said and started to weep again.

Massoud reached out and stroked her head in the way he had comforted his children when something had gone terribly wrong for them. He knew what killing did to a person's soul.

"I still remember the first man I killed," he said very softly. "It's going to stay with you. You will never be able to forget it. The best you can hope is to find a way to live with it." He gently stroked her hair away from her face. "I would give everything I own if I could take this burden from you. I am sorry."

Finally, after a very long while, her tears subsided, and she slept. Massoud, the pistol in his free hand and the Kalishnikov close by, stayed awake and listened to every sound both in and outside the cave for the rest of long night.

"Can we put our uninvited guest on the other side of the barrier?" Michelle shuddered as she looked at the body of the man she killed.

"I will bury him in the snow if you will go gather our day's fuel," Commander Massoud said. He understood her desperate need not to have the man's body confronting her every moment. He saw that she had begun to tremble again, but whether it was from the seeping cold, her grief, or her fear, he did not know.

It hurt him to see her this way. When she first came to him,

from that flame

she had been filled with confidence and humor. Now he suspected that she was only hanging onto sanity because of her sheer guts and determination. He sensed that she had lost some important part of herself at the moment she pulled the trigger and killed the would-be assassin and that she now was at a loss as to how to get it back.

Massoud signed deeply, worry etched on his face. This is what the current conditions in Afghanistan do to women, he thought with combined sadness and anger. It's a harsh, unyielding country filled with danger and brutality, and it rips all joy and comfort from its people with as little concern as a buzzard strips carrion from a dead animal. "I have to do better," he muttered under his breath. "My people deserve better."

He saw the suffering just behind her eyes although she was trying valiantly to hide it from him. Something in his heart hardened even more against the men who had inflicted this brand of misery on women. He remembered his own mother during the days of his youth when Afghanistan was still a land filled with music and laughter. She had the sweetest face and the warmest smile. Being in her presence was like basking in sunlight. When was the last time he had seen that look of happiness and joy on a woman's face? Even his own wife lived with fear—fear for him, fear for herself, and fear for their children. What would they do if something happened to him before the Taliban was ousted and al-Qaeda was vanquished? He thought about his five cherished daughters. How could he not fight until his last breath to create an Afghanistan for them where they would be free to choose their way in life, where they would be safe, where they could become all that their potential allowed?

He slipped the *paktou* from his shoulders and placed it around hers. Despite the military fatigues and *pakol* she wore, she looked more like a frightened girl than a *mujahidin*.

"This will keep you warmer," he said and smiled. She managed to force a wan smile on her own face, and again the utter enormity of what he was fighting to achieve struck him. He could not afford to fail. At that moment she personified every broken woman in his country, and he wanted to shelter and comfort them all.

There had been times, he realized, when he had lost sight of women's plight in his country. He often became consumed with

from that flame

the battle itself and with his extreme dislike of the Taliban. His rage towards the terrorists who had overrun his country blocked everything else from view. That would not happen again, he vowed to himself. He wanted to hold her so that he might comfort her and will his own strength and determination into her. Instead he simply said, "You need to carry a gun when you are outside getting more wood."

"I know. I will. And I will use it again if I must."

Those were the words he had hoped to hear. "Don't wander too far."

"I know," Michelle cut him off. "'Use the trees and rocks as cover. Don't get caught out in the open. If I see anyone, drop the wood and get back here as fast as I can. The land is heavily mined. Stick to the paths, and don't wander off them, whatever I do.'" She smiled weakly when she had finished reciting the oft-heard list of instructions.

"I think that covers it," Massoud said, relieved that even a small flash of spirit had returned to her. He watched as she flung her backpack over one shoulder, strapped on the handgun holster, and headed for the cave opening. She deliberately didn't look down at the dead soldier as she passed.

"Michelle *Jaan*?" he called after her. She turned and looked back. "Please be careful."

"I will, *Amer Saheb*. I promise." She forced another small smile before leaving the cave and trudging off into the snow.

Commander Massoud followed her to the opening and watched for a long time as she walked away from him. He knew there was nothing he could say or do that would make her feel any better about what had happened. It shouldn't have happened, and he blamed himself. He had become careless, or his rifle would never have been so far out of his reach. Had he kept the weapon near him as usual, he would have been able to defend himself. He watched Michelle walk away with her head and shoulders drooping as if her small frame was being weighted down by some impossibly heavy burden. He rubbed his tired eyes and then watched her a while longer. Finally, he decided the only thing he could do for her at that place in time was to make sure the man's body was gone by the time she got back. He wrapped his coat more tightly around himself and went outside to begin digging a hole in the snow.

from that flame

It took Michelle several trips and most of the morning to gather the wood and grass they would need to survive another night in the cave. It was beginning to snow again, and the air grew colder with each passing hour. The only relief for her was that the body of the man she had killed was no longer inside the cave. She saw an area of disturbed snow but didn't ask Massoud any questions. She was grateful for the fresh snow. It would further remove from her view the evidence of what she had done.

Inside the cave, the Commander had also been busy. Everything had been moved and neatly rearranged until every vestige of the previous night's horror was hidden from view. He didn't tell her about the small food supply he had removed from the dead man's pack. They needed the food, and he thought she might be reluctant to eat anything she knew belonged to the dead man. Instead he pretended as if it had come from his own pack. Had she asked, he would have told her the truth, but she sat quietly and asked him no questions even when he handed her a cup of hot green tea.

He sat opposite her and watched her with great concern. It was as if a switch had been thrown and all the joy and light in her had been turned off. The silence in the cave became deafening. The only indication of any life at all was the small crackle from the fire.

"Please stop watching me." Michelle turned her face and hastily wiped the tears on her cheeks. "And stop blaming yourself. It's not your fault."

"Of course it is," Massoud answered. "It is my job to protect you, not the other way around. I should have done a better job keeping my guard up."

"I'm not your 'job,' Ahmed Shah *Jaan*," Michelle answered with a hint of anger in her voice. "You didn't ask me to show up in your camp last week. I was an uninvited guest. You have been nothing but kind and generous towards me no matter how difficult the situation was for you. You wouldn't have been shot and half-incapacitated if you hadn't come after me up on that mountain. It's my fault we are in this mess in the first place." She looked at him with an odd mix of anger, hurt, and grief. "It's all my fault,

from that flame

okay? Consider yourself absolved."

Massoud set his tea aside. "Michelle *Jaan*..." he began.

"I don't need your sympathy," she interrupted him.

"Yes, you do," he said quietly, "and I need to give it to you."
Slowly, translating from Persian to French in his mind before
speaking the words, he began to recite.

Our Union is like this:
You feel cold,
So I reach for a blanket
To cover our shivering feet.

A hunger comes into your body,
So I run to my garden
And start digging potatoes.

You ask for a few words of comfort and guidance,
I quickly kneel at your side
Offering you this whole book
As a gift.

You ache with loneliness one night
So much you weep,
And I say, 'Here's a rope.
Tie it around me.
[I] will be your companion for life.'

By nightfall Michelle seemed much calmer. She had managed to seal off the part of her somewhere deep inside that was
still struggling with the horror of having taken a human life. She
knew that one day she would have to open the seal and deal with
the pain behind it, but at this moment her survival instincts had
all kicked in again, and she couldn't spare the energy required
to worry about something she could not change. Her mind had
repeated the mantra *It was either that man or Ahmed Shah, and you
chose Massoud* until her heart's cry had been silenced.

"It is time for tea," Massoud announced abruptly.

from that flame

"Are you sure you aren't British?" Michelle smiled and shook her head. "I have never seen such a penchant for tea in anyone who is not British."

"No one ever said that the Brits didn't leave behind some remnants of their culture when they, too, tried to conquer Afghanistan," Massoud quipped, delighted to see the smile even if it was small.

"No, no, wait a minute," Michelle said, shaking her head more emphatically. "I know good and well that you weren't around to fight the British during any of their three wars in this country."

"You don't think I am a well preserved eighty-year-old man?" Commander Massoud asked with a straight face.

"You'd have to be closer to ninety or ninety-five to have made the last Anglo-Afghan War, my friend," Michelle pointed out. "Unless, of course, you were born with a gun in your hands and emerged from your mother's womb ready for battle."

"I see you know some Afghan history," Massoud said. "I guess there is no point in telling you about the battles against Alexander the Great and Ghengis Kahn?"

"Not if you are going to tell me you fought in those battles," Michelle said, laughing aloud. "You are a dazzling and amazing military man, Ahmed Shah Massoud, and you're a wonderful storyteller, but even you aren't going to be able to convince me that you were at war in 1219 AD, much less 329 BC."

"No, I haven't, but my country has," Massoud said, suddenly serious. "Will you promise me something?"

"Only if I believe it is a promise I can fulfill," Michelle said sincerely. "I don't want to tell you I promise to do something and then not be able to deliver on the promise. That would be like lying to you, and I won't do that."

"I believe this is a promise you can keep," Massoud said.

"Then of course I will make that promise. What is it?"

"When you write your story, make the outside world feel the suffering as well as the courage and nobility of the Afghan people. You have experienced a little of what life in this country is like. No other Western journalist has been through what you have this past week. Make the West understand. Make them see it through your eyes. Bring it into their homes in such a way that they no longer want to turn their backs on us. Use all of your skill with words, all of your craft, to make people understand what is happening here. Will you do that?"

"Doctor Abdullah told me that every time a journalist shows up, you dare hope that your message might finally be heard. He also said that every time you are disappointed and nothing changes. How can I promise to do something no one else including you, yourself has been able to accomplish? How could I dare risk such a promise only to end up as the next journalist who has let you down?"

"You won't let me down," Massoud said with conviction. "You won't let my people down."

"How do you know that? I haven't written a word yet. I don't even have a publisher. Why should I have more success than any other journalist?"

"Because you are you and not them. Because you have courage and passion and truth. Because I believe in you and need you to do this for my people. You can. I know you can."

Michelle watched him carefully for a moment. When he looked at her the way he was looking now, she believed everything he said was possible. "Because of you I have seen not only Afghanistan's troubled past and present, but also her hope and promise for the future," she picked her words with care. "I promise you that I will write this story about you and your country with the best I have in me. I will try to infuse the words I choose with everything you have shown me and taught me. I promise I will try to make the outside world understand. But I cannot promise that anything will change. Please don't make me promise that. I don't want to fail you."

"If you do what you have said, that will be more than enough. If you do what you've said, you could not fail me, no matter what the outcome."

"You are an extraordinary man, Ahmed Shah Massoud," Michelle said with sincere respect and admiration. "Despite everything that has happened—or perhaps because if it—I will always be grateful for this time with you."

"It has been my great pleasure. While I don't normally subject journalists who visit me to conditions such as you've been asked to endure, I don't normally consider the journalist a friend by the end of the interview either," Massoud said. "I would like to count you as a friend, Michelle *Jaan.*"

"That would be my deepest honor, *Amer Saheb,*" Michelle replied, returning his smile with one of her own that was so warm, it was as if the sun had suddenly lit the cave.

Massoud left the cave to get a breath of fresh air before turning in for the night. He could hardly believe their luck that the would-be assassin had been alone, that no one had come looking for him, that they had not been attacked in a full assault by more of his determined enemy. He had nearly decided that if his men did not arrive by mid-morning, he and Michelle would begin the long, dangerous hike towards Khwaja Bahauddin. With any luck at all, they would meet his men on the way. He wished he had his maps so that he could study the best route. He had not been in this area in several years and wondered if he would remember his way. In addition to becoming lost, Massoud was concerned that they would be exposed to both the elements and the enemy once they left the relative safety and warmth of the cave. Without sufficient food or shelter, and with the continual threat of coming under fire, he wondered how long Michelle would survive. Would he? While the gunshot wound in his leg didn't bother him very much when he was mostly idle, he worried that it might open once he began a strenuous hike. In a gunfight, would he be the lone defender, or would Michelle be able to fire a gun at a human being again? Is it foolhardy to even consider hiking out? He wondered. Will a search team find us before more Taliban do? Can I risk it? He decided that he should talk candidly to Michelle about their slim options and ask for her thoughts. Based on what she said, he would at the very least be better able to gage her frame of mind.

She had seemed much better all evening. After their tea, she had asked about Taloqan again, but he changed the subject. He pressed her into telling him more about herself. He had watched her animated face as she spoke and realized that in a few, short days, he had become very fond of her. She was most assuredly unlike any woman he had previously encountered. He knew that, God willing, she would be leaving Afghanistan one day soon, and he knew, too, that he would miss her when she was gone. There was something transparent and honest about her. It made him trust her. It made him believe her when she said she would return. In this life he led, it would be good to have a pleasant anticipation.

After surveying the region one final time, Massoud ducked back into the cave. Michelle was curled up on her corner of the blanket, and at first he thought she was already asleep. It wasn't until he sat on the blanket beside her that he realized she was crying.

"Michelle *Jaan*? What has happened? Why do you weep? Are you ill?" His questions tripped over each other in his anxiety.

Michelle rolled onto her back so that she could look up at him. "I'm okay. I'm just being a silly woman."

"I don't understand," Massoud said.

"I am having what we women in America call 'a good cry.'"

"'A good cry'?" Massoud repeated. "I don't know the expression. Please explain it to me so that I will know what this means."

"You're a man. I don't know if you could ever understand why women sometimes just need to cry and why they feel better when they do." Michelle started to laugh through her tears at Massoud's perplexed, distressed expression. She sat up so that she could look into his eyes with her own, red-rimmed ones.

"I'm okay. Honestly, I am. You have to admit that the past few days have been harrowing. I have had several strange, frightening experiences." Massoud nodded in agreement. "All of these strange and frightening experiences have wrecked some havoc on my nerves," Michelle continued. "Crying helps to soothe them. That's all."

"So your crying over what happened the past few days and not because something is wrong right this moment? And this makes you feel better?"

"See, I told you it was silly and that you wouldn't understand."

"No, I do understand," he said softly. "Sometimes I want to weep when I think of all the terrible things that have happened to my people. I just have never given in to the need for tears. I didn't know they would make me feel better."

"They will," Michelle nodded sagely.

from that flame

"Then the next time I feel the need, perhaps I will try," Massoud replied.

Michelle shook her head slightly. "Thank you for not making me feel foolish. You are the kindest man I have ever known," she said sincerely.

"Kindness towards one another is what God wants from us," he answered with a smile. "Now we must sleep," he said. "In the morning we must decide whether to stay or whether to go." He tossed his pakol aside and laid down.

"You make it sound so easy," Michelle complained as she pulled her corner of the thin blanket over her shoulders. "It's not so easy." Still, she feel asleep sooner than she would have expected, and her dreams were not nightmares.

10. Found

fter a lengthy discussion of their options the following morning, they agreed to stay in the cave one more day. If Massoud's men had not come by the following morning, they would head out.

"Michelle *Jaan*," Massoud began to speak, and when she looked at him, Michelle saw a look of concern on his face. He shook his head. "No, never mind."

"Tell me," she said, sat opposite him, and looked him in the eyes. "It must be important, or you wouldn't have started to bring it up."

Massoud sighed. He had known for three days that this conversation would be necessary, and he dreaded it. He was afraid he would hurt her, and he did not want to do that.

"When we see my men again," he began slowly, carefully picking his words, "whether it is here, on the road, or at the compound in Khwaja Bahauddin, there are things about which it would be better if my men were unaware."

"I won't tell anyone what happened here. If you don't want them to know about the assassin, I won't say anything," Michelle assured him quickly.

"No, that is the one thing they should know," he said. "You saved my life. They will be grateful."

"Then what?"

"They should not see the degree to which our friendship has blossomed. They would not understand, I fear."

"Because I'm an 'infidel' in their eyes as well as a woman?"

"Among other things, yes. Not everyone would feel that way,

but some would. It would be better if what has transpired between us privately remains between us."

"But nothing transpired except friendship…" Michelle's voice trailed off. "There can't be any sign that we have become overly friendly? Is that it?"

"Yes. I am their military commander, but they look to me for guidance in many areas. I not only lead them in battle, I also lead them in prayer. I must remain what they need me to be: a moral man. Can you understand that?"

"Yes, of course I can. You are a moral man, too important to them and to all of Afghanistan. Your image and your reputation must remain unblemished, especially since nothing untoward happened between us."

"It's more than that, Michelle *Jaan*. They cannot see the man I am when I am with you. That man must be left behind in the cave the moment we leave here."

"But I like that man. He is brave and strong and good. That's who you are. Surely they already know that."

"And he laughs and feels tenderness," Massoud said. "He sometimes forgets about the war and his responsibilities. He forgets everything except how different and new it is to be with someone who loves life, embraces dreams, and finds hope where no one else could. You are like an intoxicating drug to me, a drug to which I could easily become addicted. I cannot afford that addiction. Please understand and forgive me."

"There is nothing to forgive. You have been very good to me. You trusted me with your thoughts and feelings. You gifted me with your friendship. I can carry that in my heart, and it will be enough. No one else ever needs to know."

"Thank you, my true friend," the commander replied with all sincerity.

About two hours later, Massoud heard the sound of a finely tuned engine among the coarser sound of large engines. Climbing to a higher elevation and flattening his body against the high, external wall of the cave, he raised his binoculars and searched for the source of the sound. He saw his own white Land Rover, Abdullah behind the wheel, slowly making a weaving path down

from that flame

the mountainside. Behind the Land Rover were two trucks filled with his armed men.

Massoud climbed higher up the outer bank, took off his *patou*, and waved it like a flag. As he waved he saw the Land Rover turn in his direction. He went back into the cave.

"We are found. Gather your things. Abdullah will be here in a few minutes."

Michelle hurriedly began to shove her belongings into her pack. "I'll be ready in a minute," she said.

"Michelle *Jaan*?"

She glanced up at Massoud. "I remember what you said, *Amer Saheb*. I know that my friend will remain in the cave when we leave."

"Michelle *Jaan*?" Massoud said again. Again she looked at him, this time with a question on her face. He continued. "I am supposed to attend that conference in Paris early next month, remember? Do you think you might be able to be in Paris then as well?"

"Sure," Michelle said, smiling. "I can be there, but you will probably be so busy, you won't have time for me."

"But I want you to attend the conference with Abdullah and me, at least in an unofficial capacity. I would appreciate your thoughts and input at the end of each day. I am an unsophisticated man. I don't always understand the Western mind, although I try. I trust you to tell me anything I need to know but may not hear. Will you help me?"

"Of course I will, and I am honored by your confidence in me," Michelle answered. She held out her hand to shake his. "I will see you in Paris, *Amer Saheb*. And now it is time for Commander Massoud to greet his very relieved men."

Massoud's men enthusiastically celebrated the discovery of their missing leader. The Commander had no choice but to shake the hand of each man. Finally, they fanned out in a protective circle with Dr. Abdullah, Commander Massoud, and Michelle Garrett in the middle.

"Are you all right?" Dr. Abdullah looked from Massoud to

Michelle and back again. He saw the bandage around Commander Massoud's leg. "What is this?" he asked, pointing.

"I was shot. Michelle took good care of the wound. It's been cleaned twice a day and treated with an antibiotic ointment," Massoud explained.

The doctor looked very concerned. "And the bullet?"

"It's still in there."

"You're going to have to go to a hospital in Dushanbe," Abdullah said sternly.

"I know, I know," Massoud said. He smiled and patted his friend on the arm. "I am okay."

The doctor was not going to be so easily placated. "I'll decide that when I've had a chance to look at the wound." He looked at Michelle again. "How about you? Any bullet wounds I need to know about?"

"Nope. I'm fine, thanks," Michelle assured him.

The doctor ran a practiced, medical eye over her small frame. "You look too thin."

Michelle shrugged. "Maybe I lost a few pounds. We were rationing food, you know. I'll eat more."

"Do you know the difference between junk food and health food?" Massoud asked the doctor solemnly though there was a slight twinkle in his eyes. Michelle nearly gave him a friendly poke in the ribs but remembered his warning and shook her head instead.

"What? No, but I'm sure you'll tell me," Dr. Abdullah said, shaking his head as if over a hopeless case. "Do you have any idea how worried I was about you?" he demanded.

"Of course I do, and I'm sure you'll tell me," Massoud replied with a grin. "But could you tell me in the car? I am freezing."

"Of course you are," the doctor said contritely. "Do the men need to get anything?"

"I don't think so." Massoud handed his two weapons to the doctor and took an inventory of everything he had in his pockets.

"Do you have everything?" Massoud asked, looking at Michelle.

"Right here," she said, holding up her trusty backpack.

from that flame

"What about your sleeping bag?" Dr. Abdullah asked. He saw Michelle glance at Massoud who then answered.

"Everything that is in the cave remains there," the Commander said. He leveled his gaze at his friend.

Abdullah searched his friend's eyes for a clue about what was going on, but when he saw none he simply answered, "I have a medical kit in the car, and I would like to look at your leg before we leave."

"All right," Massoud agreed. "Michelle *Jaan*, will you wait in the car where it is warm? If I don't let the doctor here look at what a good job you've been doing on my leg, he will give me no peace."

Commander Massoud went back through the shelter of the cave's opening while Dr. Abdullah and Michelle walked to the Land Rover.

"We won't be long," Abdullah said as he removed his medical kit and Michelle climbed into the back seat.

"Take your time. This is the softest, warmest place I've been in a week," Michelle said as she eased herself down onto the cushions.

"Are you sure you're all right?"

"Stop worrying about me," Michelle answered. It was good to see him again. "I'm not your favorite patient at the moment. The Commander is."

"I think he prefers your brand of medicine," Dr. Abdullah replied. "I am fairly certain he appreciates massages and relaxing music more that he is going to appreciate me digging around in that bullet hole."

Michelle grimaced at the thought. "Ouch! Well, if he gets too cranky, you'll think of some way to deal with him. You always do." Dr. Abdullah laughed as he closed the car door and went back to his friend.

"It doesn't look as bad as I feared," Dr. Abdullah said, closely examining the wound. "It doesn't appear to be infected, but that bullet does have to come out soon."

"Why can't one of the local doctors do it?" Massoud asked

as he watched the doctor apply a new bandage. "Why can't you do it?"

"If I had been here when it happened, I would have. But that bullet has been in there a long time, my friend. You are going to need a course of antibiotics, and I would rather have you in a hospital in case there are complications."

"All right," the Commander said with a sigh. "But let us go now, please. I haven't been able to bathe or change my clothes in several days."

"Are you going to tell me what happened here?" Dr. Abdullah looked at the bedding and supplies that were being left behind. He was accustomed to taking everything along when they moved. They didn't have anything to spare, and little was ever wasted.

"I'll tell you in the car," Massoud answered. "Don't look so worried, my friend. It turned out all right in the end."

Once Massoud was comfortably settled in the back seat with his leg propped up and Michelle had transferred to the front passenger seat , Dr. Abdullah called to all the men who had accompanied him. They hurried to climb into their vehicles. One pulled in front of the Land Rover, and the other one stayed behind it. Caravan style, they began the long drive to Khwaja Bahauddin.

"How did you find us?" Michelle asked. "We were beginning to think we would have to have to hike out."

Dr. Abdullah was horrified at the thought. "You would have frozen to death."

"How did you find us?" Massoud repeated from his perch in the back.

"We assembled in Kalan Eylgah the way you said we should," said Dr. Abdullah. "We waited for you to join us. I knew that Nasser had reached the helicopter and had gone out after you. Eventually, Mohammed made it to base camp. He told me that Nasser had picked you up. We waited twelve more hours for you, and when you didn't come, I sent teams out to search for you. I took some of the men and headed back to Khwaja Bahauddin to get more men and weapons to join the search.

"One of the teams found the crashed helicopter and Nasser's remains, but there was no sign of either of you. I prayed that meant you had somehow miraculously escaped. From then on it was simply a matter of developing a search pattern. We started small and spread out to look in areas where we thought you might be able to take cover. Of course, our fear was that you had been badly injured. I also knew you had inadequate supplies of food and ammunition, and I was worried what would happen if you couldn't find shelter from the cold. I thank God that everything turned out well."

"The Commander kept telling me that you would find us," Michelle told Abdullah.

Abdullah looked in the rear view mirror so that he could see his friend's face. "Is that why you were talking about hiking out?"

"I thought at worst we'd meet you along the way. I knew you'd be looking for us. One way or the other, I knew you would find us," Massoud said with conviction.

"That's easy to say now that you are on your way home," Dr. Abdullah said dryly.

"Now it's my turn to tell a story. May I, Michelle?"

Michelle leaned over the front seat so that she could see him better. "Is it necessary?"

"To tell Abdullah? Yes. No one else needs to hear it if you would prefer."

"Then tell him." Michelle settled back in her seat and looked out the window.

Massoud began to tell the tale of the assassin who found him lying in the cave helpless and unarmed. He told Abdullah about Michelle's courage in shooting the man he suspected to be a bounty hunter for the Taliban. He also told Abdullah how he had buried the body in the snow and said the ritual prayers for the dead over him.

Bouncing along over the rough terrain, Michelle listened carefully to Massoud's narration even though he was speaking in Dari, and she could not understand him. She knew he would give an accurate accounting of precisely what happened.

"You really did save his life," Abdullah said with amazement and gratitude when Massoud stopped speaking.

"I did what I had to do," Michelle said quietly. "I couldn't let him be killed. I was grateful for the gun and the shooting lessons you gave me."

from that flame

Dr. Abdullah felt Massoud's hand on his shoulder and understood that it would be better if he didn't say anything else. Still, he felt as if he had to say something.

"I am grateful you were there to protect my friend. Thank you," he added quietly.

"Me, too," was all Michelle said before looking out the side window again. The majestic beauty of the Hindu Kush mountains entranced her. Looking at them also gave her the excuse she needed to divert her attention away from the two men in the car. They had both been wonderful to her, but what she needed most at that moment was an hour or two alone with her own thoughts. She was weary to the core of her being—physically, emotionally, and psychologically. The past week had been too frantically spent surviving one crisis after another to allow for real thought and reflection. Lost in thought now, she didn't realize Commander Massoud was speaking to her until he had said her name twice.

"I'm sorry. What?" She looked over the seat back at him.

"Abdullah insists that I go to Tajikistan to have the bullet removed. Will you be able to stay in the compound until I return, or shall I make arrangements to have you escorted back to Pakistan?"

Michelle looked from Massoud in the back seat to Abdullah behind the wheel. "I would have thought you two would be eager to be rid of me after all the trouble I've caused. Should I say 'send me back to Pakistan' and let you off the hook?"

"Not on my account," Massoud said quickly. "I would prefer that you stay until I return, but if you must leave, of course I understand."

Michelle looked at the doctor. "What about you, Abdullah *Jaan*? You'll have primary responsibility for me while he's gone."

"A week ago I would have said the sooner you left, the better," the doctor answered honestly but with a laugh in his voice. "Now, if you can stay, that would be fine with me...on one condition."

"What's that?"

"That you continue to refrain from being my 'favorite' patient by staying well and unharmed," the doctor said and flashed a warm smile at the journalist.

"I'll do my best," Michelle promised with a returned smile. "It would be helpful if you stopped shoving me under tanks and on top of old mules."

"I'll give it my best effort," Abdullah laughed. "I was thinking I could scrounge up an old typewriter, lock you safely in the guest house, and let you get to work on your story."

"Except for the locked door part, that would be perfect. I'd like to be able to get a rough draft done and check all my facts before leaving."

"Then it is settled," Commander Massoud said with satisfaction. "You will write. I will go to hospital, and Doctor Abdullah will keep track of both of us."

"If that is my job," Dr. Abdullah said. "I would like you both to get some sleep now. It will take us hours to get to the compound. Use the time wisely."

Neither of his favorite patients argued with him.

At headquarters in Khwaja Bahauddin, Massoud immediately went to his office after asking Abdullah to arrange accommodations for Michelle in the small, one room guesthouse in the complex.

"I'm going to have the helicopter readied, and as soon as it is, you are going to Dushanbe," Dr. Abdullah said firmly.

"I need to write a few messages and answer a few others, and then I will be ready to go," Commander Massoud agreed.

"I'll be back in a few minutes," Abdullah said as he turned to leave the office and settle Michelle Garrett into her new quarters. "Ready or not, that is when you will leave." He didn't think Massoud heard him since the Commander was already immersed in reading a *communiqué* he had found on his desk. Dr. Abdullah shook his head and went to find Michelle in the center courtyard.

"Come with me," Abdullah said in English to Michelle. "I will show you to a room and have someone bring hot water to you so that you may freshen yourself."

"A hot bath—even a sponge bath—would be heaven right now," Michelle said, dragging her fingers through her tangled hair. After her many mishaps with French, it was a huge relief to think and speak in English again.

from that flame

They crossed the compound. "I am a little surprised you are staying here," Abdullah said. "I should think you would like to get back to civilization as soon as possible after what you have been through. Plenty of hot water, a wider range of foods, regular electricity…"

"All of that is tempting," Michelle agreed, "but I really do want to get a rough draft done and then double check all the facts. I was hoping that you might be able to help fill in some of the blanks for me."

"I will help in any way I can," Abdullah answered, "but I would think that Commander Massoud would be better able than I to discuss his various battles."

"The battles, yes," Michelle agreed again, "but he is too modest to talk about his real role in those battles, and that is something I would like to know. Who better to tell me that than you?"

"Then we will talk, and I will help you all I can," Abdullah said. He opened a narrow door in a mud brick wall of a semi-detached building. "This will be your quarters," he said, directing her in before him.

The room was small with a single window. There were several carpets on the floor, a thin mattress—a luxury after a week of sleeping on the ground—a low-lying table, a lantern, and a *sandali*. This traditional heating apparatus continued to amaze Michelle no matter how many times she saw one. On this day, she was extremely grateful for its presence and warmth.

"It is not elegant, but it is the best we have," Abdullah said.

"It's wonderful; thank you." Michelle walked into the room and set her backpack down. She walked over to the window and looked out. About fifty yards away was a brick wall, and near the wall were Massoud's *mujahidin* on patrol. Dr. Abdullah joined her and likewise looked out onto the snowy scene.

"This is the safest place in the whole country for him," Abdullah said. "And even when he is here, I worry."

Michelle looked up at the doctor who towered over her. "I understand why. If an assassin can find him out in the middle of nowhere the way that man did when we were in the cave, I think they could find him anywhere. Will he be safe in Dushanbe?"

"Yes," Abdullah said. "He is a hero in Tajikistan. The people idolize him. He will be well attended and protected."

from that flame

"Would you go with him if it were not for me?" Michelle asked. "I can go to Peshawar and perhaps return at a later date."

Abdullah shook his head. "No. He wants you here, and he needs me here, regardless. He is very fond of you. I think he will be saddened when you leave."

"He's a good man and a good friend," Michelle said. "I promised him I would return, and I will. But I will miss him...and you, too, Abdullah *Jaan*. I know that in the beginning you were unhappy about my sudden appearance on your doorstep, so to speak, but you didn't let your feelings get in the way of treating me very kindly. Thank you for that."

"I apologize if I was less than hospitable towards you that first day. I love Massoud very much. I don't like to see him hurt... in any way or for any reason," he said slightly emphasizing the final words.

Michelle met the doctor's gaze evenly. "I know. Nor do I. On this we agree completely. I understand exactly what he represents to the soldiers, the people, and you. I would never say, write, or do anything that would demean him or lessen anyone's high opinion of him."

Dr. Abdullah studied Michelle's face and eyes in an effort to understand exactly what she was saying to him. Had she picked up on his subtle hint that what might have happened in her and the Commander's relationship while they were alone in the cave for those days should remain strictly private at all costs? He was satisfied with what he found in her open, honest look. He nodded slightly.

"All is well between us?" Michelle asked as she offered her hand.

Abdullah took her hand in his. "It is well," he said with a smile.

Late in the quickly darkening day, Dr. Abdullah and Michelle accompanied Massoud to the aging M1 Soviet helicopter that would take him to Tajikistan. Michelle crammed the *pakol* down on her head and held it there while the rotating blades of the old Soviet chopper picked up speed and tried to rip it from her head.

Massoud raised his voice to be heard over the noise of the engine and said, "You'll be glad to get back into your own clothes, *nay*?"

Michelle shrugged. "I don't know. I've gotten sort of used to this look. I was thinking of spreading it to the fashion centers of Europe. Besides, this hat is great when I'm having a bad hair day."

"'Bad hair'?" Massoud and Abdullah echoed at the same time.

"Never mind," Michelle said with a laugh. "When do you think you'll be back?" she asked Massoud. "How long will he have to stay in the hospital?" she asked, looking at Abdullah.

"Barring any complications, only a day or two," the doctor answered. "Assuming he gets out of here soon." He grasped his friend's hands. "Call me if you need anything."

"You know I will," Massoud shouted. "I'll see you both in a few days." He moved deeper into the helicopter. Abdullah closed the door. He and Michelle stepped away and started to walk back to the compound's interior as the helicopter lifted off.

"May I ask you a question about English?" Abdullah asked as they walked.

"Sure."

"There is something…there must be a rule or a pattern, but I have never been able to figure out what it is. You say that you are going 'to church,' 'to school,' 'to college,' but then you also say you are going 'to the store,' 'to the hospital,' 'to the university.' How do I know when to put 'the' in the phrase?"

Michelle looked at him blankly. She considered the question for several minutes as dozens of grammar rules ran through her trained, writer's mind. "I have absolutely no idea," she admitted at long last.

"Oh, that's helpful," Abdullah said dryly. "Meanwhile, I will keep stumbling along hoping I don't make a fool of myself."

"I could make a list," Michelle offered.

"Of every preposition combined with every object in the English language?" Abdullah said and started to laugh. He held his hands a foot apart from each other. "It would require a book this big. Can you see me carting that thing around and then asking people to wait while I looked up my little phrase? Would you at

from that flame

least compile it in alphabetical order?"

Laughing loudly at the absurd mental image each conjured, Michelle and Abdullah made their way back inside the compound.

11. Abdullah

michelle reluctantly got up from the mattress to answer a knock at her door. She opened it to find Abdullah holding an old typewriter with a ream of paper stacked on top.

"I come bearing gifts," he said as he held up the typewriter.

"Come in, come in." Michelle stepped aside so that he could enter. He set the paper and typewriter down on the small table. He turned and looked around the room.

"Is everything comfortable for you?" he asked as his eyes noted the water basin, the burning embers in the brazier, and the clean sheet and blanket spread over the mattress. The lantern gave the room a warm glow.

"Perfect, thank you," Michelle said sincerely. "I was able to wash and change. It is deliciously warm, and everything is very comfortable. Have you heard anything about the Commander's surgery? Is he all right?"

"I have not heard anything yet. Will you join me for dinner? We can start replacing some of the weight you lost. I had the cook prepare some special dishes for you. You can explain to me the difference between junk food and health food since Ahmed Shah never got around to it. Will you join me?"

"I would be delighted...as long as I don't have to explain health food and junk food. It's a silly story, and I'll let Ahmed Shah tell it to you." Michelle reached for her coat and went out with the doctor into the cold, dark night.

She followed him across the compound to an area obviously used as a mess facility. She noticed that no one but the cook was there. "Did the others already eat?" she asked.

from that flame

"Yes," Abdullah answered somewhat abruptly without offering any explanation. He pointed to a small, carpeted area. "We'll sit here."

"What do you guys have against tables and chairs?" Michelle asked as she lowered herself to the ground.

"Nothing. It is simply not our custom. Western style furniture doesn't always fit with our lifestyle. Ah, here we are," he said as the cook started to set food-laden bowls in front of them. "Will you have tea or water?" he asked Michelle.

"I'm becoming quite fond of green tea," Michelle replied. Abdullah relayed her request in Dari to the cook who retreated and returned almost immediately with the customary glass mugs of steaming green tea.

"You and Commander Massoud had quite an adventure over the past few days," Abdullah commented as he reached for a piece of *nan*, the flat bread to which Michelle had become accustomed.

"'Adventure' is a perfect description for it," Michelle said, sipping her tea. "There were some harrowing, terrifying moments, that's for sure. Then there was the concern that you might not be able to find us before our food supply ran out. I was always afraid that another assassin might show up at any minute."

"I imagine you would be. The Commander told me that you were very grieved over having to take a human life. Are you feeling better now?"

"I wouldn't say better exactly," Michelle said slowly. "I have come to terms with it. I know I had to do it. Commander Massoud told me that the memory of it would probably always be with me. He was wonderfully understanding and helpful."

"He knows all about the pain and misery caused by war and killing," Abdullah said. "Tell me about an average day," he suggested to change the subject. "What did you do?"

"As you can imagine, survival activities were high on our list of priorities," Michelle said as she reached for the bowl in front of her. "What is this?" she asked with interest when she saw the unusual food.

"It is called *pilau-e-mugh-e-shekam pur*," Dr. Abdullah answered. "Doesn't that sound exotic? It is rice with stuffed chicken, a very special meal that is difficult to make. The cook heard that you had saved Commander Massoud's life and asked if he could make this for you with his thanks." Dr. Abdullah picked up another bowl and handed it to her. "And this is *yahkoot chalau*."

"Are those cherries?" Michelle asked with surprise as she looked into the second bowl Abdullah handed her.

"Yes," the doctor replied. He dipped his bread into it. "Please eat and enjoy the meal while you tell me about your adventure."

"This is amazing," Michelle said as she tasted the *yahkoot chalau*. "Especially since Commander Massoud and I would eat only a small ration of food at every meal. Before we leave, would it be possible for me to compliment your cook and thank him?"

"Of course," the doctor agreed. "That would make him very happy. Please tell me more about how you survived in the cave."

"I didn't want Commander Massoud walking very much, so I would go out and collect more dried grass and wood for our little fire," Michelle began as she continued to eat. "He tended the fire and made certain it never went out. In his old cup I would bring in snow several times a day, and we would melt it for tea or water. One day I built our door of snow. Sometimes Massoud would take his binoculars and search the countryside for you or the Taliban or both."

"That's not a day's worth of activity," Abdullah observed. "Ahmed Shah is used to being in a state of almost constant motion. Time must have rested heavily on his hands."

Michelle picked her words carefully as she spoke. She knew Massoud had only given a factual account, and that was what she intended to do too. "We talked a lot. He told me about the upcoming trip to Paris. He recited Persian poetry. I told him about my work and the places I have visited. It's funny when you think about it, Abdullah *Jaan*. How could two people on earth have less in common that he and I do? Yet we always found something of interest to both of us. Had we not been half-starved, half-frozen, lost, and vulnerable to attacks by assassins, it would have been fun."

The doctor suppressed a smile. "Under different circumstances, it might have been like one of the camping trips Americans like so much, yes?"

Michelle did smile. "Sure. I do like to go camping, as a matter of fact. Of course, I don't usually do it when it is freezing outside,

from that flame

and I like to have all the right gear so that I can be safe and comfortable."

"You did survive this unorthodox camping trip," Abdullah pointed out. "Commander Massoud was impressed by how seldom you complained about all the hardships."

"I couldn't complain to him of all people," Michelle answered. "I had to put up with a few things I consider hardships for a week. He has been doing it for over twenty years. I would have been ashamed to complain to him when my life has been so easy and safe compared to his. I go where I want and do what I want. When was the last time he had that freedom? No matter how miserable I might have been, I never would have been able to look him in the eyes again if I hadn't been able to pull my own weight for a few days."

"He does that to people, you know," Abdullah said quietly. "He inspires people to be braver and more self-sacrificing and better than they would be had they not met them. No matter how much any of us may sacrifice, he gives more. It is humbling."

"And he does it without preaching or yelling or even raising his voice," Michelle observed. "He goes through the day making life-and-death decisions, quietly giving this order or that command, and everyone looks at him adoringly and does what he says."

"Not always," Abdullah said, shaking his head. "Don't forget men like Kahn who betrayed and deceived him. Praise God they are the exception rather than the rule. You are right, though, that most men in the Alliance, whether general or foot soldier, would gladly die for Commander Massoud."

After they had finished their meal, the cook was summoned. Thanks to Abdullah's interpretation skills, Michelle was able to express her thanks and praise for the special meal. When the cook asked for permission to address the journalist, Abdullah reversed his translation from Dari to English. The cook pronounced his sincere gratitude for the opportunity to cook for the brave woman who had saved his commander's life

"**Qaabilay tashakur nayst**," Michelle said and looked at Abdullah to confirm she had pronounced the words properly. He nodded his approval, and they rose to leave.

Dr. Abdullah walked Michelle back across the compound

towards her quarters.

"You are one of the people on whom he had a profound effect," Michelle said, picking up the thread of their previous conversation. She phrased her observation as a statement of fact rather than a question.

Abdullah answered as if it had been a question. "Yes. From the first I knew that I was in the presence of a great man. He always treated me with respect and dignity. He listened when I spoke. I am his aide and advisor, and I am his friend. It is the great honor of my life to serve him and, through him, serve Afghanistan."

"I think he's lucky to have you," Michelle said sincerely when they reached her door and she turned to say good-night. "He thinks he is too."

"Thank you for having dinner with me," Abdullah said graciously.

"It was my pleasure, believe me. Are there any rules I should know about before I retire?"

"It would be best if you stayed inside unless you are accompanied by either me or someone I send to you. Also, it might be better if you had breakfast here in your room. Will that be a problem for you?"

"No, of course not. I want to start working on my notes for the article, and since you have so kindly provided a typewriter and paper, I can start early in the morning." Michelle saw the relief on the doctor's face. "I understand that my movements and interactions with the men here need to be restricted, Abdullah *Jaan*. It's okay. I don't take it personally. I respect your culture and customs."

"Thank you for that," Abdullah smiled. "At least until Massoud gets back, it would be better if the men forget that you are here. None of them would hurt you in any way, but your presence might make them feel uncomfortable. This is a barracks for them, and they behave differently than when we are in the field. I will have breakfast and lunch sent to you, and I would be honored if you would join me again tomorrow evening for dinner."

"I will look forward to it," Michelle said, offering her hand. "Good night, Doctor Abdullah."

The doctor shook her hand and turned to walk to his own quarters. He stopped and looked back at her. "I will let you know when I hear anything about his surgery."

Michelle smiled her thanks and went inside. Suddenly, sleep was the farthest thing from her mind. She wanted to begin work on her article right then. A typewriter clicking throughout the night might bother the sleeping men, but a pen on paper would serve her needs just as well. She immediately started to organize and outline her thoughts.

By eight o'clock the next morning, Michelle was happily pounding away on the old typewriter. When Dr. Abdullah knocked on her door an hour later, she was on a roll and hated having to stop.

"I spoke to Massoud a few minutes ago," Abdullah said as he handed her a tray with tea and food. He followed her into the room. "The surgery went well last night, and he is resting comfortably—. What are you laughing at?" Abdullah was perplexed by her reaction.

"I'm sorry," Michelle said as she continued to laugh. "I have spoken to doctors in a dozen different countries, and every one of them—and now you—say that the patient is 'resting comfortably.' Is that the first thing they teach you guys in medical school?

"Yes, I think it is the universal description handed out to doctors," Abdullah agreed.

"I am very relieved there were no complications during his surgery. I know you were concerned. When will he be back?" Michelle asked.

"They are giving him a course of IV antibiotics as a precaution. They will probably release him tomorrow. Sit. Eat," the doctor said, pointing at the mattress. "I will sit with you while you eat, if I may."

"Well," Michelle said, looking longingly at the typewriter, "I wasn't really going to stop right now to eat."

"Oh, but you are," the doctor said firmly. "You aren't going to regain the weight you lost if you don't eat regular meals." His voice changed and he began to coax her. "Come on, we can talk."

Realizing the determination of the man before her, Michelle sat on the edge of the mattress and brought the tray to her lap.

from that flame

Abdullah settled onto the carpet in front of her.

Michelle decided that she might as well take advantage of the opportunity to ask Abdullah some questions.

"Tell me about Taloqan," Michelle said.

"I thought you said the Commander told you about it," Abdullah replied, knitting his brow. "What did he tell you?"

Michelle picked up her notepad and flipped a few pages. "That he had his headquarters there. That the Taliban wanted to cut his supply lines. He said the battle was fierce and lasted for several weeks before he finally retreated. In October he met with Khan and Dostum, and the three of them decided to join forces. He said that they are planning to retake Taloqan when the weather gets better, and that weapons are starting to come in from various countries including the US." Michelle set the tablet aside and returned to her breakfast. She looked at Abdullah expectantly.

"That sounds like everything to me," Abdullah said with a shrug. "What else do you want to know? We are meeting with Generals Khan and Dostum again soon."

"He mentioned that, too," Michelle said as she ate. "I want to know if he was really outgunned and out-manned. Is that why he retreated?"

"I'm not sure I know what you mean," Abdullah said. "Pakistan sent in three divisions against him. That was enough to force anyone to retreat."

"Okay." Michelle shrugged and nodded her head, but her voice implied that she was unconvinced about something.

"You have never been subtle before," Abdullah said, picking up on her skepticism. "I'm not trying to withhold information; I'm just not sure what you are asking me."

"It was his worst defeat?"

"Yes."

Michelle set the tray aside and leaned forward to rest her elbows on her knees. "Here is what I don't understand. He held back the entire Soviet Union with their tanks and cannons and helicopters. Why couldn't he hold the Taliban fighters back? Why were there so many casualties? Did he have a bad strategy? Is there any chance that he is growing too weary of war to be as effective as he once was? Is he nearly played out?"

from that flame

"You are comparing two different wars in two different places," Abdullah protested. "He kept the Soviets from getting into the Panjshir Valley, not a city filled with civilians. The Soviets weren't any good at guerrilla fighting, and the Pakistani and Taliban are. The Soviets didn't usually target civilians. The Taliban doesn't care who they kill. Civilians and combatants are the same to them.

"Do you have any idea how many displaced people headed north to escape the Taliban? *Four hundred thousand!* They knew that Massoud was in the north and that life in his territories was far better. Massoud would never turn anyone away, and the people poured in. They had no homes, no food, no work, and they looked to him for help. He felt responsible for all of them. Not only did he have to worry about crafting a battle strategy, he had to do it in a way that wouldn't kill thousands of innocent people who expected his protection. He doesn't count Taloqan as his worst defeat only because he lost land and buildings. He counts it as his worst defeat because those tens of thousands of people sought his protection ended up either dead or back under Taliban control."

Michelle sat quietly for several minutes before she raised her eyes and looked at Abdullah. "I knew there was something he wasn't telling me. He had given me the facts about the loss of Taloqan before the assassin showed up. The plan was that he was going to discuss his feelings about the whole thing at a later time, but when I tried to bring it up again, he didn't want to discuss it and changed the subject. That was after the shooting."

"I'm not sure I follow," Abdullah said.

"He told me that he felt as if he had failed to keep me safe when I had to defend his life. It probably dredged up all the painful feelings he had related to the defeat in Taloqan since he felt he had failed to protect and defend the people there too. Plus, I was already feeling pretty shaky myself. He wasn't going to add to that by burdening me with more of his regrets. I knew there was something he was holding back, and that surprised me because he had always been candid and honest about everything."

"You asked your questions in such a way as to trigger an emotional response from me," Dr. Abdullah said, smiling ruefully. "You caused me to defend him when no defense was necessary."

"Yes, I did," Michelle admitted. "I needed the truth, and I

wasn't sure how else to get it. I didn't want a logical, military analysis of why the battle failed. Massoud already gave me that. I needed to know the emotions behind it all, which were what the Commander wasn't telling me. That's what you did."

"Yes, I did," Dr. Abdullah said and stood up abruptly.

Michelle hopped to her feet. "Please, don't be angry." She put a restraining hand on his arm. "I needed to know the whole story. I would have pestered him until he told me. You saved him from my nagging questions. And what you told me is not a secret, is it? If you say it is, I will strike it from the story, and no one will ever hear about it from me, I swear. But I think it makes him more human, Abdullah, and that is a good thing. Look, the man is a legend. He is practically a myth. Maybe that's why other journalists haven't been able to elicit the response to his struggle that he has hoped to get. Maybe no one believes that this mythical lion really needs help."

The doctor could not doubt the sincerity of her plea. His annoyance began to melt away.

"Let me put a human face on the legend," Michelle continued. "Let me make a mythical man capable of remorse and defeat. He remains a brilliant military mind who is completely devoted to the freedom of his people and his country. He remains all the amazing and extraordinary things he truly is. And when he also becomes human and fallible in other people's eyes, he'll still be worthy of help."

Dr. Abdullah nodded. "I understand what you are trying to do. Perhaps you are correct. He will see the draft before you leave, won't he?"

"Yes."

"Then he will decide if your approach is a good one."

"He already told me that he wouldn't influence the approach I chose to take. He told me that he trusts my decision."

"Then the matter is settled and there is nothing more to discuss. I must go now. I have work to do."

"Abdullah *Jaan*, am I forgiven?" Michelle looked up at him with genuine remorse. "I am sorry. Please don't stay angry with me."

"I am not angry. Massoud warned me that you were unpredictable and unlike anyone we have ever met before. I should have been better prepared."

"Is that 'yes, I'm forgiven'?"

"Yes, you are forgiven," the doctor said and smiled, this time genuinely. "I will let you get back to your writing. Are we still having dinner this evening?"

"I hope we are. I promise not to ask you a single question."

"I don't think that's possible," Abdullah said with a laugh.

Early on the third morning after his departure for Tajikistan, Commander Massoud returned to his compound. "Welcome back," Dr. Abdullah shouted over the engine noise as he helped Massoud step down from the helicopter. The Commander's leg was heavily bandaged almost from hip to knee, and his pant leg was cut short to accommodate the bulky wrapping. He carefully allowed his body weight to distribute evenly on both feet.

"Are you in pain?" Abdullah asked.

"Not too much." Massoud allowed Abdullah to put his arm around the Commander's waist and help support him. He flung his arm over the doctor's shoulder for extra support. "What has been happening here? What have I missed?"

"It's been quiet. We had a message from General Fahim. He is training his men together with Dostum's men as you requested."

"Good. What about Kahn's men? Are they on their way?"

"Yes. We can expect them in a few days."

"By then I will be ready for them," Massoud said. "I want you to take these drainage tubes out of my leg so the incision can start to close and heal."

"The drainage tubes are in there for a reason. I will look at the wound before deciding about when they come out," Abdullah said firmly. "Right now we are going to have you lie down and get off that leg."

"Why do doctor's always use 'we' when the patient does everything alone?" Massoud grumbled.

"Now you sound like Michelle when she complained that all doctors use the phrase 'the patient is resting comfortably,'" Abdullah said with a laugh.

"How is she? Where is she?" Massoud looked around as if he

had expected her to be part of the welcoming committee.

"Fine. She's driving everyone crazy by banging on the type-writer eighteen hours a day. I check in on her every few hours, and we have been having dinner together. Once you are settled and rested, I will send her to you if you'd like."

"I need to go to the office, not to bed," Commander Massoud countered. "I've been away for almost three days. I need to be informed about all the recent developments."

"I will send your advisors to you as well—after you have rest-ed from your trip."

"You are worse than my wife and mother combined," Mas-soud grumbled as he allowed the doctor to steer him away from the office towards his quarters.

"I'm sure I am," Abdullah said, unconcerned and unfazed by his friend's comments. "On the other hand, I wouldn't want to answer to your wife if your leg had to be amputated because I was negligent and allowed you to be stubborn. The men asked if they could have a *nazer* this evening. They want to give thanks for your safe return."

"Are you going to let me attend?" Massoud asked dryly.

"I think the guest of honor's presence is required—at least for a short while," the doctor conceded. "However, you must rest first."

"I wish to see Michelle Garrett," Commander Massoud said in reply.

"I will send her to you in an hour," said the stubborn doctor before forcing his recalcitrant patient into bed. Exactly an hour later, after quietly knocking, Michelle stuck her head in the door of Massoud's quarters.

"Are you awake? May I come in?"

"*Balay, lotfan,*" Massoud said eagerly. " Yes, please come in." He started to rise, winced in pain, and lowered himself back down. "Forgive me for not getting up."

"I'd have to knock you back down if you did. I brought you tea," Michelle said and handed him the steaming cup she carried. She settled herself on the rug next to where he was lying.

"It's good to see you. How are you feeling?" she asked.

"I feel fine. I would be up and working in my office if Abdul-

from that flame

lah was a more reasonable man. How have you been faring?"

"Doctor Abdullah is an eminently reasonable man. I am fine, thank you for asking. The article is really starting to take shape."

"Abdullah said you were driving everyone in the compound crazy by pounding on the typewriter all day and night," Massoud said with a smile.

"Maybe he isn't so reasonable after all," Michelle replied. "I haven't composed on a typewriter in years. I'm used to my computer which has a word processing program so that I don't have to start a page over every time I make a mistake."

"Even if we managed to get you a computer, you'd only have electricity for a few hours a day—hardly enough for what you are trying to do."

"I have a laptop in my hotel in Peshawar," Michelle said with a laugh. "Well, I had one two weeks ago. Remember, I sort of sneaked across the border on a whim. I thought I'd meet you, head to Kabul for that interview, and be back in Peshawar within three days. Lugging the laptop didn't seem worth the effort. I'm especially glad I didn't bring it since I doubt it would have survived these past ten days."

"You barely survived these past ten days," Commander Massoud said, shaking his head. "Are your adventures finding their way into your article?"

"Only as they apply to your struggle here. I think I am going to end up with three stories. One about RAWA that I still hope to finish. One about you I am working on now, and one strictly about my experiences since coming to Afghanistan."

"I look forward to reading them all."

"You are a central figure in them. I hope that when you read them, you don't regret letting me spend all this time with you. I don't want to disappoint you."

"I don't see how that could be possible," Massoud assured her. "I told you that I trust you. I mean that. You will tell the truth as you see it. I ask for no more than that. Where there is bad, you will find a proportionate amount of good. Where there is ugliness, you will balance it with beauty. Where there is despair, you will discover the symmetry of hope. I know these things, and I do not worry."

"Thank you for your faith in me," she said simply. "Now, I

am back to work, and you are back to recovering."

"Will you return later?" Massoud asked wistfully. "Abdullah won't let me do anything until tomorrow, and I miss our long conversations."

"I thought the men were having a celebration?"

"Abdullah will only let me go for an hour. He wants me to stay off my leg while these drainage tubes are still in."

"Then I'll be back," Michelle said as she stood up. "You still need to tell me a victory story, remember? Think about your best defeating-the-Soviets story so that you can tell it to me when I come back."

"I'll be waiting," Commander Massoud said, leaned back into the pillows, and closed his eyes. He had several memories to sift through before Michelle returned, and once the *nazer* had begun, he wouldn't have the luxury of quiet thought.

"I'm glad you're here," Commander Massoud said to Michelle when she returned later in the evening. "Is that food and tea?"

"*Balay*. Yes." Michelle carefully lowered herself and the tray to the rug. She had stayed in her room during the *nazer*, but the sounds of the men laughing, singing, celebrating, and praying reached her ears. She searched the Commander's face for signs of excessive fatigue or pain, but he looked well, cheerful, and wide-awake. She handed him the tray.

"Tea, bread, and dried mulberries?" Massoud said as he looked at the food in dismay. "Are we out of food?" His eyes met Michelle's, and he saw the laughter dancing in them.

"I thought this was your favorite meal," Michelle said, trying not to giggle. "You mean it's not?"

"Very funny," Massoud said dryly.

"You ate well at the *nazer*, didn't you?" Michelle asked innocently.

"I could eat a little more," the Commander said emphatically.

"Good, because I have a little more." Just then Abdullah came around the corner and into the Commander's range of vision. He carried another tray in his hands.

from that flame

"You are in on this, too?" Massoud started to laugh as he accepted the tray from his friend. "Are you two 'ganging up' on me again?"

"Yes," Michelle and Abdullah said at the same time.

"We are co-conspirators," Abdullah said. "I told Michelle I was concerned I would not be able to make you rest much longer. We decided to join forces and 'gang up' on you. This was a trial run. How did we do working together?"

"Well enough that I think I am in trouble. Neither of you deserves anything more than tea and mulberries for dinner," he scolded but with laughter in his voice.

"I already ate," Michelle said. It was good to hear his laugh again. "But if you promise to be good and stay still, we will keep you company while you eat."

"All right, I promise," Massoud said, picking up his tea cup, "although I have a feeling I should be negotiating a truce among us."

"No negotiations," the doctor said, shaking his head. "You are staying here until I say you can get up. Now eat your food."

Massoud arched an eyebrow and looked at Michelle. "See what happens when I leave for a few days? He thinks he's in charge."

Michelle looked over at Abdullah. "You told me you are in charge when he's gone. He seems to be disputing your claim."

"He's delusional," Abdullah said with a dismissive wave of his hand. "I've seen it happen in cases like this."

"I see," Michelle said sagely. "And what can be done about his delusion?"

"Well," the doctor said thoughtfully, "we could indulge him for a little while. It might not hurt to let him continue thinking he's in charge."

"I'm not so sure," Michelle replied. "I have heard that delusional people can be dangerous to themselves and others."

"That is true in some cases—" Abdullah stopped speaking when Commander Massoud began to laugh so hard he spilled his tea.

"You two need your own show," Massoud said as he shifted his body away from the damp spot on the bedding beneath him.

"Good job, my fellow conspirator," Michelle said as she offered her hand to Dr. Abdullah. He shook it as he laughed and stood up.

"All right, I trust you can keep him in bed while I go to the office? I'll be back in a little while."

"We'll be here," Michelle said and looked over at Massoud, who was still laughing. "Eat your food, Commander, and then tell me a story of victory."

"I know exactly the one to tell." Massoud dug into his food with a real appetite. "Facts first?"

Michelle pulled out her notepad from her coat pocket. "Yes, please," she answered. "The same five Ws."

"It's a long story," Massoud warned.

"Oh, well, then I'd better not listen to it. I have so many other places I need to be and other things I need to be doing," Michelle said with mock sarcasm.

Massoud shook his head and chuckled. This was the Michelle he feared had disappeared forever the moment she pulled the trigger and killed the would-be assassin. His felt enormously relieved that she appeared to have somehow found her equilibrium again during the time he was in Dushanbe. Perhaps returning to the work she loved had helped her. Whatever the cause, he was grateful to hear her laughing and teasing again.

Forcing his mind back to the matter at hand, he gathered his thoughts to answer her question. His face darkened, and his smile vanished. There was no way to present this story in a completely positive light.

"Afghan politics and war are a complicated tale. I told you how the Soviets came into my country to support the Communist government?"

"Yes. You had been trained as a saboteur in Pakistan to undermine the Communist government that had forced the king into exile. You must have been doing a good job if the Soviet Union had to send in their army to settle the unrest," Michelle commented.

"I hadn't thought about it quite that way," the Commander said and smiled a little sadly. He shrugged. "Whatever the reason, in 1979 they sent in a division they called the 'Limited Contingent of Soviet Forces.' They quickly moved into the populated areas and gained control. They established bases in several places. They began working with the Afghan army that was, of course, run by the Communist government. I believe that in the early stages, the Soviets hoped to avoid direct confrontation with the Afghan rebels. They thought they could use the Afghan army proper to quell our uprising."

"And the *Mujahidin* was born," Michelle said softly. "Ahmed Shah *Jaan*, what if you had known then that you would be a *mujahidin* fighter twenty years later? Would you have still joined the fight?"

"Yes, of course I would have," Massoud answered quickly, as if he had asked himself the same question many times and knew the answer by heart. "This was the path God laid out before me, to defend my people and their lands. I could not choose a different path. One of my favorite Dari poets, Jalauddin Rumi, wrote:

> Consider the difference
> in our actions and God's actions.
> We often ask, 'Why did you do that?'
> or 'Why did I act like that?
> We do act, yet everything we do
> Is God's creative action.
> We look back and analyze the events
> Of our lives, but there is another way
> of seeing, a backward-and-forward-at-once
> vision, that is not rationally understandable.
> Only God can understand it.

"I think of those lines often when I am inclined to ask 'why?'," Massoud concluded quietly.

"I know that poem," Michelle said in an equally quiet voice. "I think it is the same one." She spoke slowly as she translated the words into French.

> Ignorance is God's prison.
> Knowing is God's palace.
> We sleep in God's unconsciousness.
> We wake in God's open hand.

from that flame

We weep God's rain.
We laugh God's lightening.
Fighting and peacefulness
Both take place within God.
Who are we then
in this complicated world-tangle
that is really just the single, straight
line down at the beginning of Allah?

"You know the words by heart?" Massoud asked with delight. "You will never cease to amaze me, Michelle Garrett."

Michelle blushed under his approving stare. "You aren't the only one who likes poetry, you know," she mumbled. She glanced at her notes before meeting his gaze. "So the Soviets thought they could use the Afghan army to quell your resistance?" she asked, desperate to change the subject.

Commander Massoud smiled faintly. He understood this woman now and obediently returned to their previous discussion. "The Afghan army was not prepared well enough to do the job they were asked, and the president, a man named Karmal, asked the LCSF to fight against us. The problem the Limited Contingent had was that they relied on traditional, combined-arms tactics. We knew we would not be able to defeat them in a conventional battle, so we turned to guerrilla tactics instead. We would launch surprise attacks against them and return to the mountains before they could rally and find their guns.

"The Soviets sent in more tanks and armored personnel carriers. It didn't do them any good. We didn't try to take them head-on in a battle we could never win. Unfortunately for them but good for us, the Soviets remained conventional in their thinking and tactics. The *mujahidin* began inflicting heavy casualties against them. I have never understood why they were unable to grasp completely the concept of guerrilla fighting."

"Can you give me an example of a guerrilla operation?" Michelle asked with interest.

Commander Massoud thought for a minute before answering. "They would send a column of tanks and armored personnel carriers into very narrow mountain passages in the Panjshir Valley. We would lie low and wait until their convoy was in an area we had pre-designated and either mined or seeded with bombs on a delay switch. We would then set off the explosive device, crippling both the front and rear vehicle in the convoy. That meant all the vehicles in between were trapped. They couldn't go forward or backward, and the road wasn't wide enough to turn around. Since we were situated higher in the mountains, it was easy to pick the soldiers off one by one."

"They never caught on to this plan of attack?" Michelle asked in amazement. "I would have thought once would do the trick."

"The Soviets tried to breach Panjshir nine different times, and nine times we repelled them. Eventually they started sending helicopters in to provide air support of their convoys, but by then, as I told you earlier, we had surface-to-air missiles and US-made Stinger missiles." Massoud started to smile to himself.

"What are you recalling?" Michelle asked with anticipation.

Massoud was eager to tell the story. "One time we shot down a helicopter, but it was not seriously damaged. We captured it and managed to repair it and get it operating again. We used it to travel up and down the valley ourselves. It was demoralizing for the Soviets to see us use their helicopter that way. We knew that one day they would try to recover it."

"Did they?"

Massoud's smile broadened. "Oh, yes, they did. We left it in a place that would be relatively accessible to them. They must have felt such glee to think we had left it unguarded. What they had no way of knowing, of course, was that we had left a few supplies onboard when we abandoned it."

"Supplies?" Michelle asked, trying to coax the Commander, though he needed no coaxing.

Massoud shook his head as he recalled the triumph. "We left behind a rather large amount of explosives. It rained helicopter parts for half a kilometer."

"They must have hated and feared you," Michelle observed.

"I lost track of how many times they tried to assassinate me," Massoud rested his head on his hand. "I had good intelligence, better than theirs, and was always warned in time. Once they kidnapped the family of an Afghan man and told him they would kill his family unless he killed me."

"How horrible," Michelle gasped. "What happened? What

did the poor man do?"

"He came to me," Massoud answered with a small smile. "We set up a ruse that lasted for several days. Word spread that Ahmed Shah Massoud had been killed. I was hidden safely away, and no one but Abdullah knew where to find me. At least the Soviets honored their word. When notice reached them that I had been killed, they released his family. Once I knew he and his family were safe, it was amazing how quickly I came back to life."

The Commander saw a look on Michelle's face that he couldn't quite figure out. "What?" he asked. "Did I say something that troubles you? Or are you only surprised that the Soviets kept their word?"

"I was thinking about the man," Michelle said slowly, "and about how much he must have trusted you." Michelle looked at Massoud almost as intently as he studied her. "He knew that in the worst moment of his life—at a time when he was most afraid—he could come to you for help, and that you wouldn't let him down."

"I don't find it remarkable that one man would be willing to help another man save his family," Massoud said seriously. He was genuinely perplexed by Michelle's comment. "I know I would do anything to save mine."

"Did it ever cross your mind to tell him that you were in the middle of a war, that you had more important concerns, that this was his concern and not yours?"

"No," Massoud answered.

"That," Michelle said emphatically, "is remarkable whether you realize it or not."

"I still don't understand," Massoud said.

"I know, and that is one of the most endearing things about you," Michelle answered. "I think tonight's interview is concluded. You should get some rest." She started to put away her pad and pen.

"But there is more to tell," Massoud said quickly.

"And there is tomorrow in which to tell it. I don't want Doctor Abdullah coming in here and throwing me out."

"He will understand that we are in the middle of something," Commander Massoud persisted.

from that flame

"Are we talking about the same Doctor Abdullah?" Michelle asked skeptically. "A sort of tall fellow, balding a little, with very nice eyes? That Doctor Abdullah?

"Ah, but you said he was an eminently reasonable man!" the Commander reminded her.

"Okay, so maybe he is a little less than reasonable when it comes to risking your health and well-being. I could offer you a therapeutic back massage, but I don't think you can lie on your stomach without hurting your leg. Can you rest comfortably on your side?"

"It is not necessary," Commander Massoud said. "You don't need an excuse to stay longer. When Abdullah comes, I will tell him I insisted. That will be sufficient for him."

"I'm not worried about Abdullah," Michelle laughed. "I used him as an excuse to strengthen my argument that you should sleep now."

Massoud was irritated. "I think I am able to decide when I wish to sleep."

"All right," Michelle said, suppressing a smile. "Then we will talk a while longer. When did you say you are going to be in Paris?"

"I am scheduled to be there on April fourth, God willing. After Paris, I am going to Brussels to address the European Union. Why?"

"We talked about whether or not you would have any free time to see the city."

"Perhaps a little. If I have time, what will you take me to see?"

"Am I the tour guide?" Michelle asked.

Commander Massoud was delighted to make the appointment. "*Oui*," he replied.

"Hmmm...let's see..." Michelle said slowly as she thought. "Since you would appreciate the architecture of that grand city, we would have to take a driving tour at the very least. You would want to see some of the usual attractions such as the Arch de Triumph and the Eiffel Tower, but the drive shouldn't be limited to places like that. You should also see some of the smaller streets and neighborhoods, don't you think?"

from that flame

"That sounds very nice. I would like to see how average people live. What else? If I have only a little time, what one thing should I see first?"

"I would say the Louvre, but you couldn't possibly see it in a short time. If there is only a short amount of time, then we should go to a local restaurant to eat."

"Will any local restaurant suffice, or do you have a particular one in mind?" Massoud was enjoying this new game.

"Two actually, so we will have to make a difficult decision. One is Chardenoux on rue Jules Valles, and the other is Pharamond on rue de la Grande Truanderie. It is quite close to the Louvre. If we eat quickly, perhaps we will have time to see at least a room or two at the museum."

"What foods do these restaurants serve? And are you certain their food contains no condoms?"

Michelle swatted his arm. "They serve bread, dried mulberries, and sugared almonds, of course. The staples of life."

"And green tea?" the Commander said, laughing.

Michelle joined in the laughter. "*Certainement!*"

"Ah, Michelle *Jaan*," Commander Massoud said as he looked at her fondly, "I will miss you when you leave, but knowing that I will see you again soon in Paris makes it much better."

"For me too, *Amir Saheb*. Who knows? By then a magazine may be interested in the story, and I will be able to tell you a publication date."

"And the date when you will bring me several copies of the magazine."

"Yes." Michelle picked up her water glass and handed the Commander his. "We have a custom of touching our glasses together and making what we call a 'toast.' It is a hope for or an acknowledgment of something that is special."

"And you wish to make a toast?"

"To Paris," Michelle said, touching her glass against his and then taking a sip of the water.

"To Paris," Massoud repeated and also drank. "And now may I make a toast as well? A toast to our continued friendship."

Again Michelle tapped his glass with her own. "To our continued friendship. May it grow and prosper over the years."

198

from that flame

They both drank again.

Michelle set her glass aside. "You look tired. Are you?"

"I am," Massoud admitted, "but you should not leave yet. I do not want you walking around the compound alone in the dark. You must wait for Abdullah. He should be here soon."

"In that case, you should roll onto your side and let me massage your back. I won't be here much longer, and you should take advantage of the opportunity while you can."

"I would never take advantage of you," Massoud.

"Advantage of the opportunity, not me." Michelle corrected him. "I know that you would never take advantage of me. You are simply incapable of harming a woman, child, or elderly person. It is one of the mysteries about you I hope to understand one day."

"Mysteries?" Massoud asked sleepily.

"How the Lion of Panjshir could be ferocious enough to defeat the Soviet Union and the Taliban and then be such a pussycat to ordinary people."

"Pussycat? I don't know that term."

"Shhh …. I'll explain it tomorrow. Sleep now." Michelle noted with satisfaction that his eyes were closing and his breathing was changing. When Abdullah walked in a few minutes later, she quickly raised her finger to her lips.

"Is he asleep?" Abdullah whispered.

"Just barely," Michelle answered and stood up. "He wouldn't let me leave until you could walk me across the compound. I'm sorry to be so much trouble to you."

"He's right, of course, and it is no trouble. Are you ready to go?"

"Yes." Michelle put on her coat and picked up her paper and pen. "I don't understand the need for an escort," she said in a low voice as they left the room. "I've been with you and your men for nearly two weeks. They all know me. I can't believe any of them would hurt me."

"You are right," the doctor agreed. "Nevertheless—"

"Nevertheless, I am a woman, and women should be escorted," Michelle interrupted.

"I was going to say, nevertheless, you are our guest, and it is polite to escort one's guest rather than send her wandering around alone in the dark. That would be bad manners."

"A handsome, gallant doctor who is well-mannered to boot." Michelle slipped her arm through his and asked, "How is it you have only one wife?" she teased. "You can explain it to me as we walk."

12. Greatness

The next morning Michelle stuck her head in the door of Commander Massoud's quarters and asked, "Are you awake? May I come in?"

"Yes to both questions," Commander Massoud replied, struggling to sit up. Michelle set the tray down, reached for the pillows, and rearranged them behind him for better support. The *sandali* had fresh charcoal in the brazier, and the room was warm and comfortable.

"I brought you breakfast," Michelle said as she shoved the last pillow into place.

"You are very good to me. Thank you."

Michelle set the tray within easy reach for him. "I have an ulterior motive. I'm still unclear on a few historical points, and I was hoping you would fill in the blanks for me."

"It would be my pleasure," Massoud said, sipping his hot tea.

"Thanks." Michelle settled herself onto a nearby carpet and took out the small notepad that was now nearly full of her scribbled words. "In 1986 the Soviets replaced President Karmal with a man named Najibullah," she began. "They hoped he would be acceptable to the Afghan population, but he wasn't. The *mujahidin* continued to fight. Is that correct so far?"

Massoud nodded. "It was around that time we started to get more aid from the outside world."

"Was the US involved at that point?" Michelle asked and then wrote a reminder to check a few State Department sources after she returned to Islamabad.

from that flame

"Yes, in many ways. We worked with the CIA. They would locate weapons and ammunition and get them to us through various intermediary countries. They also arranged for us to get Stinger missiles."

"Hence the story you told me yesterday," Michelle observed thoughtfully. "But why did the Soviets want to control the Panjshir Valley so badly?"

"They couldn't fully control Afghanistan without it. They had access to the Khyber Pass which enabled them to travel back and forth into Pakistan, but to get to the Northeast—including the Silk Route to China—they had to cross the Shomali Planes, come through the Salang Tunnel, and travel through Panjshir." Massoud's hands sliced the air in a habit to which Michelle was now well accustomed but found no less compelling.

"Which you would never let them do," Michelle said factually as she wrote furiously. She glanced up at the Commander. "Are you aware that a major US newspaper, *The Wall Street Journal*, credits you as the man who brought down the Soviet Union and ended the Cold War?"

Commander Massoud smiled. "I have heard that. It is an exaggeration. Eventually the Soviet Union realized it was in a war it could never win, that's all. It decided to negotiate a means of withdrawing its troops, but it intended to keep control of the government and have Afghanistan remain a Communist-controlled country."

"Wouldn't that have still been unacceptable to you?" Michelle stumbled over her double negative. "I mean, you wanted the Communists gone way before the Soviets showed up, so you wouldn't have accepted a communist government with or without the presence of the Soviet military."

Commander Massoud nodded in agreement. "I wish the Communists had all gone when the Soviets did. However, that was not the case. In 1988, a Geneva Accord was signed that allowed for the withdrawal of Soviet troops between May of that year and February of the next year. The *mujahidin* hoped and expected that the government headed by Najibullah would collapse once the troops withdrew. It didn't. We were determined to continue our fight against the Communists."

"The Soviets were gone by February of 1989, right?" Michelle

from that flame

wanted to double-check the date.

"Yes, the military was gone, but their influence and interference were not. We *mujahidin* continued our resistance. It wasn't until 1991, when the Soviet Union was collapsing, that Boris Yeltsin began talks to end the crisis. They replaced Najibullah with a counsel of Afghan army officers and politicos still allied with them. This time the various *mujahidin* factions decided to work together to take back Kabul."

"A goal you did accomplish."

Commander Massoud sighed and looked sorrowful, a reaction Michelle had come to expect whenever the failed Rabbani government in Kabul was mentioned.

"Yes, a goal we accomplished," he said slowly. "I will always regret that we were unable to better utilize the opportunity we were given."

"I can only imagine," Michelle said softly. "It must have been extremely disappointing that after twelve years of war, you were unable to build the government you had envisioned. You have always taken responsibility for that. But didn't you also say that outside forces were once again at work?"

"Pakistan had its own plans for Afghanistan," Massoud agreed. "It wanted to use us as a rear guard in the event they went to war with India. It still does."

"And because of that ongoing effort, Pakistan is also responsible for the Taliban?"

"Yes."

"What do you do now?" Michelle watched Commander Massoud's face closely as she waited for a response.

The Commander shrugged. "Continue to resist. It's all that we have left to do. If we lay down our arms and allow the Taliban to assume control of the entire country, Afghanistan might as well become part of Pakistan completely." He scratched his beard thoughtfully. "I have wondered if we should try to establish a separate government here in the North. We could have elections, build schools and hospitals, and give the people here a better life. The people in the Taliban-controlled areas could move here if they wished."

"But would the Taliban allow that? Surely they would still try to destroy you?"

203

"Of course they wouldn't allow it, and of course we must continue to resist their incursion into our territories. I don't really want a divided country. None of us do. We have plans to take future actions against the Taliban. I have hope that we will succeed."

"Tell me," Michelle said eagerly. "What new torment do you have planned for them?"

"I told you that other commanders have agreed to join forces with me. We are having a meeting soon. I think we are talking about an additional twenty thousand fighters. Also, when I was in Dushanbe, I arranged the purchase of five transport helicopters. This will give us the added mobility that we need."

"What about firepower?"

"We have new tanks and armored vehicles coming," Massoud said, smiling mysteriously.

"Okay, I won't press you to give away secrets," Michelle said with a short laugh. She glanced over her recent notes. "What about the political aspects of forming a new government? I know you want to be careful not to make the same mistakes you have made in the past."

"No, that is one area in which we must make changes. There are two other Afghan leaders with whom we believe we can work. One man is named Abdul Haq and the other is Hamid Karzai. They are Pashtun and therefore acceptable to the majority of the Afghan people. Since they have not been living in Afghanistan in recent years, they don't have blood on their hands as I do. I will be meeting with them in the summer."

Michelle finished scribbling down her notes. "I think that is everything for the moment. If I discover that I have gaps, may I come back as I write the article and pester you some more?"

"You never pester me," Commander Massoud said sincerely.

"Then may I ask one more question? It is a question I have asked and you have answered before, but I am still not sure I understand your answer."

Commander Massoud's brow creased with concern. "What is it?"

"Where do you find the strength to keep fighting? I have been listening to story after story of battles. Twenty years of war! Don't you crave respite from the physical hardships you have endured

from that flame

for such a long time? Aren't you sick of guns and tanks, of maps and battle plans, of friends bleeding and dying? Why haven't you walked away as so many others have?"

"The *Qur'an* teaches that 'whosoever submits himself entirely to Allah, and he is a doer of good, he has his reward from his Lord, and there is no fear for him nor shall he grieve.' I am a servant of my country, my people, and God. This is the path God laid before me. Who am I to question him?"

"Okay," Michelle said slowly. "I understand how that could explain the spiritual aspects of this *jihad*." She studied Commander Massoud intently. "What else? How do you force the mind and body to go where the spirit guides when the path is fraught with sorrow and peril?"

The Commander's eyes met Michelle's with such intensity, she couldn't have looked away if she tried. There was an impassioned, smoldering fire burning deep inside those eyes. Michelle sensed it was a fire that would never be quenched until his country and fellow Afghans were free. The personal cost to him would always be consumed by the larger fire surrounding it. Did all heroes, revolutionaries, and men of vision have this look in their eyes? She knew she was in the presence of an extraordinary man, a once-in-a-century kind of man. She thought about the old saying that some men are born to greatness, some achieve greatness, and some have greatness thrust upon them. Ahmed Shah Massoud might be the first and only man she ever met who fit into all three categories of greatness.

She suddenly realized that he was speaking, and she wasn't hearing him. She forced herself to focus on his words. "Of course there are times when the daily hardships of life seem too much to bear," he was saying, "but I think once a decision is made about a certain course of action, when the determination is there, staying for the long term is easier. I made a decision many years ago that I would not stop fighting until Afghanistan is free and has the right to self-determination. That is what I now live to achieve. Everything else is secondary to that decision."

Massoud watched Michelle with amusement. "No wonder I have to answer the same questions for you more than once. You daydream in the middle of my answers."

Michelle began to blush a deep, hot red. Flustered, she gripped her pen and tablet so tightly, her knuckles turned white.

"I'm sorry," she stammered.

"*Nay.*" Massoud reached for the pen and pad she held so that she would not put them away and then leave. "I was teasing; honestly, I was."

"But I was thinking about something other than what you were saying," Michelle admitted, releasing the pad and pen to him. "It was both rude and unprofessional. I am sorry."

"It's all right," he said softly with a gentle smile and handed the items back to her. "I don't flatter myself enough to think that every thought, word, and deed of mine is worthy of attention. Do you want to tell me what distracted you? Is there some problem, some concern with which I might help?"

"No," Michelle said and stood up. "I'm going to get back to work. Abdullah insists that the sound of the typewriter is driving everyone crazy, and he asked me to stop no later than eight at night. That means I have to work double-time during the day. Thank you for your time, Commander."

She was out the door before Massoud could say anything. He looked in puzzlement at the space she had vacated and tried to figure out what part of their conversation had caused such an odd and unexpected reaction from her. He had teased her two dozen times in the past without her becoming upset. He had offered assistance numerous times. He had truthfully answered every question she ever asked. What was he missing? He was very glad she had agreed to meet him in Paris. As hard as he tried, there were still many things about the Western mind he did not understand. Michelle could explain certain subtleties to him when they were in Europe. He hoped that she would explain to him what had happened in the course of the conversation before they reached Paris, however.

Michelle glanced at her watch just as a knock came at her door. "I'm quitting," she shouted. "I need five minutes."

Massoud's voice came from the other side of the door. "I can wait five minutes."

"You're up!" Michelle shouted as she leapt to her feet and hurried to open the door. When she saw the Commander standing there leaning on a cane, her eyes narrowed. "Does Doctor

from that flame

Abdullah know you're walking?" she asked in a loud whisper as she peered over his shoulders as if she expected the other man to come bursting through the door.

"Doctor Abdullah removed the drainage tube from my leg himself, bandaged it, and gave me permission to take a short walk. As long as I use this," he said, brandishing the cane.

"And you came here? I am honored, sir. I would ask you to sit down, but I don't have any chairs—and anyway, you've been sitting for days."

"I was hoping you would accompany me on a walk around the interior perimeter of the compound. It is not terribly cold. I need to talk to you about something."

"Let's go," Michelle said, grabbing her coat. "Abdullah and I walked when you were in Dushanbe. I enjoyed it."

She walked out the door with the Commander a few steps behind. She still seemed nervous and ill at ease to Massoud.

"I know there are men out there somewhere," Michelle said, pointing to the wall that surrounded the compound, "but I've never seen them." What a stupid topic of conversation, she thought. However, nothing equally safe and nonchalant came to mind.

"Good. You shouldn't see them," Commander Massoud said and looked at her oddly.

"Are you sure they're there?" Michelle said hurriedly. Oh, shut up! she yelled at herself.

"Yes, I'm sure." Massoud was trying to figure out what this conversation was about. Did she feel threatened or unsafe? "There are men on both the interior and exterior perimeters of the wall. There are men on the rooftops. There are men stationed at the farthest perimeter of the compound. There are men at one and two perimeter outward points. is there a reason you are concerned?"

"No, just curious," Michelle said as lightly as she could considering she felt like an idiot.

"Could we walk a little more slowly?" Massoud asked.

Michelle immediately slowed down. Since he could make no sense of her conversation, he decided to initiate the one he needed to have with her.

"Your safety is exactly what I want to talk about," he began.

from that flame

"I learned a short while ago that both Abdullah and I need to leave the compound for a few days. It is time for the meeting I am having with the other commanders, and I need Abdullah to go with me."

"How long will you be gone?" Michelle asked.

"Three, maybe four days."

"Do you want to send me to Peshawar? I can leave if that would be easier for you."

"It had not occurred to me," Massoud answered, "although it is an option, I suppose. If you want to do that, I will, of course, make all the necessary preparations before I leave in the morning."

"What is another option? Going with you?"

Massoud shook his head. "Not this time. I was hoping you would stay here and wait for my return, but there are conditions that might not make that as appealing an option to you as going to Peshawar."

Curiosity replaced her discomfort. "What conditions?"

"I would want you to stay in your room. I have a trusted aide who speaks English and would make sure you had food, water, and coals for the brazier. If there is anything else you want, he will check on you several times a day, and you need only ask him. I would post someone at your door as an additional security measure."

"Why all the precautions? Your men wouldn't harm me."

"No, of course they wouldn't. My concern is that in the unlikely event the compound came under attack, they wouldn't know best how to keep you safe. They will react as they have been trained. That could result in you being left alone in the compound. I don't want that to happen. If you stay in your room, and if the man outside has special orders to protect you, I won't have to worry about leaving you here."

Michelle shook her head in amazement. "How do you do that?"

"What?"

"Think of every last detail? Plan six steps ahead of everyone else? I would hate to play chess with you."

"You play chess?" Massoud asked with delight. "We shall play when I get back."

"Didn't you just hear me say that I would hate to play that game with you?" Michelle demanded, but there was a twinkle in her eyes.

"I'll change your mind," Massoud said with a grin. "I've been told I am persuasive."

Michelle laughed and shook her head. "You are relentless. There's a difference. Does anyone ever say no to you?"

"I seem to recall you and Abdullah saying that word to me several times in the past few days." They had come full circle back to Michelle's door. "Will you stay while I'm away?"

"Yes, I would like that. Maybe I can have the rough draft ready by the time you get back. Will I see you again before you leave?"

"We are leaving at first light."

"Then I will see you when you return. Have a safe trip, Ahmed Shah *Jaan*."

"I will see you in a few days." Commander Massoud smiled at her as he turned to go.

He turned back before she closed the door. "The aide I'm sending to you is named Assem Suhail. You'll like him."

13. Meeting

Are you comfortable?"

Dr. Abdullah looked from the driver's seat over to where Commander Massoud sat in the passenger seat watching the men get into the first vehicle in their small convoy. The Land Rover would again be sandwiched in between two armored vehicles.

"I'm fine," Massoud said absently. "Please stop worrying about me."

"It's a long drive," the doctor reminded him.

"Uh-huh," Massoud agreed absently. "Is Masood Khalili going to be at the meeting?"

"I believe he is coming in from New Deli, yes. Why?"

"I think he should attend the European Parliament meeting with us," Commander Massoud answered as the caravan began its journey.

"I agree," the doctor said. "Who else?"

"Besides you, you mean?" Massoud glanced over at his friend with a smile. "What do you think about taking Generals Anwari, Qol, and Noorzai?"

"I think that would be a good delegation," Abdullah answered. "Add the five of us to Charge d'Affaires Tandar and Ambassador Farhadi, and the Afghan people will be well represented." Abdullah Abdullah cast a sidelong glance at Massoud. "Is Michelle Garrett still planning to meet you in Paris?"

"Yes." Massoud offered no elaboration.

"Do you really think it is a good idea?" Abdullah asked quietly.

from that flame

"I need her there. I want her there," Massoud said firmly. "Nothing improper has ever occurred between us. She is a trusted friend."

"Ahmed Shah—"

"*Nay*. I do not wish to discuss it further," the commander said, cutting him off. He tipped his *pakol* down over his eyes and settled back into his seat. "I'm tired and will sleep now."

Dr. Abdullah drove over the rough roads as carefully as he could so that he would not awaken his sometimes stubborn friend.

The late afternoon sun was barely peeking over the farthest mountains when the convoy reached its destination. The location had been carefully selected for its remoteness. When the most powerful warlords and commanders whose combined forces made up the United Front planned a meeting, it was well served to prevent their common enemies from locating them.

Commander Massoud, who had been awake for hours silently watching the countryside as they drove, rubbed his eyes, opened the car door, and prepared to greet all of the other men assembled there. He had barely stepped out of the vehicle when his Chief of Intelligence and one of his oldest friends, Mohammed Fahim, greeted him with an embrace and a kiss on each cheek.

"*Salaam*. It is good to see you, my old friend," Fahim said quietly. "I was worried when I heard what happened. Are you well?" He looked pointedly at the cane Massoud was using.

Commander Massoud smiled reassuringly. "Do you think Abdullah would let me come if I wasn't? I'm fine, but I thank you for your concern."

"Except for Younis, no one else knows about the incident or the female journalist," Fahim continued in a low voice.

"We shall keep it that way," Massoud said quietly before turning to greet the other men who were approaching him. The first to reach him was his old ally in the war against the Soviet Union.

"Ismail Kahn," Ahmed Shah Massoud embraced the man with genuine warmth. "When I heard the Taliban had captured you, I was afraid I would never see you again."

from that flame

"It was a fortunate escape I made, *nay?*" the older man replied with a broad smile. "I have gathered my men from Heart. They are training now. We will be ready to join you whenever you give the word."

"I can give you 20,000 men," said a deep voice behind Kahn. "The rest I must keep around Mazar-i-sharif. But 20,000 of my men are worth 40,000 of anyone else's men."

Commander Massoud looked past Ismail Kahn to see his ally-turned-enemy-turned-ally again. "Their help will be welcome; *tashakur.*" Massoud extended his hand to Rashid Dostum, the Uzbek warlord who had supported the communist Najibullah and reportedly worked for the Soviet KGB.

Abdullah and Mohammed Fahim both watched Commander Massoud's face closely, but he never showed any of his true emotions. Massoud was a practical man. He may have hated Dostum at times, but he needed his men and artillery to participate in his next major assault against the Taliban. His personal thoughts and feelings came second to that.

Standing beside Dostum was another Uzbek resistance leader who had fought against the Soviet Union. Commander Massoud offered his hand next to Mohammed Ata.

"*Salaam.* It's been a long time, my friend," Commander Massoud said, warmly shaking Ata's hand.

Ata returned the Commander's smile. "*Balay.* Yes, it's been too long,"

"Thank you all for coming." Commander Massoud said, addressing the assembled men. He motioned towards a tent that had been set up nearby. "If we can all adjourn to the tent, we will have something to eat, and then we will talk."

Younis Qanooni stayed behind so that he could catch a moment alone with Massoud.

"I was very worried during those days you were missing, Ahmed Shah. When word reached me that one of the helicopters had crashed and that you might have been in it, my blood ran cold. Thank our merciful Allah that you are all right. Where would we all be without you? You truly are all right, aren't you?" The slender, spectacled man anxiously studied his friend's face.

"Yes, I am. And you would be fine without me," Commander Massoud assured his old friend. "But now that you mention it, there are some things I would like to discuss with you, Fahim, and Abdullah privately. Perhaps we can find time a little later this evening after the main meeting."

"I will tell them," Qanooni replied.

"Thank you," Massoud said, clasping his friend's shoulder. "And now let us go eat before the food is all gone." Leaning heavily on the cane for support, Commander Massoud slowly went with his advisor and friend to join the others.

The Tajik, Uzbek, and Hazar warlords—venerable comrades and ancient enemies bound inescapably together by years of war in a county where allegiances were determined by the enemy and by the circumstances of the moment—spent a social hour swapping tales of old battles won, valued friends lost, and glorious feats both achieved and only dreamed. Their conversation were peppered with as many a "do you remember?" as their hair and beards were with gray. No longer young and in their prime, the aging warriors came together once again at the invitation of the only man whose summons they would obey.

Commander Massoud watched and listened as he ate. His piercing gaze missed nothing as it roamed from man to man seeking something in the other men only Massoud himself could detect.

"Ahmed Shah?" Ismail Kahn repeated twice before Massoud heard him.

"I'm sorry. What did you ask?"

"I heard a story, and I want to know if it is true."

"If I did something strategically brilliant, probably," Commander Massoud said, smiling at his friend, "but if I did something foolish or ill-fated, probably not." Everyone laughed with Massoud. The Commander looked at Kahn. "Perhaps you should tell me what you heard."

"I was still in the Taliban prison, and I heard others whispering of how clever the Lion of Panjshir had been," Ismail Kahn began. He looked around at the other warlords seated in a large circle around him. "We were so desperate for distraction and amusement, men would often make up stories just to pass the time, and Massoud was always a favorite character in the tales they wove." Kahn looked back at Massoud.

"You still held the air base at Bagram last year, didn't you?

And the Taliban threw a huge force against you and forced you to retreat?"

"One of the foolish and ill-fated stories, I see," Commander Massoud said dryly. "Unfortunately, yes, we were routed from Bagram and retreated into Panjshir."

Ismail Kahn waved his hand dismissively. "That's not the part of the story I want to know about. It's what comes next that's important. Is it true that 400,000 civilians followed you in an attempt to escape the Taliban?"

Commander Massoud scratched his beard. "I never counted them, but that sounds like a good estimate. I remember hundreds of thousands of people pouring into Panjshir, and I didn't know how I was going to shelter and feed them all."

"Tell me what you did next," Kahn urged Massoud. "If I hear it from you, I will know it is true."

"I dynamited the walls of the Dalang Sang gorge," Massoud said with a small smile. "I closed the route, keeping the people safe on one side and locking out the Taliban and their tanks on the other side."

Commander Massoud glanced over at Younis Qanooni and Mohammed Fahim who were seated on his right. Both of them were grinning broadly at the recollection.

"You never saw such a mess," Fahim said with a laugh as he picked up the thread of the story. "Rubble and rock everywhere. The Taliban dropped down on the other side and looked as if they would weep like old women."

All of the other warlords laughed and applauded this daring action by one of their own.

"Then he went from village to village trying to find a ways and means of housing and feeding all the refugees who had flooded the valley." Qanooni quietly added the information he thought most relevant.

"A few days later," Fahim took up the story again, "Commander Massoud gathered his best fighters, turned us around, and had us march all night. At dawn he led us out of the mountains and across the Shomali Plain to wage a surprise attack against the Taliban. They were caught completely off-guard. We cut their supply lines and began to fight. They lost hundreds of men. It was a very good fight," Fahim concluded with glee.

from that flame

"And they have never been able to recapture that land, praise God," Commander Massoud said. "Talk of the Taliban is a good place for us to start, my friends. They are our common enemy. Will you tell everyone what happened in Bamiyan, Commander Khalili?"

"We all know that they blew up the old statues of Buddha," Dostum interjected. "The whole world knows."

"Worse than that," Karim Khalili said gruffly. "Do you think I care about old statues? The Taliban started coming into my towns and villages. They began to commit widespread slaughter, rape, robbery, and arson. I have heard that as many as three hundred men, women, and children were killed. I think they are determined to drive the Hazara out of Afghanistan. We will not go."

"Of course you won't," Commander Massoud said quietly. "That is why we are all here." He looked around the gathering again making eye contact one by one with each man. "If we combine our forces and pool our weapons, then we will be stronger, larger, and better-equipped than the Taliban has ever seen us. Instead of small skirmishes in scattered provinces and villages, we will be able to confront them head-on with force and drive them and al-Qaeda from our land."

"It is a good plan, Ahmed Shah," Ismail Kahn said, nodding. "They don't think that Tajik, Hazara, and Uzbek can work together as a unified group. Our United Front will prove them wrong."

"20,000 men, General Dostum?" Commander Massoud looked at his former enemy. There was a slight hint of challenge in his voice.

Dostum shrugged his heavy shoulders. "Maybe 30,000."

Commander Massoud smiled broadly. "Doctor Abdullah, if you have paper and pen, will you please begin keeping a list? We will go around the circle and find out how many men and munitions we have among us. Once we know that, we can begin to work on a strategy."

The men stayed up late into the night counting AK-47s and the rounds of ammunitions needed for each. They counted 82mm mortar, 75mm recoilless guns, and Chinese-made ZPY missiles. They checked their inventory for SAM-7s and Stingers as well as for Egyptian-made RPG-7 antitank grenade launchers. They added together the total number of T62 Soviet tanks

and MI-24 helicopters each had. Finally, when the inventory of
the weapons was complete and the number of troops had been
counted, Commander Massoud brought out his maps and began
to explain his strategic plan to recapture Taloqan. He spoke until
his commanders began to yawn and said they would start again
in the morning.

While the majority of the commanders retired for the night,
Commander Massoud and his most trusted advisors withdrew to
a smaller tent. He looked from the face of Dr. Abdullah to those
of Generals Fahim and Qanooni.

"You have been with me for many years," Massoud began
slowly. "I want you to know that you have my complete confidence and trust. We have been through many battles together, my
friends, and *enshallah*, God willing, we will stay together in battle
until the Taliban is gone and our country is free." He accepted a
cup of tea from Abdullah and continued.

"All of you know I was recently wounded by a sniper. Mohammed and Younis, what you may not know is that while I was
hiding in a cave waiting to be found, a Taliban bounty hunter
tracked me down and nearly killed me. Had it not been for the
quick action of the Western, female journalist who was with me,
I would not be here today."

"Then we owe her a larger debt of thanks than we could ever
pay," Younis said, speaking for all of them.

"The reason I bring this up now is not because of the journalist, but rather because I think we should discuss what you will do
if something happens to me. It has been on my mind a great deal
lately. We need to devise a plan of action as well as distribute clear
responsibilities among you. Should I be killed, I know that you
will continue to fight for the vision and hope we have discussed
so many times. The well-being of this country will depend upon
you, and you must be prepared."

"How could we go on without you?" Mohammed Fahim
asked in a worried tone.

"You would because you must," Commander Massoud said
with conviction. "If you did not, everything we have fought to
achieve these past twenty years will have be lost. The cause of free-

dom and self-determination must live beyond any one of us."

"What would you have us do?" Dr. Abdullah asked quietly. He saw the expression on his friend's face and knew that no matter what his private thoughts might be, his calm help and advice was needed. He cleared his throat before making his observation.

"The first problem would be how to hold the alliance together. If we are without a leader, Dostum and others would not hesitate to attempt a takeover. You are the only one who has been able to keep him under control. What would you suggest we do?"

"You will ask Ismail Kahn to be an interlocutor. I believe that Dostum will work with him, and since Kahn is Tajik, he can prevent our men from turning against Dostum as well as prevent Dostum from trying to wrest power away from General Fahim who would replace me as the military leader."

Mohammed Fahim's head shot up. "Me?"

"Of course you," Commander Massoud said with a tender smile. "Who else? Are you not the Chief of Intelligence as well as a seasoned warrior? Who better to lead our men in battle than you? Who better to plan new attacks and create new strategies?"

Before Fahim could respond, Commander Massoud shifted his attention to Younis Qanooni.

"You, my friend, should take over the political affairs of the United Front. I will count on you to conduct meetings such as the one we had tonight. You will be the driving force behind alliances, cease-fires, treaties, and negotiations."

Commander Massoud reached out and placed his hand on Abdullah's arm while his eyes traveled back and forth between Fahim and Qanooni. "Abdullah is my most trusted advisor. Consult him on everything significant. Listen to his wisdom. Consider his opinions. Value his insights. If he strongly cautions against something, you would be wise to heed his warning. If he heavily favors a plan of action, be judicious and follow his advice. Know that when he speaks, he speaks for me. Abdullah knows all my dreams and hopes, all my successes and failures. Give him your complete confidence, as I have. He will never give you bad counsel. A more loyal servant Afghanistan does not have."

The four men sat quietly for several minutes as Commander Massoud's words pealed in their ears before drifting away into the cool night air. They were painful words for three of them to hear and yet words that had to be said.

"You know that none of us can imagine doing this without you as our leader," Abdullah finally said for all of them.. "You have always been our commander, our visionary, and our friend. But for your sake we would do as you have asked. We would do it in your memory and out of respect for your vision of a free Afghanistan. We would do it for our country."

"Thank you," Commander Massoud said gently. He looked at the other men. "Now I think we should all get some sleep. We have work to do in the morning."

"Good night, Commander," Fahim and Qanooni said as they left the tent. Neither thought they would sleep much that night. Massoud's fearsome words slipped back into their minds, and they would not leave. They haunted the sleeping men and made their rest uneasy.

In the tent Dr. Abdullah watched as his friend unrolled a blanket and prepared to go to sleep. "I should re-dress your wound," the doctor suggested.

"It's fine," Massoud assured him. "We can do it tomorrow before we leave; that will be soon enough. We should rest now."

As he laid down, the Commander glanced over and saw the worried expression on Abdullah's face.

"My words trouble you," Massoud observed. "I expected that reaction from Mohammed and Younis, but I thought you would understand why I needed to say what I did. I would be irresponsible otherwise."

"I do understand," Abdullah said slowly. He looked intently at his friend. "But there is something you must understand as well. You are the lifeblood that flows through all of us. If that blood is bled away, we may survive, but we will never completely recover. Our hearts will be broken. Victories will be bittersweet. And when Afghanistan is finally free, no amount of glad celebration will be able to drown out the bleak words, 'Massoud isn't here.'"

Abdullah turned his head away so that Massoud wouldn't see his eyes fill with tears.

Commander Massoud got up from his bed and painfully

from that flame

moved onto the small rug beside his friend. "I understand your words, and I love you for them. I would feel the same way if you were taken from me. We have been shoulder-to-shoulder for more than fifteen years. How could part of me not be lost forever if you were no longer standing there? And still, my dear friend, I would have to find a way to keep going. It would not be easy or painless, but it would be necessary. Neither of us is individually as important as the work we do collectively. No matter how much we lose or how much we have suffer, we have made a commitment to free this land and her people. Not even personal loss and grief can halt our pursuit of that goal."

"I know you are right," Abdullah answered quietly. He turned his head so that he could look his friend in the eyes. "I pray five times every day that God will not take you from us for a long time to come. I will do everything in my limited power to keep you alive and safe. But if Allah in his wisdom decides to take you to him, I swear to you that I will do everything you have asked of me. I will not fail you."

"I never thought you would," Commander Massoud said and kissed Abdullah on each cheek. "And now we shall sleep so that in the morning we can continue with our work here. *Shab bakhair*, my friend."

"Good night, Ahmed Shah. Sleep well."

Abdullah reached over and turned off the lantern. He lay awake in the darkness and thought about everything that had been said.

"I'm sorry I wasn't here last night," Masood Khalili said as he hurried up to Commander Massoud. "I was late getting out of New Delhi, and I was delayed in Peshawar."

"You are here now, and that's what matters," Massoud said warmly as he embraced his friend. "If you are going back to Khwaja Bahauddin with Abdullah and me, we can fill you in on the way back regarding what transpired yesterday."

"Fill me in on all your latest adventures," Khalili laughed. "Tell me how you managed to escape yet another Taliban assault. The Americans say that a cat has nine lives. Are you a cat, Ahmed Shah? You have had at least nine lives."

"Of course he is," Younis laughed. "He is the 'Lion of Pan-jshir.'"

"We can discuss the lives of cats and lions and escaping from the Taliban on the ride home," Massoud said. "Right now I would like you to sit in on a strategy session with me."

Dr. Abdullah hurried over to them and greeted Masood Khalili. "Did you see my wife and children?" the doctor asked eagerly.

"I did. They are all well and send their love." Khalili reached into his pocket and withdrew an envelope which he handed to Abdullah. "Your wife asked me to give this to you."

Abdullah almost opened the envelope before he remembered they were on their way to a meeting. With a sigh he started to put the letter into his pocket. Massoud rested his hand on Abdullah's arm.

"I think you should go read your letter and join us when you are finished," he said.

"You wouldn't mind?" Abdullah asked hopefully.

Massoud shook his head and smiled. "No. Your mind would be on the letter anyway. We'll see you soon." Massoud looked at Masood Khalili as Abdullah hurried off. "Ready?" he asked as he began to walk slowly in the direction of the large tent where the other men awaited him.

Khalili nodded as he fell into step beside Massoud. "Is Dostum here?"

"He's here. He offered 30,000 well-equipped men plus five tanks and two helicopters," Massoud answered.

"I don't trust him," Khalili said, shaking his head.

"Who said anything about trusting him?" Commander Massoud countered. "We know what he is capable of doing. We will always be guarded and careful around him. But as a practical matter, we need him and must find a way to work with him."

"You and Fahim can work with him," Khalili said with disgust.

"We have a common enemy," Commander Massoud reminded his deputy defense minister-turned-ambassador.

"The Soviets were a common enemy, too," Khalili snapped, "and he sold us out to them. How do we know he won't switch

from that flame

sides again and go over to the Taliban?"

"The Taliban hate him. They also know he will never willing give up control of Mazar. They know—and he knows they know—they would have to kill him to take control away from him. His best and only real chance to keep his power is with us. I know that he doesn't care about Afghanistan and her people. He cares about himself and his power. Do you think he would join us if it didn't serve his own purposes? In this case, his purpose serves ours."

"We need a spy in his camp," Khalili decided. "Someone we can trust who reports only to you. That way we would at least have advance warning if he plans to turn against us."

"Agreed," Commander Massoud said. "Discuss with Younis who it should be. It has to be someone very discreet. If Dostum becomes suspicious at all, he would not hesitate to kill him. And now let us get to the meeting. We agreed on a general strategy last night, but we need to work out the details and determine a time table before we leave."

"Come in, Assem," Michelle yelled when she heard a knock at her door. She finished typing a sentence before looking up at the young man who was smiling down at her.

"Good morning, Miss Garrett," Assem Suhail said cheerily. He handed her a cup of the ever-present green tea.

"Assem, I think I am actually going to miss this stuff when I leave this part of the world," Michelle said before sipping the steaming tea.

"I will prepare a package of it for you to take with you," the young man offered.

"Only if you teach me first how to prepare it properly," Michelle said with a laugh. "I am horrible in a kitchen. I don't think I could boil water."

"You are making a joke, yes?" the young man asked seriously.

"Partly," Michelle answered with another laugh. Over the past two days, Assem had popped in and out of her room several times, always enthusiastically cheerful, always willing to do whatever she asked. She set the tea aside and stood up.

from that flame

"Assem *Jaan*, I have been cooped up in this room for two days. Looking out the window, it is a beautiful day. Could we please take a walk around the compound?"

The young man hesitated. "Commander Massoud told me that he wanted you to stay in here. I don't think we should disobey him."

"But I have obeyed him for two days, and I'm getting cabin fever," Michelle pleaded. "Surely a short walk around the compound won't hurt anything. I've been on that walk with both Doctor Abdullah and Massoud himself. The Commander doesn't even need to know."

"I would tell him," Assem said.

"Well, then you can tell him truthfully that I decided to go out, and you couldn't stop me."

Michelle grabbed her coat and hurried to the door. She pulled it open and rushed out so quickly, she startled the guard who was posted directly outside. The man yelled something Michelle didn't understand, and she heard Assem speaking quickly and urgently to the guard as she continued walking. A moment later Assem caught up with her.

"Was he going to shoot me?" Michelle asked, only half-kidding.

"He was thinking about it," Assem answered grimly. "Commander Massoud told him that you were supposed to stay in the room. I persuaded him that it was for your own safety and not because you were under arrest. I told him that I would take responsibility for this excursion when Commander Massoud learns about it."

Michelle stopped walking and looked at Assem. "Is it really going to cause so much trouble?" she asked.

"The Commander does not like his direct orders disobeyed," Assem said.

"Oh, for heaven's sake," Michelle said, turned on her heel, and started walking back towards her room. "I didn't know the world was going to come to an end. It's no fun taking a walk if everyone is going to get this upset about it."

She brushed past the guard with a glare and slammed the door behind her. A few minutes later, the compound was filled with the sound of someone pounding especially hard on the old typewriter's keys.

14. Return

ichelle opened her eyes when she heard the sound of knocking at the door again. Looking out the small window, she saw that dusk was falling. She sat up on the mattress, a little surprised she had fallen asleep after laying down to stretch her back, which was stiff after hunching over the low table for hours. She heard the soft knocking again.

"Go away, Assem. I'm not hungry," she shouted in the direction of the door as she reached for the lantern on the floor beside her.

"I hope you were not that rude to him the entire time I was gone," Massoud said from the other side of the door.

Michelle leapt to her feet and jerked the door open.

"It's good to see you back safely," Michelle said with a smile. "And, no, I haven't been rude to Assem while you were away. We had a small misunderstanding this afternoon, and I was sulking, that's all. How was your meeting? Was it a success?"

"Yes, the meeting was all that I had hoped it would be. A misunderstanding about what?" Massoud asked.

"I wanted to go for a walk around the compound, and he didn't want me to go," Michelle shrugged. "I went out anyway, and the guard was going to shoot me, and then Assem got all upset because he thought you would blame him."

"He is right," Massoud said in a low voice.

"Oh, come on," Michelle protested. She got to her feet and went to face the Commander. "If you're going to be mad at anyone, be mad at me. Assem told me not to go, and I did anyway. What was he supposed to do? Lock me in?"

from that flame

"If necessary, yes," Massoud said, still speaking quietly. "I gave specific instructions for a reason. Why would I waste my time doing that if they weren't important? And I am angry with you as well as with him."

"I'm not one of your soldiers who has to obey your orders, Commander," Michelle said with annoyance. This was not how she expected their reunion to be.

"No, but you are my guest and should abide by my wishes, especially when everything I have asked is designed to keep you safe from harm."

The stern look of reproof in his eyes caused Michelle to take a step backwards. Finally, she took a deep sigh and looked at him squarely in the eyes.

"You're right. I'm sorry. I was feeling a little confined after two days and couldn't see any real harm in going out for just a few minutes. I should have realized that you would not have gone to such lengths to keep me indoors without a good reason. Please don't blame Assem. I really didn't give him a choice. He would have had to physically restrain me from going out that door. Please don't be mad at me."

"'Don't blame Assem.' 'Don't be angry with you.' Is there anything else you would like to tell me to do?" Commander Massoud kept his voice stern, but Michelle could see the twinkle in his eyes.

"Give me a minute; I'll think of something," Michelle said, relived.

Massoud gave up trying to remain angry. "I don't doubt that. I must go now, but I will return in a few hours if I may."

"I was hoping we could eat together."

Commander Massoud shook his head. "Not tonight. Three of my highest ranking officers came back with Abdullah and me. There are matters we must discuss over dinner. After that I will come and speak with you for a while. Will that be all right?"

"Sure, that would be great. If you want to bring your chess game along, I'll play with you. I'll even let you win."

Commander Massoud's eyebrows shot up. "Let me win?"

"Well, sure. I mean, I wouldn't want to make you look bad or anything," Michelle said with a grin. "We have to preserve your reputation as a master strategist, right?"

from that flame

"I will return in a few hours, "Massoud reiterated. "Meanwhile, don't be rude when Assem shows up with your dinner."

"I won't be rude to him if you won't be angry with him," Michelle shot back.

"Agreed," Massoud said and smiled again before leaving the small room.

Commander Massoud moved his bishop and said, "Check." Michelle moved her rook to block his bishop. The Commander scratched his head just under the curled lip of his pakol as he studied the board.

"Why did you do that?" he asked at last.

"Because I was in check, of course," Michelle pointed out. "The point was to get out of check, right? Well, I'm out of check."

"But there were other moves," Massoud said slowly as he continued to study the board. "Other moves that might have..." his voice trailed off.

"Other moves that you would have expected," Michelle chided. "Why would I want to make a move you could anticipate?"

"There is a logic to chess, a strategy," Massoud explained thoughtfully as he cocked his head, stroked his beard, and looked at the position of the pieces.

"Oh-ho," Michelle snorted and pointed at him. "You don't think I've figured out that a normal strategy would never work to defeat you? I am playing guerrilla chess."

"Guerrilla chess?" Massoud repeated as if he had not heard her correctly. Their eyes met, and he started to laugh. He laughed until his eyes filled with tears. Michelle started to laugh as well. The idea of trying to outmaneuver one of the greatest guerrilla strategists of all time tickled her funny bone. She fell over backwards onto the mattress and laughed until she was too weak to get up. Every time one of them tried to speak, they both started laughing again.

"All right, so it wasn't the most brilliant plan," Michelle gasped at last. "I had to try something. The thought of trying to play you scared me silly."

"I should keep you as my secret weapon against the Taliban,"

Massoud said, holding his side which now ached from having laughed so hard. "You are so unpredictable, you would constantly catch them off-guard."

"I think you do that well enough without my help," Michelle said, still trying to catch her breath. She looked down at the chessboard. "Go ahead and finish me off. I know you are dying to do it."

Massoud shoved his queen forward. "Checkmate," he said with a grin.

"Thank goodness," Michelle said, shoving the board aside. "Now I will pour some tea, and you can tell me how your meeting went. Is there information I can add to the article?"

"I would prefer the Taliban not know about any future plans I have to attack them. Can we keep this conversation strictly between us?"

"Oh, you assume that someone in the Taliban will read the magazine to which I finally sell this story? Highly unlikely, *Amer Saheb*, but this can be off-the-record if that is the way you want it." Michelle settled across from him again. "See? No notes. Just talk between two friends."

"Thank you," the Commander said, sipping his tea. "The meeting was productive, I think. I met with some of the other commanders, and we agreed to combine our forces and work together to defeat the Taliban. This combined effort will be known as the United Front."

"It took you two days to come to this agreement?"

"No, of course not. We had to make an inventory of men and supplies, arrange times and places for joint training, and agree on a general strategic plan. It will probably be mid– to late summer before we are ready to launch a combined offensive."

"Was anybody I know at the meeting?"

"My old friend Dostum," Massoud answered with a slow nod of his head.

"Dostum?" Michelle perked up. "As in 'he-joined-the-KGB' Dostum?"

"Yes," Massoud said slowly.

"How can you work with him again after he betrayed you?" Michelle demanded. "How could you ever trust him?"

from that flame

"You sound exactly like Masood Khalili," Commander Massoud said. "I don't trust Dostum. I never will. But I can work with him because I must. He has what I need. Wouldn't it be foolish of me to let past grievances prevent me from getting needed assistance now? I cannot afford to be foolish when many lives and the freedom of my country hang in the balance."

"You are a better person than I would be under those circumstances," Michelle said. "I admire your pragmatism and self-control."

"I am a practical man. I know my strengths and my limitations," Massoud said. "I also know that the most brilliant strategy in the world can't work without the means to execute it. Dostum would be perfectly happy to stay in his fiefdom at Mazar-i-sharif and fight the Taliban from there. I need him and what he can bring to the battle more than he needs me. I can offer the hand of friendship to him for the purpose he serves. Being who he is, he will never notice that the hand I am extending to him is cold rather than warm." Massoud raised his cup so that Michelle could add more tea. "And now tell me how the article is coming."

"I think I have written and thrown out a hundred pages," Michelle said with a sigh. "I know the approach I want to use, but there is too much material. I am having a hard time picking and choosing what should go in and what should get tossed out."

"Is there any way in which I might help?

"Not without influencing the piece," Michelle answered, "and you said you didn't want to do that."

"No, I don't," Commander Massoud said and started to put the chess pieces back in their box. "I shall retire now. Would you join me for breakfast in the morning? Younis Qanooni and Masood Khalili expressed an interest in meeting you before they leave tomorrow."

"I would be honored to meet them," Michelle said as she walked the Commander to the door. "Thank you for the invitation."

"Good. I will send Assem for you when we are ready. Good night, Michelle *Jaan*."

"Good night, Ahmed Shah *Jann*," Michelle replied. She offered her hand to him.

"A warm hand of friendship is a wonderful gift," Massoud

said with a smile as he accepted and gently shook her hand. "Thank you for your warm hand."

"It will always be a warm hand of friendship for you, *Amer Saheb*."

"As mine will be for you. *Baamaanay khuda*."

Michelle watched him walk slowly away until he vanished in the darkness. She decided at that moment how to solve the problem of having too much information for her magazine article. She would write an average-length article, and then she would write a book. It was something she had always wanted to do, something she had always promised herself she would do when she found the right topic. The right topic had just left her room.

"Are you ready?" Assem Suhail asked as he walked up to where Michelle was standing in the doorway of her room.

Michelle stepped out and pulled the door closed behind her. "Yes. Are you still speaking to me? I told the Commander that everything was my fault. Was he very angry with you?"

"He was stern," Assem answered as they walked across the compound, "...as he should have been. I made a mistake. He has a responsibility to correct me. Afterwards, however, he told me that I still have his confidence. He asked me to interpret this morning."

"Interpret?" Michelle repeated. "Interpret what?"

"Younis Qanooni doesn't speak English or French," the young man explained. "Commander Massoud will speak in Dari to him, and I will translate for you."

"Why doesn't the Commander translate himself?"

Assem stopped and looked puzzled. The thought had not crossed his mind. "I don't know. He asked me to interpret, and I never question his orders."

"If he wants to have it this way, that's a good enough reason for me, too," Michelle said and smiled at her young escort. "We'd better hurry. I don't think he likes to wait."

After the introductions had been made all around, Michelle and the six men sat down on the rugs. She suddenly felt more than a little out of place. In the past few weeks she had become very comfortable with both Massoud and Abdullah. Even sharing sleeping space with them when necessary hadn't been awkward. Sitting with these three strangers staring at her made her self-conscious and very aware of the fact that she was dressed in a way they had probably never seen and might even find offensive. This was more than likely the first time they sat to eat a meal with a female who was not a relative. She looked at Massoud across the circle from her. He was speaking to Younis Qanooni who was sitting on his left, but he was looking at her. He flashed a small, easy smile in her direction, and Michelle breathed again.

"He is telling Younis Qanooni that you are like the women of Afghanistan…filled with courage," Assem said quietly into her right ear.

A burly man on the other side of Qanooni barked some words. His voice sounded so loud in the small area that Michelle jumped.

"General Fahim asked Commander Massoud if he is permitted to speak to you directly. The Commander said that he could," Assem explained.

Both Assem and Michelle looked at Mohammed Fahim. He seemed to be choosing his words carefully. Assem leaned close to Michelle again and translated the other man's words.

"Commander Massoud told him—told them – the story about the Taliban bounty hunter who was going to kill him. He didn't know that women could shoot a gun and kill a man that way. He doesn't think it is right for women to fight in battle, but he wants to thank you for your bravery in killing the assassin."

Michelle spoke to Assem but continued to look towards the general. "Please tell General Fahim that I appreciate his kind words and that I am honored to have been able to help Commander Massoud." As Assem translated her words, she smiled tentatively. When Fahim nodded and returned her smile, Michelle's own smile became broad and genuine.

"Commander Massoud was also telling us about the many adventures you have survived since coming to our country," Masood Khalili said to Michelle in English. He repeated himself in Dari before finishing his comment. "I hope that your impression of Afghanistan is not entirely unfavorable."

"To the contrary," Michelle answered. "I have fallen in love with your beautiful country and have nothing but admiration for her people." Assem repeated her words.

The ice broken, the men visibly relaxed and began peppering the journalist with questions about what she had seen and experienced and how it would all affect the article she was writing. Sometimes Abdullah and Masood Khalili spoke to Michelle in English, and sometimes they switched to Dari so that the others would understand. Assem Suhail made a valiant effort to translate what everyone was saying as the conversation continued. At one point he looked at Michelle and translated a comment that Dr. Abdullah had made in English into Dari. Everyone started to laugh, and the young man—blushing a brilliant red—laughed at himself. It was at that point Commander Massoud stood to indicate that the breakfast meeting was over.

"Our visitors will be leaving now," Commander Massoud said to Michelle. "Will you walk with us to see them off?"

Michelle arose, indicating that she would like to do that, and the whole group then walked across the compound to the field where the helicopter was kept. After everyone shook hands, Younis Qanooni, Mohammed Fahim, and Masood Khalili boarded the chopper. Abdullah, Assem, Michelle, and Commander Massoud stood back and watched it leave before turning to go back to the compound. Commander Massoud said something to Dr. Abdullah and Assem Suhail. They excused themselves from Michelle and walked in the direction of the Commander's office.

"I will walk you to your room," Commander Massoud said. "I wish to speak to you about something."

"What's on your mind?" When Massoud didn't answer immediately, Michelle stopped walking and looked at him. "What's wrong?"

"When Mohammed Fahim thanked you for shooting the assassin, I saw your face," the Commander answered quietly. "I thought you had more or less accepted what happened, but then I realized that we have never spoken of the matter again, and I don't know what you think or feel now. Will you tell me?" Massoud studied her face for her honest reaction.

"I have accepted what happened," Michelle answered slowly and with a note of surprise in her voice, as if she hadn't come to the realization herself until that very moment. She looked up at

from that flame

Commander Massoud. "I will always regret having to take another life, but I would pull the trigger again without a moment's hesitation if I had to do it in order to save you, Ahmed Shah Massoud."

"I am relieved that you have come to peace with what happened. I saw how much it hurt your heart and spirit, and I would have been grieved to know I had been the source of your sorrow."

"Doing something for you could never be a source of sorrow," Michelle answered with heartfelt emotion. "I'm not sure I can clearly express how much knowing you has added to my life. I have never known anyone like you. I admire and respect you more than I can say. You are an extraordinary man, Amer Saheb."

"*Nay,*" Commander Massoud said, shaking his head. "I am an ordinary man in extraordinary circumstances. All I do is walk the path God has laid before me. It is the people of my land who are extraordinary. They will never be conquered. They will never stop fighting for freedom."

"Nor will they ever have to stop with you here leading them in their fight."

They arrived at the door of her room. Michelle stepped onto the threshold and turned back to face the Commander. "I want to write a whole book about you and my experiences here. Would that be all right with you?"

Commander Massoud nodded. "That would be more than 'all right,' but write the book about your experience rather than about me. That would be more interesting."

"Of course, it might mean that I would have to come back here," Michelle said as she arched an eyebrow and gave him a crooked smile.

"In addition to coming back to open a massage clinic in Kabul and to hold a seminar for the teachers?" Massoud said, laughing softly.

"And don't forget the first aid kits and the magazine article," Michelle reminded him. "With all this coming back, it might be easier not to leave in the first place."

"And yet you must...leave, I mean," Commander Massoud said wistfully. "When do you think you will want to go to Peshawar? I need to know when I will be missing the men I send with you."

"By the end of the week?" Michelle said, thinking aloud. "Your men will have prayer Friday night. So, how about Saturday?"

"Saturday will be fine," Massoud said. "It means you will be here to celebrate the new year with us. Before you leave, we will need to figure out a means to coordinate our meeting in Paris."

Michelle grinned. "I look forward to *Nowroze*, but please tell me I won't have to watch a game of *buzkashi*."

"You don't like our national sport?" the Commander said with a knowing smile. Many—most—from outside the region found the game violent and distasteful. "Think of it as a game of polo."

"Sure, there are horses like in polo, but a decapitated goat instead of a ball?" Michelle grimaced. "I don't attend bullfights, either, *Amer Saheb*. And as far as Paris is concerned, I don't think you need to worry about me meeting you. You won't be exactly hard to find. I'll just look for a huge pack of reporters and find you smack in the middle of them all." She saw an odd expression cross his face. "Okay, okay," she laughed again. "If it makes you feel better to plan everything down to the last, minute detail, then, Commander, that's exactly what we will do."

"Thank you for humoring me," Massoud answered. "Compulsive planning and attention to details are occupational hazards. You need not watch the *buzkashi* match if you do not wish it. Now, if you will excuse me, I have some matters that really do need my attention. Will you join Abdullah and me for the evening meal?"

"It would be my pleasure," Michelle said, ducked into her room, and headed straight for the old typewriter. Before Commander Massoud had crossed half way across the compound's central courtyard, he heard the clacking of the ancient machine's keys.

15. Finished

ichelle had holed herself up in her small room for days, even asking that her breakfast and midday meal be brought to her. She would come out of her room in time to join Dr. Abdullah and Commander Massoud for dinner and then hurry back to write until the eight PM curfew the doctor had given her. Sometimes she would rejoin Abdullah and Massoud for conversation or a game of chess, and sometimes she went to bed early so that she could start working at daybreak. All she would tell the men was that the article was progressing nicely and that she would let them see it when she was finished.

Wednesday was the traditional Afghan new year, *Nowroze*. Since the holiday had been outlawed in Taliban-controlled areas, the people of Panjshir, and especially Massoud's men in the Khwaja Bahauddin camp, looked forward to the celebration. The past year had been a difficult one for them. They had suffered the serious defeat at Taloqan and had lost many *mujahidin*. It had been a year of severe deprivation and suffering. The new year promised new victories as word spread of shipments of military supplies and humanitarian aid.

The cooks began preparing nearly a week in advance. Many of the ingredients needed to make the traditional dishes were hard to get, but some items had been hoarded from the previous year, and others had been acquired by clever negotiation. *Kulcha naurazee, haft miwa, shola-e-zard*, and *samanak* would grace the meal Commander Massoud would share with his top advisors and generals.

Michelle dressed in the best clothes she had brought with her from Pakistan, which was not much since she had packed enough

from that flame

for five days and had been gone nearly five weeks. She longed for the beautiful dress she had purchased in Peshawar. It was in the same hotel room as her laptop computer. The clothes and computer are probably long gone, she thought. She had only pre-paid for the week she thought she'd be away. Michelle sighed, covered her head with a bright scarf, and waited for Massoud, Abdullah, or Assem to come and escort her to the celebration.

Safely ensconced between Commander Massoud and Dr. Abdullah, Michelle enjoyed the festivities very much. Until this day, her experience with the *mujahidin* had been almost exclusively serious and grim, which was befitting the life-and-death struggle in which they were engaged. On this bright, sunny afternoon, however, she was permitted a glimpse into the other side of the Afghan personality, and she loved what she saw.

Music, laughter, dance, and song filled the compound as the feast was served picnic–style. The men, glad to have a day of fun, celebration, and good food, played as carefree children would. An impromptu soccer field was created and teams quickly formed. A few men even flew brightly colored kites, a favorite pastime in Afghanistan that had also been outlawed by the Taliban. In fact, Michelle realized, everything around her on that glorious day had been banned in Taliban-controlled parts of the country. No wonder the Afghans, by nature a people filled with the joy of life, felt oppressed by the group of religious zealots who had overrun and controlled their country.

"Are you enjoying yourself?" Commander Massoud asked Michelle.

"Very much," Michelle smiled and nodded. "Of course you realize that you have created a new problem for me."

Massoud's brow furrowed. "In what way?"

"I need to go back into the article and find a place to insert a paragraph or two about this aspect of the *mujahidin*, a side I have not seen before. I like this fun-filled, playful side of your men, Commander."

"This is what the Afghan spirit is at its very core," Massoud said, looking out over the group of men gathered there with a smile on his face. "Their delight in life is based on the belief that all good things come from God. How can the Taliban be so blind to that fact?"

234

from that flame

"I hope that is a rhetorical question because I certainly don't have an answer. Given a choice, I think everyone would prefer this way of life. And now, Ahmed Shah *Jaan*, if you will permit Assem to take me back to my quarters, I would like to return to my work. I see the goat being brought out, and you promised me I wouldn't have to watch the *buzkashi*."

"I will stop by later in the evening, if I may," Massoud said, motioning to Assem as he spoke. "Perhaps a bloodthirsty game of chess will be more to your liking."

"How bloodthirsty can it be when you always checkmate me in under ten moves?" Michelle demanded with a laugh. "I'll see you then, Commander. Enjoy the *buzkashi*, and thank you very much for allowing me to participate in today's celebration."

Before long, Massoud's complete attention was focused on the game being played in front of him. Yet between the thundering hooves of the galloping horses and the excited shouts of the men, he was aware of the constant, rhythmic click of Michelle's old typewriter in the background.

Commander Massoud was beginning to wonder if Michelle was going to finish when she expected. He walked out onto the sheltered porch and looked around the grounds as he drank his morning tea. The snows of winter had done little to quench the earth's thirst. If it was as dry a spring as the previous two had been, he wondered how the farmers would survive yet another failed crop. When he gathered the men for evening prayer, he would pray for rain.

He looked across the compound in the direction of Michelle's room and realized that the incessant tapping of the typewriter keys had ceased. As he stood watching her door and wondering what the silence meant, the door opened, and Michelle stepped into the bright sunlight. She had a stack of papers in her hands.

Michelle saw Massoud standing across from her. "Commander," she said, waving the papers at him, "I'm finished!" Her voice was high with excitement, and an enormous smile covered her face. She started to run across the center courtyard of the compound as Massoud started walking towards her. Suddenly she was falling forward, and for a brief moment Massoud thought she had tripped on something. A split second later he heard the report of a gun being fired. Instinctively, his head turned in the direction from which the sound had come. He saw the sniper at the exact moment his own guards returned fire.

Without considering his own safety, Massoud thought of Michelle and looked back at the courtyard. She was lying motionless where she had fallen, her papers starting to scatter across the cold ground.

Massoud broke into a run despite the pain that shot through his back and leg. When he reached the fallen woman he saw a large bullet wound directly in the center of her back. He rolled her over to face him, pulled her to her feet, lowered his shoulder to her midsection, and lifted her over his back. His leg and back both screamed in protest, but he ignored the pain and held firmly onto the woman.

Unsure about the sniper's location or whether there was more than one, he moved as quickly as possible towards his Land Rover which was parked near an interior wall. He stopped in the narrow space between the vehicle and the building wall and carefully laid Michelle down. Her eyes were still open but had begun to glaze over. After twenty years of war, Commander Massoud could recognize a dying person, but now, with this woman, Ahmed Shah Massoud denied what his own eyes told him.

"Abdullah!" he screamed for his friend. "Help! *Eenja Beyaa!*" He sat on the ground and pulled Michelle onto his lap so that he could cradle her against his chest. He was oblivious to the gunfight that was still going on around the compound. God, please don't let her die. Don't die, he prayed and then pleaded silently. Aloud he said to her, "Abdullah will be here in a moment, and you will be all right."

Michelle choked and her mouth filled with blood. She tried to speak, but all that came out was little more than a gurgling hiss.

"Don't talk. Save all your strength," Massoud urged her.

Abdullah squeezed into the space between the car and the wall and dropped to the ground beside Massoud. He saw blood all over Massoud and Michelle and could not tell whose it was. "Who is hurt?" he asked breathlessly. "Are you hurt?"

"She is," Massoud said, looking at his friend with desperation on his face.

"Are you hit too?" Dr. Abdullah asked calmly as he reached to feel Michelle's pulse. The amount of blood lost was a very bad sign. There was barely a pulse, and the doctor saw more blood spilling from her mouth, an indication of massive internal bleeding.

"No, just her. We need to get her to a helicopter that can take her to a hospital in Tajik."

"Ahmed Shah, look at her," Abdullah said in a very low voice that was barely above a whisper. "There is nothing we can do now. I'm sorry."

Massoud looked down at her again, and this time he saw what his friend saw. Had they been some place where an ambulance could have whisked her to a hospital, she might have had a chance, but even then he was doubtful. He gathered her more closely to him and gently brushed the dirt from her face. He knew that all he could do for her now was give her a comforting place to die. He kissed her on the forehead, held her tightly against his chest, and prayed that her spirit would go straight to a merciful God.

When he looked down, he saw that she was looking at him. She knew she was dying, and she was unafraid. He brushed her hair from her face and stroked her cheek.

"*Vous vivrez dans ma mémoire,*" he whispered softly. "You will live in my memory."

Michelle managed a weak smile and tried to say something, but she was unable to speak. Massoud cradled her, rocked her, and watched her die. He had lost so many people he loved that he had fooled himself into actually believing he could face death on all levels and remain relatively unscathed. He feared now that the source of his strength was his ability to shove his personal pain behind a wall and imprison it, and that one day—maybe even this day—it would crush the wall with its horrible weight, rush down on him as an unstoppable force, and drown him forever in an ocean of grief and sorrow and loss.

Michelle was no longer breathing. A low moan escaped Massoud's lips as tears filled his eyes. He buried his face in her hair and wept. Abdullah put his arm around his friend's heaving shoulders and held them both as he silently prayed.

from that flame

Minutes passed, and still Massoud sat with the dead woman in his arms. He knew what he had to do. They would have to helicopter her body to Tajikistan and find a US consulate in a nearby country. He and Abdullah would have to fill out a thousand forms and papers. Michelle Garrett's body would be transferred from the Tajik hospital, and the consulate would make arrangements to have her taken home. He would never even be able to visit her grave the way he might if she was buried in his land. But sending her home was the right thing to do; he knew that. He knew everything he had to do, and still he sat and held her. He finally realized that there was silence in the compound.

Massoud looked at his friend who had been sitting silently beside him. "Did we get all the attackers? Who did this?"

"I'll go find out," Abdullah said and stood up. "Are you going to stay here?"

"For a little while longer, yes. Abdullah? The papers of her article are blowing all over the courtyard. Will you make sure they are gathered up? Don't let any get lost."

"All right. I'll be back for you soon."

"I'll be here," Massoud said.

The dullness in his voice worried Abdullah, but he left to do what he had been asked. Massoud continued to sit and hold Michelle in his arms. There were a dozen things he needed to do. His own men might have been hurt or killed in the attack. He needed to send troops to check the perimeter of the encampment. He needed to help bury the dead on both sides. He needed to open the armory and re-supply his fighters in case there was a second attack. He needed to take his binoculars to a higher point and scan the countryside. He needed to make sure that if there were more Taliban on the way, his forces would be ready to repel them with RPGs. He needed to do all these things and more, and still he simply sat holding Michelle's body. He felt more tired, drained, and empty than he had ever felt in his life. He thought he might simply lean against the building and sleep. He closed his eyes and didn't open them until Abdullah came back with a pile of dirty, bloody papers.

"Are you sure you got them all?" Commander Massoud asked.

"I think I did, but I'm not sure. Ahmed Shah, this may have

only been the first wave. We need to go. There is work to do. The men are awaiting your orders."

"We have to get all the pages," Massoud said as if he didn't hear the second half of what his friend said. "I need to save the article for her."

"There are more urgent things to be done now, Ahmed Shah," Abdullah spoke sharply. The commander he knew was not acting at all like himself.

"Can't you do what needs to be done?" Commander Massoud asked dully. "You know what needs to be done."

Abdullah hesitated as he continued to study the Commander. Was he in some kind of shock? Abdullah could not recall his commander ever reacting this way to someone's death before, and it unnerved him. He started from his thoughts when he realized Massoud was speaking to him.

"I will take her body to the medic's clinic and meet you at the armory. Meanwhile, make sure you have all the pages. Every last one of them." Massoud's voice was mechanical.

"Are you all right?" Dr. Abdullah asked.

"No, but I will be," Commander Massoud answered with grim determination. He would find a way to push this grief behind the wall too and then pray that the wall sprung no leaks.

Abdullah helped Massoud struggle to his feet with Michelle still in his arms. For a brief instant the doctor wondered if he should offer to carry Michelle's body, but he dismissed the idea almost before it finished forming in his mind. He watched Massoud begin the slow, painful walk across the compound before he turned his attention to other urgent matters.

Massoud did all the things he needed to do. He made all the decisions and gave all the orders. It was night by the time the area was secured enough for everyone to take a breath without having to worry about another unexpected attack. Numb and wooden, he had gotten through the day, but as soon as it was possible, Massoud headed back to the medic's tent where Michelle's body lay.

Sensing that his Commander wanted privacy, the medic left when Massoud entered. The Afghan Commander went to where

from that flame

Michelle was lying and removed the cloth that covered her face. His breath came sharply when he saw her. The medic had cleaned her face and hands and arranged her in a peaceful pose. Had she not died in his arms, Massoud might have thought she was merely asleep the way he had seen her asleep a dozen times in the past weeks. He touched her cheek. Although he knew that it would be cold, the fact that it was stiff stabbed like a knife in his own heart.

"You were worried about failing me, and it was I who failed you," he said quietly. "I am very sorry, *Amer Saheb*, that I didn't keep you safe. How did I let this happen? You weren't supposed to get caught in the crossfire of this war. I wish that bullet had found its way to me rather than to you." He tentatively reached out and stroked her hair. He softly smiled as he remembered her silly explanation of what it meant to have a 'bad hair day.' To him, her hair with blood in it was the worst bad hair he could imagine.

"Did you know how much you meant to me?" he said barely above a whisper. "Did you know that I dreaded the day you finished the article because that would mean you were leaving? Even though I expected to see you in Paris in a few weeks, I would have missed you for those weeks, and now I will miss you for the rest of my life. I will miss the way you always made me laugh. I will miss your courage and your kindness. I will miss your unique perspective. I will miss your humor, unpredictability, and fearlessness. I will miss everything about you, my dear friend."

Massoud leaned over and kissed Michelle's forehead. His lips close to her ear, he continued. "Thank you for your open mind, your warm heart, and your loving friendship. Thank you for coming to my country and for caring so much about what you found here. Thank you for the hope you gave me. *Inna lillahi wa inna ilayhi raji'un*, Michelle *Jaan*. Verily we belong to Allah, and truly to Him shall we return."

He kissed her forehead again, straightened himself, and covered her with the white cloth. Then, as Ahmed Shah Massoud did every night, he faced Mecca and knelt to say his prayers. This night he added the oft repeated prayers for the dead.

from that flame

Massoud found the pages Abdullah had gathered neatly stacked near the typewriter on the desk in Michelle's room. The dirty pages, the ones splattered with her blood, were written in French. An English version on pristine, white paper sat beside them. He picked up the French version and sat near the lantern to read what she had written.

It was all there, everything he had hoped for and more. She had captured the spirit of the country, the struggle and bravery of the Afghan people, and the complexities of the political situation. She wrote with knowledge, passion, and conviction. Her words rang with undeniable truth. She was fair and honest about the things with which she disagreed, but she was never judgmental. The story pulsed with excitement during the passages that relayed some of the events the two of them had lived through. It was a story about war, occupation, and resistance. It was also a story about human dignity, loyalty, friendship, and courage.

As he read about himself as seen through her eyes, he thought at first that she had lionized him. He knew that he was the lynchpin in her story, but he never wanted his actions to overshadow the larger story. As he continued reading, the truth began to dawn on him. She admired him as a leader of men, and she honored him as a military hero. She respected his devotion to his faith, his family, his friends, and his duty. She praised his intellect and strategic abilities. She appreciated his bravery and credited him with saving her life. And she loved him. This underlying thread was unmistakable.

He sat stunned by the revelation. He knew she would never have told him this in person. She never would have imposed herself on him in that way. She would never have burdened him with anything that might have confused or worried him. He had craved her friendship, and she had been content to give it to him. But she loved him; he knew that now.

He set aside the papers, picked up her passport, and looked at her picture as he reflected on what he had intuited. Would it have changed anything if he had discovered her secret while she was still alive? Would he have cherished her even more, or would the knowledge have caused a rift between them? He never would have allowed any feelings beyond friendship, and Michelle instinctively knew that. All of his being was focused on the war he waged and the men who answered to him. He could never dishonor his wife nor betray his God. She realized that too, and still she loved him.

"I didn't know" he muttered under his breath to her picture. "I looked in your eyes a hundred times and saw friendship shining back at me. Was that all I wanted to see? You took my blindness in stride just as you did everything else." He touched her picture and smiled sadly. "I loved you too, Michelle *Jaan*. Perhaps not in the same way you loved me, but in a way that was no less real. I think you understood and accepted my limitations. Women are much wiser than men, and I am more stupid than most men."

He folded the papers and put them into his pocket. He would take the nice, clean English version to Paris with him. Other journalists would be there, and he would ask one of them for help in finding a publisher. These papers in French, the ones stained with her blood, would be his to keep, a part of her that belonged to him alone.

He found her backpack and began to gather up her things. They would all be sent to Tajikistan with her body. He intended to accompany her there. It was the last thing he could do for her. He picked up her journal and remembered the conversation they had had when they discovered that each of them kept one. They had talked about the importance of being able to organize one's thoughts, feelings, and experiences at the end of each day. It was a sanity maintenance device both employed for balance and reason. He knew he would be writing about her that night.

Massoud flipped trough the book. Written in English, he could only pick out a word here and there. He saw his name repeatedly in the last several dozen pages. He sat again on the edge of the bed as he pondered what to do with it.

He supposed he should send it back with everything else. But to whom? Would she want someone else reading her private thoughts? Would she want even him to read them? Probably not. These were her personal thoughts and feelings, and that made them sacrosanct. He set the journal next to the backpack, his decision made: he would keep the book himself, but he wouldn't ask Abdullah for one of his English dictionaries. He would simply add the book to the collection in his library, and when he thought about Michelle and missed her, he would hold her book in his hands and feel that part of her—a very special part of her—was with him still.

from that flame

There were several rolls of film neatly stacked beside the typewriter. Massoud smiled as he recalled how many times she had asked to wander off in order to take photographs. "I may never come this way again," she had said on more than one occasion. Her prophesy had been too true. He set the film with the English language manuscript. They would also be handed over to the foreign journalist he would ask for help. Perhaps a few of her pictures could be used in the article.

Dr. Abdullah appeared in the doorway. "The helicopter is ready," he said quietly.

Massoud stood up and reached for Michelle's backpack and journal. "All right. I need to drop some things off in the office and change into clean clothes. I will meet you at the pad in fifteen minutes. Is her body already onboard?"

"Yes. Ahmed Shah, perhaps it would be better if you didn't go to Tajikistan right now. The men feel you should stay here where they can protect you. I can go with her."

"The men know she saved my life. They will understand why I am obligated to accompany her body."

"Is that what it is? An obligation?" Abdullah, still worried about Massoud's frame of mind, asked with bewilderment.

"Why do you ask me this now?" Massoud demanded. "Why does it matter what I call it? I must go with her."

"I only want to help you."

"Then give her back her life. That's the only thing that can remove this boulder from my chest." He looked at his friend. "Do that to help me, and if you cannot, then let me pass so that I can do what I must."

Abdullah took a step backwards.

"Ahmed Shah," he said to the Commander's retreating back, "I am sorry for your loss, but you must know you are not the only one who grieves. She was my friend, too."

Massoud stopped walking and looked back at Abdullah. "Yes, she was. I'm sorry for your loss." The words fell from his lips by rote.

"You couldn't have known this would happen," Abdullah called after Massoud.

Again the Commander stopped and looked back. "How

could I not? After fighting wars for twenty-two years, after two dozen assassination attempts on my life, after knowing full well that the Taliban would consider her a worthy target...How could I have not known? How could I have let this horrible thing happen?"

"She knew the risks of being in a war zone," Abdullah began, but a sharp gesture by Massoud silenced him.

"I will not have this conversation with you," Commander Massoud replied harshly. "I am taking her to Dushanbe now."

He turned and crossed the compound towards his office so that he could leave her journal, the two versions of the article, and the film canisters there.

It was on the short helicopter flight back from Dushanbe that Abdullah finally dared to question his friend again. He had silently watched as Massoud made all the arrangements to have Michelle's body sent to the US embassy in Germany. He handed over her passport and visa (but not before he had a copy of her picture made), confirmed her address in the United States, paid everyone who needed to be paid, and gave the official her belongings. Finally, having conducted all the business, Massoud hurried away as quickly as he could and sat mutely in his seat on the chopper. Abdullah joined him a few minutes later, and the pilot lifted off.

In the dim light from the control panel, Abdullah saw that Commander Massoud's eyes were filled with tears. As Abdullah watched, one tear broke free and rolled down Massoud's cheek. Abdullah reached out and put his hand on the Commander's shoulder in silent sympathy. Massoud swiped at the tear.

"She told me that allowing tears to fall would make me feel better. She was wrong. They burn and hurt." He averted his face and looked out of the chopper's side window.

Abdullah was shaken to see his Commander and friend so distraught. It frightened him, in fact, to the core of his being. If Massoud broke, if he reached a point where he could no longer fight, what would Afghanistan do? Would the death of this woman be the thing that finally made the Lion of Panjshir retreat into his den?

from that flame

"We can talk about it—" the doctor began cautiously.

"No," Massoud said, shaking his head and cutting him off. "These are matters private to my heart that are only to be shared with God." He looked at his friend and forced a small smile to his haggard face. "I know you're worried. Can you give me this one night to grieve for what has been lost? Tomorrow I will do all that I must; I promise you."

He turned his head to look out the window again, and nothing more was said, even after the helicopter landed back at the compound.

In his quarters, Massoud knelt and prayed long into the night. When he opened his door the next morning, he was tired and wan, but he was also composed and ready to work.

16. Tribute

"We are going to be in Paris in less than a week," Dr. Abdullah said to Commander Massoud. "Are your opening remarks for the European Parliament meeting ready?"

"Nearly so," Massoud said absently.

"Don't you think you should finish them?" Abdullah asked a little impatiently.

"Can we do that later this evening? I'm working on something else right now."

"What else?"

"Something I need to do for Michelle Garrett."

"You asked for a night, Ahmed Shah. It's been a week," Dr. Abdullah said with empathy. "You can't keep torturing yourself this way."

Commander Massoud rubbed his hand over his eyes and shoved aside the folder containing his remarks for next week's meeting. "I had asked her to meet me in Paris next week. It will be difficult being there without her. Perhaps we should not go."

"We have to go. A lot depends upon it. I am your foreign minister and your friend. I will be there with you," Abdullah said.

"Don't misunderstand me, Abdullah. You are my dearest friend and most trusted confidant. I could not get through a single day without your advice on matters both foreign and domestic. I trust you with everything I hold dear, with all of Afghanistan. But you are like me: born here. How many hours have we spent together struggling to understand the Western mind and all its nuances? Even with all your travel, can you tell me you always understand? Michelle would have been a Western voice from which

from that flame

I could have derived truth. She was not mired in politics or diplomacy. She would have given me—us—her honest thoughts on matters we need to understand."

"It is the loss of her usefulness alone that you mourn? I don't believe it," Abdullah said. "There is more that you are not telling me. Tell me now so that I can help you."

"My personal feelings are private," Massoud said firmly.

"Not when they keep spilling over into our work."

Commander Massoud got up and began to pace around the room. Finally, he turned to face the doctor. "I haven't yet let you read the article she wrote. Will you read it now and tell me what you think?"

He took out the English version of Michelle's article from the desk drawer and handed it to Abdullah, who accepted them, settled into a chair, and started to read. After a few minutes he looked up at Massoud with a smile on his face.

"I can actually hear her voice in my head saying these things," he said. "I can almost hear her laugh. I miss her laugh. It was contagious."

Massoud smiled and nodded in agreement. Abdullah went back to his reading. Massoud watched Abdullah's face as he read. He could almost tell what Abdullah was reading just by the various expressions on his friend's face. Twenty minutes later, Abdullah handed the pages back to Commander Massoud.

"She writes wonderfully well. I could see and hear everything. She captured you and me and the war very accurately. It's a beautifully done piece. I hope that you can find someone to publish it."

"That's all?"

"What else? It's a piece that needs to be read by the world. I remember being very hard on her when she first arrived. I told her I didn't want you to have false hope that something she would write might be heard since nothing else ever had been. I was wrong, and I wish she were here so that I could apologize. This article might actually make a difference. It even manages to give me hope."

Commander Massoud resumed his seat behind the desk, reached for the folder he had shoved aside, and withdrew a piece of paper. He handed it to Abdullah.

from that flame

"I've been writing this. I would like to have it added as a post-script to Michelle's article. Will you translate it into English for me?"

Several words had been scratched out or written over, indicating that Massoud had struggled to express what he wanted to say. Abdullah raised the paper and endeavored to read it. It said:

> Michelle Garrett was killed 24 March, 2001 by Talban forces in Afghanistan. She was a courageous journalist of the highest integrity. Her work on this article stands as a testament of her bravery and honesty. She was a cherished friend who will be missed.
>
> Ahmed Shah Massoud,
> Commander of the Northern Alliance
> 31 March 2001

"I would be very happy to translate this for you," Abdullah said when he had finished reading. "Michelle would be proud to have these words appear at the end of her article."

"Thank you," Commander Massoud said quietly. "Once you finish that, we can finish the opening remarks for the European Parliament next week."

"I'll see you soon," Abdullah said and left the Commander's office.

Once alone, Massoud took out the French version of the article. He smoothed the crinkled papers gently. He was determined to find someone who would help have Michelle Garrett's final article published. It was the last thing he could do for her, and it would stand as a tribute both to her and the Afghan people.

17. Paris

Commander Ahmed Shah Massoud, Dr. Abdullah Abdullah, Masood Khalili, General Sayed Anwari, General Piram Qol, and General Arif Noozai took Massoud's helicopter to Dushanbe, Tajikistan and they traveled from there by plane to Paris. While Dr. Abdullah and Masood Khalili had traveled to Europe before, this was the first trip out of the region for Commander Massoud and the others.

The generals chatted nervously among themselves. Dr. Abdullah and Masood Khalili talked about life in New Delhi, India. Ahmed Shah Massoud sat quietly as he looked out the window at unfamiliar terrain slipping past him. He ran the speech he would give over and over in his mind and prepared answers for the scheduled press conference that would follow.

The plane landed at Le Bourget military airport outside Paris, and the Afghan delegation was taken to the Hotel Plaza Athénée by a full diplomatic escort. Addressed as "Commandant," Commander Massoud found large crowds of cameramen, journalists, photographers, supporters, and admirers at every turn. Nothing would do except for him to stop, answer questions, and pose for pictures. He barely managed to make his breakfast meeting with the French foreign minister, Hubert Vedrine, on time.

Sandwiched between official meetings was the press conference. Humayun Tandar, an Afghan Charge d'Affaires to the UN, served as translator when necessary. Massoud answered questions as they were put to him, constantly stressing the main points he wanted to make, particularly that there was an enormous need for more humanitarian relief and that the West should pressure Pakistan to stop backing the Taliban. If that happened, he as-

from that flame

serted, the war would end in a year. When asked if he was able to overcome the infamous ethnic divisions in Afghanistan in order to form a single, cohesive fighting unit, Massoud smiled and pointed to the generals he had brought with him: a Hazara, a Pashtun, and an Uzbek. Dr. Abdullah suppressed a smile. Massoud had thought of everything.

"But Commandant Massoud," a French reporter shouted, "isn't your war against the Taliban futile? It controls ninety percent of your country. Can you really hope to win it back?"

"I would say they control more like seventy percent. No, this fight for freedom will never be called futile," he answered firmly, "and we will 'win it back,' as you say."

"Commandant Massoud, you are entering your third decade of war. Have you any regrets over the path your life has taken?"

Massoud studied his hands. He interlaced them, loosened them, and interlaced them again. This was the question he had asked himself so many times in recent months. Finally, he looked up and brought the full intensity of his eyes onto the man who had asked the question.

"I'll tell you what I think: life goes by whether you are happy or not. Any man who looks back on his past and feels he has been of some use need have no regrets. I have no regrets."

When it was time for lunch, Massoud and company were whisked away to dine with the head of France's National Assembly, Raymond Forni. After lunch he had a meeting with the President of the Senate, Christian Poncelet, followed by a press conference. He answered many questions ranging in topics from the Soviet Union's occupation of Afghanistan to the current situation in his country. Throughout the arduous day, he was consistently gracious, charming, and diplomatic. He smiled, shook hands, and posed for pictures until he was nearly blinded by the flashes before going to a new location and repeating the entire ordeal again. No matter what was asked of him, he obliged with humility, patience, and confidence. This trip was too important for a single misstep, and he did not intend to make one.

In the evening, Commander Massoud and his party met with six hundred members of the Afghan community who resided in Paris. Massoud shook hands, listened to the people's stories, accepted their good wishes, and assured them that one day soon they would be welcome and safe back in Afghanistan.

At the end of an 18-hour day, Commander Massoud was relieved to finally return to the hotel. He had barely sat down before there was a knock. Exhausted, he crossed the room and opened the door.

"Based on some of the questions asked today," Abdullah spoke as he strode into the room, "I think we need to make a few minor adjustments in your answers when we get to the meeting in Strasbourg."

"No more tonight, Abdullah," Massoud said grumpily. "I'm tired. I want to bathe, pray, and sleep. Go away."

"But we must be prepared," Dr. Abdullah protested.

"Didn't I do well enough today?"

"Well, yes, of course, but the main event is yet to come. You must be your most persuasive. Everyone must exactly understand our intent."

Massoud sighed. "Do you think I don't know this, my friend? Do you think I traveled this far after finally being offered a world stage on which to plead our position, only to make a mistake?" He patted Abdullah on the arm. "You have prepared me well. If there are any details I forget to mention, you can add them. After all, you will be beside me the whole time just as you always are, my right arm. Now go away and let me sleep so that I don't nod off in the middle of someone else's speech."

Abdullah admired the beautiful suite in which Massoud was being housed. "We should have rooms like this again in Kabul, huh?"

"Perhaps some day," Massoud said, yawning. "After the children are fed and in school. We must not forget our priorities." He made a great show of yawning again.

"All right, I'm leaving," Abdullah smiled. "Unless, of course, you want to go out and see the night life of the city. It would be a shame to visit Paris and not see anything except the inside of government buildings."

"I wouldn't know where to go even if I was so inclined—which I'm not. Aren't we scheduled for some sightseeing over the weekend?"

"If you stop working long enough to go," Abdullah answered, shaking his head.

from that flame

"Good night, my friend," Massoud said firmly.

"Good night," Abdullah said. "We can go over my notes on the way to Strasbourg."

He stopped with his hand on the doorknob and looked back at Massoud. "Are you all right?" he asked, and Massoud knew his concern.

"Nothing will interfere with what I need to do."

"That's not what I meant."

"I know, but it is the only answer I have. Good night."

Abdullah nodded. "Good night, Ahmed Shah."

After his bath and prayers, Massoud stood at the window and peered out onto the twinkling ocean of lights. He did want to see the city, but he wanted to see it with his friend the way they had planned. It would seem disloyal to her if he went out to celebrate the day's victories without her there to be a part of it. He knew his thoughts were foolish. He had done well and made every point he had come to the country to make. If he was equally persuasive in Strasbourg, it might make a real difference in the war he waged and in the lives of his people at home. That was his mission and goal in coming here, and, in the end, it was the only thing that really mattered.

Despite that, the ache in his heart prevented him from feeling the sense of accomplishment he would otherwise have. He had an odd feeling he couldn't identify. Certainly he had never felt it before. Is it loneliness? he wondered.

"I can't keep doing this," he muttered to himself. "Abdullah is right in all his concerns." He opened the door and walked out onto the balcony. The cool, April night air caressed his face. He leaned against the balcony and looked out over the city.

"I have to leave you here, Michelle *Jaan*."

He spoke as if she were there with him and could hear his words. Perhaps it was he, himself, who needed to hear the words spoken aloud.

"I can't take you back to Afghanistan with me. My life is there, but you are not part of it any longer. I have to say *baamaanay khuda* to you. It's the only way I can go forward because the guilt of your death is crushing me. I know you understand why I must do this, just as you understood everything else.

from that flame

"Tomorrow I will hand your story over to a respected journalist and ask his help in having it published. Once that is done, our last connection will be severed. I will force you from my thoughts because I must. I cannot allow this sorrow to pervade and cloud my mind."

He went inside. As he locked the door, he allowed himself one final, sweeping glance.

"But in a tiny, most private corner of my heart, there you will always live and laugh, my dear friend, my *Amer Saheb*," he murmured softly.

Commander Massoud went to bed but couldn't sleep because the room was haunted by the sound of a contagious laugh.

Abdullah dumped a large stack of newspapers on Massoud's bed the next morning.

"I went out to get these. You are on every front page."

"My picture or my words?" Massoud asked and reached for the papers. "My picture doesn't matter, but my message does."

"One of them described you as a 'wiry man with a scruffy'— or was it 'scraggly'?—beard," Abdullah said, laughing. "Oh, and the writer said you looked like the American singer Bob Dylan."

"Bob Dylan?" Massoud repeated absentmindedly as he continued reading through the newspapers. He looked at Abdullah. "Who is Bob Dylan?"

"An American singer. You look like him," Abdullah chortled.

"Do I?" Massoud was lost in an article again. "I am wiry. Did you see this?" He pointed to the article he was reading. "He got it all, word for word. Not a summary, but everything I said, every point." He looked at his foreign minister and smiled. "What was that you were saying about going over notes again? If not another word is printed, this will be enough."

"But more will be printed; that's exactly my point," Abdullah said, wagging his finger at his friend. "And we will go over the revisions on the plane."

"Yes, yes," Massoud waved him off and went back to reading. "By the way," he said without looking up, "your tie is crooked."

He smiled broadly but didn't lift his eyes from the paper

when he heard Abdullah drop the papers he had in hand and start fumbling with the tie in front of the mirror. It always worked as a momentary distraction. Abdullah was a fastidious clothes-horse.

In the lobby of the hotel, Massoud rose as a man approached him. "Mr. Chaliand, thank you for coming to see me."

The Commander offered his hand to the noted French journalist.

"It is an honor, sir. I must say I was a bit surprised. After all the press you had to handle yesterday, I could not imagine why you would want to see another reporter."

Commander Massoud gestured to a chair near the window. "Please, sit down. I don't have much time, and I must ask you to forgive me for getting straight to the point of our visit. I have a request to make of you. A favor."

"If it is within my power to do something for you, Sir, it would be my pleasure."

"Are you familiar with an American writer, a woman named Michelle Garrett?"

"Yes, I am. I heard that she was killed in Afghanistan a few weeks ago. Was she with you? If I heard that, I had forgotten. I thought she was writing about Afghan women?"

"Her story changed after we met." Commander Massoud took the stack of papers from the small table between them and handed them to Christophe Chaliand. The canisters of film were perched on top of the papers. "This is her article and film. She had no publisher for it but believed she could find one who would be interested. I am asking for your help in finding someone, some respectable magazine, perhaps, who would publish it."

"This is the piece she was working on when she was killed?" Christophe started flipping through the pages with great interest. "Is it complete?"

"Yes to both questions. Will you help me?"

"Of course. It shouldn't be difficult at all. Not only was Michelle Garrett well-respected as a journalist, this is her last article. Her death got a good bit of press coverage. I wouldn't be surprised if more than one magazine is interested in it, especially considering the attention you are getting right now."

"Thank you," Massoud said quietly. "There is one more thing. I have written a brief statement," he said, handing another paper to the Frenchman, "that I would like to have included at the end."

Christophe Chaliand scanned the translated words Massoud had written. "That is a fitting ending, Commandant. I think any magazine interested in the article would be interested in your eulogy of Michelle as well."

"Thank you very much. Now we must discuss your fee for this service."

"No, that isn't necessary. It would be my privilege to do this for both you and for my colleague. I am honored that you thought to ask me, Sir."

"You have a fine reputation, and I believe I can trust you." Massoud rose and offered his hand again. "This is important to me."

"You can trust me. Do you think I'd want a warrior like you chasing me down?" Chaliand laughed as he again shook the Commander's hand. "I will do as you ask, I promise. Perhaps one day you will permit me to visit you in your Panjshir Valley? After you have defeated the Taliban?"

"I would be very pleased to have you as my guest."

Massoud saw Dr. Abdullah frantically gesturing for him from where he stood near the hotel doors.

"May I ask one more question, Commandant?" Chaliand said quickly. Massoud nodded, and the journalist asked his question. "Why are you doing this for her?"

"Miss Garrett was my friend," Massoud said softly. "It's the least I can do for her. And now if you will forgive me, I am already late. I am to be in Strasbourg within the hour. You will keep me informed of your progress with Miss Garrett's article, won't you?"

"As soon as I know anything, I'll be in touch."

"Thank you again, and now I must fly. Goodbye."

Massoud hurried toward Abdullah feeling relieved that he had been able to fulfill the last promise he had made to his lost

from that flame

friend.

In Strasbourg, Massoud was brilliant. His remarks to the European Parliament were interrupted many times by thunderous, standing ovations. He made his message loud and clear: "The Taliban, along with the Pakistani military and Osama bin Laden are facing the Afghan nation. Very soon you will witness popular uprisings on several fronts, and the Taliban will lose ground. Our enemies claim that our struggle is ethnic in nature, pitting one group against the other, but even now in the worst conditions inside the country, all ethnic groups are still together and standing next to each other. There are works underway to build a 20,000-man army, and we will expand the national resistance movement. We consider this our duty: to defend humanity against the scourge of intolerance, violence, and fanaticism. We will build a democratic Islam in which the rights of all citizens, both male and female, are protected and in which all are free to determine their political leadership by ballots, not bullets.

"The international community must support us in our struggle. They must provide aid to both our internal refugees as well as those refugees who have who have fled the brutality of the Taliban and the war by moving to Pakistan and Iran. There is famine and disease. My people are starving and dying. We need your help, and I humbly ask you for it.

"Finally, I have words of caution for you. If the West does not help us eliminate al-Qaeda, if they do not help us rid our land of those terrorists who have invaded it, there will be a tragedy, a horror visited on you that is beyond comprehension or endurance. Help us, and by doing so, you will help yourselves."

"I don't know what is left to say," Commander Massoud wearily said to Dr. Abdullah as the Afghan contingent made the short trip from Strasbourg to Brussels. "I have said everything at least a dozen times already."

"Then say it a dozen and one times," Dr. Abdullah argued. "Since Foreign Minister Louis Michel, Policy Chief Javier Solana, and the European Union have asked to meet with you, it will be

from that flame

a perfect opportunity to press them for funds and humanitarian aid."

Commander Massoud rubbed his eyes and sighed heavily. "I will, my friend. You know I will. Allow me to sleep for five minutes, all right? Once I am rested, I will do all that you ask."

Commander Massoud looked out over the sea of friendly faces. He could not help but feel encouraged. He had given his speech, and it had been very well received. His exhaustion had turned to elation as he carefully listened to the words Dr. Abdullah was translating into his right ear. There would be help coming. He had received promises now for all sorts of humanitarian aid. No matter how many more people fled the Taliban and poured into the Panjshir Valley, they would have food, shelter, and medicine. The commander nodded in agreement when Dr. Abdullah told him that a request for a question and answer session had been made.

"Commandant, could you please explain why the Taliban destroyed the Buddha in Bamiyan?"

Massoud shoved his *pakol* back a little farther and scratched his head where the hat's lip had been.

"It is difficult for a rational man to explain the actions of an irrational man," he said dryly, "but I will try. I was told that Mohammed Mullah Omar, the head of the Taliban, said that some people pray to the statues as if they were God, and that is against Islam. He also said that if people say the statues are not connected to religious beliefs but are only part of Afghan history, then all the Taliban was destroying were stones. The world told him that he was wrong, but he refused to listen. It was cultural genocide he committed."

"A follow-up question?" the man asked. When Massoud nodded, the man smiled. "I take it you don't think very highly of Omar or the Taliban?"

"The Taliban practice a distorted, radical form of Islam I neither know nor understand," Commander Massoud answered. "There is nothing in the *Qur'an* that supports their treatment of women. Women are equal to men in God's eyes. Women should be educated and should work if they wish. Women should again

257

be part of Afghan society and government as they once were and will be again once the Taliban is driven out.

"The nature and the true face of the Taliban is now known by all our people. In the near future, you will witness popular movements against the Taliban. Help us be rid of them. Be part of the movement."

"Do you mean that the European Union should supply you militarily as well as with humanitarian aid?" someone else asked.

Commander Massoud shrugged. "Do the European leaders want to defend the just cause of the Afghan people, or are they satisfied by mere declarations of support? In addition, we need the international community to apply pressure on Pakistan to stop supplying the Taliban. If they would stop, the Taliban would be gone in less than a year."

"You have mentioned Pakistan's interference on more than one occasion," a newsman observed. "You blame Islamabad for creating an Afghan government subservient to Pakistani interests. What do you see in the future for your relationship with them?"

"Pakistan is the main reason for the conflict in my country. I have said this many times. We will never become the slaves of Pakistan. We could become good friends with Pakistan, but this is only possible if the leadership changes its attitude towards the Afghan conflict and stops supporting the Taliban."

"Do you believe there is only a military solution?" a woman asked.

"No," Commander Massoud answered. "I would prefer a political solution. Too many people have died already. We have millions of Afghans displaced in Iran and Pakistan. I want them all to return home safely. I have tried to negotiate with Mohammed Mullah Omar, but he refused to hold elections. I call upon the United States and fellow Muslim nations to increase their efforts for peace and democratic elections in Afghanistan. Their lack of support in the past has been disappointing. If they determine to help now, they can make a large impact for good. They can help pave the way for a *Loya Jirga*, a grand council, that will reflect the true will of the Afghan people."

"If your conflict continues, would you want foreign troops and advisors to assist you in your fight?"

from that flame

"As was the case during the Soviet occupation, the people of Afghanistan are ready to resist and defend their country against the aggressor from the South. The way to restore peace is to strengthen the resistance and exert pressure on Pakistan."

"What can you tell us about Osama bin Laden?" someone called out from the back of auditorium.

"Bin Laden is a terrorist," Commander Massoud stated flatly. "What more needs to be said of him? He has formed an unholy alliance with the Taliban. He supplies them with money, weapons, and fighters in exchange for a safe place from which to launch his terrorist attacks. Like Mohammed Omar, bin Laden embraces a false interpretation of Islam that he has used as a justification for his terrorism."

"It has been rumored that the United States Central Intelligence Agency has approached you in their efforts to get bin Laden. Is that true?"

Commander Massoud smiled a little and shrugged. "I meet many people from many lands. I listen to everything they have to say. That does not mean I choose to act."

"Is that a 'yes'?"

"I did not say that. I said that I meet many people and listen to what they say. I am aware, of course, that the CIA is very interested in locating Osama bin Laden; however, since the United States does not have a clear policy regarding Afghanistan, it presents problems. The United States must decide if it is on the side of freedom or oppression."

"If you could send a message to President George W. Bush, what would it be?"

"My message to President Bush is the following: If he isn't interested in peace in Afghanistan, if he doesn't help the Afghan people arrive at their objective of peace, the Americans and the rest of the world will have to face the problems."

"Would you care to elaborate?"

"No." Commander Massoud glanced at Dr. Abdullah indicating he was ready for the press conference to end. Dr. Abdullah immediately stood up.

"Thank you all very much for attending and for your interest. Thank you, also, for inviting us to your lovely city. It has been a pleasure for all of us to be here."

from that flame

Amid continued shouted questions, Abdullah helped Commander Massoud escape the hall and return to their hotel where the whole delegation collapsed in exhaustion.

"The Taliban is not happy with the Europeans," Abdullah said as he tossed a newspaper to Massoud the next morning. "They accuse the European Parliament of 'fanning the fires of war' by inviting you here. Let's see…Rahimullah Yusafzai wrote, and I quote: 'By shunning one armed faction, the Taliban, and befriending another, the Northern Alliance, the European Parliament and Western countries may be stoking the fire of continued fighting in war-ravaged Afghanistan.' Of course he would like it much better if there was no war because the Taliban has overrun the whole country," Abdullah concluded with disgust.

Commander Massoud scanned the article himself. "The Taliban also issued a warning to the European Parliament to remain neutral. Did you see what someone from the French Foreign Ministry said? 'This visit is taking place within the framework of our policy of keeping contact with all parties to the Afghan conflict.' They also say they 'hope to maintain contact with the Taliban in the hopes of convincing them to do more for their suffering people.' What does that mean? Are they inviting Omar next?"

"I don't think he meant that," Dr. Abdullah said, rereading his copy of the newspaper. "I think they are simply trying to sound diplomatic and not look as if they are taking sides."

"Are you certain?" Massoud read the article for a third time in an effort to glean its true meaning. He looked up at his friend. "Do you see why I wanted Michelle Garrett here? She would understand this and explain it to us. I don't understand this double-speak." He threw the paper down in disgust. "I felt as if we had made good progress here. Now I am uncertain. Perhaps we were foolish to come."

"No, we weren't," Abdullah Abdullah protested strongly. "You laid out our case clearly and well, and you were heard—of that I am convinced. Don't allow a few words tossed as a bone to the Taliban undermine all the good you accomplished here." The doctor looked at his friend's dejected face. "You are tired, and you've been under a lot of stress these past few days. It has colored your view of things. Today is a day of rest for you. Relax. Read your poetry. Take a nap. By the time we are ready to go back to Paris, your balanced perspective will have returned."

"Is that your medical advice, Doctor?" Massoud said, managing a smile.

Abdullah patted the Commander on his shoulder. "And my friendly advice as well." He gathered up the newspapers. He would read every word in all of them, but not in this room, and not with Massoud. "If you feel like it, someone has offered to take us on a driving tour of the city this afternoon."

"Perhaps." Massoud picked up a book from the nightstand. "My doctor has advised me to rest, and that is what I intend to do."

"Good. I will check in on you later."

Abdullah went to the door. He had a few phone calls he wanted to make in private. There were a few other Western minds he trusted, and he intended to get their interpretation of the news articles.

"Listen to what Hafiz says," Massoud read aloud from his book so that Abdullah would hear the words that seemed amazingly appropriate for the moment:

> Then to the rolling Heaven itself I cried,
> Asking, "What Lamp has destiny to guide
> Her little children stumbling in the Dark?"
> "A blind understanding!" Heaven replied.

Massoud looked up from the page to Abdullah. "It is, indeed, a 'blind understanding' sometime, isn't it, my friend?"

"It often seems that way," Abdullah agreed with a smile. If Massoud was absorbed in his beloved poetry, for a while at least he would find comfort. Abdullah closed the door quietly behind him.

Dr. Abdullah entered Massoud's hotel room. "The people from Azadi Afghan Radio are waiting for you in one of the meeting rooms downstairs."

from that flame

The Commander had just finished putting on a cream-colored *shalwar-kamiz*, the traditional Afghan garment for men.

"Before you go down, you need to know that the forces of Dostum and Kahn had some sort of battle with Taliban forces. I don't have the details yet."

"You are certain it was the combined forces of Dostum and Kahn?" Commander Massoud asked with concern. "How did that happen? Have you spoken to General Fahim? Can we get in touch with him?"

"I will get as much information as I can," Dr. Abdullah assured Massoud. "I realize you didn't want the Taliban to know that the Northern Alliance has joined forces with Dostum and Kahn, but does it really matter if they find out?"

"I wanted to keep the information—*all of it*—secret," Commander Massoud sighed deeply. "I wanted to have the element of surprise. Well, what is done, is done. Find out as much as you can. I will try to cut this meeting short."

"Don't forget that King Zahir Shah's men are here from Italy to see you too," Dr. Abdullah reminded Massoud.

"I did forget," Massoud sighed again. "They have probably been dispatched by the King to make a formal visit because of my father's service and loyalty to him for so many years. All right, well, I will see them as soon as they arrive and then return here as soon as possible."

"I think they are going to invite you to visit the King in Rome," Abdullah said. "It might well be worth making that trip in the summer or fall. Having the support of the King could be valuable propaganda for us."

"We'll see," Commander Massoud answered. "Perhaps by autumn the Taliban will be defeated, and we can invite the King to come home at last."

With that, he hurried from the room and went downstairs to conduct yet another meeting.

"The Western press is saying that you pulled off quite a coup by enhancing your stature as a political leader," one of the Afghan media said with a smile once Commander Massoud had settled in his chair.

262

from that flame

"It is very good news for the men and women of Afghanistan to see that Europe and the European Parliament have shown an interest in Afghanistan and the condition of the Afghan people, and that they are thinking of taking a step in the direction of peace," Commander Massoud said, modestly deflecting the praise from himself to those who had hosted him. "Positive steps have been made this week that will hopefully put an end to the agony and troubles faced by Afghans."

"Another paper suggested that you successfully articulated an alternative political vision for Afghanistan, and that Europeans will find it more palatable than that of the Taliban."

"That is good news," Massoud said. He appeared very relaxed. "What the Taliban did in Bamiyan got them some very negative attention from the world."

Massoud saw the French journalist Christophe Chaliand appear at the back of the room and waved to him to come forward and join them. Instead, Chaliand approached the Commander and bent to whisper something in his ear. As Chaliand straightened, Commander Massoud stood.

"Please excuse me for just a moment. I'm sorry. I will return immediately," Massoud said to those gathered before him before he hastily followed the journalist out into the hall. He closed the door behind him and faced Chaliand.

"You have news about Miss Garrett's article? Have you found a publisher so quickly?"

"I've been doing two things simultaneously," Chaliand answered. "I have located and spoken with her attorney in the United States and received the authority from him to handle the sale of Michelle's article here in Europe. He knows contacts of hers at various magazines in the States, and he will talk to them directly.

"I have also been talking to several magazine publishers here in France as well as in Great Britain, Belgium, Italy, and Germany. I am receiving a great deal of interest. Marketing the article at the same time you are all over the newspaper headlines makes my job easy."

"That is good news," Massoud said, smiling broadly. "Thank you very much."

"It is my pleasure," Christophe returned the other man's

smile. However, it was quickly replaced by another, more serious expression. "Commandant, there is something else. I have been debating about whether or not I should tell you now or wait until you hear from Michelle's attorney directly, but there is something else you need to know."

"What is that?" Massoud's eyebrows knit in concern. "Is there a legal issue because she is not living?"

"No, it's not that," the journalist said, shaking his head. "Apparently Michelle had sent her lawyer a letter while she was still with you in Afghanistan."

"Yes, I remember that she added a few pieces of mail to some things I was sending to Peshawar. Is this letter important?"

"Well, in the letter she told her lawyer about the article and said that she intended to have all the proceeds from its sale go directly to you to use as you see fit. The lawyer showed Michelle's letter to her parents, and they want to honor her wish. All the money from the sale of the article will be sent to you through her attorney. You will get something from him in writing, and perhaps I shouldn't have said anything, but, well, I thought you might want to know." When Chaliand saw the Commander's blank expression, he added one more remark. "Commandant Massoud, we are easily talking about a six-figure number here. The British magazine alone offered £100,000."

Commander Massoud closed his eyes as he endeavored to order both his thoughts and emotions. At a time when scraping up the $400 needed to fill the tank of one helicopter was a daunting task, the idea of £100,000 took his breath away. He would accept the money in the same spirit it was being offered by Michelle's parents. It was a means of honoring her wishes. And yet…he had wanted to leave her behind in Paris. Accepting her money would guarantee that she returned to Afghanistan with him. It would mean that she would be there with him every time he refueled a helicopter or bought meat for his men. It would mean that she would be there with him every time he paid for a school or built a clinic. It would mean that every day he would have to face anew the loss and responsibility he felt over her death. Slowly he opened his eyes; his decision was made. He smiled at Christophe Chaliand.

"Michelle Garrett was one of the bravest, kindest, most generous people I have ever met. It was a privilege to know her. I will accept her gift with heartfelt thanks because it is a way to honor her memory in my country. Thank you. Now, if you will excuse me, I must go to my room."

"But your meeting..." Chaliand said, gesturing towards the door behind Massoud.

"Oh, yes, the meeting," Commander Massoud repeated. He forced a smile to his face. "I have had so many meetings this week, surely you can't blame me for trying to duck out of at least one?"

"I hate meetings, too," Chaliand said. "Well, I'll be on my way." He offered his hand to the Afghan commander. "I intend to take you up on the invitation to visit you one day."

Commander Massoud accepted the journalist's hand and shook it warmly. "I look forward to that day. Thank you again for all that you are doing."

"You are very welcome, sir. Good-bye."

Chaliand slipped his hands into his overcoat as he turned away. Immediately he turned back and called to Massoud.

"Commandant, I forgot. There is one more thing." Chaliand withdrew his hand from his pocket and offered a photographer's envelope to Massoud.

"I had the film developed to see if there were any usable prints for the article. When I saw these, I had duplicates made. I thought you might want them."

Commander Massoud accepted the envelope and slid a few photographs out of the protective covering. The first picture was one of Massoud and Dr. Abdullah standing shoulder to shoulder. The second was of Massoud and Michelle Garrett. The Commander immediately remembered when and where it had been taken. Silently, he slid both pictures back into the envelope and tucked them into his pocket. He would look at the rest when he was alone.

"Thank you," he said with a catch in his voice. "I hope there were some usable prints in those roles of film. She was forever wandering off taking pictures..." He looked at the Frenchman. "I have my meeting," he said, waving vaguely at the door behind him.

"Yes, of course. Good-bye, Commandant," Chaliand said as he turned again and left.

from that flame

Massoud also turned and went back into his meeting, grateful he had already answered the same questions so often that he would be able to talk his way through the rest of the time without really thinking. His mind was far away from the current activity. Burned into his mind's eye was a picture of a small woman in camouflage clothes with wild hair only partially tucked beneath a battered *pakol* and a disarming, crooked smile on her face. Leaving her behind when he returned to Afghanistan might have been his idea, but she, apparently, had another. He had made a promise to her that she would live in his memory. She intended for him to keep that promise.

Abdullah stuck his head in Massoud's hotel door. "Ready? The car is waiting to take us to the airport."

"I'm ready," Massoud answered. He laid the last of the newspapers in his suitcase, closed the lid, and snapped it shut.

"It was a good trip, a worthwhile trip," Abdullah pronounced. "I just wish we could stay longer."

"I will leave this city with few regrets," Massoud answered. He glanced around the room one last time. Nothing has been forgotten. "Shall we go?"

The car ride to the airport was silent most of the way. Massoud looked out the window as the streets rushed passed, and he did regret a little that he had not been able to see more of the beautiful city. Paris filled him with a bittersweet longing. Under other circumstances, he would have liked to spend more time there. Later, as the plane departed the area and flew over Paris to carry him into the Eastern sky, he again looked out the window at the twinkling lights.

He had hoped to leave Michelle Garrett's spirit behind when he left only to discover that it was impossible. Whether he had received the money for the article or not, she would have been with him. Whereas a short time ago she had been a vital, living force in his life, now she was a cherished memory he would quietly carry in his heart. She would also serve as an additional inspiration as he continued his fight against the Taliban. He lived for the day when Afghan women, already courageous, would be as free, well-educated, and filled with the joy of life as Michelle had been. He

from that flame

regretted that her story on the women of RAWA would remain unfinished. It was a story he would have to finish for her as well as for the Afghan women. As Michelle had observed, his progress on the battlefield would determine whether the RAWA story would have a happy ending or not. He would not fail any of them.

"Are you ready for more meetings and another press conference?" Dr. Abdullah asked, glancing over at Commander Massoud in the seat beside him. "We are landing in a few minutes."

Massoud opened his eyes, closed them again, rubbed them hard with his thumb and forefinger, and finally looked over at the doctor. "How many meetings and how many press conferences?" he asked wearily.

"Two meetings. The public meeting with President Rakhmanov and the private one with Minister Shoigu. Only one press conference."

"I can do that," the exhausted commander said, forcing a smile to his haggard face.

When their small chartered plane landed in Dushanbe, a large crowd of Afghans—hundreds and hundreds at first guess—greeted Ahmed Shah Massoud as a conquering hero. Fatigue fell away from him and was replaced with new vitality and determination. More of his Afghan kinsmen would be able to return home safely, and soon; this he vowed to himself as he shook every hand outstretched to him.

At the public meeting with the president of Tajikistan, Emomali Rakhmanov, the two men assured continued cooperation between their governments. At the private, secret meeting with Sergei Shoigu, the Russian Emergencies Minister, Commander Massoud was assured of the delivery of certain munitions and vehicles he had acquired. Although both sides would later deny that the meeting had taken place, Commander Massoud did make a statement that he was grateful to Russia for its assistance in settling the Afghan conflict and praised Russian efforts to mediate a settlement in the civil war.

"Despite all the existing problems, we have always been ready to sit down at the negotiating table. We may even accept the creation of a provisional government, but for no longer than

from that flame

six months or a year," he said. "After that time, it would be necessary to hold general elections under the aegis of the United Nations and the six-plus-two formula which would include Iran, China, Pakistan, Tajikistan, Turkmenistan, Russia, and the United States."

At the press conference the next day, everyone wanted the Commander to estimate the success of the trip to Europe. Commander Massoud refused to go into specific details about private discussions, but he did highlight many of the comments he had made repeatedly to his audiences there. He concluded with several warnings.

"The Taliban wants to spread its radical ideas not only in Afghanistan, but, with the help of the drug trade and terrorism, into the rest of Central Asia as well. We prescribe against the cultivation and trafficking of illegal narcotics. As during the *jihad*, we fully oppose terrorism and terrorist activities. No one ever witnessed a terrorist attack by a *mujahidin*, even when the Soviets were in Afghanistan. Terrorism is wrong, and we are against it. We do not want to see Afghanistan become a base for terrorism. In an Afghanistan we may guide, there will be no room for terrorists or Osama bin Laden.

"Control of Afghanistan by the Taliban will not result in stability, peace, and prosperity in the region. The people of Afghanistan will never accept such a repressive regime. Regional countries will never feel secure and safe. The goal is clear. The international community and democracies of the world should not waste any valuable time and begin to provide critical assistance to the Afghan people who are making valiant efforts to overcome obstacles that exist on the path to freedom, peace, stability, and prosperity.

"Allow me to make one final observation: terrorist operations will spread throughout the world. Osama bin Laden is in search of opportunity and a base of operations. Afghanistan provides him with that base. The longer this opportunity is given to him, the more he will fan the flames of terrorism all over the world. The world needs to join us now in removing bin Laden from his base and in denying him the opportunity to spread his terror."

Amidst more handshakes, backslaps, and cheers, Commander Massoud made his way out of the room. He turned to Abdullah who was directly behind him.

from that flame

"Are we done here now?"

"Yes, officially we are. Why? Is there someone else you want to see?"

Massoud shook his head emphatically. "No. What I would like to do is leave for home tonight rather than wait until morning. Is that possible?"

Abdullah shrugged "I suppose it is. The helicopter is probably refueled and ready to go. Are you sure you wouldn't rather get a good night's sleep and leave in the morning?"

"I would rather get back to Khwaja Bahauddin tonight. After a week away, I am anxious to get caught up on everything that's happened while we've been gone."

"All right," Dr. Abdullah nodded agreeably. "I'll get a driver to take us to the helicopter and send someone to get our luggage from the hotel. We can be home in a few hours."

"Good. I need to see some people in the next few days, but after that, what do you think about both of us taking a couple of days off to see our families?"

Dr. Abdullah grinned broadly. "Those are travel plans I will gladly make."

"And travel I will gladly make," Commander Massoud said, returning his friend's smile. Spring would come to them soon, and that would mean an increase in military activity. If they didn't get to their homes now, another opportunity might not present itself for months. He yearned to hold his wife and tuck his children into bed. It had been a long, difficult winter. Being surrounded by his family was a respite he needed more than he could express.

He put his hand on his friend's shoulder. "Let's go." There were few things in life on which he could count, but having Abdullah Abdullah at his side was one of them.

18. Hamid

"Well, you did it again," Dr. Abdullah said as he approached the desk where Commander Massoud sat reading his mail. The commander looked up.

"What did I do?"

"Got the Pakistanis in an uproar," Abdullah said with a laugh as he tossed a newspaper in front of Massoud. "Their propaganda machine is working overtime trying to denigrate your trip to France. Since you're just a 'minority figure' as they insist, I don't see why they are so worried, do you?"

"I don't know, and I don't care," Commander Massoud answered as he shoved the newspaper aside without reading it.

"Here is something you'll care about." The doctor settled into a chair across from Massoud. "There's a young man outside who says he defected from the Taliban. He wants to talk to you and says he has information about an upcoming attack."

"That is interesting, indeed." Massoud looked past Abdullah and addressed one of his bodyguards. "There is a stranger out there. Bring him to me."

"Search him," Abdullah called over his shoulder to the departing man. He looked back at Massoud. "Besides this Hamid, there are several citizens waiting to see you. Will this be a good afternoon, or should I tell them to come back another time?"

"Let's see what this newcomer has to say, and then I'll decide."

Commander Massoud watched as his bodyguard escorted a youth towards the end of the room where the commander and doctor sat.

from that flame

"You were with the Taliban?" Commander Massoud asked without preamble. The young man nodded his assent. "Why did you leave them?" Massoud maintained a steady gaze on Hamid, determining the measure of the man as much by his body language as by the words he spoke.

"I never wanted to join them in the first place," Hamid said, steadily returning Commander Massoud's intense look. "They came to my town and dragged all the men out into the street. They told us that we either had to join them or be killed. My father said that if he and I both had to leave my mother and sister, the women would have no one to care for them. So the Taliban shot my father." Hamid's eyes filled with tears. "Then they said they didn't want me to have my father's concerns for my mother and sister and shot them too." The tears overfilled his eyes and rolled down his dusty, thin cheeks. He shifted his gaze to the floor as if he was ashamed for everything that had happened.

"I went with them," Hamid continued in a shaky voice. "There was no reason to stay home since my whole family was dead. I pretended to be a good soldier for them. I listened and I learned. They hate and fear you. I knew that I wanted to join you and fight against them. One night when I was supposed to be on guard duty, I managed to slip away. I didn't have any food or water. It took me four days to walk here." He looked back up at Massoud. "I don't care if you feed me or not, just say that you will let me join your forces so that I can fight against those who murdered my family."

Massoud stood up and walked around the desk with his hand outstretched towards the young man. "You are welcome to join us," he said with a smile, "and I think we will even manage to feed you, if little else."

A sob broke in Hamid's throat as he grasped the Commander's hand. "Thank you," he managed to say as he struggled to fight back more tears. "I will be a good and loyal *mujahidin* for you, Commander Massoud. I have information I think will be helpful to you."

"Later we will talk again, and then you shall tell me everything you know," Commander Massoud said quietly as he motioned to his bodyguard to approach. "First you will go and get some food and water and sleep. When you have rested, we will talk. Go with this man now. Relax. Feel safe. You are among friends."

from That Flame

Massoud sat on the edge of his desk and watched Hamid and the bodyguard walk out of the office. When they were gone, he looked down at Abdullah who had been sitting quietly throughout the exchange.

"I don't think I will ever understand the Taliban no matter how many stories I hear," he said with a deep sigh. "Their cruelty is beyond comprehension." He shook his head and returned to his chair. "You are very quiet," he said as he settled in behind his desk again.

"I was thinking," Abdullah said quietly.

"That could be dangerous," Massoud teased, but when he saw how serious Abdullah's expression was, he leaned across the desk. "Tell me, my friend. What worries you?"

"I didn't say I was worried. I said I was thinking," Abdullah said. "There is a difference, you know."

"All right," Massoud said, suppressing a smile. "Are they thoughts you choose to share?"

"I was thinking about what was written in that newspaper I brought in this morning."

"Why waste your time thinking about that propaganda?"

"It angers me that people who don't know you, who have never even met you, write those lies, and other people who have never met you, read and believe them. Why don't they write the truth? Why don't they tell stories about the Taliban like the one Hamid just told us? Why don't they tell stories about the hundreds of thousands of people who have fled the Taliban and found their way here to Panjshir because they trust you to make wise decisions and help them?"

"The truth doesn't serve their purpose," Commander Massoud answered quietly, "and while I genuinely appreciate the loyalty and friendship that lies beneath your anger at these lies, I ask you not to waste your thoughts that way. In the end, when all is said and done, the truth will come out. Then everyone will know the true face of the Taliban as well as the true face of the United Front. Until that time, we must keep our focus on the task at hand and not be distracted by the malignant lies of bitter foes."

"Yes, you are right," Abdullah agreed, although he sighed as he spoke. Another thought entered his mind and a smile crossed his face. "When Michelle Garrett's article comes out, it will be a

from that flame

blow for the truth."

Massoud glanced at a bookcase shelf containing Michelle's journal and the French copy of the article. He nodded in agreement but said nothing. He began to sort and organize the papers on his desk. The Pakistani newspaper was tossed into the trash. When he was finished, he looked at Abdullah.

"I think we should see as many citizens as possible this morning. Helping them will restore our determination, refresh our spirits, and remind us that no matter how much cruelty there is in our country, there is also much goodness."

"I'll go get the first person in line," Dr. Abdullah said with a smile as he rose. "If I recall what he told me earlier, he needs help removing land mines from a field he wants to use to expand his grape crops. Oh, and there is a woman waiting who needs work. She arrived from Kabul while we were away."

"Bring her in first," Commander Massoud said. "Perhaps she will be qualified to teach my daughters' math class."

In addition to helping the woman in search of work and the farmer who needed help clearing his field, Commander Massoud also mediated a boundary dispute between two farmers with adjoining land, accepted the volunteer services of three brothers who wanted to join the *mujahidin*, discussed the correct dimensions of children's school desks that a carpenter was building, went over a list of supplies needed for the clinic, welcomed a new refugee family to their group, and considered a proposal for a new bridge across the river. Finally, he and Abdullah broke for lunch.

"Are you going to interview Hamid after we eat?" Dr. Abdullah asked as he reached for bread and a cup of tea.

"Yes," Commander Massoud answered thoughtfully. "It will be interesting to hear what he has to say."

"You sound skeptical," Abdullah observed. "Don't you think he is legitimate?"

"Oh, yes," Massoud assured him. "I believe every word he said. I am puzzled why we haven't received this information about a pending attack from any of our usual sources, that's all. I thought we had infiltrated every major Taliban group."

"We could train Hamid and send him back in as an operative," the doctor suggested.

"He doesn't have the temperament for espionage," the Commander replied. "You saw how emotional he was. I think he has exerted all the control he could muster in order to survive the Taliban camp. Now that he is free to express his grief and rage, I doubt he could bottle it back again. I also doubt that he will be fit for battle without a few weeks time to come to grips with everything that has happened to him." Massoud passed the bread to the doctor. "No, my friend, this boy may best serve us this day with the information he already has. After that, let's send him as far from the front line as we can. Maybe Ata can put him to work as a messenger going back and forth to Peshawar."

"He's going to want to fight for you," Abdullah said, arching an eyebrow. "He's going to want revenge for his family. He's not going to be happy if you send him away."

"He doesn't have to be happy." Commander Massoud had finished his sparse meal and shoved the empty bowl aside. "He only has to follow orders. I'll go get him while you finish your meal. If you're done before I get back, pull some of the maps out, will you?"

Massoud spread one of his many Soviet-era maps in front of Hamid. "Can you show me where the Taliban had their camp set up?"

The youth stared at the map with alarm before looking shamefaced at Massoud. "I don't know how to read a map," he said in a low voice.

"That's all right," Commander Massoud said kindly. "Don't worry about the map." He passed it to Abdullah who, he knew, would try to figure out where the boy described. "Just tell me what you heard. Do you know the name of the town or region where you were stationed?"

"I think we were in a place near the Farkhar Gorge," Hamid answered. "I heard some of the commanders talking about an access point to a valley, and I heard about a town called Abee."

"That's good," Massoud said as he glanced over to see Dr. Abdullah quickly pinpoint the gorge. It was, indeed, a key access point between Taloqan in Takhar province and a valley leading into Badakhshan province in the northeast and into Panjshir in the south. They had fought over that land several times in the past year. He looked at Hamid. "Were there only Afghan Taliban in the group?"

Hamid shook his head emphatically. "*Nay,* there were a lot of Pakistani soldiers, and many Arabs, too. There were fighters from places I didn't know."

"Do you know what kinds of weapons they have? How did they travel?"

"We brought SAMs and RPGs and PKM light machine guns. They have 4X4s, armored personnel carriers, and tanks. They talked about bringing in fighter bombers."

Commander Massoud and Dr. Abdullah exchanged concerned glances. A bombing campaign was something against which they were ill-prepared to fight. Their supply of Stingers was low, and they were unsure of when they would be re-supplied.

"Do you have any idea about when they plan to launch this offensive?" Abdullah asked Hamid.

"In about a week, I think. They were waiting for more troops to join them."

"Do you know how many troops they expect to have when everyone has amassed?"

"Between five and six thousand, I heard," Hamid answered. "Minus one. Me."

The Commander smiled and nodded at the youth. "Yes, thank God for that. You have been very helpful to us. Go rest from your journey. I will call you again later if I have more questions."

Massoud waited for Hamid to leave before turning to Abdullah.

"I think General Daoud can be here in a day's travel. We need to send runners to get him and General Fahim. There is not enough time to call Kahn or Dostum." The Commander started adding men and munitions totals in his head. He looked closely at the map again. "Our front line will be here," he said, tracing a path with his finger across the old creases. He glanced at Abdullah again. "A week is not much time to prepare for a battle of this size. Will you find runners to send to Daoud and Fahim? On second thought, bring me Abdul and Zahir. They have proven trustworthy in the past. Think about who we can send in as a double agent. While you are doing these things, I will study the maps and begin plans for our offensive. Let's see if we can't give the Taliban a surprise welcome to the neighborhood."

Commander Massoud looked from Abdul to Zahir and back. "You know that I prefer to send runners in teams. However, in the past few days I have allowed several of our fighters to return to their homes and farms for a week. I have summoned them back, but meanwhile I need everyone here and can't spare teams for this mission. You will each have to go alone. It is imperative that you locate General Daoud," Massoud said, nodding to Abdul, "and General Fahim," he added, nodding to Zahir. "Can I count on you?"

"You know you can, *Amer Saheb*," Zahir said as Abdul nodded in agreement.

Commander Massoud smiled encouragingly and said, "All right." He motioned for them to join him at the map. "Abdul, General Daoud is in Dormim. I think you can get there in a day or less. Tell General Daoud to deploy his men here, to Elmarzan. It is very important that the troops only move under cover of darkness. Bring the general back with you as quickly as possible.

"Zahir, General Fahim is here in Dudga. I need him here with me by mid-week at the latest. You will have to travel quickly. Ask him to send his men to Kangurch. That will put them close enough to where the front will be, but I don't think troop movement will be noticed. Fahim will give them specific orders if he deems it necessary. Do either of you have any questions?"

"No, *Amer Saheb*," Zahir said. "We will do as you ask. We won't fail you."

"I know you won't." Commander Massoud embraced Zahir and then Abdul. "We will get your provisions, pray together, and then you will be on your way, God willing, with all my trust and confidence."

"I think we have to use him, Ahmed Shah," Dr. Abdullah argued. "No one we have here right now is better situated for the job than Hamid."

from that flame

Massoud shook his head. "Not better situated, perhaps, but certainly better suited. Can you think of no one else?"

"You sent Jabir and Anwari back to Kabul. Ustad is in Marzar. Abu is in Peshawar. Omar was captured and killed a month ago. Maulana is ill with a high fever. Last week you dispatched Zardusht to Kandahar. Am I forgetting anyone? Ah, yes, Daqiqi decided he would rather join the Taliban than be killed by them. Hamid is our best chance."

Commander Massoud sighed deeply and dropped into his chair. "The boy is fragile, Abdullah. I'm not sure he has the fortitude. I don't want to send him to an automatic death."

"I asked him to come here in a few minutes. Talk to him at least, Ahmed Shah. Discuss it with him. If you still feel he is not capable of doing this, then somewhere—somehow—we will find someone else. "

"All right," Massoud said with resignation just as Hamid appeared in the doorway.

"Did you wish to see me, Commander?" the youth asked anxiously.

"Please, come in. I need to talk to you about something very serious."

Massoud welcomed Hamid into the office and pointed at a chair near Dr. Abdullah. Massoud returned to his seat and studied the face of the young man before him.

"First, I want to tell you how much we appreciate the information that you provided us. Based on what you told us, we now have time to plan an offensive strike against the Taliban. In fact, plans are already underway."

"I am grateful to be of help, and I pray to Allah for another opportunity to serve you," Hamid said sincerely. "Is that why you called me here? Is there something I can do?"

"It is a dangerous mission," Massoud began.

"I don't care," Hamid said fervently as he eagerly leapt from his seat. "I will do anything you ask. I will do anything to defeat the Taliban."

"Listen," Dr. Abdullah said as he laid a restraining hand on the younger man's arm. "Sit and listen quietly to what the Commander says."

"I will. I'm sorry." Hamid took his seat again and looked steadily at Commander Massoud.

"We rely a lot on intelligence gathering," Massoud began again. "The fact that we didn't know about plans for this Taliban strike before you told us causes me great concern. It means we don't have enough saboteurs among the Taliban ranks. It means we need to recruit more men who are willing to take on this most risky assignment: that of a double agent."

"Is that what you want me to do?" Hamid asked in amazement. "You want me to be a spy for you? I will."

Commander Massoud raised his hand to stop the youth's eager words. "It isn't that easy. It means that you have to go back among the Taliban and convince them you are truly on their side. You have to keep your eyes and ears opened for any information that would be valuable to the resistance. Periodically, you will have to get away from the Taliban to report the information you've learned, and then you will have to go back into their ranks and start all over again. If they become suspicious of you at any point, do not doubt for a moment that they will kill you. It is one of the most dangerous jobs anyone can do."

"How can I just walk back into the Taliban camp after being away for a week? Won't they be suspicious?" Hamid asked.

"Of course they will be," Massoud said. "You will have a story in your mouth and papers in your pocket. If they disbelieve either, they will kill you on the spot. You will have to convince them that the reason you were gone was because you were captured and imprisoned by my men. You will tell them you managed to escape, but before you did, you sneaked into my office and have brought 'stolen' papers back to prove your loyalty to them."

"Will you give me the story and the papers?" Hamid asked.

"Yes. The story will be taught to you word for word. You will repeat it until the words become your own. We will give you the names of locations where we have had men on patrol so that they will be able to check with their own men and learn there was Northern Alliance activity in the area. You will use some of the truth. You will say that after you were captured you were brought to me. You can say that in an effort to lure me into trusting you, you told me the story about how your family was killed and that you hated the Taliban. Of course I would want to believe this

from that flame

story and, in time, security around you was lessened, and that allowed for your eventual escape. Don't tell them that I believed you completely or that you were free to roam the camp. They will never believe that. Say only that you were not guarded as closely. Then, after being around me and my men for a week, say that you have come to understand that it is the Taliban who is on the side of Allah and that you want to be a martyr in God's own cause. When you saw an opportunity to escape, you took it, but only after you risked your life to break into my office and grab all the papers on my desk. You don't know what the papers are, but you hope they are important and will help the Taliban defeat me."

"What will the papers be?" Hamid asked with great interest.

"Communications between General Fahim and me containing information I would never want the Taliban to know. Very carefully crafted with exactly the information I want the Taliban to know. A map that shows my plans to move my troops in a direction I would only want them to think we were moving," Massoud said as he arched an eyebrow.

"I will do it," Hamid said with passion. "Teach me the words and give me the papers. I will make the Taliban believe me."

Massoud and Abdullah exchanged glances. It was Abdullah's turn to raise an eyebrow as if to say, "I told you so." The Commander looked back at Hamid and again studied the young man's face and eyes. He shoved his *pakol* back a little and scratched his head. Next he scratched his beard. Finally, he closed his eyes and rubbed them with his thumb and fingers. He looked back at Hamid again still without speaking.

"You doubt my ability, don't you?" Hamid said. "I can do this, Commander Massoud."

Massoud shook his head, still unconvinced. "It's dangerous. The risks—"

"Commander," Hamid interrupted in a low, firm voice, "the worst thing they could do is kill me. I would rather die at their hands serving God, you, and Afghanistan than fighting for them in a battle against you, my country, and God. Death is not a terrible fate. I would be reunited with my family in God's Paradise. Please, Commander Massoud, allow me the honor of serving in this way. I will be a good *mujahidin* for many years if you and God are willing."

from that flame

Commander Massoud nodded in silent acquiescence. He had reservations and prayed that he was not sending this young man to a certain death.

"All right," he said at last. "Doctor Abdullah will take you to the man who will help you with the story. I will begin work on the documents. Plan on leaving the day after tomorrow." He stood and came around the desk as Hamid rose. He opened his arms to the young man and embraced him.

"I will pray to Allah every day that you are both safe and successful. Thank you for your courage and sacrifice," Massoud said quietly.

"It would seem that Pakistan has decided to ignore international pressure and, rather than end their support of the Taliban, go ahead and launch a new initiative," Commander Massoud said to the circle of his generals and advisors a few days later.

"There was a meeting I heard about," Mohammed Fahim said. "Pakistani advisors think that Pakistani logistical support will enable the Taliban and bin Laden's men to route us by fall. They feel that is a reasonable timetable to stall public opinion, and if they obliterate us before the snow falls, the whole issue will then become moot."

"We'll see if we can't change their perception," Massoud said wryly. "I have an idea that might work."

He drew his generals and advisors closer to the map and began to talk.

"General Fahim, have you dispatched your men to Kangurch?"

"Yes, with all the weapons and munitions we have at our disposal. They will stay out of sight until I meet them there with their specific orders."

Massoud nodded thoughtfully. "Good. And General Daoud, will your men arrive in Elmarzan by week's end?"

"Yes, *Amer Saheb*. I instructed them to travel only at night, but they should make it on time. I will join them as soon as we are finished here."

"How well-armed and supplied are they?"

280

from that flame

"Reasonably well," Fahim answered. "We had a small skirmish last week and picked up eight more ZU-23 twin barrels, three GAZ light trucks, and a cache of Katyusha rockets. The Taliban will receive an unhappy surprise."

"Too bad for the Taliban," Massoud said sarcastically. He turned their attention back to the map spread before them. "The front line is going to be approximately sixty kilometers long. With your men at this end, Dostum," Massoud said, pointing to a spot on the map, "and yours here, Fahim," he continued moving his finger down several inches on the map, "we can pinch them once they cross the gorge."

"What about the bridges?" General Fahim asked. "We can't cover all three from those positions."

"No, we can't, which is why we are going to blow these two," Massoud said and lightly tapped the small lines that had been drawn in by hand to indicate the location of two recently built bridges. "With snow melting in the mountains, the water has risen. I don't think they will try to cross without bridges, but just in case they do, we'll mine the banks at any likely crossing points. I need a few more days to work out all the details. Right now, General Fahim, I need you to write a letter to me."

19. Battle

It was a frantic several days for the Commander and his men, but Massoud did work out the details. Quietly, under the cover of darkness, in many of the small towns lower in the valley and closer to where the fighting would occur, civilians were evacuated into towns and camps higher up and farther away. A few volunteers stayed behind to provide the appearance that people were still living and going about their normal daily lives. They would build fires, start engines, move vehicles around, shout to each other from different parts of town, and change clothes and houses—all in an effort to deceive any of the Taliban who might be watching. Once Massoud himself made the long trek down to the valley so that the Taliban's advance men would have the opportunity to see him and report back that Commander Ahmed Shah Massoud was, indeed, in the valley.

As civilians left, Massoud covertly moved some military units into a forward posture. They would be in position to resist an early assault. Quietly and carefully light trucks with the ZU-23 twin barrel 23mm cannons were moved into place and camouflaged. These had proven to be effective weapons against Taliban sniper dens and forward positions. Men began laying land mines by the light of the moon.

Hamid was given the carefully fabricated letter exchange between Commanders Massoud and Fahim and the map which indicated Massoud was planning to send his men towards Taloqan. With a final warning, he was sent back. When he returned to the Taliban after having successfully "escaped" and "stolen" Commander Massoud's letters and maps, he pleaded his case most convincingly. The misinformation was passed along, and the Taliban began to alter their approach based on it. Meanwhile, actual

from that flame

orders were sent out to Generals Kahn, Ata, and Dostum with the date and time of attack against southern positions in the regions of Andarab, Khenjan, Burka, and Chal. They were again sent by runners so that there would be no risk of an intercepted radio communication.

In the darkness of midnight, Massoud's men brought weapons, supplies, food and water to fortified positions on both sides of the valley. From these natural bunkers, they would be able to wait in relative safety if the Taliban decided to use air strikes. Their precious T-62 tanks were moved and half-buried in the ground with only the cannon sticking out and pointing in the direction from which the Taliban would come. The more common T-55 tanks were camouflaged and placed in strategic positions. The helicopters, which would not be used in this fight, were moved to a higher elevation where they would be safe. Finally, Commander Massoud sent out two divisions of 2,000 men each that would assume positions for a flanking maneuver once the battle began.

From the information he had gathered, Commander Massoud determined that the Taliban planned to launch its attack midweek. By Monday night the great chess master had all of his pieces in place and was ready to give the order to begin his preemptive assault. He lead his men in prayer before heading into his command center and giving the word to begin.

The first wave of the Northern Alliance Attack began when small bands of *mujahidin* fighters in Ural trucks outfitted with ZU-23 cannons overran and captured nearly three dozen Taliban forward posts. The second wave blew up two of the three bridges in the lower regions of the gorge. This left the one bridge across which the Taliban would have to pass. The land at the ridge of the gorge had been heavily mined. Any tank hitting one of the mines would be disabled. Any man stepping on one of them would be dead. By the time the bridges were blown, the Taliban knew it was fully engaged in battle no matter how unprepared the fighters were.

Lead in the field by General Fahim, the battle waged for a week. By day, the Taliban called in its fighters to carpet bomb large areas in an effort to soften the front line. They destroyed dozens of empty houses and buildings whose occupants had long been evacuated. During the day the *mujahidin* would retreat to their caves and come out only occasionally to fire a SAM or Stinger at the planes overhead. At night, the fighting became intense. The fire of Chinese-made MRL rockets and 120mm mortar sent bright orange tracers streaking across the sky in every direction. Low rumbles from D-20 cannon fire echoed through the gorge and valley. The higher pitched shriek of a 75mm's reverberation sometimes sounded like a woman screaming in pain too terrible to be borne. The mountains shook in fury at being assaulted yet again. Landslides became a hazard with which to contend.

Fahim would allow the Taliban troops to move across the bridge and come into the valley for a few kilometers before he ordered tank turrets turned on the first and last vehicle, which destroyed them and then effectively trapped between them all of the other vehicles. Once this was accomplished, it was a simple matter to take out the Taliban fighters one by one as well as lob mortar, grenades, and Katyusha rockets at the trapped vehicles. Taliban soldiers died by the dozen. The Panjshir was proving itself as unassailable to theTaliban as it had been to the Soviets a decade before, and Commander Massoud's tactic still worked well.

From his command center, Massoud stayed in constant touch with his generals by radio. Updates came to him moment by moment, and he carefully charted everything on his maps. When fine adjustments were needed, he would decide what should be done. The decisions would then be relayed to the generals who would implement them. The rear troops swung in from both sides like heavy doors slamming shut and cutting off the means of a Taliban retreat.

Massoud made certain that food and supplies were sent forward to the troops and that the troops themselves were rotated so that each man could get a few hours of sleep before returning to the front line. He also arranged for food and housing to be provided for the civilian refugees who poured into his region at an alarming rate. He watched the supplies dwindling quickly and dispatched Dr. Abdullah to Dushanbe to plead for more. Whenever possible, he visited the field hospitals not only to encourage the injured, but also to keep track of the casualties.

Finally, after a full week of battle in which the Northern Alliance lost many but the Taliban lost five times more, word came of assaults by *mujahidin* warriors belonging to Generals Kahn, Ata, and Dostum in regions surrounding the battle area. The towns of Andarab, Khenjan, Burka, and Chal fell quickly to the combined forces. Supply lines for the Taliban were effectively severed. With no hope of reinforcement troops arriving for them and with a fear that Kahn, Ata, and Dostum's forces would soon advance to join Massoud's troops, the Taliban went into full retreat. It was haphazard and clumsy as many of their fighters were conscripts who had been forced into service and never well trained. Without the passion for the fight that Massoud and his men held, they were less willing to die in the Taliban *jihad*. Many simply turned and fled.

As the Taliban retreated, the Northern Alliance advanced, claiming territory as they went. Civilians followed closely behind the Alliance soldiers, happily moving back into their homes and towns. Those communities newly liberated from the harsh control of the Taliban celebrated in the streets, threw flowers at the Alliance troops, played music and danced, and agreed they all felt a new wind of hope sweeping down from the Panjshir Valley and into their communities. They had little food, and their houses and villages had been flattened, but they were free of the brutality they had known at the hands of the Taliban, and for the moment that was enough.

"Congratulations, Ahmed Shah," said Dr. Abdullah, who had just returned from Tajikistan where he arranged for a convoy of supplies that would soon arrive. He moved aside an old Enfield rifle and sat down. They had just finished listening to final reports from the most forward fighters and felt confident that the Taliban would be completely gone from the area in less than a day. "Your strategy worked as perfectly as it always does."

"Not always." Massoud forced a small smile to his heavily lined face. He had slept in increments no longer than five minutes for the past week and was exhausted. "Let's not congratulate ourselves until we know how many of our men we have lost."

"However many that may be, the Taliban's number is much higher, and the immediate threat is over," Abdullah reminded his friend. "I know you mourn each life lost, and I do as well, but I think you can take a moment to feel good about what you have accomplished. More towns, more people are free than there were a week ago thanks to you."

"Praise to God and thanks to the martyrs who gave their lives," Commander Massoud said quietly. "I will pray, eat, and sleep. I will help bury the dead. I will count the wounded, the homeless, and the displaced. I will listen to damage reports about how much equipment has been lost and try to figure out a way to replace it. Perhaps after all that is done, I will find time to think about celebrating a victory."

Abdullah watched his commander and friend walk out of the command center, his prayer rug in one hand and his *tasbih*, prayer beads, in the other. Beyond the obvious and explainable exhaustion, he feared there was some other cause for Massoud's low spirits. However much Massoud might want to ignore the matter, it was a conversation they would have, Abdullah determined.

20. Weary

Your spirits are downcast, Ahmed Shah," Abdullah said quietly. It had been a long day during which Massoud had managed about two hours of sleep before his many responsibilities forced him into action again. Dr. Abdullah remained convinced, however, that fatigue alone was not causing the weary look in his friend's eyes.

"I suppose they are a little," Commander Massoud agreed absently as he continued to look over written reports of the recent battles. He looked up at Abdullah. "General Daoud reports that he lost fifteen men. The number is bad enough, but it easily could have been worse. Best estimates put the Taliban losses at close to one hundred and seventy, and they had heavy damage to their artillery, tanks, and planes."

"And yet you find neither comfort nor relief in those numbers," Abdullah observed. "Will you tell me what troubles you, *Amer Saheb?*"

Commander Massoud shoved aside the rest of the papers in front of him, folded his hands together, and looked steadily at Abdullah. He sighed deeply as if unsure of the words.

"I think I am having a fit of self-pity," he stated honestly. "I am ashamed of it, and I am praying that it will pass soon."

"Self-pity?" Abdullah repeated in surprise. "You are incapable of self-pity."

"Don't ask me to tell you how I am feeling, and then, when I do, tell me that is not how I feel," Massoud grumbled and then frowned. He pulled the papers back in front of him to resume his reading.

"I'm sorry," Abdullah responded quickly. "I only meant to

say that in these past fifteen years, I have never seen you indulge in self-pity. I find it difficult to believe that is what you are doing now."

"Well, it is," Massoud insisted grimly. "I am weary to the core of my being of this never-ending war against one foe or another. I am losing hope that it will end in my lifetime, and I wonder why God has not found the means to give me some respite after twenty-two years."

He rose and began to slowly pace around the room. Abdullah wisely said nothing and did not move except to allow his eyes to follow the Commander as he walked.

"I am growing old, Abdullah. Is it terribly wrong of me to desire some peace and comfort in my old age? I want to go home to my family. I want to tend a garden, read my books, watch my children play, and eat my wife's dinner. I want to sleep in my bed in my house every night without hearing a single explosion. I want to visit friends and play long, leisurely games of chess. I want to pray in a mosque five times every day. I want to go back to Europe as a tourist and visit all the beautiful cities there. I want to grow old and die in peace.

"I don't ever want to see another person with a leg blown off by a land mine. I don't want to hear the cries of another mother when I tell her that her son was killed in action. I don't want to count any more rounds of ammunition for guns and shells for cannons or worry how many rations of food there are for the men. I don't want to be responsible for feeding, clothing, and housing hundreds of thousands of people. I don't want to make truces and negotiations with men I neither like nor trust. I don't want to be accompanied by bodyguards every time I take three steps outside the door. I don't want to lose any more friends and people I love until they die peacefully in their old age. I don't want to decide on one more strategy or plan one more battle." Commander Massoud dropped back into his chair and stared mournfully at Abdullah. "I don't want to command this war anymore, my friend. I think I am all fought-out. There is nothing left inside me that wants anything but peace."

Dr. Abdullah sat quietly for several minutes as he thought about everything Massoud had said. He wanted to say the words his friend needed to hear, but he wasn't sure exactly what those words should be. He studied Massoud's face and saw the complete and utter exhaustion there. It was possible that eight hours of sleep would solve the problem, but he doubted it. This was more than a depletion of physical resources. This was a depletion of emotional, psychological, and spiritual strength as well.

"Ahmed Shah," the doctor began slowly, "I don't think what you are feeling is self- pity. I think it is self-doubt. I think you have given so much to your country and your people for such a very long time, you are beginning to wonder if you have the strength and determination to continue dealing with all the problems, difficulties, worries, and hardship this war inevitably brings. You can hardly be blamed for feeling this way. No one has sacrificed more than you. No one deserves the peace you crave more than you, yourself." Dr. Abdullah reached across the desk and put his hand on Massoud's arm. "You are weary to the core of your being. You don't trust yourself at the moment. If you can't trust yourself, then trust me. No one knows you better than I do. No one knows the forged steel from which you are made better than I. Let me tell you what will happen, shall I?"

Commander Massoud frowned, but he didn't move his arm out of his friend's grasp. He nodded slightly to indicate he would listen.

"Tomorrow or the day after that, you will hear children laughing and playing. They may not be the children of your body, but they will be the children of your heart and soul. They will be the children of Afghanistan. And when you hear those children laugh, you will find deep inside yourself a new strength and determination to resist and fight, to make any sacrifice until all the children of our land have enough joy in their lives to laugh in that same way. You are exhausted, and your outlook is bleak, but that's not going to last. You don't give up. You never give up. That's who you are, Ahmed Shah Massoud. That is who you will be until the day you die."

"Maybe you're right." Massoud was too tired to argue with his friend. Besides, it didn't matter how he felt or what he said. Tomorrow, somehow, he knew he would find a way to get up from his pallet, drink some tea, and go back to work. Perhaps the day after tomorrow would be the day he could no longer fight, but tomorrow he would.

"Find something to make me laugh, Abdullah," he said, resting his heavy head on his hand. "I need to laugh long and hard.

We haven't laughed in weeks."

"I miss her, too," Abdullah said quietly. "We have never laughed so often or so heartily."

"I said make me laugh, not make me weep," Commander Massoud said as he stood up abruptly. "I'm going for a walk to clear my head. We'll go over the rest of the written reports when I get back. Oh, and see if you can find out anything about young Hamid. I would like to know if he is among the listed dead of the Taliban." Massoud picked up his *tasbih* from the desk. Rolling the small prayer beads between his fingers, he slowly looked at Abdullah. "Every day I pray that I will stop feeling such sorrow over her death, and still it does not get easier."

"It has only been a few weeks. Give yourself more time. Besides, I don't think you are struggling with only sorrow, my friend," Abdullah said gently. "I suspect you are still struggling with guilt because you were unable to keep her safe, and I think you are also angry the way you always are when an innocent dies. You wouldn't want to forget her, would you?"

"No, of course not," Massoud answered. "I long for the day when I can remember her with joy rather than sorrow, that's all." He came around the desk and clasped Abdullah's shoulder. "You are a very wise man. Thank you for the good counsel you always give me. I'm going for that walk now. See what you can find out about Hamid, will you?"

"Only if you promise not to beat yourself up with more guilt if he is dead too."

"If he is dead, and I pray to our merciful Allah he is not, then we will discuss his death, and you will be wise again, and we will go on as we have for these past fifteen years."

"Enjoy your walk, Ahmed Shah. It's a beautiful day outside. Find a few moments of peace and comfort."

Abdullah watched Commander Massoud leave the office and step out into the bright sunlight. As he watched he saw the Commander square his shoulders and raise his head. The lion may be weary and worn, but he was not finished fighting yet, of that the doctor was certain.

"There is only one way we are ever going to have peace, Abdul-

from that flame

lah," Commander Massoud said resolutely after he returned from his walk, "and that is to defeat the Taliban. I think we need to build on the advantage we just gained at Farkhar Gorge and launch new offensives before the Taliban has time to recover and regroup. Let's get all the generals in here for a strategy meeting. I think we can take territory in Baghlan." He grabbed one of his ever-present maps and unrolled it with a flourish across his desk. "We'll start here, with Lataband." He glanced over at the doctor. "Did you learn anything of the fate of young Hamid?"

"He lives, Ahmed Shah," the doctor said. "He lives."

At Abdullah's words, Massoud turned back to his maps with new resolve.

21. Letter

may brought intense fighting to the northeast and central regions of Afghanistan. Casualties numbered in the thousands on both sides. One day land was gained by Massoud's troops, and the next day the Taliban took it back. Lataband, Hazarbagh, and Chal changed hands repeatedly as first one side and then the other claimed victory. By the end of the month, the Taliban had sent three waves of attacks backed by heavy artillery fire and sporadic air bombardment, and all three times they were repulsed by the Northern Alliance. Taliban casualties were extremely heavy, and Massoud's jails began to overflow with the ever-growing number of captured Taliban and al-Qaeda fighters.

The Alliance gained lands in the Chaal and Samand Aab regions. As June was drawing close, Massoud and his commanders again met and planned.

"We are making good progress in Bamiyan," General Karim Khalili said. "I think we need to keep up the pressure."

"I agree," said Ishmael Kahn. "We have them on the run; let's not stop now."

"I have no intention of stopping that front from developing," Commander Massoud assured the generals. "In fact, I have received word just today that we will have three hundred new *mujahidin* coming from Andarab. General Khalili, if you will see to their training, I would like to deploy them and others of your men here," said the Commander, pointing to a region south of Bamiyan known as Daikundi. "I believe you should have success in driving the Taliban from this area. We will discuss a particular strategy I have in mind at a later time."

from that flame

Commander Massoud peered more closely at the map spread before them. "I also want to open another front farther north. I want to retake Taloqan. I want all Taliban and al-Qaeda out of Takar Province."

"That would be good," General Dostum said. "It is difficult to travel between Mazar-I-sharif and Khwaja Bahauddin while the Taliban still holds Taloqan."

"It is difficult to travel anywhere while the Taliban holds so much of our country hostage," Massoud replied in sharp agreement. He looked around at the stern-faced men who surrounded him. "Their days are numbered," he added with grim determination.

Ishmael Kahn spoke up. "I think I would like to take my troops on a little Taliban-rousting mission in Yakawlang. My intelligence tells me they are weaker than they appear."

"Then you must move against them now," Commander Massoud agreed. "I have new T-55 and T-62 tanks as well as armored fighting vehicles coming through Dushanbe. We will decide how best to use them to our advantage." He looked around at the men again. "Let us break for dinner now and return here in a few hours...unless there is anything else that is immediate?"

"I think we should release a list of names of the 107 Pakistani POWs we have," Younis Qanooni said.

"Why?" General Dostum demanded. "Who cares about POWs? I don't know why you make us feed and house them. Why can't we just shoot them?"

"It would serve two purposes," Qanooni replied calmly and reasonably. "First, it proves what we have been saying all along: Pakistan is providing military support to the Taliban despite their constant denials. Second, it will work as a psychological deterrent against those who may have grand thoughts of dying a martyr's death for al-Qaeda but who might not find the thought of spending a long time in prison nearly as alluring."

"I agree it is a good idea," Commander Massoud said. "Will you prepare a press release? If you can get the prisoner's names, hometowns, and the battles in which they were caught, that would prove the authenticity of the list." The Commander gestured toward the door. "And now let us go and eat." He hung back as the other men filed out.

"General Dostum, a word with you, please," Massoud said before the burly man followed the others out of the room.

"I know what you are going to say," Dostum rumbled in his gravel-sounding voice. "I haven't killed any surrendering men or any POWs since you were so insistent about it the last time. I don't understand why you are so touchy on this issue, but I go along with it rather than argue with you every time we meet."

"I appreciate your cooperation," Commander Massoud spoke in a calm, quiet voice. "I know how difficult it is to feed prisoners when you can barely find enough food for your own men. I also know that there are times when you would like to take men off guard duty and assign them to other details. Nevertheless, if we desire that the Taliban treats our captured fighters humanely, we must do the same."

Commander Massoud flashed his most disarming smile. "Will you walk with me to the dining area? I want to tell you about some of the newly added features on the T-62 tanks since some of them will be headed in your direction."

All through June and July the war waged. Especially heavy fighting continued in both central and northeast territories. Land was won and lost and won again. Life continued as usual in Afghanistan. One day in early August, a large wooden crate was delivered to the headquarters in Khwaja Bahauddin. It had been dragged overland after its delivery to Islamabad, Pakistan. A little worse for wear, it was still sturdy and bore Massoud's name as well as numerous American Customs seals, stamps, and US postmarks. The men in the compound examined its exterior along with the papers and stamps it bore with great interest and curiosity, but they did not dare open it until Massoud himself returned from Tajikistan later in the day. It was carefully moved to his office.

Before Massoud arrived, a French journalist showed up at the command center and asked to meet with Commander Ahmed Shah Massoud. He was directed to Dr. Abdullah.

"Ah, I see the package got here," Christophe Chaliand said and slapped the box with delight. "Commandant Massoud is going to love this," he said to Abdullah after he introduced himself.

"Then you are the one who sent it?" Abdullah asked as he sat back down into the chair behind Massoud's desk.

"Let's just say I had a part in getting it here," Chaliand said with a grin. "I didn't send it directly. It came from the United States. I believe you knew the sender? Michelle Garrett? Well, actually, her attorney made all the arrangements to have it sent per her instructions."

"I knew Michelle. She was a good friend." Dr. Abdullah looked at the crate with greater curiosity. If it was from Michelle in some way, it might prove interesting. The doctor turned his attention back to the French journalist. "I thought you looked familiar. You are the journalist Commander Massoud saw in Paris last April, are you not?"

"Yes. The Commandant gave me *Mademoiselle* Garrett's article on him. I have news, but I would prefer to tell the whole story when the Commandant is here, if that's all right with you."

"He will be here soon," Abdullah said agreeably. He looked at the stamps and stickers on the crate again. "May I ask the contents of this crate? It is large and heavy."

"Presents," Chaliand answered. "I don't know what else to call them."

"Presents?" Abdullah repeated in surprise. "I can't imagine."

"Be patient, Doctor," the French journalist said. "I think this afternoon will be filled with pleasant surprises."

"Pleasant surprises are always welcome," Abdullah said as he eyed the crate with uncertainty. "Commander Massoud should be here momentarily." The doctor looked at the journalist and settled back into the chair to wait.

"*Comment allez-vous?* It is good to see you again, Commandant Massoud." Chaliand shook Massoud's outstretched hand when the Commander entered his office.

"*Très bien, merci*. Thank you for coming all the way here, Mr. Chaliand. Were you able to find a publisher for Miss Garrett's story?"

The journalist dug in his attaché case and pulled out two

magazines. He handed them to Massoud. "Advance copies. Two magazines, one in the United States and one in France, decided to run the story concurrently. As you see, the French magazine even gave you the cover. The British also bought the story, but they didn't have the cover done yet. We still have ongoing negotiations with a German magazine for a reprint later in the fall."

Massoud accepted both magazines and looked at them carefully. He handed the English language version to Abdullah and then began to search the index of the French magazine for the article. Upon finding it, he sat and read, his attention completely absorbed. In his mind he could hear Michelle's voice as if she were speaking the words written on the page, and a small smile crossed his face. Five months after Michelle's death he was finally able to remember the time spent with her without the horrible grief that had haunted him for months. Yet, when he reached the end of the article and read the endnote he himself had written about Michelle's death, the smile fled his face. Michelle's picture appeared at the very end of the article. In it, she, smiling broadly, was filled with the joy of life he had found so irresistible. Massoud closed the magazine abruptly and glanced at Abdullah, who was still reading. He turned his attention to the Frenchman.

"Thank you very much for bringing these to me," Massoud said sincerely. "This article means a great deal. Thank you."

"There's something else, Commandant," the journalist said and pointed to the large crate.

Massoud looked over at the box. "What is it?"

"Before I could do anything with Miss Garrett's story, I had to contact her lawyer in the United States. I found her agent through an older publication of hers, and through the agent, I found her attorney. Remember I told you in Paris that I had spoken to him? Well, apparently he had received a communication from her that was mailed a few days before her death. It arrived at his office shortly after we last spoke."

"Yes, I remember," Commander Massoud said.

"In the course of the letter, she told her attorney about a plan she had to give you first aid kits you had wanted for your fighters. She said she didn't want to wait until the article sold, and she authorized him to make the purchase from her existing accounts."

Massoud's back teeth clenched a little. "Is that what's in the

from that flame

crate?"

"*Oui,*" Chaliand said. "There are 1,500 medical first aid kits here. There are personal gifts for both you and Doctor Abdullah as well. There is this, too," he said and handed an envelope to Commander Massoud.

Massoud looked at the envelope. "What is it?"

"A letter from her attorney. It is sealed, and of course I didn't read it. And then there is this." He produced another envelope. "These are the checks for the article as negotiated with the two magazines. I will send the rest of the payments as they come in."

Commander Massoud was feeling overwhelmed. "Did you deduct the cost of the medical kits from these payments?" he asked. "Surely she did not mean for me to have both?"

"I think that's one of the things the lawyer writes about," the Frenchman replied. "He is the executor of her estate and will explain all the terms to you. But, no, there was nothing deducted from those payments. It's all there. $175,000."

Massoud paled. "*Pardonnez-moi*? Pardon me? There must be a mistake." He tried to hand the envelope with the check back to the journalist.

Chaliand shook his head. "There is no mistake, Commandant. Read the attorney's letter. She left everything to you personally."

"Well, thank you again," said a stunned Massoud putting both envelopes in his pocket. "Now, while I send someone for a crowbar to open the crate, would you like to have some tea? I would like to hear all the details about what happened after I gave the manuscript to you in Paris."

"You are very quiet," Abdullah observed later in the evening when he and the Commander were alone in Massoud's office.

"I'm tired," Massoud answered. "And my back hurts."

"That's all?"

"Yes, that's all." Massoud glanced at his friend and saw his disbelief. "No, that is a lie," he said softly. "I am overwhelmed by Michelle *Jaan's* generosity. I feel as if we should give the money back. It is too much. This is enough," he said, touching the portable CD player and stack of CDs on his desk. Beside them was a pile of batteries large enough to last for months as well as an adapter, battery charger, and rechargeable batteries. "She thought of everything," he said with a sad smile.

"Yes, she did." Dr. Abdullah's long fingers caressed the stethoscope he had around his neck. "She was an amazing woman. I wish she was here so that I could tell her thank you."

"You know she would make some funny remark and laugh off your words of gratitude," Massoud said quietly.

Abdullah smiled softly in agreement. "*Balay*. Yes. We were lucky to have known her, although I can't imagine I ever would have believed that possible the very first night she showed up in our camp."

"You were going to throw her out," Massoud said with a laugh, but then his face sobered. "She would still be alive if I had let you do that."

"Don't tell me you are still beating yourself up with guilt?" Abdullah asked with concern. "Nothing that happened was your fault. Michelle would be very distressed to know that you are still blaming yourself. I doubt she would ever blame you."

"No, she wouldn't. Perhaps it is an accumulation of responsibility I feel and not just the guilt caused by her death alone. I have made mistakes, and my mistakes caused people to lose their lives. I made miscalculations, and it caused us to lose more land to the Taliban. The guilt and sorrow and regret I carry after twenty-two years of war are too heavy to lay at the feet of Michelle Garrett."

Massoud walked over to the open crate, lifted out one of the first aid kits, and looked at Abdullah. "We need to figure out how best to distribute these."

"It was a very kind thing of her to have those sent," Abdullah acknowledged.

"She was a very kind person." Massoud remembered the letter in his pocket. After taking it out and opening it, he handed it to Abdullah. "It's in English. Will you translate it for me, please?"

"Dear Commander Massoud," Abdullah slowly began to translate into Dari.

I write this letter to you with a full heart.
Three months ago, I attended the funeral of Mi-

from that flame

chelle Garrett. Please accept my heartfelt gratitude for your efforts in having her body returned to the United States. It would have been much easier for you to have her buried there, but the grief to her parents, family, and friends would have been increased had you chosen that easier option. Now all of us who loved her can at least visit her final resting place.

I must also thank you for making certain that Michelle's final work was given to Christophe Chaliand. He has been in contact with me, and I am working with him to make every effort to find publishers for the story. My hope is that by the time you read this letter, Michelle's article will have been contracted for sale with a reputable magazine. Since Michelle was killed while writing this final piece, I feel that its publication is as much a tribute to her as it is to you. Nevertheless, for you to have gone to such effort on her behalf, knowing the heavy responsibilities you have, tells me much about the caliber of man you are. I understand why she wrote about you in the glowing terms she did.

While Michelle was still in your camp, she wrote to me and asked that I purchase on her behalf 1,500 first aid kits. I have complied with her wishes. If the medical kits are not there yet, you may expect them soon. Please know that she wanted you to have them because during the short time she was in your country, she learned to care deeply for your people, your *mujahidin*, and your cause.

After a discussion with her family, everyone agreed that it would best serve Michelle's final wishes to bequeath her entire estate to you for use as you see fit. At this writing, I am unsure of the final amount of money that will be paid for the article. However, the rest of her estate in cash and assets will be in the approximate range of $250,000. Michelle mentioned your frequent trips to Dushanbe, Tajikistan. Perhaps if you send me your bank account information, I can have the money wired there. I will need a little longer to liquidate some assets, so there is no urgency.

I must tell you in all honesty that none of us wanted Michelle to go to Pakistan and Afghanistan. We all feared it was much too dangerous for her. Sadly, our fears proved accurate. But anyone who knew Michelle knew that determination was her middle name, and none of us, no matter how we argued, could dissuade her from her quest. She believed there was a story to be told and that she was the one to tell it. Despite the tragic end of Michelle's life there with you, I cannot help but be glad that her last days were spent doing the thing she most loved to do.

She wrote to me that never had she been as inspired or challenged as she was by the story she was writing about you and your struggle. She believed it would be her best work. She wrote to me of your 'fierce determination, relentless sacrifice, unblinking vision, and devout devotion to duty.' She admired you more than my poor words can express. You touched something in her heart that as a journalist she always tried to shield from the subjects of her work.

I will not comment on events themselves. Michelle did that already. The story speaks for itself and does not need me to enhance it in any way. But again, I find I owe you thanks for all that you did to protect and care for her while she was there. She wrote to me that you were generous, kind, and supportive of her efforts even when the cost to you was high. I believe, Commander Massoud, that because of you, Michelle's final days were fulfilling ones.

I will close now having taken far too much of your time already. I wish God's blessings on you and your people. I will pray for peace to

from that flame

come to Afghanistan soon. If you ever visit the United States, it would be my distinct honor and pleasure to meet you at any place of your choosing. Should you wish to visit Michelle's grave, I would accompany you there with gratitude.

Warmest regards and best wishes,

Lewis Hanrahan, Esq.

Dr. Abdullah folded the letter, put it back in the envelope, and handed it to Massoud, who carefully placed it in his pocket.

"Will you make a written translation for me tomorrow?" Massoud asked.

"Of course. I think I should wish you good night now."

"Yes," Massoud answered. "There is much work to be done tomorrow. Thank you, my friend, for your efforts tonight."

"Will you be all right? I can stay if you wish." Abdullah scrutinized his friend's face for signs of stress and anxiety.

Massoud patted the pocket containing the letter. "I'm fine. I am going to sit here and listen to some of this beautiful music sent to me, and then I will sleep and have a pleasant dream of the friend who brought bountiful laughter and extraordinary generosity to my life." He smiled at his friend. "Good night, Abdullah *Jaan*. Sleep well."

"I'm going to dream that you decided to give me $400,000. Then I will dream that I buy an island in a tropical paradise and live the rest of my days in peace and quiet with my family," Abdullah said.

"Yes, by all means, keep dreaming," Massoud said, smiling in spite of himself. "That is a wild dream and one worth having."

After Abdullah left, Massoud took both envelopes from his pocket and turned them over in his hands. He set them on the desk next to the Panasonic CD player. Next he took the magazines from a drawer and laid them beside the envelopes. From another drawer, he withdrew the copy of Michelle's passport photo, the photograph of the two of them, her journal, and the blood-splattered, original manuscript. These he laid neatly beside the other items. He sat for several minutes simply staring at the small pile of things that would not be in his possession if Michelle Garrett hadn't come into his life.

from that flame

He leaned forward and carefully removed the CD player from its packaging. He figured out where to insert the batteries and plugged in the headset. He glanced through the stack of ten CDs and recognized the one by Andrea Bocelli that Michelle had loaned him and he had enjoyed so much. He placed the disc into the player, put the headset on, and pushed buttons until he found "on." The magnificent voice filled his ears.

As the CD played, the Commander reread Michelle's article first in the original manuscript and then again in the French magazine. Satisfied that nothing had been changed or left out, he set the magazine aside and picked up the passport picture. He studied it closely, and a gentle smile crept to his mouth. He lightly traced the outline of her hair before slipping the picture into the pocket where the envelopes had been. With his hand over his heart, he leaned back in the chair and allowed the music to take him away.

22. Allies

Commander?" Assem Suhail said, sticking his head in the door of Commander Massoud's office. Massoud and Abdullah sat at the desk making up a list of items they needed to purchase on the Commander's next visit to Tajikistan.

"Commander, I received a radio communication from a US Army helicopter that just departed Dushanbe. They are asking for permission to land," Assem reported.

"Yes, I have been expecting them," Massoud said. "Bring them to me as soon as they land. Thank you, Assem."

"Will you need for me to stay and interpret?" Assem asked.

"No, thank you. Go back to your duties. Doctor Abdullah can handle that for me," the Commander answered.

"Do you know what they want?" Abdullah asked Massoud when they were alone again.

"Not specifically," Massoud replied. "My guess is that this will be a combined military and intelligence committee coming to talk over some new plan with us."

"The CIA again?" Abdullah asked with ironic amusement. "Perhaps you had better call Assem back to interpret. They didn't seem to understand when I repeatedly told them 'no' during our last meeting."

"I remember the frowns on their faces when they left," Commander Massoud said, laughing. "They understood our 'no' quite well; they just didn't like it very much."

"It will be interesting to learn what new incentives they have added to their latest offer," Abdullah said.

from that flame

"We'll know soon enough. I hear the helicopter now," Massoud said, pointing North. He and Abdullah continued their work as they awaited the arrival of the Americans.

"Commander Massoud, it is good to see you again," said an unusual looking man in military fatigues who offered his hand to Massoud. Dr. Abdullah began translating immediately.

Massoud accepted his hand and shook it. "Welcome back, Colonel Brinkman-*Jaan*."

"May I introduce my intelligence operative, Sam Snipes? He would like to have a candid discussion with you if he may."

"Indeed he may. Please sit down." Commander Massoud indicated some chairs opposite his at the desk. Dr. Abdullah pulled up another chair close to but slightly behind Massoud. In this position, he would be able to translate easily, and Massoud could turn back to him and speak quietly in Dari without the others hearing. It was a position that in the past had proved to be both efficient and practical.

"Please begin," Massoud said in Dari. Abdullah repeated the command in English.

"The President of the United States would like us to develop a plan with you that will bring down not only Osama bin Laden but his entire al-Qaeda terrorist network in Afghanistan."

"That is a change in policy," Massoud observed, keeping his surprise to himself. "The last time the Colonel was here, the US only wanted my help to assassinate bin Laden. What has changed?"

"Let's just say that since we last discussed the matter with you, we have had additional intelligence that makes your recommendation to have all of the al-Qaeda and the Taliban eliminated a better scenario than killing just bin Laden." Sam Snipes withdrew a cigarette from his pocket, lit it, and inhaled deeply. "Do you mind?" he asked after the fact as he waved the cigarette in Massoud and Abdullah's direction. He continued speaking without waiting for an answer. "We now agree with you that the threat is larger than just bin Laden. The Taliban must go as well."

"What intelligence? Specifically?" Massoud wanted to know.

"What difference does it make? You were right all along,

from that flame

Commander."

"I'm right, but you don't trust me with your intelligence?"

Sam Snipes and Colonel Brinkman exchanged glances. The colonel nodded slightly.

"We intercepted some transmissions between al-Qaeda operatives. They were discussing a major attack against the United States. There was also discussion of a possible hijacking."

"One man said the attack would be devastating," Colonel Brinkman added. "As devastating as Hiroshima. And, we have come to understand that—as you always maintained—it is impossible to separate al Qaeda and the Taliban. The groups are now almost completely interwoven."

It was Commander Massoud and Dr. Abdullah's turn to exchange glances. Massoud turned back to the Americans. "Why have you suddenly changed your minds about helping me rid the country of the Taliban? Previously you always said you didn't want to do that. Why not bring in your own troops to take out al-Qaeda? You already have bin Laden under indictment in your country. You have shot missiles at him before. Why do you want the Northern Alliance to fight a surrogate war for you?"

"Because you're here, and we're not. Because no one knows the terrain better than your *mujahidin*. Because you have as much to gain—if not more—than we do in ridding Afghanistan of al-Qaeda. Because you have always demanded help getting rid of the Taliban in exchange for helping us get bin Laden. Because we don't want to be seen as an invading force. Good reasons all, don't you agree?" Snipes said, looking at the Northern Alliance leader.

"You forgot a reason," Commander Massoud replied, arching an eyebrow. "You don't want to cause an international incident. You don't want to appear to be at war with Afghanistan without an overt provocation."

"That is true, too," Colonel Brinkman agreed. "Look, Commander, we worked well together when we supplied you and helped you drive the Soviets out. We both know that you don't really want US troops on the ground here. Let's make an arrangement similar to the one we had ten years ago."

"Ten years ago, after hundreds of thousands of my people died in battle, after Afghan blood was spread from one end of the land to the other and Soviet weapons of war littered the landscape like tree stumps in a clear-cut forest, the United States turned its back on my country and my people and walked away. Your goal had been met, and you had no further interest in us." Commander Massoud's voice carried an undercurrent of cold fury that was not lost on the Americans even though Abdullah was translating his words. "We needed every kind of help: food, medicine, clothing. We needed grain to grow crops in our fields. We needed to rebuild our infrastructure. We needed to have the tanks, burned-out helicopters, and land mines removed from our countryside. We needed help establishing a central government, a central bank, a viable economy, and a strong currency. We had been brutalized by invaders and used by our allies. And then we were dismissed and forgotten. Why should I help you now? And if you swear this time it will be different, why should I believe you?"

Sam Snipes angrily raised his arm and opened his mouth to speak, but Colonel Brinkman touched the other man's arm and pressed it back down. The colonel looked steadily at Commander Massoud and spoke in a low voice.

"I understand both your anger and mistrust, Commander Massoud. I am an old warrior too, and I have seen too much death and destruction. We need to believe that we can count on our friends and allies in times of trouble. I agree that my country failed to provide yours with the support it earned and deserved to have. However, that is in the past, and there is nothing either of us can do to change what happened." The colonel leaned forward in his chair and spoke earnestly.

"As well as being old warriors, you and I are both realists and pragmatists. We know our strengths and limitations. We have a clear vision of what needs to be done, and then we set about doing whatever we must in order to accomplish our goal.

"In this case, Commander, our goal is identical: the destruction of al-Qaeda and Osama bin Laden, and the removal of the Taliban from power. Surely we can continue to be pragmatic and find a way to work together to accomplish our mutual goal?"

"What assurances will I have that the past will not be revisited?" Massoud asked. "If we go down this path again, what assurance will I have that this time will be different? What assurance will I have that this time you will stay to help reconstruct all that you have destroyed?"

from that flame

"I will not insult you, sir, with false promises," Colonel Brinkman replied. "We both know that there can be nothing in writing between us. But I can give you my word and my hand as an officer that I will do everything in my power to make certain that this time the United States is a better friend and ally." Brinkman stood and reached his arm across the desk. "One old warrior to another, I give you my word."

Commander Massoud had been studying the colonel's face as he listened to Abdullah's translation. He liked the steady gaze of the other man. He sensed this American military man was a man of honor and integrity. He didn't know for a fact he could trust the colonel, but he believed he could. He decided it was worth the risk. Massoud stood and accepted the proffered hand.

"Allies and friends," Massoud said as he shook the other man's hand.

"Good," the colonel said and smiled before taking his seat again. "Now you can begin to tell us what type of logistical support you want. How many American operatives will you allow us to send? What types of munitions do you have at your disposal, and what additional supplies and ammunition will you need? Is your intelligence on the location of the al-Qaeda training camps up-to-date?"

"May I ask if you have a time in mind for all this to begin?" Dr. Abdullah asked, breathless at how quickly events were unfolding.

"Before the end of the year," Sam Snipes answered. "I don't have anything more definite than that. It will depend on how long it takes us to get coordinated."

"Every month you wait makes al-Qaeda more of a threat and the Taliban more entrenched," Commander Massoud added with a grim expression. "And you know how brutal our winters can be. The sooner the better is my opinion."

"Then let's get to work," Colonel Brinkman replied. "I haven't had any of your wonderful green tea in ages. Do you suppose I could have a cup? And I would like to see your maps, Commander. You can show me where your front line currently is. We have been hearing reports about your victories all summer."

from that flame

"Do you think I made the right decision," Massoud asked Abdullah after their guests had gone. The night's darkness wrapped around them as they took a short stroll around the compound before retiring.

"I think you made the only decision you could," Abdullah answered. "How could you say no to help from the Americans? Escalating the war with their help and support is our best chance of ending the fighting once and for all."

"What if we do manage to oust both the Taliban and al Qaeda? Have we learned enough from our mistakes not to make them again? We will be able to build a functioning government and keep a peaceful land? Will we really be able to bring about the reforms we want? Will we be able to build schools and hospitals and factories?"

"All in the first week? Probably not," Abdullah answered patiently. "In time? Yes, I believe we can do all those things with God's help."

"I need to send a message to Rabanni. He may be our interim president again sooner than he expected."

"Tomorrow, my friend. Tomorrow you can defeat the enemy, restore peace to the land, and build a government. Right now it is time to sleep."

"What would I do without you to remind me of practical matters?" Massoud smiled fondly at his friend.

"Never remember to sleep or eat," Abdullah said with a laugh. "Come on. The hour grows late, and I still want to write a letter to my wife."

"Another winter will be on us soon," Massoud observed as he looked up into the blue September sky over Khwaja Bahauddin. Then he looked down at the parched earth. "We must start pleading with the international relief agencies again. Our people are going to need food and warm clothes."

"Will you be meeting with any of the relief agency workers during this trip to Tajikistan?" Abdullah asked.

"I will try," Massoud said.

"How long do you think you'll be gone?"

from that flame

Massoud shook his head. "I don't know. A few days. Why?"

"We have a lot of journalists who have asked to see you. After the successes we've had this summer, there has been a renewed interest."

"Journalists from where? Which countries? People who can help us?"

"An American and a Russian. An Uzbek. Two Frenchmen, two Arabs from Morocco. And don't forget, you told that group of American women that they could come too."

Massoud laughed and then shrugged. "Why didn't you stop me before I agreed to all this? Don't worry. Arrange a press conference. I'll talk to them all at once and get it done."

"That would be great if they would all agree to it, but you've promised one-on-one interviews, remember?"

Massoud patted his friend on the arm. "What can I tell you? I have a soft spot in my heart for journalists."

"A soft spot in your head is more like it," Abdullah countered.

"I have every confidence that you will work out all the logistics, foreign minister of mine," Massoud said with an air of certainty. "I have to leave."

"Of course you do." Abdullah was trying be aggrieved but couldn't stop a smile from creasing his face. "Go on, get out of here. I'll figure it out—just as I always do."

"And you will have my everlasting appreciation—just as you always do."

23. Lion

The journalists were piling up. Dr. Abdullah was running out of places to put people. Commander Massoud had been gone for several days. "But he is expected soon," Abdullah assured everyone. When a severe windstorm began to kick up the sandy, dry earth, everyone knew there would be a delay in Massoud's return. The American decided to travel down into the Panjshir Valley and asked if any of the others wanted to go along. Several agreed that it would be a pleasant way to pass the time until the Commander arrived back. The Arab journalists decided that they would rather wait there for Massoud to return.

"Hoping to scoop us, huh?" one of the French journalists tried to tease. In response he received only surly looks. The Frenchman shrugged and walked off.

"See if you can reach the Commander," Abdullah said to Assem Suhail. "Find out if he has any idea when he might be able to get back. Tell him that if the helicopter can't fly because of the sandstorm, I can pick him up in the Land Rover."

"You worry too much," Masood Khalili said, patting Dr. Abdullah on the back. "He'll get here as soon as he safely can. Relax."

Abdullah frowned. "That's easy for you to say. All you have to do is translate for him when he meets with the journalists. I have to make sure they all stay safe, sheltered, fed, and patient."

"Then you translate, and I will look after the journalists," Khalili said with a loud laugh that boomed and reverberated through the small room.

"If my Arabic was as good as yours, I would take you up on

from that flame

the offer."

"I have a better idea," Khalili said, still laughing. "Let us both go away and leave the Commander to handle the journalists all alone. That will teach him to agree to all these interviews."

Abdullah looked heavenward. "The flaw in your plan is that he would figure out a way to handle them all alone, and then forever after we would have to listen to him tease and torment us about his accomplishment."

"I have the Commander on the line," Assem said, handing the satellite phone to Abdullah.

"Commander, do you have any idea when you will return?" Abdullah spoke loudly into the phone. Massoud's voice seemed distant and hollow to him. "What?" he shouted. "I can hardly hear you. On the ninth? All right. Yes, I will tell them. Most of them have gone to Panjshir, but a few are still here, and the others will be back in a few days. Yes, I understand. Of course. All right. We'll hope to see you then." Abdullah handed the phone back to Assem.

"He thinks there will be a window in the weather on the ninth. He should return then. He asked if you would both please wait for him." Abdullah looked from Assem to Khalili.

Assem smiled. "I don't have anywhere else to be."

"I can stay a few more days," Khalili said. "If the Lion wants me to wait, I will wait. But where is the tea?" he asked as he wandered out of the room.

"I'm glad you're back," Abdullah said, embracing Massoud on his return the morning of 9 September 2001. "Was it a successful trip?"

"Yes, it was. Nothing breeds success like success. Our progress against the Taliban this summer has been well noted. We will be re-supplied soon whether or not the Americans help us. I bought boots and blankets with some of the money Michelle Garrett gave to us."

"What about food? Boots and blankets won't fill empty stomachs."

"I bought a flock of sheep, too," Massoud answered. "What

is on my schedule for today? Are the journalists back from Panjshir?"

"No, but the Arabs are still here and are insisting that they can wait no longer. I don't want to sound biased, but there is something about them that strikes me as peculiar."

"I'm sure they are all right. I remember processing their request last month. Moroccans, correct?"

"Yes," Abdullah answered as the men began to walk towards Massoud's office. "Moroccans with Belgian passports. They haven't been behaving like journalists usually do, that's all. They are tense and impatient. They were in Panjshir two weeks ago when you and the leadership council were meeting. Sayyaf told me that on three different occasions, they asked to take a joint photo of all the top leadership."

"But they were denied permission. We were too busy and didn't want to be disturbed," Massoud said, thinking back. "If I recall correctly, they are making a documentary?"

"So they say."

Massoud smiled. "You worry too much, my friend. Where are Assem and Khalili?"

"Assem is in my office. Khalili is around somewhere. Shall I find him for you?"

"Yes, please. Ask him to arrange the interview with the Moroccan journalists for one o'clock. I'll wash, and then we'll do the interview. Send them to the guest house. We'll conduct the interview there."

"All right. I forgot to mention that Faheem Dasty is here now too. In fact, Khalili is probably off somewhere with him."

"Well, send my young friend along too. I am curious how Faheem's own documentary is coming along. Perhaps he and the Moroccans would like to compare notes," Massoud suggested.

"Oh, absolutely," Abdullah said dryly. "I'm sure Faheem would be delighted to share all of the unique insights he's gained over the years first working on your newspaper in Kabul and in the time at the Ariana since then."

"I see your point," Massoud smiled. "All right, then. If you will round everyone up and get them situated, I will join them shortly."

from that flame

"It's good to see you, my friend," Massoud said, extending his hand to Masood Khalili who was waiting for him in the guest house often used to conduct interviews with the press.

"How have you been, *Amer Saheb*?" Khalili said, embracing his longtime friend.

"Well, thank you. Is Faheem with you?"

"I'm here, Commander," said the young Afghan journalist as he came into the room with the Moroccan journalists following behind him.

Massoud also embraced the 28-year-old journalist who had been a close ally throughout his adult life. Faheem then introduced the Moroccan journalists to the Commander.

"Shall we begin?" Massoud asked. "Where is Assem?"

"I'll get him," Faheem Dasty said and hurried out of the room. He returned a moment later with Assem in tow.

"Now we can begin." Massoud took his place behind a table. Khalili took the seat beside him on one side, and Assem sat on the other. The Moroccan journalists were setting up their camera, and Faheem Dasty set his own up slightly behind theirs. One of the Moroccan journalists began to ask the first question in halting English. The other Arab journalist stopped him and turned to Massoud. He said something in Arabic. Khalili translated for the Commander.

"He said that the table is blocking the camera's view. Can we move it out of the way?"

"Of course," Massoud agreed and stood up so that the others could shove the table aside. They all sat down again, arranged their chairs, and looked at the cameras once more.

Again the Moroccan camera operator began to adjust his equipment.

"I got a new passport," Masood Khalili said, took the booklet from his pocket, and handed it to Commander Massoud. "I think it is a better picture. What do you think?"

"I think you look older," the Commander teased. Rather than hand the passport back to his friend, he reached over and slipped it into Khalili's breast pocket himself. "Handsome, but older." He patted Khalili on the shoulder.

Khalili laughed before turning his attention back to the journalist. The camera operator indicated that he was ready to begin, and the journalist began asking his questions. As Khalili listened to the questions, the smile left his face. He did not like the angry, aggressive tone the other man used.

"On your recent trip to Europe," the journalist said, "you criticized Osama bin Laden. You said he is a terrorist. Why do you hate him so much? What would you do to him if you captured him?"

Khalili turned to Massoud and translated the questions. Surprised by the abrupt, condemning nature of these questions, Commander Massoud threw his head back in surprised laughter.

Masood Khalili's attention was drawn from the cameraman when he moved unexpectedly. He saw a deep, dark blue fire coming from the lens just as an explosion ripped through the small room.

No, please God, not now! Commander Massoud thought with sorrow as he felt shrapnel pierce his face and body. He saw Khalili start to fall and reached his arm out towards his friend before the pain from his wounds made it impossible for him to move. His whole body was on fire. He felt burning in his head, chest, and legs. The sound of his heart thundering in his chest filled his ears as his blood rushed out of his body. He tried to open his eyes, but when he did, all he saw was an agonizing red. His spirit began to reach out for the God to whom he had devoted his life. Despite his initial plea, Massoud was ready to accept what God planned for him.

Across the compound, Abdullah turned at the sound of the explosion. When he realized that its source was the building in which Ahmed Shah Massoud was conducting the interview, horror overtook him. Without a thought for his own safety, he began to run towards the burning building. He ducked flying pieces of charred and splintered wood, spinning shrapnel, and detached body parts. All he could think about was getting to Massoud.

"Dear, merciful Allah, please let him be alive," Abdullah prayed as he fought his way through the destruction and debris.

from that flame

He ran passed Assem's broken, burning body. He saw the legs of another man but realized they were not Massoud's. Out of the corner of his eye, he saw someone running away from the building with Massoud's bodyguards in pursuit. He saw a bleeding, burned, but obviously alive Khalili. If he had survived, God willing, Massoud had too! Faheem Dasty, who had been behind the cameras, screamed that he was on fire. Men rushed to help him. But where was Massoud?

Abdullah started grabbing and hurling pieces of charred wood and crumbled brick aside. His hands were burned in the process, but he didn't notice. All that mattered at that moment was finding Massoud. His prayer was urgent and constant as he hunted for his friend. "Ahmed Shah!" he screamed in the desperate hope that Massoud would answer.

Others hurried over and joined in the search. Every second could mean the difference between life and death for their *Amer Saheb*—if he was still alive at all.

"I have him," Abdullah screamed, casting aside a piece of the table that had been moved out of the way. What he saw terrified him. Massoud was lying unconscious, his body apparently bleeding from two dozen different places. There were pieces of shrapnel buried in Massoud's head and leg, and an entire starburst of pieces was embedded in his chest around his heart.

Abdullah fell to his knees and gathered his friend into his arms. His fingers sought and found a very faint pulse. He was alive!

"*Help me!*" Abdullah screamed. "Bring bandages, blankets, and the car. We have to get him to the helicopter." He held Massoud carefully and willed his friend to stay alive. He glanced over to where others were tending to Faheem and Khalili. He thanked God that they were alive, but when he thought about the precious man he held in his arms, he knew that he would have traded any of their lives—including his own—for his.

If he dies, Afghanistan's hopes and dreams die too, Abdullah thought. God help us, where will we all be without him? Where will I be without my dearest friend? Tears began to stream down his cheeks. He dropped his mouth close to Massoud's ear and spoke to him softly but firmly.

"You have to live, Ahmed Shah. I know you are badly hurt,

and I know how weary you are, but you must find the strength to survive this. Our people need you. Our troops need you. Your family needs you. I need you. Please don't leave us. Life here without you would be unendurable. Do you hear me? We'll get you help soon. Don't let go of life, my friend, I beg you. I beg Allah. Stay with us. I love you. Don't leave me to fight this war without you. I wouldn't have the courage."

Abdullah wiped the blood from Massoud's motionless face and kissed him on the forehead. Massoud's hair, freed from the confines of his *pakol*, glistened in the September sun, and Abdullah realized with dread that the shiny droplets all over his head were blood.

The Land Rover came to a screeching halt nearby. Someone began to remove the back seat as others hurried towards Abdullah with a stretcher on which to lay Massoud. They would get him into the car and from there drive to the helicopter. With luck and good weather, they would have him in Dushanbe within half an hour.

"Be careful!" Abdullah ordered as hands took Massoud's body from his grasp and laid him on the stretcher. He looked around and realized that Khalili was also being put onto a stretcher. Both men were covered with blankets. Carefully, the two stretchers were placed in the Land Rover. Dr. Abdullah started to climb in, but a restraining hand stopped him.

"You can't go," Faheem Dasty said.

"What do you mean I can't go? Of course I'm going. Get out of my way; we are wasting precious seconds."

"You are needed here, Abdullah. You are in command for now. What if there is another attack? What if the Taliban planned this as a diversion as well as an assassination? We need you to stay here and take command."

Abdullah understood the truth of the words even though they made him feel sick to his stomach. Faheem was right. He was in command until General Fahim and Younis Qanooni were located and brought to the camp. He leaned into the car and kissed Massoud's cheek. "Fight one more time, my friend. Fight for your life."

Abdullah stepped away from the vehicle and helped Faheem climb up into it. Abdullah closed the door. "*Go! Hurry!*" he shout-

from that flame

ed to the driver. At least five minutes had passed since the initial explosion. It is too long. Too much time has past, he thought and prayed he was wrong. He glanced through the window at Massoud's beloved, bloody face. Abdullah wondered if he would ever see that well-loved face again.

The car raced away, kicking up dust that mixed in with the smoke and smell of burning flesh that already filled the air. In the distance shouts followed by a scream of anger and the clatter of an AK-47 being discharged were heard. Abdullah guessed the other assassin had been killed.

Masood Khalili lie on his stretcher in great pain as the Land Rover bounced over the rough terrain. He looked down and saw shrapnel embedded all over the left side of his body. Many pieces were stuck in the leather cover of his passport where it still rested over his heart where Massoud had placed it. He managed to turn his head and look in the direction of his longtime companion. Ahmed Shah Massoud was lying with closed eyes and a peaceful expression on his ravaged face.

"Ahmed Shah?" Khalili managed to croak.

There was no response. No flicker of an eyelid, no slight movement of a finger that would indicate Massoud had heard him.

Ahmed Shah Massoud, *Mujahidin* warrior, the Lion of Panjshir, he who defeated the Soviet Union and prevented the Taliban from taking over all of his country, was sitting in a cave at a small campfire. He looked across the cave and saw a woman sitting and smiling at him. As he watched, Michelle Garrett extended her hand to him, and he clasped it in his own. His friend had come to help him in this last moment of human need.

He felt joy course through his spirit. Soon he would be face-to-face with the Beloved, and he would receive the reward given to those who devoted their lives submitting to God. The man who had longed for peace yet spent a lifetime in war, knew that he would never have to fight again.

"How is he?" Khalili demanded of Faheem Dasty, who had painfully made his way over to where Massoud was lying. Khalili saw tears streaming down Faheem's scorched cheeks and knew the answer before his friend spoke.

"He's gone," Faheem replied, stumbling over the words. "May Allah take our beloved *Amer Saheb* straight to Paradise for his martyrdom."

Khalili wept too. His own pain and suffering was forgotten for the moment. All that mattered was that he prayed for the soul of the greatest man he had ever known.

Faheem Dasty called Dr. Abdullah as soon as possible after the helicopter landed in Tajikistan. He had never dreaded making a call as much as that one.

"He's gone, Abdullah. He is with God."

There was a long silence on the phone before Abdullah answered. Abdullah wiped the tears that had filled his eyes upon hearing Faheem's words. He struggled to control himself and took a deep breath.

"There are four dead here as well including Assem. You must tell no one about Commander Massoud," he said in a strained, choked voice. "No one must know that he is gone. This is very important. Do you understand?"

"I understand what you want, but I don't understand why."

"Because no one—especially our enemies—must know that we are without a leader. We need time to regroup and prepare to defend ourselves. If our fighters think they have no leader, terrible things will happen. If they know Massoud is dead, they will want vengeance, and I don't want anyone rushing off on his own before we have a plan in place. Also, think what the Taliban and bin Laden will do if they know Massoud is dead."

"They will think we are weak and attack us."

"Exactly. They must not know," Abdullah repeated firmly.

"Do you think bin Laden was behind it?"

"Is there any doubt in your mind?" Abdullah replied flatly.

"What do you want me to do?" Faheem asked.

from that flame

"We have friends in Dushanbe. Take Massoud to someone you trust and make them understand that his death must be kept a secret for now. Then go to some of your friends in the press. Start a false story. Say there was an attack by suicide bombers in which Massoud was seriously injured, but that he is expected to recover. Tell them he is being treated in a hospital there in Tajikistan, and add that because of security concerns, you must remain vague on his exact location."

"What if they don't believe me?"

"Stick to that story. No one will be able to prove you wrong, although rumors will fly. I will contact Ahmad Wali Massoud and have him issue a statement that he spoke to his brother by phone. We will have the Afghan Embassy in Moscow make the same statement. We will all say that Ahmed Shah received severe shrapnel wounds, but that he is expected to make a full recovery. Can you do this for me—for all of us? Can you get me the time I need?"

"I will try my best," Faheem said passionately.

"Good. I will need Haroun Amin, too. Do you know where he is?"

"In Germany, I believe."

"He can make a statement from there as the Alliance's spokesman. After he has made a public statement, ask him to return here. I will need him when the truth comes out. All right, Faheem. Please do as I have asked."

"I will. May God be with you and grant you wisdom and guidance."

"Faheem?" Abdullah asked before the other man could hang up the phone. "Are you all right? Have you heard anything about Masood Khalili's condition?"

"I've been burned but have only minor shrapnel injuries. Ambassador Khalili is in much worse shape. The doctor said he will probably be deaf and blind on one side and may never walk again."

"But he will live?"

"They seem to think so. He is taking Commander Massoud's death very badly."

"As we all are," Abdullah answered. "I thank God that you and he were not killed. As soon as you are able, do the things

from that flame

I have asked. After that, do everything required to get well, my friend."

24. Losses

bdullah had many matters to attend. He couldn't even imagine how difficult the next days would be. He started to get up from his seat behind Massoud's office desk when his eye caught a glimpse of a framed picture there. It was one that Michelle had taken and that Massoud liked very much. In it, the two friends stood shoulder to shoulder with broad smiles on their tired but happy faces.

Abdullah picked up the picture and looked at it closely. He sat back down as he returned the frame to its exact spot. He stared at it until tears started to roll down his cheeks, and he buried his face in his hands and wept. It felt as if his chest bore a weight that was crushing him with terrible force.

Afghanistan had lost her greatest warrior, protector, and hero. Abdullah had lost all that and his best friend, his dearest, most well-loved friend, as well. Somewhere deep inside he feared that he would never be able to recover from this terrible loss. How could he? Who would he be if he was no longer the friend, advisor, and confidant of Ahmed Shah Massoud? A strangled cry ripped from his constricted throat.

He couldn't catch his breath. He couldn't stop shaking. He opened his eyes, but they were blinded by tears, and he could see nothing. Grief washed over him in wave after wave that pounded him until he collapsed forward onto Massoud's desk. Without looking he reached out for the framed photograph he had looked at a moment before. He found it, grasped it, and grieved for all that had been lost that day.

from that flame

Half an hour later, a pale and still shaken man reached for the phone. He had the unhappy responsibility of telling Ahmad Wali Massoud that his brother was dead but that no one could know. Perhaps Ahmad Wali would prefer to tell Massoud's wife himself. If not, Abdullah would have to think of whom best to send to break the news to the family.

Later that day, the news went out around the world that Northern Alliance Commander Ahmed Shah Massoud had been seriously injured in an assassination attempt. Ahmad Wali Massoud assured interested parties that he had spoken to his brother on the phone. Rumors about Commander Ahmed Shah Massoud's death were reported on all major television news stations. There was great suspicion that the stories of his survival were false, but no one was able to receive a definitive answer. Rumor and speculation ran rampant.

Once stabilized, Masood Khalili was transferred to a hospital in New Delhi so that he would be closer to his family. Faheem Dasty was sent to Paris where he could receive better treatment for his burns. In Khwaja Bahauddin, General Fahim and Younis Qanooni arrived to rage and grieve with Massoud's inconsolable *mujahidin*.

At a meeting held the day after the attack, Dr. Abdullah looked from the grim face of Mohammed Fahim to the grief-stricken face of Younis Qanooni. "We know exactly what he wants us to do," Abdullah said in a low, measured tone. "He made his wishes very clear. You, General Fahim, are to assume responsibility for the military aspects of our resistance, and you, Younis, you are to assume responsibility for the political aspects."

"How can we?" Younis asked as tears streamed down his face. "How can we continue the resistance when our hearts have been removed? The resistance is as dead as our beloved friend. I have nothing left inside me. Let the Taliban come. I don't care any more." He removed his glasses and wiped tears that would not stop.

"That is your grief speaking, not you," Abdullah said gently. "I know this because my own grief said exactly the same thing to me. It is hard—nearly impossible—to imagine continuing with-

from that flame

out him, and yet that is exactly what we must do. I remembered something Ahmed Shah said to me when we discussed his plans for after his death. I told him then what you are saying now. I remember his exact reply. He said, 'None of us individually is as important as the work we do. No matter how much we have lost or how much we have suffered, we have made a commitment to free this land and her people. Not even personal loss and grief can break our dedication to that goal.' Younis, he needs us to carry on for him. It's all we have left to give him. It's the only way we can prove that he did not spend his life fighting for all of us in vain."

"I can never replace him," General Fahim said very quietly. "I don't have the brilliant military mind he had." Fahim looked from one man to the other. "But if both of you promise to help and advise me, I will try to prove he was right when he chose me for this position. I will try to confirm his faith in me."

"We will help each other," Abdullah replied in a voice barely above a whisper. "It will take all three of us to do the work he did. Massoud trusted us to keep his vision of a free Afghanistan alive. I am not prepared to disappointment him."

The three friends agreed. The fight for the freedom of Afghanistan would continue. Massoud's dream would live.

Dr. Abdullah sat at Massoud's desk. He had volunteered to gather together any personal items it might contain so that they could be sent to Massoud's widow. He would ask to keep the picture on top of the desk, the one of him and Massoud, for himself. He had other pictures, but that one reminded him of a happier day when everything still seemed possible.

He found Massoud's *Qur'an* and several books of poetry. He uncovered a photo album that had been given to Massoud by the famed Italian photographer Reza. It contained some of the best and most widely recognized pictures of Commander Massoud and the Northern Alliance which Reza had taken over a period of twenty years. Massoud had cherished the album because it contained images of friends long dead.

Dr. Abdullah opened another drawer and realized that it contained Massoud's memories of Michelle Garrett. The doctor withdrew the CD player and CDs. The Commander's children would enjoy them as much as their father had. Abdullah placed them in the container with the other items being sent to the Massoud family. To that pile he also added the French magazine that contained Michelle's article and which had Massoud's face on the cover. He thought it would be all right if he kept the English version for himself.

He found the bank book into which Massoud had deposited the money Michelle Garrett had left him. Abdullah decided at that moment to give fifty thousand of it to the Commander's wife and children. It would take care of them for life. He thought Michelle would approve wholeheartedly.

Finally, he withdrew from the drawer the blood-and-dust-covered manuscript, Michelle's journal, the photo of Massoud and Michelle, and her passport photo. He set aside the manuscript and photos and turned the journal over and over in his hands. He had known of its existence, but he had not seen it before. He opened it to a random page near the back and looked without reading the words written in her neat, upright handwriting.

He saw his name and that of Massoud sprinkled several times over the open pages. Part of him wanted to know what Michelle had written about them. He almost allowed his eyes to focus on the words before he remembered how Ahmed Shah Massoud felt about his own journal. It was a private place to express private thoughts. Abdullah snapped the journal shut. He added it to the photos and manuscript. These he would keep himself—for both his dead friends' sake and for his own. When he found Massoud's journal, he set that as well among the things he would keep safe.

25. Al-Qaeda

"octor Abdullah?" a soft voice said as a hand shook his shoulder. He struggled to consciousness. It had been a late night, and he felt as if he had been asleep for mere minutes.

"*Chee shod*? What happened?" Abdullah opened his eyes.

"Al-Qaeda made a strike against the United States," Hani said in amazement.

Abdullah was fully awake now. "What are you talking about? How could they?" He sat straight up in his bed.

"Suicide attackers hijacked planes and flew them into the World Trade Center towers in New York City. Tens of thousands are thought to be dead. It's on the news."

Abdullah got up and reached for his clothes. "Find a radio for me. Get the commanders. Have them meet me in Massoud's office."

"I'm worried," Hani admitted before he left to do as Abdullah asked.

"You should be," Abdullah said. "This changes everything."

Abdullah, General Fahim, Younis Qanooni, and an assortment of Massoud's commanders sat around the office, carefully listening to every word that came from the tinny-sounding portable radio.

The news from the United States became increasingly grim. Another plane had crashed, this time into the Pentagon in Washington, DC. A fourth plane crashed in a field in Pennsylvania. As they listened in horror, word came that one of the World Trade towers had collapsed. Firefighters and police reportedly had been trapped by the falling tower.

"No wonder they had to get rid of Massoud," Abdullah observed grimly.

"What do you mean?" someone asked.

Abdullah looked around the room at the men assembled there. "Don't you see? This attack on the United States will bring a military response from the Americans. And where are they going to strike? Here. Here because this is where Osama bin Laden and his al-Qaeda dogs live. This is why they killed Commander Massoud. The Taliban and bin Laden knew that he would be a rallying force within the country to help the Americans. They had to eliminate him."

"What are we going to do?" Hani asked.

"Help them," Abdullah said firmly as he rose from the chair.

"Where are you going?" Younis asked.

"To Dushanbe. I need better news access. Television. Better communications. The Americans will want to talk to us again. Younis, I think you should accompany me. You, too, General Fahim. The Americans will want to talk to you."

"Are we going to tell the truth about *Amer Saheb*?"

Abdullah shook his head vehemently. "Not yet. If anyone asks why we are going to Dushanbe, tell them we are visiting Commander Massoud."

"But we need to bury him," another man protested. "This delay is in violation of Islamic law."

"Don't you think I know that?" Abdullah said angrily. "Don't you think I want to bring him home to the land he loved and lay his body to rest? What *I* want—what *you* want—doesn't matter right now." The doctor paused and spoke more calmly.

"What if the Americans decide to strike right away, and we are unprepared? What if they wait until they can coordinate with us? We need to focus our attention on what has happened today. We cannot allow the Taliban or al-Qaeda to think that we are weak in any way. It is what Massoud would want. It's what he would have done." His voice softened a little. "I know how much you grieve; I do, too. I loved him as I would my own brother. But he is gone, and the thing we can best do to honor his memory is win this war

from that flame

and free our land, God willing. Are you with me?"

"We are, Abdullah," someone said, and everyone else nodded his head.

"May Allah go with you," another man said.

They turned back to the radio as Abdullah left the room. The second tower of the World Trade Center had just collapsed.

The next few days went by in a hectic, headachy, tension-filled whirlwind for Abdullah. He struggled to quell the terrible surges of grief that strangled his words and forced him to stop and catch his breath. More than once his eyes unexpectedly filled with tears, and he fought them back with all the determination he could muster. For Massoud. For Afghanistan, he thought over and over again as a mantra. It didn't assuage his grief, but it did allow him to keep going when all he wanted to do was bring home Massoud's body, bury him, and weep openly.

Abdullah, Fahim, and Qanooni were in near constant communication with the Americans. Much of the initial planning had been done in August when General Brinkman and Sam Snipes visited, but other details needed to be worked out. Yes, as Massoud had promised, the Northern Alliance would be able to supply intelligence about the locations of the hierarchy of both the Taliban and al-Qaeda as well as the al-Qaeda training camps. Yes, also as agreed by Commander Massoud, they would be willing to fight a surrogate ground war, but they would need every kind of armament: SAMs, RPGs, tens of thousands of rounds of bullets for their Kalashnikovs, tanks, mortar, and armored vehicles. Dr. Abdullah gave them the entire shopping list Commander Massoud had been trying to get them to fill for five years. The difference was that this time they agreed. The US would contact the governments of the north-lying countries, especially Russia and Tajikistan, and somehow they would work out a deal to pay for all the supplies needed by the Northern Alliance. The United States agreed to provide close air support for Northern Alliance troops. General Fahim agreed to have CIA operatives with him in a matter of days. They would work together to develop a plan of action. No, they did not need new maps, but satellite photos might be useful. Finally, every question that could be asked

327

from that flame

and answered at that moment had been asked and answered. The US attaches and CIA officers would surely have more questions, but that was days away, and there was another pressing matter to which Dr. Abdullah had to attend.

Word was sent out around the world that Ahmed Shah Massoud, the legendary Afghan resistance leader, had died of his wounds. The story was picked up by every major news agency in every country. What his death meant now that the unthinkable terror attack had occurred on US soil was a question often asked without a satisfactory answer. He would have been the natural ally of the United States as they prepared their anticipated retaliation against al Qaeda in Afghanistan. Would his Northern Alliance and the United Front be a functioning force without him? Annalists around the globe speculated, but a consensus could not be reached. The only thing upon which all could agree was that Massoud's assassination was a terrible blow to Afghanistan's future, if, indeed, Afghanistan was going to have a future.

Accusations that Osama bin Laden had sent the suicide bombers followed close on the heels of the announcement. Younis Qanooni, as the new political face of the Northern Alliance, was sent out to make the Alliance's official statement.

"The people of Afghanistan, the Islamic community, and the world have lost a great, historical figure," Qanooni said in a clear, calm voice. "I send my condolences to all the people of Afghanistan for their loss of this beloved and heroic man.

"We are convinced that the Pakistani-backed Taliban and Osama bin Laden's terrorist al-Qaeda network are responsible for this tragedy. We are also convinced there is a connection between the assassination of Commander Massoud and the terrorist attack on the United States that took place two days later. We wish to extend our deepest condolences to the people of the United States for the terrible loss they have suffered. We ourselves are victims of international terror and share in the Americans' grief.

"The Afghan resistance is totally ready to cooperate with the international community to combat terrorism and is willing to use all means at its disposal to assist in the fight against terrorism. The United Front is politically and militarily prepared to with-

328

stand Taliban and bin Laden offensives. Now all of us will follow Ahmed Shah Massoud's vision. Massoud was not only the name of a great man; it is now a school of thought and a system that will not die."

Abdullah looked from General Fahim to Younis Qanooni and said, "We will take his body back with us. His wife will want to see him and spend some private time in mourning. We can have the funeral on the sixteenth."

"It's not fair," Mohammed Fahim said softly as tears filled his eyes. "He's supposed to be here with us. Now that everything he spent his whole life fighting to achieve is going to happen, he is supposed to be here. How can we do this without him?"

"I don't know," Abdullah answered in an equally quiet voice. "I only know we have to try. We owe him that. We have to try."

"He will be with us," Younis Qanooni said in a hushed tone. "He will be in all of us. We will all be Massoud. His physical life is over, but his courage and determination, his ferocity and drive, his goodness and hope, his dreams and plans for Afghanistan... those things are in all of us. A million suicide bombers couldn't blow that apart for us."

"You are right," Abdullah managed to say around the painful lump in his throat. He looked back and forth between his friends. "The men are going to look to us both as Massoud's closest friends and as the men he trusted to carry on his work. It's up to us now. We can prove that Commander Massoud's confidence in us was well placed. We can be strong for the men who are soon going out yet again to risk their lives for Massoud's dream of a free Afghanistan. It's the least we can do for our friend Ahmed Shah Massoud."

26. Dream

Finally, a full week after the death of Ahmed Shah Massoud, Dr. Abdullah decided it was time to have the body of the Lion of Panjshir brought home at last so that he might be taken to his resting place in the valley for which he was nicknamed.

It was on a Sunday morning that a helicopter carrying the flag-draped coffin of Ahmed Shah Massoud landed in his ancestral village of Jangalak in the Panjshir Valley. When the dust and the wind subsided, 24,000 people pressed forward against the helicopter. They all wanted the honor of carrying the coffin of their hero, Commander Massoud. The moans and cries of the heartbroken people made a sound like thunder that echoed through the valley.

Dr. Abdullah, tears streaming down his face, pleaded for the people to stand back so that the helicopter door could be opened. The weeping crowd chanted endearments and verses from the *Qur'an* and continued pressing against the helicopter. Finally, as gently as possible, a security force began to move them back. The beloved of them all finally had his coffin removed and handed over to those who would carry him on his final journey. Thousands of people reached out to touch the coffin tenderly as it passed as if the act of touching it would give them a piece of him that would last forever. Others threw flowers onto the coffin of Afghanistan's most cherished son.

The most powerful, honored people in Afghanistan had gathered for Massoud's funeral. The president of the recognized Afghan government, Burhanuddin Rabbani, spoke to one of the commanders, and in turn Younis Qanooni climbed onto a Jeep

from that flame

with a loudspeaker in his hand and implored the people to put down the coffin and kneel in prayer. For a while, as the long rows of people in a prayerful position remained in prayer, all was calm and quiet. The moment the prayer ended, however, the emotional, heedless crowd again pressed forward in an effort to reach the coffin. All wanted to carry it to the armor-plated personnel carrier that would bear Massoud's body to his grave in Saricha. The outpouring of grief and love threatened to flood the plain in the Valley of Panjshir in a way the rains never could.

Afghanistan, known far and wide for its tribal infighting, had Pashtuns and Hazara, Uzbeks and Turkmens, Tajiks and Baluchis walking shoulder to shoulder as they honored their fallen comrade. On this day, the Afghan mosaic was a single tapestry, unified in their grief and bonded together by their memory, respect, admiration, and love for Ahmed Shah Massoud.

The mountaintop village of Saricha was several hundred feet higher than the surrounding villages. It had as its vantage point the mountains that had made Afghanistan unconquerable for centuries. It was a fitting place for Afghanistan to hold in her arms forever her undefeated son.

Five villages had to be crossed as the procession made its way up the steep hill of the Hindu Kush. As the procession passed through each town, more and more people joined. They were inconsolable in their grief.

Ahmed Shah Massoud's twelve-year-old son stepped forward to speak, and to those who heard him, it was the voice and words of his father. Ahmad said, "My father's killing was unjust and despicable. Now the world knows that his struggle was just and his words true. His untimely death will not cut short our fight for an independent Afghanistan. We will continue with more fervor. I will not rest, but work to realize his dream."

Epilogue

On 7 October 2001, two weeks after the funeral of Ahmed Shah Massoud, American bombs began to fall on Afghanistan. Massoud's well-loved, well-trusted *mujahidin* fighters went into battle again. Their leader was gone, but his hope and dream for Afghanistan still burned in their hearts. They put his picture on their tanks and vehicles and thus carried him into battle with them. They would fight to the death for the man they called *Amer Saheb* and for the dream of a free Afghanistan he had instilled in all of them.

Additional Reading

Articles

Davis, Anthony "Interview: Ahmadshah Massoud." *Jane's Defense Weekly*. London, July 4, 2001
and
"UF in Crisis Over Massoud." *Jane's Defense Weekly*. London, September 19, 2001

DeBay, Yves "Guerillas in the Midst." *Special Ops: Journal of the Elite Forces and SWAT Units* Vol. 8. Concord Publications, Hong Kong 2000

Geer, Galen L. "Afghan Jihad." *Soldier of Fortune.* August 1985

Girardet, Edward "Eyewitness Afghanistan." *National Geographic National Geographic, Inc.* December 2001

Junger, Sebastian "The Lion in Winter." *National Geographic Adventure.* March/April 2001

Junger, Sebastian "Massoud's Last Conquest." *Vanity Fair.* February 2002

"National Geographic: Afghanistan Revealed: The Untold Story of a Land and Its People." *National Geographic, Inc.*, 2001

Winchester, Mike "Hard-Pressed Massoud Holds Panjshir." *Soldier of Fortune.* August 1985

Anderson, Jon Lee "Letters from Kabul: Who Killed Ahmed Shah Massoud?" *The New Yorker.* June 10, 2002

Books

Ghost Wars: The Secret History of the CIA, Afghanistan, and bin Laden from the Soviet Invasion to September 10, 2001 by Steve Coll, The Penguin Press, New York, 2004

The Afghan Rebels: The War in Afghanistan by DJ Herda Franklin Watts Press, NY, 1990

The Taliban Phenomenon: Afghanistan 1994-1997 by Kamal Matinuddin, Oxford University Press, New York, 1999

Afghanistan: Mullah, Marx and Mujahid by Ralph H. Magnus and Eden Naby Boulder, Colorado, Westview Press, 2000

Alien Wars: The Soviet Union's Aggression Against the World, 1919 to 1989 by General Oleg Sarin and Colonel Lev Dvoretsky Presidio Press, Novato, CA, 1996

Afghanistan's Endless War by Larry P. Goodson, University of Washington Press, Seattle, WA, 2001

Soldiers of God: with Islamic Warriors in Afghanistan and Pakistan by Robert D. Kaplan. Vintage Books New York, 2001

About the Author

maryAnn T. Beverly is an Ohio native who has made her home in Columbia, SC for the past 25 years. A former high school English teacher, she left teaching to write and direct a documentary movie, "The Arts in Education," in Cali, Colombia, South America. *From this Flame* is the first published novel for this married mother of two. Ms. Beverly is currently working on a new novel.

A percentage of the author's proceeds from the sale of *From that Flame* will go to the Ahmed Shah Massoud Foundation, administered by Ambassador Massoud, to help the people of Afghanistan in their quest for freedom.

For more information, please visit *www.maryanntbeverly.com*.